TOGETHER FOR KEEPS

"Wake up, Selina," Layne whispered. Leaning over her, he lightly kissed the tip of her nose. "Open your eyes, sleepy-head. It's time to leave."

Her long lashes fluttered open, and she regarded him through half-lowered lids. Slowly, she laced her arms about his neck. "Let's stay here . . . a little longer."

He grinned expectantly. "Are you seducing me?"

"Well, I'm certainly trying," she answered. "You won't be difficult, will you?"

"You will be tender, won't you?" he asked, his dark eyes twinkling.

"Yes, trust me," she purred, raising her lips to his.

He smiled against her mouth, then kissed her demandingly, urgently. Then, pulling her close, he pressed every inch of his body to hers.

"Selina . . . Selina," Layne whispered, his warm lips traveling to her neck, covering her throat with feather-light kisses.

They made love blissfully, cresting love's apex together, finding breathless, rapturous fulfillment.

"I could make love to you for a hundred years," Layne said, "and still want more."

She laughed softly. "Greedy, aren't you?"

As his arms encircled her, he placed his lips against her ear. "I love you, Selina."

His words were music to her heart. "I love you, too," she murmured. "I always will."

HISTORICAL ROMANCES BY EMMA MERRITT

RESTLESS FLAMES (2203, $3.95)

Having lost her husband six months before, determined Brenna Allen couldn't afford to lose her freight company, too. Outfitted as wagon captain with revolver, knife and whip, the single-minded beauty relentlessly drove her caravan, desperate to reach Santa Fe. Then she crossed paths with insolent Logan Mac-Dougald. The taciturn Texas Ranger was as primitive as the surrounding Comanche Territory, and he didn't hesitate to let the tantalizing trail boss know what he wanted from her. Yet despite her outrage with his brazen ways, jet-haired Brenna couldn't suppress the scorching passions surging through her . . . and suddenly she never wanted this trip to end!

COMANCHE BRIDE (2549, $3.95)

When stunning Dr. Zoe Randolph headed to Mexico to halt a cholera epidemic, she didn't think twice about traversing Comanche territory . . . until a band of bloodthirsty savages attacked her caravan. The gorgeous physician was furious that her mission had been interrupted, but nothing compared to the rage she felt on meeting the barbaric warrior who made her his slave. Determined to return to civilization, the ivory-skinned blonde decided to make a woman's ultimate sacrifice to gain her freedom — and never admit that deep down inside she burned to be loved by the handsome brute!

SWEET, WILD LOVE (2834, $4.50)

It was hard enough for Eleanor Hunt to get men to take her seriously in sophisticated Chicago — it was going to be impossible in Blissful, Kansas! These cowboys couldn't believe she was a real attorney, here to try a cattle rustling case. They just looked her up and down and grinned. Especially that Bradley Smith. The man worked for her father and he still had the audacity to stare at her with those lust-filled green eyes. Every time she turned around, he was trying to trap her in his strong embrace.

Available wherever paperbacks are sold, or order direct from the Publisher. Send cover price plus 50¢ per copy for mailing and handling to Zebra Books, Dept. 2865, 475 Park Avenue South, New York, N.Y. 10016. Residents of New York, New Jersey and Pennsylvania must include sales tax. DO NOT SEND CASH.

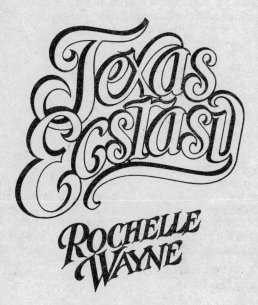

TEXAS ECSTASY

ROCHELLE WAYNE

ZEBRA BOOKS
KENSINGTON PUBLISHING CORP.

ZEBRA BOOKS

are published by

Kensington Publishing Corp.
475 Park Avenue South
New York, NY 10016

First printing: January 1990

Printed in the United States of America

For Cassie Edwards — with thanks
for always listening, caring, and understanding

Part One
Louisiana

One

Selina Beaumont paced her bedroom restlessly. She sensed that Harold Chamberlain's visit was not a social one, but that he had called to inform her mother that he was about to purchase this house and also Cedar Hill.

Selina had been in the parlor with her mother when the butler announced Mr. Chamberlain. Following social courtesies, Chamberlain had requested that he speak privately with her mother.

Leaving the two alone, Selina went upstairs to her room and began to pace. Now, stepping to the window, she drew back the lace curtain and glanced outside.

The house was in the heart of town, and the New Orleans streets were crowded with people. Although the city was considered enticing, it held little charm for Selina; she preferred to live in the country. Her mother had always favored this house over their plantation, Cedar Hill. Unlike Mrs. Beaumont, Selina disliked crowded and noisy city-dwelling and stayed at Cedar Hill as often as possible. She'd be there now if circumstances were different.

Selina turned away from the window, moved to her dressing table, and sat down. Giving her reflection little thought, she picked up her hair brush and began running it through her long, chestnut-brown tresses.

Selina Beaumont wasn't impressed by her own beauty and was totally unaware of the astounding effect it had on others. Her sky-blue eyes were framed by naturally arched brows and thick, sooty lashes. Her face was lovely, and her slender frame was seductively curvaceous.

Selina was twenty-one years old and had never had a serious romance, let alone contemplated matrimony. She knew her mother was extremely concerned, for in her opinion her daughter was quickly overtaking the ideal marrying age. Considering her daughter's startling good looks, she couldn't fathom why Selina hadn't chosen a husband. After all, her beauty attracted eligible bachelors like bees to honey. She'd had numerous suitors, young, wealthy men of good families. However, to her mother's dismay, Selina hadn't taken a serious interest in any of them.

Putting down the brush, Selina rose and walked over to her bed and sat on the edge. She supposed that her mother blamed her in part for their present situation. If she had married one of her rich suitors, her husband could now take over and pay the debts her father had accumulated before his untimely death.

Selina gave a heavy, depressing sigh. She wished she didn't feel guilty, but she did. Her mother had never come right out and accused her of being too choosy, but Selina knew how she felt. They were about to lose their townhouse in New Orleans and Cedar Hill as well. Despite the fact that her father had been the one to mortgage the properties for gambling expenses, Selina's mother had managed to place a large part of the blame on her daughter. If Selina was married to a wealthy husband, he certainly wouldn't allow his wife to lose her inheritance.

A petulant frown creased Selina's brow as she silently

berated herself. She should have encouraged the well-to-do swains who had come calling at her door. But she had been determined to marry for love, not for convenience. She shrugged tersely. Well, now it was too late for her to entice a rich husband, for the Beaumonts' reduced state was well known. If she were to try and inveigle one or more of her former suitors, they would suspect that she was simply after their money.

Selina's frown turned thoughtful. Could she possibly bring herself to marry a man for his money? The mere idea was disturbing. Not only did she abhor dishonesty, but she also wanted desperately to be in love with the man she married.

Suddenly, her blue eyes narrowed angrily. She could hardly believe that her father had so thoughtlessly gambled away their fortune. Josh Beaumont had kept his debts concealed from his wife and daughter, with the hope of someday regaining his losses. He certainly hadn't imagined that he'd die unexpectedly of a heart attack, leaving his family so heavily in debt that the bank would decide to foreclose on his mortgaged property.

Still curious about Chamberlain's visit, Selina rose from the bed and continued pacing. The man's image came to her mind. Harold Chamberlain was indeed a handsome aristocrat. His tall frame was masculine, and his hair and well-groomed moustache were as black as ebony. At the age of thirty-five, he was considered one of the most eligible and richest bachelors in New Orleans.

Because Selina spent most of her time at Cedar Hill, she had only come into contact with Chamberlain a few times; once she had spoken and danced with him at a ball, and twice her father had invited him to their New Orleans home for dinner.

On the occasions when Selina had found herself in

his company, she had thought him dashingly handsome, but there had been something about the man that she hadn't liked.

Now, she tried to pin down exactly why Chamberlain affected her so adversely. But it wasn't concrete, it was just a feeling she had. She somehow sensed that his elegant manners were a facade.

A knock on her bedroom door interrupted Selina's thoughts. Hurrying across the room, she admitted her personal maid, who was an attractive Negro slave two years younger than her mistress.

"Miz Selina," Dottie said. "Your mama's a-wantin' you to come to the parlah."

"Is Mr. Chamberlain still here?"

"Yes'm. He's in the parlah with your mama."

A look of resignation fell across Selina's face. "I suppose he came here to let us know that he's buying our property."

Dottie's large eyes filled with sudden tears, and fear crept into her voice. "Oh Lawdy, Miz Selina! What's gonna become of us? What you and your mama gonna do? Where's ya'll gonna go? And what's Masta Chamberlain gonna do with us? You reckon he'll sell us?"

"Don't worry, Dottie," Selina said. "I'm sure Mr. Chamberlain has no intentions of selling any of father's slaves. I don't know where Mama and I will go, but wherever we go, you'll come with us."

The girl's relief was evident "I's glad you gonna keep me, Miz Selina."

"What would I do without you?" Selina said warmly. She reached over and patted Dottie's shoulder affectionately, then hastened to the spiral stairway and descended.

Selina's heart was pounding as she opened the parlor door and stepped inside.

"Selina, darling," her mother said sweetly. She was

12

sitting on the rose-colored settee and patting the cushion beside her, as she urged, "Come, sit down."

As Selina crossed the room, she cast Chamberlain an inquisitive glance. The man was standing in front of the open window, a glass of brandy in his hand. Catching Selina's eye, he gave her a charming smile.

Taking her place on the settee, Selina returned his smile somewhat hesitantly, then turned to her mother.

Although Elizabeth Beaumont was an attractive woman, she was obviously frail. Since her husband's death, her health had declined drastically.

"Selina," Elizabeth began with excitement, "Mr. Chamberlain made me a most generous offer."

Selina was surprised to see that her mother was actually beaming and that a bright sparkle was in her eyes.

"An offer, Mama?" she asked, watching the woman curiously.

Elizabeth drew a deep breath. "Mr. Chamberlain is the answer to my prayers." She turned, smiled gratefully at Harold Chamberlain, then looking back at her daughter, remarked, "He's offered to take care of your father's debts."

Selina was confused. "I don't quite understand. Are you saying that he's willing to lend us the money to pay off the mortgage on this house and on Cedar Hill?"

"No, that's not what I mean," Elizabeth answered, her voice tinged with joy. Taking Selina's hands into hers, she squeezed them tightly. "Darling," she went on eagerly, "Mr. Chamberlain wants to marry you."

Shocked, Selina could only stare at her mother, her mouth agape. Marry her! But she and Harold Chamberlain barely knew each other! Why would he want her as his wife?

Elizabeth, impatient with her daughter's silence, said pressingly, "Selina, say something! Aren't you pleased?"

The woman glanced quickly at Chamberlain. Oh, he's such a handsome gentleman, she thought. Selina should thank her lucky stars that a man so rich and elegant wants to marry her! He'll make an ideal husband!

Elizabeth turned back to Selina, somewhat annoyed that the young woman was still unresponsive. Sternly, she demanded, "Selina, say something!" She was finding her daughter's lack of enthusiasm embarrassing. After all, Harold Chamberlain was the most sought after bachelor in New Orleans.

"I'm sorry, Mama," Selina murmured. "But . . . but I'm shocked."

"Of course you're shocked," Chamberlain spoke up. Moving away from the window, he walked over and sat in the wing chair facing the settee. His gaze swept appreciatively over Selina. Her blue gown, edged with guipure lace, was the exact shade of her eyes, and her full, dark tresses framed her face beautifully.

"Miss Beaumont," Harold began, "although we've only met a few times, I fell hopelessly in love with you at first sight. Please excuse my boldness, but considering your pressing debts, there's no time for me to court you in a leisurely fashion. I know that the bank is threatening to foreclose and that you and your mother will lose this house and your country plantation. Before coming here, I went to the bank and talked to the president, Mr. Heymann. He has agreed to accept my promissory note to cover the mortgage on this house and on Cedar Hill. On the day we are married, the mortgage will be paid."

Suddenly, Elizabeth was overcome with a coughing fit, and when it finally passed, Chamberlain used it to his advantage and said to Selina, "If you'll agree to marry me, I'll arrange immediately for your mother to receive a generous monthly allowance. I'm sure her

14

doctor bills are enormous."

"We're already heavily in debt to Doctor Wilkerson," Selina murmured. She was gravely worried about her mother's poor health.

"I'll take care of the unpaid bills," Chamberlain was quick to say.

Selina's shock was beginning to wane. "I don't understand why you're willing to be so generous."

"I think I made that quite clear. I adore you and want to marry you." His tone, however, was in stark contrast to his amorous intentions. He'd spoken crisply, as though he were merely conducting a business proposal.

Selina looked away from his questioning gaze. "I . . . I don't know what to say." She stared down at her lap.

"You can be totally honest with me," Harold encouraged. "Please, tell me how you feel."

"I don't love you," Selina replied, raising her gaze to his. "I barely know you."

"My dear," he began, as though speaking to a child, "sometimes love comes after marriage."

"Mr. Chamberlain is right," Elizabeth inserted. "Selina, darling, I wasn't in love with your father when we were married. Our marriage was arranged and was one of convenience. But, Selina, I soon learned to love Josh very deeply."

"I don't want to learn to love my husband," Selina said firmly. "I want to fall in love!"

Harold, getting to his feet, chuckled arrogantly. "Apparently, Mrs. Beaumont, your daughter has been reading too many romantic novels, and they have filled her head with nonsense. I'll leave you two alone so that you can fully discuss my offer. I'll return tonight at six, by then I'll expect you to have a final answer."

Elizabeth started to rise, but Chamberlain gestured for her to remain seated. "Don't bother, Mrs. Beaumont. I can show myself out."

15

The moment the parlor door closed behind their guest, Selina's mother remarked crossly, "I can't believe you were so inconsiderate. The man not only admits that he adores you, but his generosity is a godsend. What's wrong with you, Selina? Don't you realize Harold Chamberlain is our salvation? Furthermore, he's a perfect gentleman and will be a loving, considerate husband."

"But, Mama, I don't love him," Selina murmured lamely.

"You'll learn to love him," Elizabeth persisted.

Rising, Selina moved slowly to the open window and gazed vacantly outside. She didn't want to marry Harold Chamberlain. Also, she doubted that it was possible for her to learn to love him. Despite his good looks and gentlemanly decorum, there was something about the man that she didn't like. However, she knew it would be futile for her to say anything about this to her mother. Elizabeth would insist on knowing why she disliked Chamberlain, and she wouldn't be able to give her a valid reason.

As Selina was gazing outside, Elizabeth was watching her thoughtfully. Although she was upset with her daughter, she nonetheless studied her with motherly pride. Selina was such a lovely young lady! If one didn't know her well, one would mistakenly believe she represented the proverbial Southern belle, beautiful and fragile. Although Selina was beautiful, she certainly wasn't fragile. As a child, she had been a tomboy. Despite Elizabeth's attempts to turn her daughter into a well-behaved young lady, Selina had remained spirited and unbridled. To make matters worse for Elizabeth, Josh had encouraged his daughter's unruly behavior.

Elizabeth had given her husband two sons, but both of them had been born prematurely. The firstborn had died while only a few hours old, and their second son had only lived three days. Four years passed, and Elizabeth and Josh had begun to despair that they'd never have any more children when, joyfully, Elizabeth conceived. Unlike her brothers before her, Selina was a full-term, healthy baby. However, her birth had been a difficult one for Elizabeth, and the doctor had regrettably told the Beaumonts that this child should be their last; the next time, Elizabeth could very well die in childbirth.

Josh, knowing he'd never have the son he craved, bestowed all the attention that he'd ordinarily have given a son upon his daughter. He taught Selina to ride a horse as well as a man, and to shoot a rifle with the accuracy of a marksman. Selina was anxious to learn and was an astute pupil. She loved the outdoors, and she preferred riding her horse to sitting in the parlor doing embroidery or learning some other feminine activity.

Elizabeth found her daughter's boyish behavior mortifying and convinced her husband that Selina should be sent away to school. Against Selina's blatant protests, she was enrolled in Miss Blum's School for Young Ladies in Baton Rouge. At the time, Selina was twelve years old, but the five years she spent under Miss Blum's strict tutelage were beneficial. She was an intelligent, well-mannered student and graduated at the top of her class. Through the duration of her school years, she was allowed to visit home six weeks at Christmas and three months during the summer. So, although she received an education and learned proper etiquette, her vacations gave her the opportunity to ride across the fields with her father and to practice her marksmanship. Josh would try to entice his daughter to join him on his hunting trips, but Selina wanted no part of killing animals and restricted her shooting to man-made targets.

17

Selina was her father's pride and joy, but she was an enigma to her mother. Elizabeth loved her child dearly, but Selina's apparent disinterest in becoming a perfect, genteel lady was beyond Elizabeth's comprehension.

Once Selina's schooling was completed, Elizabeth was certain that her daughter would marry a wealthy aristocrat and take her proper place in society. Knowing Selina's choices for a husband were limited at Cedar Hill, Elizabeth insisted they leave the plantation in the overseer's capable hands and take up permanent residence in New Orleans. Josh, fighting his compulsive gambling, was reluctant to make such a move. New Orleans was overflowing with gaming houses, and he was afraid, rightfully so, that they would prove to be too much of a temptation. But his wife held firm, and giving in to her demands, Josh agreed to move to the city.

Selina's amazing beauty drew several eager beaux to her door. She was always polite and charming, but one by one, they failed to spark an ardent response. Selina liked most of them well enough, but for some reason she couldn't return their amorous feelings. As time passed, she began to worry that she might never find the right man. But she held tenaciously to her resolve to marry for love and for no other reason. Surely, someday, she'd meet the man of her dreams, they'd fall passionately in love, get married, and spend the rest of their lives together!

As Selina was turning away disappointed suitors, her father was gambling compulsively, and his enormous losses finally compelled him to borrow money on his townhouse, and, eventually, on his beloved Cedar Hill.

Unaware of her husband's huge gambling debts, Elizabeth's only worry lay with her daughter's refusal to choose a husband. Added to Elizabeth's dismay, every chance Selina got, she went running back to Cedar

Hill, causing Elizabeth to make the tiring journey to the plantation in order to bring her rebellious daughter back to New Orleans. Finally, admitting defeat, Elizabeth gave up trying to wed her daughter and allowed her to move back to Cedar Hill. Selina was perfectly content to stay there, and although her parents remained in the city, she made as few trips back to New Orleans as possible.

Now, as Elizabeth remained on the settee watching Selina stare blankly out the window, her anxiety increased. Harold Chamberlain was not only wealthy, but he was also a gentleman. Surely, Selina wouldn't foolishly turn down his marriage proposal!

Tears welled up in the woman's eyes, and surrendering to her distress, she covered her face with her hands and began sobbing.

Selina rushed to her mother, sat down, and drew her into her arms. "Mama," she pleaded, "please don't cry."

"Oh Selina!" Elizabeth sobbed. "Darling, what's to become of us?" Another coughing spasm overtook the woman, the violent bout leaving her obviously weak. Breathlessly, she implored, "Selina, you must marry Mr. Chamberlain! If not for my sake, then for your own. We need his help . . . you need his help . . . desperately!"

A foreboding shadow fell over Selina. I don't want to marry Harold Chamberlain! she cried inwardly. Her inner cry, however, was hopeless. She knew that, logically, she had no choice but to accept Chamberlain's proposal. Not for her own sake, though, but for her mother and for her father's slaves. If the bank were to foreclose, a cruel master might purchase her father's property, and then what would become of the house servants and the numerous field workers?

Selina's narrow shoulders literally drooped under their heavy burden. She was not only responsible for herself, but also for her mother and their many slaves. Given the grave consequences, she couldn't very well think only of herself. To do so would be a terribly selfish act.

"Mama," Selina murmured timorously, fighting back her own tears. "Everything will be fine. You don't have to worry. I will marry Mr. Chamberlain."

Elizabeth's joy was instantly apparent. "Selina, darling, you won't be sorry. Mr. Chamberlain is such a nice man. He'll be a doting, caring husband. You'll learn to love him very quickly."

Selina thought otherwise. She didn't believe learning to love a husband was possible. You either loved him or you didn't. Love wasn't an emotion one could simply acquire. It came from the heart, not from a sense of obligation. Keeping these thoughts to herself, Selina hugged her mother briefly and said, "This house, Cedar Hill, and our slaves will not fall into somebody else's hands."

"Selina, don't make your decision to marry Mr. Chamberlain sound so unromantic. Aren't you the least bit excited about marrying a man so charming?"

Excited? Selina mused bitterly. She could feel only a heavy, depressing dullness filling her heart and burying her dreams of love.

Not wanting to worry her mother, Selina pasted a false smile on her lips and answered evasively, "I'm still shocked by Mr. Chamberlain's proposal. In time, I'm sure I'll be delighted."

Poised at the very edge of her chair, Selina watched William Stratton anxiously as she awaited his reply.

Earlier, when Elizabeth had retired to her bedroom to take her customary nap, Selina had left the house in a flurry and had walked to Stratton's home. William

Stratton was the Beaumonts' attorney and good friend. Selina was extremely fond of the man and had always thought of him as a member of her family. The moment the lawyer had shown her into his office, Selina, her words racing, had proceeded to give him a full account of Chamberlain's extraordinary proposal.

Stratton was a distinguished-looking man in his late fifties, and as he studied Selina, across the span of his desk top, a warm twinkle came to his hazel eyes. "My dear," he began, smiling paternally, "I'm well aware of the man's proposal. Because I'm your attorney, Mr. Chamberlain came to see me before he visited you and Elizabeth. Since you obviously came here for my advice, I'll give it to you quite candidly. In my opinion, you should readily accept the man's proposal. Not only is he willing to save your mortgaged properties, but he's also a reputable gentleman. My dear, surely you must realize how fortunate you are to have Mr. Chamberlain so smitten with you."

"Fortunate?" Selina murmured. "But I'm not in love with him."

He waved aside her words as though they held no importance whatsoever. "Selina, once you and Mr. Chamberlain are married, you'll soon. . . ."

"I know. I'll soon learn to love him," she interrupted flatly.

"Dear, heed my advice and your mother's. We know what's best for you."

Selina firmly disagreed. "I don't think either of you knows what's best for me. However, my mother's welfare, our property, and our slaves are very important to me. I know the only way I can save them is to marry Harold Chamberlain."

Rising, Selina placed her hands on the desk top, leaned forward, and looked unflinchingly into the attorney's eyes. "But I don't believe for one minute that sharing a marriage bed with Chamberlain will make me fall in love with him."

Stratton blushed beneath his gray-streaked goatee. His feelings toward Selina were in full accord with Elizabeth's. The young lady was too outspoken, unruly, and needed firm discipline. He felt that Harold Chamberlain was the perfect man for the job. A smile touched the corners of his lips. Chamberlain would find his spirited bride quite a handful.

"I'm sorry if I spoke out of turn," Selina apologized. "But I've always had a habit of saying exactly what I think."

"Yes, that I know," Stratton replied.

Knowing there was no reason to linger, Selina bid the attorney a warm goodbye and showed herself out of the office.

Preoccupied with her turbulent thoughts, Selina totally missed seeing the tall gentleman who was ascending the steps. She collided with him blindly and would have fallen if the stranger hadn't caught her in his strong arms.

"Whoa there, little lady," the man said with a deep Texas drawl.

Regaining her balance, Selina gazed upward into a pair of dark brown eyes that were twinkling with amusement. She stepped back from the man's supportive hold and was about to murmur an apology when, suddenly, the stranger's striking good looks hit her with a startling force.

He was hatless, and she could see that his hair, worn to collar length, was a sandy blond. His face was deeply tanned; apparently, the man spent a lot of time outdoors. As Selina's eyes traveled boldly over his tall frame, she noticed the way his bulging muscles were clearly outlined beneath his dark, expensively-tailored suit. Selina had never seen a man so ruggedly handsome, or so blatantly virile.

Meanwhile, the stranger was finding Selina equally attractive. Her head barely reached the width of his broad shoulders, and he had to descend a couple of the porch steps to see her at eye level. He found her so incredibly beautiful that his gaze raked over her with a fiery intent.

Selina suspected that his piercing eyes were mentally undressing her. She knew that she should find such conduct insulting and should coldly shun him; but for some mysterious reason she was helplessly mesmerized.

Slowly, the man raised his gaze to hers, then smiling indolently, he stepped aside, giving her ample room to pass.

Regaining her composure, Selina lifted the hem of her long skirt, hurried down the steps, and started for home. She didn't dare glance back to see if he was watching.

Two

Layne Smith entered the Hotel St. Louis, crossed the plush lobby with long strides, and vaulted up the carpeted stairway to the second floor. He moved quickly down the long hall to the room located next to his own. He announced his arrival with a short rap on the door before opening it and stepping inside.

Layne glanced briefly at his friend. The man was sitting in a chair placed in front of the French doors that led onto a balcony.

Removing his suit coat, Layne pitched it on the bed. The air circulating through the open doors couldn't prevent the room from being uncomfortably warm, and Layne wiped a hand across his damp brow. As he rolled up the long sleeves of his shirt, his tanned, muscular arms were revealed. He was strikingly attractive. His sandy-colored hair, usually unmanageable, fell across his forehead in curly disarray, and his blatant masculinity was enhanced by his tall, powerfully-strong build.

Stepping to a small mahogany table that held four glasses and a bottle of whiskey, he poured himself a drink and carried it over to where his friend was seated, pulled up a hard-backed chair and sat down.

"Did you see Stratton?" his friend asked.

24

Layne looked at the man and smiled faintly. "Yeah, I saw him. When I told him I suspected Chamberlain of murder, he said I was out of my mind."

"We're only goin' to be here two more days. You don't have time to find any proof that Chamberlain killed your father."

When his friend said no more, Layne asked archly, "So?"

"So, why don't you forget it?"

Layne's answer was a shrug of his shoulders.

"Besides," the other man continued, "maybe your father did take his own life. After all, you read the suicide note and said it was your father's handwriting."

"I said it looked like his," Layne clarified.

"Same difference," mumbled his companion.

Taking a drink of his whiskey, Layne studied his friend over the rim of his glass. Doug Thompson's face was expressionless, but Layne could discern the man's thoughts. "You're convinced my father committed suicide, aren't you?"

Doug sighed heavily. "I don't know, Layne. But, yeah, I guess I am. And apparently the law agrees. But more importantly, why would Chamberlain murder your father? They were partners, true, but he didn't gain anything by your father's death."

"Dammit!" Smith cursed, his tone carrying a note of desperation. "Dad wasn't the kind of man to take his own life!"

"You hadn't seen him in five years. A lot can happen to a man in that amount of time. He obviously had problems you know nothing about."

Doug left his chair and crossed the room to pour himself a drink. His tall, brawny frame moved gracefully for its huge size. Doug Thompson exuded a forbidding aura that was misleading. He was basically a gentle man, and he went out of his way to avoid trouble. But when confronted with violence, he met it with a deadly response. His grandmother had been a full-blood Apache, and Doug's dark complexion, broad features, and black hair were traits of his Indian heritage. His face wasn't handsome, nor was it especially unattractive. He had once tried to grow a beard to help conceal his plainness, but his Indian blood had made it difficult to grow a full beard. Giving up, he had shaved off the stubble; thereafter, he had remained clean-shaven.

Doug, a taciturn man, had been a loner and a wanderer when, three years ago, he rode up to Layne's ranch in Texas to ask for a job. Layne had taken an instant liking to Doug and had hired him on the spot. As time passed, a warm friendship developed between the two, and last year, when Layne's foreman had quit, the job was given to Doug. Their friendship hadn't been the main factor behind Layne's promoting Doug to foreman; Doug Thompson had been the best man for the job.

As Doug fixed himself a drink, Layne became buried in his thoughts. The breeze wafting through the open doors felt cool on his warm brow, and he leaned back, relaxing in his chair and stretching out his long legs.

Layne was ridden with guilt, and he couldn't shake it. Regardless of the personal differences between himself and his father, he should have made more trips back to New Orleans to visit him. Five years! God, it was hard to believe that so much time had passed since he'd last made the effort to see his father. A frown furrowed his brow as he remembered their final visit. It hadn't been a pleasant one for Layne, for, as always, his father had spent their time together complaining about Layne's move to Texas.

Howard Smith had never understood, or forgiven, his son for taking no interest in the Smith-Chamberlain

Shipping Company. Howard had labored arduously to build an empire to hand down to his only heir; and when Layne, at age twenty-one, had informed his father that he wanted nothing to do with the family business, Howard's disappointment had been enormous. The harsh arguments that eventually erupted between father and son finally convinced Layne to leave New Orleans and head for Texas.

Now, as Layne's frown deepened with regret, he wished he had found a way to make his father understand that a man had to follow his own dream. Just because a shipping line was Howard Smith's dream, didn't necessarily make it his son's as well.

From the time Layne was a young boy, he'd had visions of moving to Texas. Men like Davy Crockett, Jim Bowie, William Travis, and Sam Houston had been his heroes. Sitting behind a desk while operating his father's business held no interest for the young Layne, and as he grew older his feelings failed to change. He not only longed for adventure and excitement, but he detested living in the city. Furthermore, he found Southern society superficial, his peers boring, and the typical Southern belle too pampered.

Returning to his chair, Doug asked, "What did Stratton have to say about your father's property?"

"He said that Dad's will left his half of the shipping company to me." Layne sighed deeply. "I don't want it. Stratton offered to buy it, and he made me a fair price."

"Did you sell?"

Layne nodded. "I also sold him Dad's house."

"I guess he wondered why you're staying here at the hotel instead of at the house."

"He mentioned it. I told him the truth. The place holds too many unpleasant memories." Layne changed the subject abruptly. "Before going to Stratton's, I saw Dr. Wilkerson. He invited me to his home tonight for dinner. When I told him I have a friend traveling with me, he extended the invitation to you."

Doug withdrew into silence for a long moment, then said, "Count me out."

Layne studied him questioningly. "I don't understand. Why don't you want to go?"

Doug quaffed down his whiskey. "I don't belong in New Orleans society. I wasn't born and raised here like you were. Hell, I grew up in the wilderness. Although my mother managed to drum some education into my thick head, I'm a far cry from a polished Southern gentleman. Also, my Apache blood's so obvious that the New Orleans citizens stare at me as though they're afraid I'm goin' to scalp 'em."

Layne chuckled. "You wouldn't exaggerate, would you?"

"A little, maybe," Doug admitted, grinning. "But at that dinner, I'd feel like a fish out of water. Furthermore, I doubt if the Wilkersons would be comfortable with an Apache's grandson sitting at their table." Doug shook his head emphatically. "No, you can count me out. While you're dining with the New Orleans upper crust, I'll be having a good time at Belle's."

"If I felt I had a choice in the matter, I'd go to Belle's with you. A whorehouse sounds more appealing than spending an evening with the Wilkersons. However, we'll be leaving soon, and I haven't even seen Janet yet." A deep frown crossed Layne's brow. "I'm certainly not looking forward to having a woman traveling with us." He shrugged briefly. "But I promised her father. . . ."

Janet's father, Bart Wilkerson, owned a ranch north of Layne's. Janet had been three years old when her mother died, and her father, believing she should be raised by a woman, had taken her to New Orleans to live with his brother and sister-in-law. Thereafter, Bart's fatherly duties consisted of visiting New Orleans twice a year to see his daughter. Eventually, he had remarried and was considering fetching Janet back home, but when his wife died giving birth to his still-born son, Bart decided to leave his daughter in his brother's care. Janet, now eighteen, had recently written to her father, asking for his permission to come back home. Bart was pleased by his daughter's request, and when he learned that Layne was traveling to New Orleans, he asked him to escort Janet back to Texas. Layne had agreed reluctantly. Such a journey always included a certain amount of danger, and Janet's safety would be a big responsibility. Bart Wilkerson, though, was a good friend and neighbor, so Layne acquiesced, but with strong reservations.

"I don't know about you," Doug began, stifling a yawn. "But I'll be glad to get back home. New Orleans is too noisy and crowded for me. I sure miss the wide open plains of Texas."

"My sentiments exactly," Layne remarked. A warm twinkle came to his eyes as he said, "New Orleans, however, does have its assets."

"For instance?"

"At Stratton's home, I literally collided with the most enticing woman I've ever seen."

Doug arched a brow. "This could be interesting. Who was she?"

"I don't know. There were no introductions."

"You didn't quiz Stratton about her?"

"I didn't see any reason to. We'll be leavin' soon, so why should I go to the trouble to meet her, only to leave her?" Layne finished his whiskey, sighed heavily, and murmured, "But she sure was a vision of loveliness."

Harold Chamberlain returned to the Beaumont home at six o'clock sharp. He had expected the butler to receive his knock and was surprised when Selina admitted him instead. He erroneously took her answering his call as a sign that she had been eagerly awaiting his return.

As Chamberlain followed his hostess into the parlor, he was gloating with confidence. He inwardly chastised himself for his earlier doubts. When Selina had shown no enthusiasm over his proposal, he had been mystified by her indifference. Didn't she realize that he was the most sought after bachelor in town? Surely she was aware that he could have his pick among the unmarried ladies in and about New Orleans.

Now, however, Harold's questions surrounding Selina's peculiar behavior were quickly dissipated. Earlier, apparently, she had been too incredulous by his generous offer to display her gratitude openly.

Selina led her guest to the settee, and gesturing for him to sit beside her, she said with a composure she was far from feeling, "Mr. Chamberlain, I'm very grateful to you for your generosity. You have lifted a heavy burden from my mother's shoulders."

She had purposefully omitted any reference to herself, for Selina felt as though the burden she had carried since her father's death had merely been replaced by another one; this burden heavier than the first. Marrying a man she didn't love was a cross she found almost impossible to bear.

Averting her eyes from Harold's expectant face, Selina lowered her gaze to her lap and murmured, "Mr. Chamberlain, I have decided to accept your proposal." A painful lump rose in her throat. She felt as though she had just sentenced herself to a lifetime of unhappiness.

Her brand-new fiancé smiled complacently. "Selina, my love, I knew you'd say yes."

"Mr. Chamberlain . . ." she began.

"Don't be so formal. Please call me Harold."

Selina started over. "Harold, I feel that I must be totally honest with you."

Again, he interrupted, "I already know what you're about to say. You don't love me and you are marrying me for your mother's sake, and also to keep the bank from taking your property. Am I right?"

She nodded listlessly. "Yes, you're right."

Chamberlain's confidence was still soaring. "Selina, believe me, within an incredibly short time you'll fall deeply in love with me."

"But what if I don't?" she asked bluntly.

"Then that, my dear, will be your misfortune. Marriage is more pleasant for a woman if she loves her husband." He shrugged as though unconcerned. "However, a marriage doesn't need love to be successful."

He rose abruptly, took her hands, and drew her to her feet. "Dr. Wilkerson invited me to his home tonight for dinner. He said I could bring a guest, so hurry and change clothes. We're supposed to be there at seven."

Selina didn't feel up to socializing. "I'd rather not go, if you don't mind."

"But I do mind. After dinner, we'll announce our engagement." He gave her a gentle push toward the parlor door. "Dress ravishingly, my love. I want to show off my beautiful fiancée."

Selina relented. "I'll be as quick as I can. Do you want me to ask Mama to come sit with you while I dress?"

"That won't be necessary." He had spoken hastily, for he found Mrs. Beaumont's company enormously tedious.

As Selina hurried from the room, Chamberlain's eyes bore into her departing back. He was well satisfied with his choice of a bride. Selina Beaumont was extraordinarily beautiful but, just as important, she had

31

no male kin to intervene with his treatment of her. When she became his wife, she would be his to do with as he pleased.

As a vision of their wedding night flashed before him, Harold Chamberlain's lips curled into a cunningly lustful grin.

"Oh Janet!" Melody Harper exclaimed. "You're so courageous and daring! I'd be terrified to make such a journey. I hear there are hostile Indians in Texas! Aren't you scared the savages will attack you?" The young woman shuddered visibly, moaning gravely, "Or even worse! A warrior might abduct you and . . . and force himself on you!"

Janet, who had been sitting at her dressing table, stood up quickly and faced her companion. Her chin lifted with a defiant tilt. "Of course I'm not scared," she remarked with forced bravo. "Furthermore, it might be exciting to be abducted by a warrior. I've read that some of them are savagely handsome."

Melody was aghast. "Janet, surely you aren't serious!"

Janet pouted sullenly. "Why not? It'd serve Uncle Fred and Aunt Effie right if I were to be molested. Then they'd be sorry that they treated me so unfairly."

"Unfairly?" her friend questioned, astounded. "Why, Janet Wilkerson, everyone knows that your uncle and aunt have spoiled you extravagantly."

Stamping her foot immaturely, Janet retorted, "They treat me like I'm still a child!"

"Maybe that's because you still act like one," Melody pointed out.

Janet was furious. "How dare you! We're the same age, but just because you're married you think you know so much more than I do!" Tossing her head petulantly, Janet stormed to the bedroom door, opened it, and ordered, "I want you to leave!"

Melody was sorry that she had angered her friend. "Please don't be upset," she pleaded, hurrying to Janet's side.

As usual, Janet's anger vanished as quickly as it had arisen. "I'm not upset."

"Are you sure?" Melody pressed.

"I'm sure," Janet assured her, smiling freely. "But you do have to leave. We're having guests for dinner. Layne Smith, who's taking me to my father, and Harold Chamberlain are due at seven."

"Harold Chamberlain!" Melody sighed. "He's so suave and handsome!"

"Why, Melody Harper!" Janet teased. "Such shameless behavior for a married lady! And still a bride, no less!"

The other woman giggled merrily. "I love my husband, as you well know." She hugged Janet, then left quickly.

Janet pushed the door closed with a solid bang. Melody Harper was such a silly goose. She liked her well enough; after all, they had been friends since childhood. But they were as different as night and day. Melody had no gumption, no craving for excitement. In Janet's opinion, her childhood friend was hopelessly dull.

Returning to her dressing table, Janet sat down on the velvet-covered stool. Dismissing Melody from her mind, she glanced carefully about her room, its expensive furnishings reflecting the Wilkersons' devotion to their niece. It was hard for Janet to believe that she'd soon be leaving such familiar surroundings. Contrary to the brave front she had presented to Melody, traveling to Texas was somewhat frightening. Resolutely Janet transferred her fright to the far recesses of her mind. After all, people frequently made the trip from New Orleans to Texas without losing their scalps. The journey might contain a certain amount of risk, but apparently it wasn't all that dangerous.

Several times Janet had questioned her decision to visit her father, and again these doubts came flooding back. Maybe she should reconsider and stay here where she was safe.

Safe, yes! she thought testily. But bored!

Doubling her small hand into a fist, she slammed it consecutively against the dresser top, grumbling, "Bored! . . . Bored! . . . Bored!"

Janet blamed her aunt and uncle entirely for her dreary existence. If they weren't so overly protective, and if they didn't watch her like a pair of hawks, then surely her life would be filled with fun and excitement.

She wasn't sure if it was possible to find this fun and excitement in the Texas wilderness, but she was so desperate to free herself from the Wilkersons' supervision that she was willing to take her chances. She realized, of course, that her father would most assuredly guard her paternally, but operating a large ranch was probably a full-time job. She doubted if he'd have time to closely scrutinize her activities.

But what if I hate living in Texas? she wondered. I might be more miserable there than I am here. She considered the possibility for a moment, then dismissed it. If she didn't like staying with her father, then she'd simply return to New Orleans.

"Nothing ventured, nothing gained," she reminded herself.

Turning toward the mirror, she peered closely at her reflection. Janet Wilkerson was exceptionally pretty, and although she took great pride in her beauty, her vanity was within reason. Her heart-shape face was framed by golden-blond tresses, and dark, long lashes shadowed her jade-green eyes.

Standing, Janet studied her full appearance. She turned this way and that, studying herself from different angles. She was pleased with what she saw, although she wished her breasts were more voluptuous.

She was already dressed for dinner, and her evening gown was snowy white with an overdress of white crepe. Its voluminous skirt, falling gracefully past her ankles, barely touched the tops of her dainty slippers.

Her hair, pulled back into a cluster of long curls, displayed the pair of diamond earrings that adorned her ears. A matching diamond pendant came to rest above the cleavage between her breasts, the expensive piece of jewelry adding a tasteful touch to her off-the-shoulder evening gown.

Deciding she was presentable, Janet crossed the room and hastened downstairs to join her aunt and uncle. She suddenly became curious about the man who was escorting her to her father's ranch. A hopeful gleam shone in her green eyes. If Layne Smith was young and handsome, then the trip to Texas might be a delightful experience.

Three

Fred Wilkerson ushered Layne into his study, saying briskly, "I'm glad you arrived before the others, it gives us time to talk."

"Others?" Layne questioned. He'd gotten the impression that he was the only one coming to dinner. He hoped the Wilkersons weren't having a lot of company. He wasn't in the mood for socializing.

"I invited Harold Chamberlain, and I think he's bringing a young lady," Doctor Wilkerson replied, as he showed his guest to a chair.

Chamberlain! Layne groaned inwardly. He certainly didn't relish spending an evening in the man's company. When seated, he glanced about the spacious room as his host poured two tumblers of brandy. The study reflected a masculine decor, with furniture of large pieces and walnut bookshelves. A matching pair of criss-crossed sabres hung over the fireplace, and a fully stocked gun cabinet stood in the far corner.

Doctor Wilkerson handed Layne a drink, then moved behind the desk and eased his tall, lanky frame into the leather-bound chair.

"Mr. Smith," he began, "I need to talk to you about my niece."

Layne nodded. "I figured as much."

"My niece," the doctor proceeded hesitantly — he was uncomfortable discussing Janet with a stranger, "is a very spoiled young lady."

An irritable frown wrinkled Layne's brow. Escorting a spoiled Southern belle to Texas didn't sit well with him. He had a sinking feeling that the girl would be nothing but trouble. If only he hadn't promised Bart Wilkerson!

The doctor continued, "My wife and I have spoiled our niece terribly. We never had any children of our own, and we were so overjoyed to have Janet that we foolishly doted on her. I'm afraid we gave her too much love and not enough discipline. I'm telling you this because I believe you're going to have a difficult time. She's never had to lift a finger to do anything for herself, and she's never done without all the luxuries money can buy." Wilkerson sighed heavily. "Mr. Smith, under the circumstances, I don't think Janet can endure the demanding trip to Texas."

"She'll have to endure it," Layne said dryly. "Once we leave, I'm not turning back."

"I understand," the doctor replied. "But, Mr. Smith, please be patient with her."

Layne held back the impulse to tell the man that he could damn well keep his pampered niece. Through gritted teeth he promised with honest intent, "I'll try to be patient."

"Janet will take her personal maid. The servant's presence will make the journey less tiring for Janet, for the wench will be there to take care of her mistress's needs."

"Her maid's not going," Layne remarked tersely.

Wilkerson was confused. "I don't understand. Why not?" All at once his eyes narrowed disagreeably. "Mr. Smith, are you opposed to slavery?"

"My beliefs on slavery have nothing to do with this."

"Then why are you against Janet's taking her maid?"

"The maid's safety is an added responsibility I intend to do without."

"But, sir, it wouldn't be proper for Janet to travel alone with you and your friend. For propriety's sake, you must allow Janet's maid to accompany her."

"I'm sorry, Doctor Wilkerson. But my mind's made up." Layne's tone was final.

A few minutes later as Doctor Wilkerson was escorting Layne into the parlor, he saw that his other guests had arrived.

Mrs. Wilkerson was sitting on the sofa beside her niece as she spoke to Chamberlain and Selina. The couple, sitting close together on the loveseat, were listening politely to their hostess's trivial colloquy.

Selina, though, was finding it extremely difficult to give Mrs. Wilkerson her full attention, for Harold's proximity made her uneasy. She wished he'd move over and not sit so close. An imperceptible shudder ran through her. If sharing a loveseat with the man bothered her, then how in heaven's name was she going to share his bed?

Selina stopped listening to her hostess, for she was now totally engulfed in her troublesome thoughts. Harold Chamberlain was such a handsome man, so why did he affect her so adversely? What's wrong with him? she wondered intensely. Then she told herself impatiently, there's probably nothing wrong with him. It's me! I'm the problem! Maybe I'm incapable of responding ardently to a man. After all, I've had numerous suitors, most of them handsome and charming. Yet I didn't fall in love with any of them. Why? If I only knew why?

"Selina? . . . Selina?" Doctor Wilkerson's voice cut

into her reverie.

Startled out of her deep thoughts, Selina was surprised to find her host poised in front of her, watching her expectantly.

"Are you all right, my dear?" Wilkerson inquired.

"Yes . . . I'm sorry, my mind wandered," she apologized, embarrassed that she had been caught daydreaming.

"I was about to introduce you to my other guest," the doctor explained.

Becoming aware of the man standing at Wilkerson's side, she recognized him as the gentleman she had collided with at Stratton's home. A warm blush started to color her cheeks.

"Selina," her host began, "this is Layne Smith." He turned his introduction to Layne. "Mr. Smith, may I present Miss Beaumont."

A wry grin touched the corners of Layne's lips as he lifted Selina's extended hand and placed a light kiss upon it. "Miss Beaumont, it's a pleasure to make your acquaintance."

"Thank you," she murmured. She wondered why her heart was suddenly beating so rapidly, and why the touch of his lips had caused such a delightful tingle.

A few moments before, when Layne had entered the parlor, he'd found Selina's presence a pleasant surprise. However, he'd been sorely disappointed to find her with Chamberlain.

Now, unmindful of the others in the room, Layne's piercing gaze swept over Selina openly. She was just as beautiful as he'd first thought.

Selina was indeed a fetching sight. Her evening dress of sea-green silk was trimmed with a darker shade of velvet and white crepe. Her ears were pierced with a pair of emerald stud earrings. Her hair was unbound, and the dark tresses fell past her bare shoulders in lustrous fullness.

Doctor Wilkerson, growing quite uncomfortable with Layne's apparent fascination with Selina, was greatly relieved when the butler announced that dinner was served.

Tearing his eyes away from Selina, Layne stepped to Janet and offered her his arm. "Ma'am, may I escort you to the dinin' room?"

Delighted, Janet bounded gracefully to her feet, slipped her hand in the crook of Layne's arm, and smiled coquettishly. "I'd be honored, Mr. Smith."

Meanwhile, Chamberlain assisted his fiancée from the loveseat, slipping an arm familiarly about her waist. He drew her close to his side, too close for Selina's comfort. As they followed the others to the dining room, Selina dreaded the rest of the evening. She had a feeling it would drag on interminably.

Much later, when Janet offered to take Layne outside and show him the flower garden, he accepted readily. He needed a breath of cool air; and while following Janet through the patio doors, he loosened his tight-fitting cravat. The stuffy confinement of the house had begun to close in on him. He was an outdoor man, used to the wide open plains.

As they crossed the patio, Layne turned briefly and glanced back into the parlor. He caught a quick glimpse of Selina. She was again sitting on the loveseat with Chamberlain. Layne was puzzled to note a touch of sadness on her face.

His thoughts now exclusively on Selina, Layne tuned out Janet's constant chatter as she led him to the wrought-iron bench that overlooked her aunt's luxuriant garden. Sitting beside his young hostess, Layne wondered why there seemed to be an aura of sadness about Miss Beaumont.

Following dinner, Chamberlain had announced that he and Selina were engaged, and they planned to marry in the near future. Layne's puzzlement deepened. Selina Beaumont didn't seem very happy for a woman who was about to be married.

Chamberlain's fiancée isn't my concern, Layne told himself, banishing her from his thoughts. In an effort to keep Selina out of his mind, Layne turned to Janet and gave her his undivided attention. However, it was disconcerting to find that she was discussing Selina and Chamberlain.

"When Mr. Chamberlain announced his engagement to Selina," Janet was saying, "you could have knocked me over with a feather. I mean, I always knew that someday he would marry—but Selina Beaumont? She's very beautiful, of course, but everyone knows she's a little strange."

"Strange?" Layne questioned.

"She's almost a recluse. She seldom comes to the city, but spends all her time at the Beaumonts' country plantation. I ask you, why would a woman want to be stuck in the country with a bunch of nigras? Her parents even resided here in town, yet Selina stayed at Cedar Hill. Her father died recently, and I'm sure his death is the only reason she's here instead of at the plantation."

"How well do you know Miss Beaumont?"

"I barely know her at all. We've only talked a few times. As I said, she spends all of her time at Cedar Hill. I heard that a few years ago she had several rich suitors vying for her hand. She lived in the city at that time, but she didn't marry any of them. I understand that her poor mama was driven to distraction. Imagine having a daughter so . . . so odd? Rumor has it that Mrs. Beaumont finally gave up trying to marry off

41

Selina and allowed her to move permanently back to Cedar Hill."

Janet clucked her tongue. "There's no accounting for taste. Mr. Chamberlain could have his pick of unmarried ladies, yet he chose Selina Beaumont." Changing the subject, Janet went on eagerly, "Mr. Smith, do you have any instructions for me concerning our journey?"

"As a matter of fact, I do," he replied.

Janet flashed him a radiant smile. She was thrilled that her escort was so handsome and intriguing. She wondered if he'd fall passionately in love with her. Would she love him in return? Yes, she decided, it would be very easy to fall in love with Layne Smith. He's so ruggedly attractive—and so excitingly male!

"I bought a canvas-top wagon for the trip," Layne began.

"A covered wagon!" Janet cut in gaily, clasping her hands together. "How quaint! My goodness, I feel like a pioneer!"

Layne, his jaw clenched, held back a testy retort. The young lady's foolishness was exasperating. He continued, his voice on an even keel, "I insist that you pack lightly. If you decide to reside permanently with your father, you can always send for the rest of your things. Also, your maid will not be accompanying us."

"But why not?" she gasped. Was he that determined to get her alone? Although Janet was flattered, she was also apprehensive. She was a shameless flirt, but she somehow sensed that Layne Smith was not a man to trifle with.

"I don't want to be responsible for your maid's safety," Layne explained.

"Oh?" she asked archly. "Are you sure you don't have an ulterior motive?"

Layne was perplexed, but only for a moment. "Miss Wilkerson, I can assure you that I don't plan to take

42

advantage of you."

"But it'll only be the two of us," she reminded him.

"Three of us," he corrected. "My foreman, Doug Thompson, is traveling with me. Didn't your uncle tell you?"

"No, he didn't." Janet's eyes widened with wonderment. Heavens, she'd be traveling alone with two rugged Texas cowboys! She could hardly wait to tell Melody Harper! Her humdrum existence was certainly becoming a thing of the past.

As Layne and Janet returned to the parlor, Layne immediately noticed that Chamberlain was nowhere in sight.

Explaining the man's absence, Doctor Wilkerson said, "One of Mr. Chamberlain's employees stopped by while you two were outside, and he was called away unexpectedly on a pressing business matter. Mr. Smith, would you mind escorting Miss Beaumont home?"

"That won't be necessary," Selina remarked, not giving Layne time to reply. "I can walk home alone."

"Nonsense!" the doctor declared. "My dear, I insist that you allow Mr. Smith or myself to see you safely home."

"Very well, Doctor Wilkerson." She looked at Layne. "Mr. Smith, if you don't mind?"

"I'd be honored to accompany you, ma'am," he said, bowing gallantly from the waist. His conduct was that of a chivalrous gentleman, but Selina thought she detected an amusing twinkle in his brown eyes.

Anxious to leave, Selina murmured departing courtesies to her host and hostess. Smith quickly followed suit.

Her strides were unmistakably hurried, and to stay

abreast of her Layne picked up his pace. The residential area was a fine one, and wooden sidewalks ran along the streets.

Layne wanted time to get to know her a little better. "Why the rush? Are you eager to get home or to get rid of me?"

Slowing her strides somewhat, Selina apologized. "I'm sorry, Mr. Smith. But, yes, I am eager to reach home."

"Would it be too forward of me to ask why?"

"Well, for one thing, I want to get out of this confining corset. I hate wearing the dadblasted thing!"

Taken aback, Layne's steps halted abruptly. He was astounded that this southern-bred lady had made such a straightforward declaration.

Pausing, Selina asked point-blank, "Did I shock you, Mr. Smith?"

"A little, I guess," he stammered.

Suddenly, Selina laughed infectiously, and Layne found himself joining her.

"Mr. Smith," she said, her laughter fading, "you should've seen the look on your face. I'm afraid my frankness took you completely off guard."

"That's puttin' it mildly," he answered. His gaze went to her slim waist, and smiling indolently, he remarked, "If you ask me, you don't need a corset. Also, the garments are a lot of trouble to get off."

"Oh?" she questioned pertly. "And I suppose you have removed your share of them?"

He looked deeply into her sparkling blue eyes. He wondered what had happened to the sadness that had seemed to surround her at the Wilkersons'. Or had the sadness only been his imagination?

Selina resumed her steady strides, and Layne fell into step beside her. She was acutely aware of his closeness, and it had an exhilarating affect on her.

"When you and Janet were in the garden, I'm sure she told you all about me." Selina's tone was even, and Layne was totally unaware that she was finding his presence stimulating. "Did she tell you that I'm . . . different?"

"She used the words 'strange' and 'odd,' " Layne answered, smiling uncertainly.

Selina wasn't offended. "I prefer different. Strange and odd makes me sound a little demented. But believe me, there's nothing wrong with me. Ladies like Janet can't understand why I prefer my plantation over New Orleans."

"Why do you?" Layne asked.

"I love Cedar Hill, Mr. Smith."

For an instant a despondent shadow seemed to darken her face, but the moment was gone so quickly that Layne couldn't be sure.

Her mood again cheerful, Selina said saucily, "Speaking of Janet, you'd better be on your guard, for she's a flirt. If you aren't careful, she'll have a wedding ring on your finger before you reach Texas."

"No chance," Layne answered flatly. "I'm not the marrying kind."

"Why aren't you?"

"I relish my independence. Besides, a rancher's life is a demanding one. Also, parts of Texas are still untamed. It takes a special breed of woman to settle for that way of life. She has to have a lot of grit, stamina, and courage."

He touched her arm, bringing their steps to a halt. "I suppose someday you'll find out what it's like to be a rancher's wife."

"Why do you think that?" she asked, thoroughly confused.

"Your fiancé owns a ranch in Texas. In fact, it borders on my own." Seeing her bewilderment, he queried,

"You didn't know about his ranch?"

She shook her head. "No, I didn't."

They continued walking.

"A few years ago," Layne explained, "Chamberlain came to Texas, bought a large spread of land, and filled it with cattle. He has a prosperous ranch, and his home is quite elegant."

"Who takes care of his ranch?"

"Jessie and Larry Harte. They're brother and sister."

"Do you know Harold well?"

"No, not really. He and my father were business partners."

"Then your father was Howard Smith?"

"Yes," he replied.

"Please accept my condolences. You must be devastated over your father's suicide."

Layne drifted into silence for a long moment, then said kindly, "Janet said that your father also died recently. I'm sorry."

They had reached her home, and Selina stopped, gestured tersely toward the house, and said, "This is where I live."

Layne was disappointed. He wished she lived farther away. He had found their short walk a pleasant one, and he had enjoyed her company so much.

He touched the brim of his hat. "Well, ma'am, it was a pleasure meeting you."

She extended her hand. "Good night, Mr. Smith, and thank you for seeing me home."

His large hand slipped into her small one, and he was about to kiss it when he suddenly changed his mind. Believing he'd never see this enticing young woman again, he was determined, just once, to taste the sweetness of her lips.

Taking Selina completely unaware, Layne's arm went swiftly about her waist as he drew her flush to his tall frame. Bending his head, his mouth captured hers in a sensuous, demanding caress. Desire coursed through him so strongly that he had to release her brusquely in order to control the fiery longing stirring in his loins.

Layne girded himself for the slap he was sure was now coming. But instead, Selina simply whirled about, unlatched the gate, and rushed into the house.

Racing up the stairs and to her room, Selina rushed to her bed and fell across it. She held back the tears that were threatening to overflow.

His kiss had been thrilling! She had kissed former suitors, but no one's kiss had ever aroused her so intensely! Thinking back, she decided that her past kisses were less than nothing when compared to Layne Smith's.

Frustrated, Selina pounded her fists against the mattress. Life was so unfair! She had finally found a man she could respond to, but he could never be hers! She was engaged to Harold Chamberlain, and she'd soon be his wife. In every sense of the word!

Giving in to her despair, Selina released her bottled up tears.

Meanwhile, Layne was walking toward the hotel, silently berating himself for his behavior. He inwardly cursed himself for desiring Chamberlain's fiancée. Unfairly, he aimed his anger directly at Selina. He rationalized that any woman who agreed to marry Chamberlain had to be as unsavory as her intended. Layne had no proof that Chamberlain was unsavory, it was merely speculation. But he knew the man well enough to form his own opinion of him, and Layne found him a pompous, conceited bastard. He doubted if Selina was blind to Chamberlain's character, which meant she was probably just like him. Furthermore, she was evidently insincere; otherwise, she would have

47

rebuffed his kiss and reminded him that she was engaged. Apparently, Chamberlain's fiancée was not a woman the man could trust.

Layne cast Selina out of his mind and turned his thoughts to Texas—to his ranch. Home! He'd be glad to get back.

Four

Hattie's face was sympathetic as she gazed into Stella Larson's tear-glazed eyes.

"Oh Hattie!" the young woman cried brokenly. "If it wasn't for my son, I'd wanna die! I just wouldn't wanna go on livin'!"

The rotund Negro woman placed her hands on her broad hips, a gesture she always used when she was about to speak reproachfully. "Miz Stella, I ain't gonna listen to that kind of talk. And the good Lord, he don't like that kind of talk neither. You got to believe that someday things is gonna get better."

"Better?" Stella remarked bitterly. "The only way things is gonna get better is for Harold Chamberlain to up and die!"

"Well, he ain't gonna die just to oblige you," Hattie humphed. "So you may as well get that hope right out of your head."

Stella turned to her son's crib and lifted the child into her arms. She hugged him lovingly; and as he wrapped his chubby little arms about her neck, she was suddenly reminded of those days when he had been painfully thin. She embraced the child tighter; she'd never let him go hungry again! No matter what!

She placed a kiss on the baby's rosy cheek before

49

returning him to the crib. He rolled onto his stomach, then maneuvering himself into his favorite slumbering position, he drew up his knees and stuck his plump bottom in the air. Within moments, he was sound asleep.

Smiling, Stella affectionately patted his uplifted rear, whispering, "Good night, Paul. Mommy loves you."

She turned about to leave her bedroom, but seeing Hattie standing behind her, she flung herself into the older woman's embrace.

Hattie's arms went about her companion, drawing her close. Stella cried until her tears ran dry.

Then, sniffling, she stepped back and murmured, "I don't know what's wrong with me. I mean, it ain't as though today's any different than most of 'em."

"I think, honey, that you's about to reach a breakin' point. You cain't take much more of Masta Chamberlain's abuse." Hattie's voice deepened gravely. "I's afraid that one of these days that man's gonna go too far, and he's gonna hurt you real bad. Maybe even kill you. Masta Chamberlain, he's a devil, through and through."

Stella moved sluggishly to her dressing table; and peering into the mirror, she examined the ugly, discolored bruises on her arms and neck. There were more such bruises, but they were hidden beneath her dress.

"God!" she groaned. "Mr. Chamberlain don't give my old bruises time to heal before he's inflictin' new ones."

"Miz Stella, I's gonna fix you a cup of hot tea. You got time to drink it 'fore you has to leave."

"Thank you, Hattie," Stella murmured, smiling fondly. Hattie believed firmly that a cup of hot tea was a remedy for whatever ailed a body; whether it be physical or emotional.

As the woman left the room, Stella moved to her bed

and sat on the edge. Her thoughts meandered back into the past.

Stella Larson was born into poverty; her parents were what was referred to as poor white trash. Stella was never offended by the commonly used term, for in her opinion her mother and father were just that—poor, white, and trash. The small, dilapidated cabin where she grew up was overly crowded, for Stella shared the home with five siblings and her parents.

Her father, Joe Larson, tried half-heartedly to scratch out a living on his few acres of farm land. The dried-up soil could barely produce a marginal crop; but even if it were fertile, Joe Larson didn't have the energy, nor the initiative, to toil his land and bring in a full harvest. More often than not, his children went to bed with their stomachs gnawing from hunger. Stella, being the oldest, comforted the younger ones, often saving her cornbread from supper and dividing it among them. It did little to satiate their hunger.

Joe Larson had only one ambitious drive in life—drinking. He drank to excess. Too poor to buy liquor, he brewed his own. His wife, Alice, was a compatible mate, for like her husband, she drank from sunup to sundown.

Stella despised her parents, loathed her way of life, and spent her adolescent years deeply depressed.

Her father was visited regularly by an itinerant slave dealer. The trader, Ben Chadwell, swore up and down that Joe Larson made the best homebrew in Louisiana. Ben, the same age as Larson, was as uneducated as his drinking companion and just as lazy. Never having much money, he could only afford to buy maimed or elderly slaves—so his coffle was always a pitiful one.

The summer when Stella turned sixteen, Chadwell

stopped by on one of his regular visits. For the past year or so, Stella had begun to dread the man's arrival. She didn't like the way he looked at her. Her young body had bloomed voluptuously, and Ben's beady eyes were always traveling over her full breasts and down to her womanly-shaped thighs.

On this particular visit, Ben Chadwell, liquored-up, offered Joe Larson twenty-five dollars for his daughter. Larson, equally as drunk, agreed unhesitantly.

Stella begged her father not to send her away with Chadwell, but he turned a deaf ear; and her mother told her sternly that she was now a full-grown woman, and it was time for her to move on. Did she expect her parents to feed and clothe her forever?

Stella's life with Ben Chadwell was oppressive. His home, located on the outskirts of New Orleans, was a rundown cabin in dire need of repairs.

Stella was miserable living with the slave-trader, and she hated sharing his bed. He never mentioned marriage, and neither did she.

When Stella realized that she was pregnant, she plunged into a deeper depression. She didn't want Chadwell's child. She even considered getting rid of it, but she didn't know who to contact; and even if she did, she had no money to pay someone to abort her unwanted baby.

As the weeks passed and the baby began moving inside her womb, Stella's feelings changed drastically. Her unborn child became the center of her lonely life. She now wanted the baby with all her heart and was anxious for its birth.

When Stella went into labor, Ben had just returned with a new coffle. Fortunately, an elderly midwife was among the slaves, and she ably delivered Stella's son.

The child brought a ray of sunshine into Stella's otherwise dismal existence. She loved her son and lived exclusively for him. Having no friends or close neighbors, Stella's whole life was wrapped up in her child.

It was Chadwell who insisted that they call the baby Paul. Stella didn't object; she had always liked the name.

Paul was fourteen months old when his father was murdered. Ben, delivering a coffle to New Orleans, was waylaid on a rural road by five runaway slaves. The fugitives, five strong and violent men, killed the slave-trader without mercy. The sheriff's report read that Ben Chadwell's body was so badly butchered that identification was extremely difficult.

Stella felt no grief over Ben's death. She had always loathed the man, he had been a repulsive, despicable human being.

She suddenly found herself alone, however, with a child to support. Stella was totally unqualified for employment, she couldn't even read or write. Her only skill was housekeeping. There was no one to watch her son, so taking him with her, she trudged through finer neighborhoods, knocking on each door along the way, asking for domestic work. None of the residents needed a white woman to clean house; they all had Negro slaves to do the job.

Desperate, Stella visited restaurants, even saloons, asking if they needed a dishwasher, or perhaps a waitress. A few of the proprietors had considered hiring her until they learned that she had no one to watch her son and would have to bring the baby to her job. She begged them to hire her anyhow, pointing out that it'd only be a temporary situation. When she started earning a salary she could pay someone to keep the child. Although a few of the proprietors actually felt sorry for her, they nonetheless turned her away.

Finally, penniless, her kitchen cupboards bare, Stella was driven to begging in the streets for handouts. The charitable donations were few and far between. Helpless, Stella watched her son become thinner and thinner.

The day Stella met Hattie, she hadn't eaten in over four days. The little food she had managed to come by through begging, she had given to the child.

Stella was standing on a street corner, Paul balanced on her hip and a tin cup in her hand, when Hattie, on her way home, came walking by.

Weak from hunger, Stella's head began to swim, and her balance became precarious. She was on the brink of fainting when Hattie's arms suddenly steadied her. Taking the child from Stella's feeble hold, she cradled him gently.

Stella, taken with the middle-aged woman's kindness, found herself confessing her destitution.

Hattie took Stella and Paul to her home in the colored section of town. Hattie's rundown shack was in even worse condition than Stella's; however, unlike Stella's home, the kitchen cupboards weren't bare. She fed the starving girl and her son, assuring Stella that she and the child were welcome to share her food for as long as it lasted. Lasted? Stella had asked. Hattie then explained that her late mistress's will had set her free. Since then, she had been working as a cook, but last week she had lost her job.

The two women, developing an instant friendship, decided to stay together. Because Stella's home was in somewhat better condition, they chose to live there. It was also understood that Stella would find employment and Hattie would stay home with Paul.

Now that she had someone to watch her son, Stella was sure that she'd find work. Job hunting, she was passing a seamstress's shop when a flashy-dressed woman suddenly stepped through the doorway. Stella and the customer collided.

Stella's collision with New Orlean's most infamous Madam was a turning point in her life. Belle's experienced eye quickly measured the young woman, and despite Stella's cheap, unbecoming apparel, Belle could see that she was exceptionally beautiful. The Madam was very impressed with Stella's voluptuous curves, her dark auburn hair, and her pretty face. The girl's large gray eyes were especially captivating. Belle was a shrewd and cunning businesswoman, and she manipulated Stella into prostitution with relative ease.

Stella could hardly believe that bedding men could be such a lucrative profession. With no qualms whatsoever, she agreed to work for Belle. Selling her body was nothing new to Stella; her father had sold her for twenty-five dollars.

Although Hattie disapproved of Stella's line of work, she didn't verbally reproach her. She understood her friend's desperation. Prostitution paid more than menial labor, and Stella was determined that her son would never again go hungry.

Being intimate with different men made little impression on Stella. Knowing nothing of love, she simply accommodated her customers and pretended to enjoy the act. To Stella, it was a job that kept food on the table. Her son was healthy and well fed. And that was all that mattered.

Unlike the other prostitutes, Stella refused to live at Belle's. She spent her days at home with Hattie and Paul. Within a few weeks, she was financially able to lease a better house. It was modest but comfortable; more important, though, it was located in a respectable part of town.

Stella had been at her new profession for two months when Harold Chamberlain spotted her. Taken with her seductive beauty, he informed Belle that, hereafter, the young woman would be his exclusively. The Madam didn't argue, for Chamberlain owned the controlling interest in her business.

Harold Chamberlain turned Stella's life into a living nightmare. The man's sexual acts were eccentric and cruel. Stella, hating his abuse, threatened to leave New Orleans, but Harold quickly thwarted her threat. If she dared to run away, he'd hunt her down, then kill her and her son.

The beaten woman soon lost the will to live, and Chamberlain's threat to kill her meant nothing. Paul's life, however, was precious. Thus, protecting her son's safety, she submissively suffered Chamberlain's cruelty.

Bringing herself out of her reverie, Stella rose from the bed, stepped to the crib, and checked her sleeping son. Then, leaving the room, she found Hattie in the parlor. A cup of hot tea was on the coffee table.

"You best hurry and drink your tea," Hattie said, moving to the window. Parting the drapes, she glanced outside. "The carriage, it'll be here most any minute."

Stella's rendezvous with Chamberlain never differed. He always sent a public conveyance to her house, instructing the driver to deliver his passenger to Belle's.

Chamberlain had his own quarters at Belle's establishment, and Stella's orders were to go straight to his rooms. When he was finished with her, she was sent home in another public conveyance. Her salary was paid by Chamberlain. He gave her barely enough to support herself, her son, and Hattie.

Sitting on the sofa, Stella stared blankly at the cup of tea. Cold sweat broke out on her brow as she thought about the upcoming evening. She knew she couldn't take anymore! She was at the end of her rope!

"Hattie, you was right. I've reached my breakin' point. I gotta get away from that man! If I don't, I'll lose my mind!"

Standing, Stella looked resolutely at her companion. "We're gonna leave this town. I don't know how, but somehow we'll find a way."

Hattie smiled broadly. "Miz Stella, I's been waitin' a long time for you to get the courage to run away."

"If that's how you feel, how come you ain't said nothin' sooner?"

" 'Cause I knew it wouldn't do no good. Honey, you had to make that decision on your own."

"Well, my mind's made up. Just as soon as I come up with a plan, we're leaving."

"What about Masta Chamberlain's threat to kill you and little Paul?"

"To kill us, he's first gotta catch us." Stella thought quickly. "When we leave, we're heading west. He'd never expect us to take that direction.

"West?" Hattie questioned with reservations. "Just how far west are you plannin' to go? They's wild Indians out in them Plains."

"Don't you see? We have no choice. We must head west."

"Lord help us!" Hattie groaned.

Five

Selina slept late, and when she awakened, her maid informed her that Elizabeth wished to see her. She dressed quickly and hurried downstairs. Entering the parlor, she found her mother sitting on the settee.

"Did you want to see me, Mama?"

"Yes, dear." Getting to her feet, she hastened to her daughter, grasped her hands and asked eagerly, "Did you have a nice time last night at the Wilkersons'?"

Selina shrugged listlessly. "It was all right. But Harold was called away. He claimed it was a pressing business matter. But, of course, he went to Belle's."

Elizabeth was abashed. "Selina Beaumont, how dare you mention that wicked woman's name in this house! And how dare you accuse Mr. Chamberlain so wrongly!"

Selina sighed tediously. "Oh Mama, everyone knows he goes there all the time. He even has his own quarters at Belle's house."

"Where did you ever hear something so outrageous?"

"I heard it from Papa."

Elizabeth scowled deeply. "Your father had no business discussing something like that with you. I do declare! Sometimes, he treated you more like a son than a daughter!"

Increasing her grip on Selina's hands, she went on anxiously, "But, darling, even if Mr. Chamberlain did go to that awful place, you mustn't be upset. Men, especially bachelors, often frequent such establishments." Finding the topic embarrassing, Elizabeth blushed. "Selina, men have certain appetites. . . ." Not knowing how to continue, her voice faded.

Smiling amusedly, Selina went over to the settee and sat down, and remarked, "Mama, I know what you're trying to say."

"Then you aren't perturbed with Mr. Chamberlain?"

"Of course not. As far as I'm concerned, he can go to Belle's and stay there forever."

Elizabeth hurried over and sat beside her daughter. She was visibly distraught. "Oh Selina, from the moment you decided to marry Mr. Chamberlain, I have been so happy and so greatly relieved. But, honey, when you talk about him so unfeelingly, well I start to worry."

"Worry about what, Mama?"

"That you'll change your mind and break off your engagement."

"And if I did?" she asked, watching her mother carefully.

"I'd be absolutely shattered! Lord, within weeks we'd be homeless! I couldn't take such destitution! I'd die! I'd literally give up and die!" Tears appeared in the woman's eyes.

"Don't worry, Mama," Selina said comfortingly. "I don't intend to break my engagement." Her heart had sunk. For a moment she had actually hoped that her mother would understand. But Selina admitted to herself that her mother wasn't capable of comprehending her daughter's reluctance to marry Harold Chamberlain. In her mother's eyes, the man was handsome, a gentleman, rich, and the answer to her prayers. With her daughter wed to the wealthy shipping tycoon, her own life would be secure and comfortable.

Selina looked closely at her mother. The woman's poor health had taken its toll. Elizabeth's face was pallid, her cheeks gaunt. Selina was trapped into marrying Chamberlain, she knew there was no way out unless she wanted to gamble with her mother's well-being. If she and Elizabeth were to find themselves homeless and destitute, Elizabeth might very well sink into a state of malaise so severe that it would eventually cost her her life.

"Mama," Selina said, patting the woman's hand. "Please don't get upset. I told Mr. Chamberlain I'd marry him, and have you ever known me to break my word?"

Elizabeth smiled timorously. "No, darling, I haven't."

They were interrupted by the butler's sudden appearance. "Excuse me, mistress ma'am," he began, speaking to Elizabeth. "Masta Chamberlain is here."

"Send him in," she hastened to say. "Don't keep the gentleman waiting."

The ladies stood as Harold came into the room. He greeted Elizabeth cordially. "Good morning, Mrs. Beaumont." Then, stepping to Selina, he took her hand and kissed it lightly. "My love, you look very beautiful."

"Thank you," she murmured. Selina gestured to the chair facing the settee and invited him to sit down. He waited until the women were seated, then complied.

"Please pardon my intrusion," Chamberlain began.

Interrupting, Elizabeth assured him, "Why, Mr. Chamberlain, you could never be an intrusion. You're welcome to stop by anytime you wish. After all, you'll soon be family."

Chamberlain thanked her politely, although he was inwardly annoyed at being interrupted. He turned to Selina. "I'm afraid, my love, that I have some disturbing news. I've been called to London on business. I learned this morning that I must make this trip. I hope you won't be too distressed."

Distressed? Quite the contrary. Selina was delighted. "How long will you be gone?" she asked, her even tone concealing her joy.

"Two, maybe three months."

"So long?" she responded, smiling secretly.

"I'm afraid so. My business can be very demanding. But, while I'm away. . . ." He hesitated.

"Yes?" Curious, Selina encouraged him to continue.

"I don't know if you're aware of this, but I have a ranch in Texas."

"Yes, I know. Last night when Mr. Smith walked me home, he mentioned your ranch."

Learning that Layne had taken her home irked Chamberlain. He had thought Dr. Wilkerson would escort her. He reproached himself for leaving her at the Wilkersons', but he'd been overly anxious to see Stella. His fiancée's seductive beauty had aroused his passion, and he'd been eager to use Stella to appease it.

Elizabeth had been listening attentively, and she now asked, "Who's Mr. Smith?"

"Layne Smith," Harold clarified. "Howard Smith's son."

"So Mr. Smith's ungrateful son is in New Orleans, is he?"

"Why do you say he's ungrateful?" Selina queried.

"I met Howard Smith on several occasions. He talked to me often about his son. Layne actually had the gall to inform his father that he wanted no part of the shipping company. Well, needless to say, Howard was absolutely devastated. They had quite a few heated arguments; then, one day, Layne simply packed up and moved to Texas."

Elizabeth smiled brightly at Harold. "While your

dear father was still alive, he must have been enormously proud of you. Unlike Howard Smith's son, you abided by your father's wishes and joined his business. I suppose Layne's here to get Howard's affairs in order?"

Chamberlain nodded brusquely. "He sold his father's half of the business to your attorney."

"To William?" Elizabeth declared. "Why do you suppose William wanted to make such a purchase?"

"The shipping business is a very lucrative one." Chamberlain's attention returned to Selina. "While I'm away, I want you to stay at my ranch."

"What!" Selina and her mother exclaimed in unison.

Before they could state their objections, Harold held up a hand, blocking their words. "Please, ladies, let me explain." He looked at Elizabeth. "Mrs. Beaumont, now that your husband is gone, Selina has no male guardian. It's not safe for her to stay here in New Orleans. A young lady as beautiful as your daughter should be well sheltered. Otherwise, some man might very well take advantage of her innocence. Also, Selina has promised to marry me. How can I be sure that while I'm away, someone won't come along and claim he'll pay off her father's debts in return for her hand in marriage?"

"Sir, my daughter and I would never break our word to you," Elizabeth remarked strongly. "I can assure you that Selina will marry you."

"Nonetheless, I insist that she be secure during my absence. I have decided to send her to my ranch."

Selina was bristling. "I refuse to go to your ranch. If you're so worried about my virtue and my loyalty, then I'll move back to Cedar Hill. My plantation is very safe, and I'll be quite isolated there."

"Mrs. Beaumont, may I speak to Selina privately?" Harold requested.

"Yes, of course," she said, standing. Worried that this

unexpected turn of events would change her daughter's mind, she looked at Selina and said firmly, "Mr. Chamberlain is now the man in this family. You'll do well to keep that in mind and abide by his wishes. I'm sure he knows what's best for you." With that, she left the parlor, closing the door behind her.

"Selina," Harold began sternly, "I insist that you do as I say, or else!"

"Or else, what?" Her tone was unmistakably defiant.

"Or else you can find someone else to pay off your mortgage and take care of your mother."

Rising, Selina placed her hands on her hips and remarked angrily, "Don't threaten me! And furthermore, your reasons for insisting I move to your ranch are utterly ridiculous!"

Harold also rose to his feet. "It's your attitude that is ridiculous. You are being totally unreasonable. I'm sending you to my ranch for your own protection. New Orleans is overrun with unsavory rogues who might very well take advantage of you." His face reddened with barely restrained rage. "You'll do as I say!"

She eyed him cunningly. "Are you that determined to marry a virgin?"

He decided to answer frankly. "Yes, I insist that my bride be a virgin. It's no more than any man expects."

"Well?" Selina remarked crossly.

"Well, what?"

"Aren't you going to ask me if I'm still innocent?"

"Aren't you?"

Whirling about, she stepped to the center of the room, turned, and spat irritably, "Yes, I'm still a virgin!"

Crossing the floor, Harold went to her side and grabbed her arm firmly. "I don't have time to bicker with you. Now, are you going to my ranch or not?"

"Why will my virtue be safe at your ranch?"

"Because you're going to pretend to be my wife."

Selina was astounded. "Your wife! You can't be serious!"

"I'm very serious. I'd marry you now if I thought there was time. But Smith's leaving in the morning, and I plan to send you with him."

Layne? Recalling his kiss brought a hot flush to Selina's cheeks.

"Smith's taking Janet Wilkerson to her father," Harold continued, too preoccupied to notice his fiancée's sudden blush. "You and Janet can chaperone each other."

Selina cleared the exciting Layne Smith from her mind. "I refuse to move to your ranch. I have no desire to live in Texas. I'm returning to Cedar Hill."

"Very well, my dear. But I withdraw my offer to pay your mortgage and an allowance for your mother. I also call off our engagement. When I leave here, I'll stop at the bank and tell Mr. Heymann that he's free to foreclose on your property. By this time next week, you and your mother will be out on the streets, homeless and penniless. You'll be forced to go to your friends and beg them for charity."

"Beg!" Selina exclaimed. "Never!"

"We'll see about that," he retorted, heading toward the door.

"Wait!" she called.

Pausing, he turned and faced her.

Selina hated herself for submitting. But what could she do? She'd rather die than see her mother homeless and dependent on the charity of friends. There were also her father's slaves to consider. They were now her responsibility, and she must protect them.

"Very well," Selina said collectedly. "You have won. I'll go to your ranch."

Harold smiled smugly. "I'm glad you came to your

senses."

Moving to Chamberlain, she looked him directly in the eyes and asked, "Why do you want to marry me? And please don't insult my intelligence by telling me that you're in love with me. I somehow sense that you're too much in love with yourself to love anybody else."

He laughed briefly. "Selina, I wouldn't dream of insulting your intelligence. However, you might be too smart for your own good. Someday, it could get you in trouble."

He suddenly wrapped an arm about her waist, drawing her close. "My love, I want to marry you for more reasons than one. I crave a son, but his mother must be well bred. I also insist that my wife be beautiful. You, my dear, are well bred and beautiful."

"There are plenty of unmarried women who are well bred and beautiful. So why me?"

"Because you're the most desirable one among them."

Selina tried to squirm free, but his arm tightened about her waist. "I also expect my wife to be obedient. Can you be obedient, my spirited beauty?"

"I wouldn't count on it, if I were you."

Chuckling, Harold released her. "We'll see about that when the time comes." He was confident that he'd have no problem breaking her rebellious spirit.

"If you'll excuse me, my dear, I need to pay a visit to Smith. I'll return this evening. In the meantime, I suggest you start packing." He went to the door and left.

Layne was taken aback by Harold Chamberlain's request to escort Selina to Texas. "I already have one woman to take care of," Layne objected. "And one woman is one too many!"

"I'll pay you handsomely. Furthermore, I can't believe one more woman would make that much of a

65

difference."

Layne's thoughts were churning as he began pacing his hotel room. Chamberlain, seated on a chair, watched him anxiously. Meanwhile, Doug was standing leisurely in front of the patio doors. He hoped Smith would refuse, for they were already responsible for Janet Wilkerson, and they didn't need an added responsibility.

Layne's feelings, however, were mixed. A part of him wanted to jump at the chance to be with Selina. He hadn't been able to get her out of his mind, and sharing a long journey with her was tempting.

But she's Chamberlain's fiancée, he told himself testily. And if I were better acquainted with her, I probably wouldn't like her anymore than I like her future husband. But what if I'm wrong about her? What if I'm wrong?

Halting his pacing, and reminding himself that all's fair in love and war, Layne turned to Chamberlain and said, "On second thought, I might consider taking her."

Harold was relieved. "Does two hundred dollars for your trouble seem like a fair offer?"

"I don't want to be paid."

"But I insist."

"Insist all you want, but I won't change my mind."

"Very well," Harold yielded.

Not giving his better judgment a chance to alter his decision, Layne said hastily, "Tell Miss Beaumont that we'll pick her up in the morning at seven. Also, tell her to pack lightly and to leave her maid behind."

Standing, Harold said with a smile, "I'll be sure and tell her. By the way, tomorrow morning she'll no longer be Miss Beaumont."

Layne looked at him questioningly.

"The young lady and I are getting married tonight."

Layne inwardly cursed his hasty decision. So all's fair

in love and war, eh? Dammit! Where married women were concerned, he drew the line!

He was about to renege, to tell Chamberlain he had changed his mind when, suddenly, his thoughts raced shrewdly. Chamberlain's bride might prove to be useful. If he played his cards right, he could extract certain information from her.

"I must leave," Harold spoke up crisply. "I have a busy afternoon facing me. I'll see you in the morning when you come for Selina."

"Will she be at your home?"

"No, she'll be at her mother's house."

"Spending your wedding night at your mother-in-law's, are you?" Layne taunted.

"Of course not! But I'll have my bride back at her mother's by seven in the morning."

"See that you do. 'Cause if she's not there at seven, we'll leave without her."

Chamberlain departed, and the moment the door closed behind him, Doug asked gruffly, "Layne, what's wrong with you? We sure as hell don't need two women taggin' along on this trip."

"I have a good reason for agreeing to take the soon-to-be Mrs. Chamberlain to Texas."

"Like what?"

"If Chamberlain murdered my father, he had to have a motive—he had to gain something through his death. I intend to pump Selina for that information. She might very well know something."

"And if she doesn't?"

"Then to hell with it. One woman or two, in the long run what difference does it really make? Two probably won't be any more of a hassle than one. Either way you look at it, it's a long trip, and a real pain in the rear."

"Two women will make it a double pain in the rear."

Chuckling, Layne wished he felt as unconcerned as

67

he sounded. But knowing Selina would soon be sharing Chamberlain's bed not only depressed him, but it also ignited a spark of anger.

To hell with Chamberlain and his bride! he decided irritably. Then, glancing at Doug, he suggested, "Let's get drunk and celebrate our last night in New Orleans. You wanna go to Belle's?"

"Naw, I went there last night. Let's try a different place."

"Suits me," Layne answered.

The full moon shone down softly on Selina's face as she stood on the front porch. She watched unemotionally as Chamberlain stepped up into his buggy and directed his driver to leave. She continued to look on until the carriage was out of sight. Then, turning, she went into the house and up the stairs to her bedroom.

She moved lethargically to her wardrobe, from which she removed several dresses and spread them on her bed. She looked them over thoughtfully, which ones should she take and which ones should she leave? Her interest waned, for she didn't really care. She didn't want to go to Texas. She wanted to flee to Cedar Hill. The peaceful plantation had always been her haven, and she wished desperately that she was there now.

She slumped down on the edge of the bed and thought about Harold's short visit. He had informed her briskly that Layne Smith had agreed to escort her safely to his ranch, which he called the Circle-C. He'd then relayed Layne's instructions to pack sparsely and to leave her maid behind. A large and pompous smile had crossed Harold's lips when he told her that Smith believed they were getting married tonight. He had assured her that her marital status would dissuade men such as Layne Smith from trying to take liberties with her. Harold had then left in a flurry, promising Selina that he'd return in the morning.

She wondered why he had been in such a hurry. Was he on his way to Belle's? He most likely had a favorite prostitute there and was anxious to be with her. She hoped he'd continue to see his harlot after they were married, then maybe he'd leave his wife alone! She had a feeling, though, that she wouldn't be so lucky.

Would I feel this way if I were married to Layne Smith? she suddenly puzzled. She didn't think so, for his kiss had been too thrilling, too exciting! No! If Layne were her husband, she'd never share him with another woman!

As her thoughts turned to the upcoming journey, her doleful spirits lifted considerably. Traveling to Texas with Layne might be very pleasant. She enjoyed his company immensely, and his mere presence excited her.

Will he kiss me again? she wondered. No, of course not! He'll believe I'm married! Her uplifted mood took a downward plunge. Lord, she moaned inwardly, Layne will see me as a married woman! Maybe this trip won't be so pleasant after all.

Selina glanced up as her bedroom door opened. Dottie, hurrying into the room, said hastily, "Miz Selina, you ain't got no business packin' your own clothes. That's my job."

Selina hadn't forgotten her promise to keep Dottie with her. Now, she dreaded telling the servant that she had to leave her behind. Drawing a deep breath, she was about to break the news; but before she could, Dottie burst into unexpected tears.

Covering her face with her hands, she sobbed hysterically, "Oh Miz Selina! . . . Please don't make me go to Texas with you! . . . I's scared to go out there! . . . I heard they's wild Indians in Texas! . . . I's scared of

Indians, Miz Selina!"

Standing and patting the maid's trembling shoulder, Selina said soothingly, "Stop crying, Dottie. You aren't coming with me."

Her tears abated at once. "I ain't goin'?"

Selina smiled affectionately. "No, you aren't. Mr. Smith sent orders that you were to be left here."

A note of panic came to Dottie's large eyes. "I's gonna worry 'bout you, Miz Selina. What if you's captured by savage Indians?"

"I'm sure I won't be captured by Indians. There's no need for you to worry. The trip from here to Mr. Chamberlain's ranch may be tiring and tedious, but I doubt if it's all that dangerous."

At least I hope so! Selina thought with apprehension.

Selina had guessed correctly about Chamberlain, he was indeed in a hurry to reach Belle's. He was anxious to get Stella into his bed, but as he was entering the establishment, he ran into William Stratton. The two men decided to have a drink, and over their brandies, their conversation turned to the prospect of war between the North and the South. As they became thoroughly absorbed in their speculations, they ordered several more drinks. By the time their lengthy discussion ended, both men were feeling their liquor.

Stratton chose a pretty prostitute and went upstairs with her. Meanwhile, Chamberlain, his movements unsteady, made his way to his private quarters. The door opened into a sitting room, and Stella was there waiting for him. As he entered the room, he stumbled awkwardly.

Seeing this, Stella smiled. She was glad that he was intoxicated. Too much liquor always rendered him impotent. Tonight, she'd be spared his sexual assault.

Meandering to his liquor cabinet, Chamberlain poured himself a glass of brandy, clumsily spilling part of it. Swaying, he turned and looked at Stella. She was watching him from the sofa. His eyes raked over her lustfully. The little tart was remarkably beautiful. He despised the flashy, revealing gowns worn by prostitutes and insisted on Stella dressing tastefully.

Now, as his gaze continued to sweep over her, he found her very desirable. Her blue, modestly-cut dress enhanced her appeal, and he silently cursed himself for drinking so much brandy. The damn liquor always made it impossible for him to achieve an erection.

He frowned irritably. Well, he was already disabled, so he might as well continue drinking. Putting the glass to his lips, he drained the contents, then poured another one. He drank the second one slowly, studying Stella as he did so. As he thought about the long, tedious voyage across the ocean, he contemplated taking Stella with him. If he had the little whore at his disposal, the days wouldn't be so long and boring.

Stella soon grew uncomfortable under his constant scrutiny. She wished she knew what was going through his mind.

Putting down the glass, Chamberlain went over and sat beside her. "I've been thinking, Stella. I've decided to take you with me."

"Take me where?" she asked.

"In a couple of days I'm leaving for London. Why should I make that long, boring voyage by myself, when I can take you along for entertainment?"

"London!" Stella gasped, leaping to her feet. "I cain't go to London! I cain't leave my son!"

"Of course you can. You have that nigra woman to take care of him. My mind's made up, Stella. You're coming with me. We'll only be gone two or three months."

Stella couldn't fathom being away from Paul for so long. Two, three months! No! No! It would be more than she could bear!

"I won't go!" she shouted.

Enraged, Harold bounded from the sofa, drew back his arm, and slapped her sharply across the face. "You damned little slut! How dare you defy me!" Dammit! The bitch was as defiant as Selina! With Selina he'd had to keep his anger subdued, but with Stella he showed no mercy.

He slapped her again, this time so powerfully that she was knocked to the floor. Releasing his pent-up rage made him feel somewhat better.

Standing over Stella, Chamberlain glared down at her coldly. When he married Selina, this cheap piece of trash could go back to whoring for Belle; but in the meantime, he needed her to appease his sexual appetites.

Chamberlain's second slap had bloodied Stella's nose, and wiping at the blood, she sat up and pleaded, "Please don't make me go to London! I don't want to be away from my son!"

"You'll do as I say!" he growled, jabbing his foot into her rib cage. "Now, get off the floor and fix me a drink!"

His head suddenly started swimming and, moving uncertainly, he lumbered to the sofa and stretched out on it.

By the time Stella brought him his drink, he had sunk into a liquor-induced sleep and was snoring loudly.

Putting down the filled glass, Stella knelt beside the sleeping man. Moving stealthily, she unbuttoned his suit jacket, reached into the inside pocket, and withdrew his wallet. Opening it, she took out his money, folded the bills, and stuffed them in the bodice of her dress.

Stepping furtively across the room, she opened the door carefully. She turned and looked disdainfully at the man who had made her life a living hell. She hated him with every fiber of her being.

Praying that she'd never see Harold Chamberlain again, she darted across the threshold, closing the door quietly behind her.

Rushing into Hattie's bedroom, Stella lit the bedside lamp. Hattie had been sound asleep, but the sudden light brought her awake with a start.

Sitting up, she asked, "Miz Stella, is somethin' wrong?" Then, noticing the young woman's swollen nose, she gasped, "Damn that Masta Chamberlain! Honey, is you all right?"

"I'm not hurt very bad." A shudder ran through her, and her words suddenly raced anxiously, "Oh Hattie, I've done something real bad! We gotta get out of here before Mr. Chamberlain wakes up!"

"Calm down, honey. Tell me exactly what you done."

"Mr. Chamberlain said he's going to London, and he said he was taking me with him. I can't go to London! I couldn't stand being closed up in the same room with that monster all the way across the ocean! Oh God! It'd be more than I could bear! I know it would! I just know!"

"Try to stay calm, and just tell me what you done that was so bad."

"Mr. Chamberlain was drunk, and when he fell asleep, I stole his money."

Hattie's eyes widened frightfully. "Miz Stella, that man's liable to kill you for that!"

"But don't you see? I had to take his money! We need it to get out of this town. And we gotta leave tonight!"

"How we gonna do that? Just walk out of here?"

"No. I stole a carriage."

Hattie groaned raspingly. "Lawdy mercy! Does this carriage have horses to pull it?"

"Only one. It isn't a very big carriage, but it was all I could get. I left Belle's by the back door, and this buggy was just sitting there."

"So you just helped yourself."

"Hattie, we don't have time for chit-chattin'. Get out of bed and help me pack."

When the woman didn't move, Stella cried wretchedly, "God Hattie! You're coming with me, aren't ya?"

Flinging aside the covers, she heaved her huge frame off the bed. "Of course I's comin'. You think I'd let you and little Paul take off without me? But I's not as young as I used to be, and it takes me a little while to get to moving."

Throwing her arms about the woman, Stella cried sincerely, "Oh Hattie! I love you so much!"

"I know you do, honey-chile. And I loves you and little Paul. You two's my family."

Stella hugged her friend tightly, then she said briskly, "First town we come to, we'll sell the carriage, then buy us a wagon and fill it with supplies."

"Miz Stella, just where is we goin'?"

Her eyes shining brightly, Stella remarked, "We're goin' to Texas!"

Six

Admitting Chamberlain into her home, Elizabeth said warmly, "Please, come in. Selina's in her room, but she'll be down very soon. Come into the parlor and have a cup of coffee."

As Chamberlain entered, his outward composure completely hid his inner rage. This morning he had awakened to find Stella gone and his wallet empty. He was furious, and if he wasn't leaving for London, he'd hire a couple of men to track her down and bring her back. However, he had no choice but to let the little thief escape. But if he ever saw her again, he'd make her pay dearly.

"Cream and sugar?" Elizabeth asked.

"No, thank you," Harold replied. He cleared Stella from his mind and turned his thoughts to the matter at hand. "Did Selina tell you that Smith believes we were married last night?"

Handing him his coffee, she answered, "Yes, she did. I must admit, though, that I'm confused. Why do you want Mr. Smith to think she's your wife?"

"Mrs. Beaumont, your daughter is a very desirable young lady. Living in Texas has made Smith somewhat coarse but, still, he isn't the type to make overtures to a married lady. If he knew Selina was only my fiancée —

well, one never knows. He might try to take advantage of her."

Elizabeth smiled radiantly. "Oh Mr. Chamberlain, you're so protective of Selina! You'll make such a wonderful, considerate husband."

"Thank you, madam. And won't you please call me Harold?"

"Of course, and you must call me Elizabeth."

At that moment, Selina entered the room. Harold put down his cup and hurried to her side. "You look tired, my love. Didn't you sleep well?"

"No, I didn't."

"Oh?" he questioned archly. "Why did you have insomnia?"

She answered coolly. "I don't like moving to your ranch. I would prefer to live at Cedar Hill. The dilemma kept me awake."

Chamberlain sighed audibly. "Must you be difficult? I thought everything was settled."

"It is settled. But you asked why I couldn't sleep, and I merely answered your question."

"Selina," Elizabeth interjected buoyantly. "Why don't you think of this trip as an adventure? You've never been to Texas, and you might find that you like the place."

"Maybe," she relented lamely. "But I'll still miss Cedar Hill." She turned her attention to Harold. "Speaking of Cedar Hill, our overseer is very capable, but there must be somebody in complete charge."

"Mr. Stratton has agreed to handle the plantation during your absence. You trust your attorney, don't you?"

"Yes, of course I do."

"Then there's no need for you to worry about Cedar Hill." Chamberlain sounded complacent.

The man's smugness irritated Selina. "You've taken

76

care of everything, haven't you? When you become my husband, I won't even have to think for myself. You'll do all my thinking for me."

Elizabeth, finding her daughter's behavior disrespectful, said sternly, "Selina, for heaven's sakes! Must you sound so rude and . . . and ungrateful!"

"Don't chastise her, Elizabeth," Harold said evenly. "Selina's pertinacious nature is part of her charm." He smiled inwardly. He was looking forward to taming this high-spirited beauty. She wouldn't submit easily, but eventually he'd break her—and take great pleasure in doing so!

Wondering what was keeping Layne, Harold stepped to the front window. As he parted the drapes, he caught sight of Doug bringing the covered wagon to a stop. Layne, riding horseback, was dismounting.

"Smith's here," he announced.

"I'll let him in," Selina said quickly.

Layne was bounding up the porch steps as Selina opened the front door. Seeing her brought his long strides to a sudden halt.

Although Selina's dark traveling dress was conservative, it nonetheless hugged her ripe curves. Her hair was pulled back from her face and worn in the popular chignon fashion. On some women the style was unbecoming, but it merely enhanced Selina's classical features.

Layne found her fascinating and was smiling at her cordially when, all at once, he remembered that she was now Chamberlain's wife. His smile twisted into a cynical sneer.

Tipping his western-style hat, he said with emphasis, "Good morning, *Mrs. Chamberlain.*"

Selina stiffened. Mrs. Chamberlain! The title was depressing. "Come in, Mr. Smith. I'll have the butler bring down my luggage." As Layne stepped across the threshold, she asked, "Have you picked up Janet yet?"

"She's in the wagon."

"I'll ask her to come in," Selina said, moving to do so. Layne's hand on her arm impeded her. "We don't have time for visitin'. We're leavin' as soon as I load your luggage."

"Very well," she replied, drawing away from his hold. His grip had been uncomfortably tight.

Without being summoned, the butler suddenly appeared in the foyer. "You wants me to bring down your baggage, Miz Selina?"

"Yes, please."

"I'll give you a hand," Layne offered, following the servant upstairs.

Selina returned to her mother in the parlor. She went over to her and hugged her tightly. "I'll miss you, Mama. Please take good care of yourself."

"I will," she murmured tearfully. "And you do the same." Releasing her daughter reluctantly, she looked at Harold, then back to Selina. "I'll leave, so that you two can have a moment alone."

Selina watched her mother as she left the room. A couple of rasping coughs shook the woman's frail shoulders. Selina hoped, prayed, that her health would soon improve.

"My dear," Chamberlain began, reaching into his jacket pocket, "I have something for you." He drew out a gold wedding band, then lifted her hand and placed it on her finger. "This belonged to my mother, so take good care of it."

Selina studied the ring dispassionately. "Your mother died when you were a baby, didn't she?"

"Yes, she did." He reached back into his jacket and took out an envelope. "This is a letter to the Hartes. They're taking care of my ranch. See that they get this."

She accepted the sealed envelope, slipping it into the

78

pocket of her dress. "Did you tell them that I'm your wife?"

"Naturally," he answered. "But, love, this charade is only temporary. As soon as I return from London, we'll be married here in New Orleans. No one in Texas will be the wiser."

The butler, poised in the open doorway, cleared his throat to make his presence known. "Excuse me, Miz Selina, but your things is loaded. Masta Smith said he's ready to leave."

Slipping an arm about Selina's waist, Chamberlain ushered her outside and onto the front porch. Layne was waiting at the bottom of the steps.

Bringing Selina into his embrace, Harold murmured passionately, "My darling, I'll see you in two or three months. Remember, I adore you."

Chamberlain's lips suddenly swooped down on Selina's, his kiss demanding and hard. She wanted to struggle free, but decided it would be best to simply submit and get it over with.

Layne turned away from the clinging couple. Jealousy was a new emotion to him, and he silently cursed himself for coveting Chamberlain's wife.

Harold finally released Selina, and she hurried down the steps. As Layne took her arm to escort her to the wagon, Chamberlain called after them, "Smith, I'm holding you responsible for my bride's safety. If anything happens to her, you'll answer to me."

"I'll keep that in mind," Layne muttered flatly.

Doug's horse was tied to the rear of the wagon, and Layne nudged the animal to the side. He lifted Selina into his arms, swinging her over the backboard, and placed her none too gently inside. She was puzzled by his curt treatment, but he was gone before she could question him.

Janet was sitting on a bed of blankets. Reaching over

and grasping Selina's hand, she said excitedly, "Layne told me that you and Mr. Chamberlain were married last night. Is that true?"

Damn Harold! Selina swore inwardly. She hated lies! She started to say yes, but couldn't bring herself to do so. Quietly, so the driver wouldn't overhear, she replied, "No, we aren't married. I can't lie to you. But, Janet, you mustn't tell anyone."

"Why in the world are you two pretending to be married?"

The wagon lurched forward, and losing her balance, Selina fell against Janet. Righting herself, she said somewhat irritably, "Harold thinks if men like Layne Smith believe I'm married, they won't try to take liberties with me."

"How romantic!" Janet exclaimed. "Mr. Chamberlain must simply adore you!"

Selina frowned testily. "You might think it's romantic, but I think it's a bunch of hogwash!"

"Honestly, Selina! Such crude language. One would think you've been associating with poor dirt farmers."

"Maybe I have," Selina mumbled brusquely. Withdrawing into a sullen silence, she moved to the rear of the wagon and watched forlornly as her house faded farther and farther into the distance.

The sun was midway in the sky when Layne decided to stop for lunch. They were now miles away from New Orleans and were on a dusty, rural road. There was no need to build a fire, for Effie Wilkerson had sent along a basket filled with fried chicken, biscuits, and honey.

Doug lowered the backboard and assisted the ladies from the wagon. Needing privacy, they walked toward the surrounding foliage.

His expression thoughtful, Doug watched them until

they disappeared into the overgrown thicket.

"What are you thinking about?" Layne asked, joining him.

"Our passengers are beautiful, too beautiful. All the no-account drifters we run across will probably have only one thing on their minds—sneakin' back and grabbin' the women." He sighed heavily. "I have a feelin' those two ladies are gonna be nothin' but trouble."

"Doug, you worry too much. Besides, we can handle trouble." Layne reached inside the wagon and picked up the lunch basket. "Come on, let's eat."

When Selina and Janet returned, the men had the food spread out on a blanket. The fare was tasty, and as they ate lunch, there was little conversation.

Finishing, Janet declared, "I can't eat another bite." She wiped her mouth daintily with a napkin. "The day is only half over, and I'm already looking forward to a bath and a soft bed. I'll be glad when we reach an inn and stop for the night."

"We'll be camping out tonight," Layne told her.

"What!" she cried. "But why?"

"The next inn is only three hours away, and I don't intend to stop that early."

"Surely there's another place farther down the road."

"There is," he answered. "Eight more hours down the road."

Janet's mouth pursed into a sullen pout. "But I don't want to sleep outdoors."

"You'll be sleeping inside the wagon," Layne replied.

"But what about a bath?" she demanded querulously. "I simply can't go to bed without washing first."

Chuckling, Doug asked, "Miss Wilkerson, have you ever heard of a sponge bath?"

"Yes, of course I have," she snapped. She found his laughter offensive.

"Well, ma'am, during this trip you got a choice between takin' a lot of sponge baths or goin' unwashed."

Janet's eyes squinted angrily into Doug's. She thought the man ill bred and a ruffian. Under normal circumstances, he wouldn't even be allowed to speak to her. In her opinion, Doug Thompson was far below her aristocratic status.

Getting to his feet, Layne said to Doug, "Let's water the horses." He made a sweeping gesture toward the lunch paraphernalia. "You ladies get this cleaned up."

Janet waited until the men had walked away before saying crankily, "If you ask me, Layne Smith and his friend are impertinent."

"No one asked you," Selina remarked petulantly. She began wrapping the left-over chicken.

"My goodness. You're in a mood, aren't you?"

Selina didn't comment. But she was indeed in a bad mood. Layne's cold, indifferent attitude was annoying. That night when he had walked her home, he had been warm and friendly. She had even believed that Layne's presence would make this trip tolerable. Apparently, though, she had been wrong.

Grudgingly, Janet pitched in and helped Selina, and they soon had the chore completed.

The ladies were about to climb back inside the wagon when they heard the sounds of approaching horses. Layne and Doug were at their sides so quickly that it seemed as though they had materialized out of thin air.

There were three riders, and as they drew closer to the wagon, they slowed down their mounts.

Pulling up, the largest man of the three, said cordially, "Good afternoon, folks."

Layne nodded affably. "Good afternoon to you, sir."

"Have you seen any suspicious-lookin' nigras travelin' this road?"

"No, we haven't," Layne replied.

"We're patrollers, and we keep an eye on this here

area. There's been a lot of runaway nigras lately. Them damned Northern abolitionists has got our darkies all stirred up." He touched the brim of his hat. "Well, you folks take it easy, you hear?"

With that, he and the others rode away.

Layne assisted the ladies inside the wagon, then as he and Doug walked to the front of the wagon, Doug asked quietly, "What do you think?"

"I doubt if they're patrollers."

"Did you notice the way they made a point of not looking at the women?"

"Yeah, I noticed."

"Do you think that was to throw us off?"

"That'd be my guess. I have a feelin' that tonight we'll have some uninvited guests."

The remainder of the day passed slowly and uneventfully. Riding in the jolting, confining wagon was uncomfortable, and when they stopped for the night, Selina and Janet were happy to leave the wagon and stretch their cramped legs.

Camp was set up close to the river, and the women were anxious to wade in the cool water. They were sorely disappointed, however, when Layne forbade them to leave the camping area. They insisted on an explanation, but Layne didn't want to alarm them, so he didn't tell them his suspicions concerning the three "patrollers." Instead, he simply demanded that they obey his wishes.

The travelers had just finished cleaning up after supper when a large group of riders approached the camp. Layne sent the women to the wagon.

They complied reluctantly. Concealed beneath the canvas-top, they couldn't see the visitors, but they could hear what was being said.

"Evenin'. I'm Sheriff Rawlins. My posse and I are lookin' for three men. They broke into the Widow Johnson's home, stole her money, then beat her up and left her for dead. She's alive though and was able to give me a full description."

"What do these men look like?" Layne asked.

The sheriff told him.

"They passed us 'bout seven hours ago. They claimed to be slave patrollers."

"Which way were they headed?"

"They were goin' west."

"Thank you, suh. We'll be on our way, then."

As the sheriff and his posse were leaving, Janet looked wide eyed at Selina and exclaimed, "Heavens! I'm glad those men didn't try to rob us, aren't you?"

"They were probably too cowardly to try and rob Layne and Doug. They'd rather steal from helpless widows."

A thought suddenly occurred to Janet, and she reached over and grasped Selina's hand. "Do you realize how easy it would be for us to sneak out of this wagon and down to the river? If the men are still at the campfire, they won't be able to see us."

Selina considered the idea. The front of the wagon faced the fire. Janet was right, they could leave without being spotted. Sensibly, though, she dismissed the notion.

"Janet, I don't think we should leave. Not with those three men out there somewhere."

"Nonsense!" her companion declared. "Why would they still be in this vicinity with a posse chasing them?"

"I suppose you're right. But all the same, I think we should forget going to the river."

"But it's so hot!" Janet complained. "Wouldn't it be heavenly to splash in the river? We won't take off all our clothes, of course. We'll only strip down to our petti-

84

coats."

Selina was weakening, and as she wiped a hand across her perspiring brow, the cool river did indeed seem tempting. However, her better sense prevailed. "I'm sorry, Janet. But Layne told us not to leave the camping area, and I think we should follow his orders."

"Stay here if you want," Janet fussed. "But I'm going to the river."

"Don't be a fool!" Selina remarked, grabbing at the woman's arm.

Avoiding her touch, Janet climbed swiftly down from the wagon. Before Selina could ask her not to leave, she turned and fled into the surrounding woodland.

"Darn it!" Selina mumbled angrily. She left the wagon and followed the direction Janet had taken. She hoped to catch up to her and persuade her to come back.

The sky was cloudless, and the luminous moon cast a golden hue over the land, making it easy for Selina to see where she was going.

"Janet?" she called softly. "Where are you?"

Steadily, she made her way farther into the thicket, and farther away from camp. The sounds of the lapping river grew closer, and when she stepped into a clearing, she found herself almost at the water's edge. She had expected to come upon Janet, but she was nowhere in sight.

Becoming worried, Selina was about to call loudly for her friend when a large hand suddenly clamped over her mouth.

Standing behind her, the attacker wrapped his arm about her waist and drew her flush against his brawny chest.

Two men, one of them restraining Janet, emerged from the thick shadows. Recognizing their captors as the men the posse were chasing, Selina knew they were ruthless and dangerous, and her fear rose.

The man holding Janet had his hand over her mouth, so neither woman was free to scream for help.

"Let's get these women to the horses and get the hell out of here," said the one with Selina. His hand moved slightly, giving her an opportunity to sink her teeth sharply into his flesh. The unexpected pain caused him to draw his hand away.

Taking advantage of his carelessness, she screamed as loudly as she could.

"You damned bitch!" he raved, grabbing her and reclamping his hand over her mouth.

"We gotta get outta here!" one of them shouted.

Knowing the men traveling with these women were now alerted, Selina's captor ordered roughly, "Leave that other bitch. We're gonna have to ride fast, and two women will slow us down." He jerked his prisoner into the foliage, forcing her to keep up with his long strides. "I'm gonna pay you back for bitin' me, you little slut!" His lips were so close to her ear that she could feel his breath. "I'm gonna pay you back real good."

The man restraining Janet released her, then drawing back his arm, he hit her with his fist. The vicious blow knocked her unconscious, and she dropped limply to the ground.

Layne and Doug, believing the women were inside the wagon, had been sitting by the fire drinking coffee when Selina's scream pierced the still night.

Drawing their pistols, they dashed into the woodland, arriving at the clearing moments after Selina was taken by her captors.

Doug hurried over to Janet, who was lying on the ground, and knelt beside her.

"How is she?" Layne asked.

"She's been knocked unconscious," he answered, lifting her into his arms and standing.

"We'll take her back to camp, then I'll go after the others."

They returned quickly, and as Doug carried Janet inside the wagon, Layne mounted his saddled horse.

Riding to the rear of the wagon, he said briskly, "I'll be back as soon as I can." He turned his horse and galloped away at full speed.

Doug prepared a basin of water, then wet a cloth and washed Janet's face gently.

Consciousness returned gradually to Janet, causing her to mumble lucidly one moment, then be completely irrational the next.

Finally she came fully awake and, looking into Doug's sensitive eyes, she asked hoarsely, "Wh . . . what happened? Where are those horrible men?"

"They're gone," he replied softly.

"And Selina?" she gasped frightfully.

"They took her with them."

"Oh no!" Janet groaned. "Poor Selina!"

"Don't worry, ma'am. Layne's gone after her."

"Don't worry!" she cried. "But Layne's alone, and he's pursuing three men."

Doug grinned wryly. "Yeah, I know. Kinda makes the odds unfair. Those men will need help."

Janet was amazed. "Is Layne Smith a gunfighter?"

"No, ma'am," he drawled. "He's a Texan. And those three scroungy bastards don't stand a chance against 'im." His grin turned apologetic. "Excuse my language, Miss Wilkerson."

Janet's jaw was throbbing painfully, and she moved a hand gingerly to her face.

"You're gonna have a dilly of a bruise," Doug told her. "You're lucky your jaw wasn't broken."

Tears came to her eyes, and in a trembling voice she

murmured, "Nobody has ever hit me in my life — until now."

"You'll be all right," he said, hoping to soothe her.

His kindness only brought on tears. Sobbing heavily, Janet moaned, "I was so scared! So terribly scared!"

Moving hesitantly, Doug drew her into his arms. Needing his comfort, she nestled her head on his wide shoulder. As she cried, he continued to hold her tenderly.

When her tears subsided, Janet was annoyed at herself for allowing this man to put his arms about her. After all, he was a ruffian, and most likely a half-breed! Furthermore, not only was he not handsome, he was quite common looking.

Stiffening, she pushed out of Doug's gentle embrace. "I'm all right now, Mr. Thompson. You don't have to sit with me."

He understood the reason behind her sudden reserve, but it didn't anger him. He was used to such treatment and had been expecting it.

Lying back on her pallet, Janet watched Doug as he left the wagon. A part of her wanted to call out to him and ask him to stay, but the other part demanded that she keep him at a respectable distance. He was not of her social class, and she must maintain an impersonal relationship with him. Otherwise, he might try to get too friendly.

Doug banished from her mind, her thoughts went to Selina. A pang of guilt shot through her conscience. She was to blame for Selina's abduction. Desperately, she prayed that Layne would find her and save her.

Selina had been flung face down across the man's saddle, and his horse's jolting gait jabbed painfully into her stomach. Worse still, the position made her feel sick, and more than once she came close to losing her supper.

The outlaws guided their horses off the rural road and into the bordering foliage. They rode a short distance, then pulled up. Selina's captor told the others to hide in the shrubbery so they could ambush anyone who was following. He promised to wait for them farther back from the road. Taking their horses with him, he soon rode out of sight.

Meanwhile, Layne was easily following their tracks. When he came upon the spot where they had ridden off the road, he reined in. He sensed a trap.

The two men had detected his presence, and crouching behind a heavy bush, they pulled their revolvers and waited expectantly. When Layne's black stallion charged through the thicket, they stood and fired two shots a piece before realizing that the horse was riderless.

Layne had stealthily circled the men and had their backs covered. "Drop your guns," he ordered. Then move away from 'em. And don't turn around."

They wisely obeyed.

Moving to stand close behind them, Smith asked, "Where's your friend and the woman?"

"He took her farther back in the woods," one of them answered. "He said he'd wait for us."

Layne suddenly whistled. His stallion was well trained, and he promptly trotted over to his master. Taking a long strand of rope from his saddlebags, he drew back his prisoners' arms and tied the two men together. Using his bowie knife, he severed the excess rope, shoved the men to the ground, and deftly bound their feet.

Then, he swung up onto his horse and rode away.

The man with Selina had heard the shots and was certain that his men had killed anyone who was following. Thinking it was safe to stop, he dismounted and drew his captive off the horse and into his arms.

"I'm a-warnin' you," he snarled. "If you scream, I'll knock the livin' hell out of ya!"

He threw her brutally to the ground, and pinning her beneath his burly frame, he tried to kiss her. She turned her head and avoided his assault.

He laughed gruffly. "Gonna try and keep me from kissin' ya, huh? Good! I like a woman with spunk."

Selina was not one to submit without a fight, and when the man moved to lift her skirt, she brought up her knee and slammed it into his groin.

Moaning with pain, he rolled off her.

Leaping to her feet, Selina ran frantically toward the horses. Despite his discomfort, the man gave pursuit. He was faster than his prey and caught her before she could escape.

Grabbing her arm, he swung her around and flung her to the ground so powerfully that, for a moment, she couldn't catch her breath.

"I'm gonna beat ya to a bloody pulp!" he raged. "No woman's gonna jab me in the privates and get by with it!"

Selina knew her only chance was to scream, and she did just that, as loudly as she could.

Dropping to his knees beside her, he put his hand over her mouth. "Shut up, you bitch!" His lips curled into a cruel grin. " 'Fore I give ya the beatin' of your life, I'm gonna hump you, then I'm gonna let my men hump you."

Seeing repulsion in her eyes, he threw back his head and laughed gleefully. "You uppity bitch, I'm gonna be stickin' it to you real good and real deep."

Layne's voice came out of the dark shadows, "Move

90

away from the woman, or I'll be stickin' my gun where you're gonna find it mighty uncomfortable."

Jumping up, the man drew his pistol, but Layne shot it out of his hand. Coming forward and into the moonlight, Smith ordered dryly, "Mount up, and if you try anything, I'll kill you."

Layne waited until Selina had gotten to her feet, then turning his steely gaze upon her, he said coldly, "Don't say a word. You and I will tangle later, Mrs. Chamberlain."

Seven

Layne brought Selina and her abductors back to camp. He sent Selina to the wagon, then leaving the men under Doug's guard, he left to catch up to the posse and bring them back.

Janet and Selina talked a few minutes before Janet fell asleep. Quietly, Selina washed from the water basin and changed into her cotton nightgown. She was in bed when she heard Layne return. He was accompanied by the sheriff and his men, and their loud arrival awakened Janet.

Getting up, Selina moved over and sat beside her.

"What's going on?" Janet wanted to know.

"Layne's back, and he has the posse with him." Studying Janet's swollen jaw, she asked, "Are you in much pain?"

"A little." She smiled gingerly. "But I'll survive."

"I hope this incident taught you a valuable lesson, and that hereafter you'll obey Mr. Smith's orders."

"Selina," she began sincerely, "I'm truly sorry. I wanted to tell you earlier, but I fell asleep. Please forgive me. I know you came to the river looking for me. If anything had happened to you, I'd never have forgiven myself. Thank God, Layne rescued you in time!"

Selina patted Janet's hand. "Well, fortunately, nothing too terrible happened to either of us."

The posse left, taking the three men with them, and Selina wondered if Layne planned to reproach her and Janet tonight, or if he'd wait until morning. She dreaded the inevitable scene.

However, Selina didn't have long to wonder, for, at that moment, Layne's voice sounded from outside, "Ladies, may I come in?"

"Just a minute," Selina called back. Janet was also in her sleeping gown, so Selina handed her a blanket, then slipped a robe over her own gown.

"You may come in," she said to Layne.

He entered, but his tall frame was too large for the confining wagon, and he was forced to stoop. He knelt beside Janet, and as his eyes flitted from one woman to the other, the kerosene lantern illuminated the anger burning in their dark depths.

Selina swallowed heavily. She had a feeling that the lecture they were about to receive would be severe.

Layne's anger mellowed somewhat as he studied Janet's discolored jaw. "I'm sorry you were hurt," he told her gently.

"Thank you," she murmured hesitantly, for she too had been expecting a firm reprimand.

"I hope," he began sternly, "that your injury has taught you to obey my orders. You could've been hurt a lot worse, maybe even killed. This journey is not a game. One careless mistake could cost you your life."

"I know," she whispered. "I promise I won't disobey you again."

He scrutinized her doubtfully.

"You believe me, don't you?"

"We'll see," he mumbled tersely. He looked reproachfully at Selina. "I want to see you outside."

"Whatever you have to say to me, you can say right

here."

He scowled deeply. "Mrs. Chamberlain, you can either leave this wagon voluntarily, or I'll carry you out. Now, which one will it be?"

"Force won't be necessary, Mr. Smith," she responded, lifting her chin defiantly. She left the wagon with Layne following close behind.

Taking her arm, he began leading her toward the edge of camp, but she drew back.

"Where are we going?" she demanded.

"Where we can talk privately."

She was about to protest, but he increased his hold on her and ushered her to the bordering foliage. Then, releasing her, he folded his arms across his chest and eyed her harshly.

She met his hard gaze without flinching.

"Mrs. Chamberlain, sneakin' down to the river was a very childish prank. I'm not surprised that Janet did something so reckless, for she can be very immature. However, I admit that I thought you had more sense. After all, madam, you're a married lady."

Selina was steaming. How dare he question her maturity! "If you're through insulting my intelligence," she spat angrily, "I'd like to return to the wagon!"

He moved suddenly and grasped her shoulders. "You little fool! Don't you realize how important it is that you do as I say?"

She flung off his hold. "Of course I realize it's important!"

"Then why did you disobey me?" he thundered.

Tossing her head, she retorted, "Since you're so smart, Mr. Smith, you figure it out!"

She whirled about and headed back. Deciding she was too upset to fall asleep, she went to the campfire and sat down beside Doug. Her thoughts were racing. Leaving the wagon to search for Janet had been dangerous. She was willing to admit that. But how dare Layne speak to her as though she were a child and, furthermore, damn him for demeaning her intelligence. Men! They think themselves so superior to women!

Meanwhile, as Selina was fuming, Layne walked past the wagon. Janet appeared at the backboard and called softly, "Layne?"

"What is it?" he asked more sharply than he had intended.

"I think you should know that Selina was against sneaking to the river."

"What do you mean?" he questioned, his interest piqued.

"It was all my idea, and I tried to talk Selina into going with me. But she refused. She said we should obey your orders. I was determined, though, and I left without her. She came down to the river looking for me because she was worried."

"Thank you, Janet," he murmured.

As Layne ambled over to the fire, he was regretting speaking so harshly to Selina. He had judged her unfairly.

"I need to talk alone with Mrs. Chamberlain," he said to Doug.

"Sure," his friend replied, taking his cup of coffee with him to his bedroll.

Layne sat down beside Selina. Before he could attempt an apology, she said irritably, "Whatever you have to say, I don't want to hear it!"

A disarming smile touched his lips as his gaze inspected the young woman at his side. The light from the flickering flames sent reddish highlights streaking through her brunette tresses, which were falling gracefully past her shoulders. When she turned her face to his, he thought he detected a wounded look in her blue eyes, but the expression was gone so quickly he couldn't be sure. Now, he could only see a smoldering anger in their depths.

"Mrs. Chamberlain," he said haltingly—apologies didn't come easy to him—"Janet told me what really happened. I treated you unfairly, and I'm sorry."

Selina hadn't been expecting an apology, but she was pleased to receive one. "That's all right, Mr. Smith. I understand," she murmured, hoping to put the unpleasant incident to rest.

"Then you aren't angry?" he asked, grinning wryly.

She saw only sincerity in his smile. "No, I guess I'm no longer angry."

"When Janet ran off, you shouldn't have followed her. If anything like that happens again, I hope you'll come to me, Mrs. Chamberlain."

That name grated on her nerves. "Please call me Selina."

Layne arched an eyebrow quizzically. "I thought brides liked being addressed by their new names?"

Selina shrugged evasively. "I guess I'm an exception."

"Why aren't you goin' to London with Chamberlain?"

"It's a business trip," she mumbled, in lieu of anything better to say.

"But it could be a honeymoon too. He won't be conducting business on the voyage."

"I get seasick," she said impulsively. Selina despised herself for fibbing. Seasick? She'd never been on the ocean! Anxious to change the subject, she said quickly, "Mr. Smith, tell me about your ranch."

"My ranch?" he queried. "Aren't you more interested in your husband's?"

"Well . . . yes, of course," she stammered, trying to cover her blunder. "But Harold has already told me about the Circle-C."

96

The night when Layne had walked her home, she hadn't even known that Chamberlain had a ranch. Recalling this, he questioned, "When did he tell you about the Circle-C?"

"Last night," she decided to answer.

"On your wedding night?" Layne remarked. "Believe me, madam, if you were my bride, last night we'd been too busy to talk about any ranch."

"Well, I'm not your bride!" she retorted testily, blushing in spite of herself.

Layne's gaze raked her intently. "Your husband is a fool. Apparently, he doesn't appreciate what a prize you are."

Her embarrassment deepened. "May we please talk about something else?"

"Of course," he answered. "What did you want to know about my ranch?"

"Does it have a name?"

"Certainly. It's called the Diamond-S."

"Why the Diamond-S?"

"That's the brand I put on my cattle. A diamond with an S in the center."

"Are your cattle Texas Longhorns?"

"None other. Have you ever seen one?"

"No, I haven't. But I've heard about them. Is your ranch very prosperous?"

Layne smiled pleasantly. "Well, it keeps a roof over my head, food on the table, and clothes on my back."

"Harold's land borders on yours, is that right?"

"Yes. His ranch is west of mine."

"And where exactly is Janet's father's ranch?"

"North of the Diamond-S."

"Then all of you are neighbors?"

"I guess you could say that."

"Is there a town close to these ranches?"

"Yeah, but it's not much. It's small and rowdy. But

San Antonio's about fifty miles away. When I have a lot of merchandise and grain to purchase, I go there."

"What's the name of this town close to your ranch?"

"Originally, it was a small Mexican settlement called Ciudad De Paso, which means, 'city that is passed.' People who drifted in never stayed 'cause they were merely passin' through. Now, the town's called Passing Through."

"Are people still passing through?"

Layne nodded. "They're usually on their way to San Antonio or farther west."

"Are there hostile Indians in the vicinity?"

"There's the Comanches. However, they usually stay on their own side of the Brazos River. Sometimes a raiding party will cross over and steal a few steers."

"These Indians, are they violent?"

"With the Comanches, you never know. If they get riled, they'll cross the river as a war party, then there's always violence. But that doesn't happen too often. Mostly the Comanches stay in their own territory, where they wish to be left alone."

Selina was finding their discussion interesting and was becoming totally involved. "Have you ever fought Indians?"

"A few times. I'm a volunteer Texas Ranger, and I ride with them when there's Indian trouble."

"What exactly is a Texas Ranger?"

"Well, the Rangers were organized when Texas was still a part of Mexico, and they provided settlers protections against Indians. Sam Houston has reorganized the rangers, and now they've grown in size and power. We aren't a military army by any means. Every man provides his own horse and weapons, and we don't wear uniforms."

Layne looked at her admiringly. "You're really interested in all this, aren't you?"

"Of course. If I'm going to live in Texas, I want to know what I'm up against."

"Texas might not be the safest place in the country, but as far as I'm concerned, it's the only place."

"How did a New Orleans-bred gentleman manage to flee to Texas and build himself a ranch?"

"I wish I could impress you with a story of my uncommon valor and determination, but I can't. When I turned twenty-one, I came into a trust fund from my mother. She died when I was a child. I bought my land and my cattle, and built my house with my inheritance."

"But I'm sure it's taken a lot of work and determination to keep your ranch." She sighed wistfully. "I understand why you love the Diamond-S, for I feel the same way about Cedar Hill."

"Your plantation?"

"Yes. I'd be there now if Harold hadn't insisted that I go to the Circle-C." She looked curiously at Layne. "Why in the world did Harold buy a ranch in Texas?"

"He hasn't told you?"

"If he had told me, I wouldn't be asking."

"You don't know your husband very well, do you?" He studied her thoughtfully.

"No, I don't know him well at all."

"Chamberlain believes that a war between the North and the South is unavoidable. He also believes that the South will lose and will be left ravaged and destitute. Before the first shot is fired, he plans to sell his half of the shipping business and move to his ranch. He hopes to dodge the upcoming war and keep his riches intact. I'm sure the bulk of his money is in a London bank."

"Do you think war is inevitable?"

"Yes, I do," he answered somberly.

"But you don't think the South will lose, do you?" Her tone was tinged with a note of desperation.

"If the war drags on for years, the South will surely lose. It has no factories and no arsenals. It only has cotton and slaves. You can't win a war with cotton and slaves."

"If there were a war and the South were to lose, what would happen to Cedar Hill?"

"It'd probably fall to ruin, perhaps be totally destroyed. But don't look so crestfallen. Your husband will have the money to rebuild your plantation. Cedar Hill could flourish again."

"If war breaks out, will you return to New Orleans and join the army?"

"No, ma'am," he answered flatly.

"But why not? It's your birthplace!"

"I may be Louisiana born, but I'm a Texan at heart. When Texas or my ranch are threatened, that's when I take up arms. Whether it be Indians, Mexicans, or desperadoes. If there's a war, I hope Texas will remain neutral. Then I won't be forced to fight fellow Americans."

"This is all speculation," Selina remarked. "Maybe there won't be a war."

"Maybe," Layne mumbled lamely. "Well, ma'am, you'd better turn in. Tomorrow's a long day."

Layne stood by, then taking Selina's hands, he helped her up. As he gazed down into her lovely face, he controlled the desire to take her into his arms.

Selina's feelings were the same as Layne's. She longed to be in his embrace, to have him kiss her again. She stepped back from his disturbing closeness. Her eyes, with a will of their own, traveled over him boldly. His sandy-colored hair fell over his brow, lending him a boyishly sensual appeal. She wished she wasn't so attracted to this daring, Texas rancher, but his tall, muscular build and handsome face were irresistible. However, she knew that it wasn't simply his good looks

100

that had captivated her; she sincerely liked him.

Afraid she might throw herself into his arms, she mumbled hastily, "Good night, Mr. Smith." Turning, she fled to the wagon.

"The name's Layne," he called after her.

Sitting back down at the fire, Layne poured himself a cup of coffee. His thoughts began to run deep, and a sudden look of determination radiated from the depths of his eyes. Regardless of how attracted he was to Selina, he'd keep his feelings in check. She was Chamberlain's wife, and he wasn't about to become involved with a married woman.

A puzzled frown creased his brow. He wondered why Selina didn't seem to care that she and her brand-new husband were separated. He figured there was only one explanation that made any sense. Most likely, Mrs. Chamberlain wasn't in love with her husband.

He shrugged aside these speculations. She was still a married woman, and he was determined not to cross the line.

It took Selina quite a while to put her mind to rest and fall asleep. Shortly thereafter, she awoke with a start. Sitting up on her pallet, she was wondering what had awakened her when, all at once, she remembered her nightmare. It was so horrible! No wonder it had brought her awake.

Recalling the disturbing dream in detail sent a foreboding chill coursing through her.

In the dream, it was her wedding night and she was truly Mrs. Chamberlain. Harold carried her into a bedroom, and without giving her a chance to undress, he ripped away her wedding gown and undergarments, leaving them in torn shreds. Then, sneering demonically, he lifted her onto the bed. Staring up into his face, she saw that his eyes were gleaming like a devil's. She was frightened, and seeing her fear, he threw back his head and laughed viciously.

It was at this point that Selina awakened.

Now, she tried to shake the nightmare, but it kept flashing through her mind. Hoping fresh air might clear her head, she left her bed and slipped quietly outside.

Stepping away from the wagon, she glanced upward at the vast sky. The moon was surrounded by a myriad of twinkling stars.

"Couldn't sleep?" Layne asked, his presence startling her. His approach had been soundless.

Selina whirled about. "No, I couldn't. But I'm sorry if I awakened you."

"I wasn't asleep. Doug and I are taking turns standing guard." He studied her with genuine concern. "Why couldn't you sleep?"

"I had a bad dream."

"Care to tell me about it?"

She blushed. "No, I'd rather not."

"That bad, eh?" He smiled tenderly. "Did you dream that you were being attacked by Comanches? When you asked me about them, maybe I shouldn't have answered your questions quite so truthfully. I didn't mean to frighten you."

"I didn't dream about Indians. However, I do appreciate your honesty, and I hope you'll continue to answer my questions candidly." She smiled warmly. "Believe me, I don't frighten that easily."

A gentle breeze stirred the hem of Selina's gown, reminding her that she had forgotten to put on her robe. Feeling a little self-conscious, she stammered, "Well, good night . . . for the second time."

Layne was also acutely aware of her attire, for the moonlight sifting through her thin gown silhouetted

102

her soft, feminine curves. Resisting temptation, he tried to look elsewhere, but with little success.

"Good night, Selina," he murmured, wishing he didn't find her so damn desirable.

She was barefooted, and as she moved to the wagon, a pebble dug into her foot. "Ouch!" she cried in pain.

Instantly Layne was beside her, his hands bracing her shoulders. "What's wrong?"

"I stepped on a stone; that's all."

Her eyes were drawn helplessly to his face, and as she studied his full lips, she longed desperately to feel them pressed against her own — to find out if his kiss were truly as thrilling as she remembered!

Driven by a power she could no longer control, Selina took Layne by surprise, flung herself into his arms, and kissed him soundly on the mouth.

His surprise waned quickly. Returning her kiss passionately, he brought her close to his tall frame, molding her thighs to his.

Selina's heart pounded madly, and her head spun with rapture as she surrendered breathlessly to the ecstasy of the moment.

Coming to his senses, Layne released her so brusquely that she tottered before retaining her balance.

"What is it?" she asked, wishing he'd resume their embrace. She wasn't sure why, but she felt as though she belonged in his arms.

Layne was upset with Selina and disgusted with himself. He had no right to kiss another man's wife!

A frigid look came to his eyes, and it was so cold that it chilled Selina's heart. His tone was icy, "You would do well, madam, to remember that you're a married woman!"

He left without further words.

Selina wanted to run after him and tell him that she

103

wasn't married, but she refrained from doing so. She might not be married now, but she soon would be. Her mother's welfare, and that of her slaves, had to come first; even over her own heart.

Furthermore, she told herself, even if she weren't engaged, she could never have a future with Layne. The first night they met, he made a point of informing her that he wasn't the marrying kind.

Her mood disconsolate, Selina returned to her bed, where she finally drifted into a restless slumber.

Eight

The next morning, Selina was apprehensive about facing Layne. Her behavior the night before had been entirely too bold. He probably thought she was no better than the women who worked for Belle. No, she was even worse, for they weren't supposed to be married ladies.

As it turned out, Selina's concern was for naught, at breakfast Layne acted as though nothing had transpired between them. Selina said little during the morning meal, and Layne said even less.

The men hitched up the wagon as the women washed the breakfast dishes. Selina had emptied the washtub and was carrying it to the wagon when she noticed that Doug was tying Layne's horse to the backboard.

As Doug took the washtub and hung it on the side of the wagon, she asked, "Aren't you driving the team?"

"Layne and I plan to take turns."

"I see," Selina murmured. Sharing the wagon with Layne made her feel uncomfortable. Although she was reasonably sure he wouldn't mention the night before, she would still find his closeness unnerving.

Catching a glimpse of Smith climbing up onto the

105

driver's seat, Doug said, "We'd better get the wagon loaded, it's time to pull out."

Within minutes they had broken camp, and Doug assisted Selina into the back of the wagon. When he turned to give Janet a hand, she remarked brightly, "I've decided to ride with Layne."

She moved swiftly to the front, and lifting the hem of her long dress, she heaved herself onto the seat.

"You don't mind, do you?" she asked, favoring Layne with a pretty smile.

Smith preferred that Janet ride in the back, and he was about to tell her so; but reading his intent, she continued sweetly, "Please let me stay! I hate being confined!"

"All right," Layne relented.

Meanwhile, Selina had positioned herself as far to the back as possible. She preferred not to hear Layne's and Janet's conversation, however, she could still overhear what was being said.

She knew why Janet had joined Layne, she intended to flirt with him. Selina refrained from passing judgment. After her own shameless behavior, she had no right to judge anyone else. Furthermore, she didn't blame Janet. Layne Smith was irresistible!

Layne slapped the reins against the horses, and the wagon rocked into motion. He steered the team away from the camping area and back onto the dusty road. Doug rode a short distance in front.

"It's gonna rain," Layne mumbled, more to himself than to Janet.

She glanced up at the sky. Dark clouds were beginning to form. The impending weather didn't interest her; but the man at her side did.

Pursing her mouth into one of her prettiest pouts, Janet asked, "Do I look terribly dreadful?" She rubbed her injured jaw gently. She had covered the bruise with face powder, and it was barely noticeable.

Layne smiled easily. "I can hardly see the bruise, besides it'd take more than a bruise to mar your beauty."

Janet was flattered.

In the meantime, Selina was still wishing she could move far enough away not to hear them.

"Layne, you're such a flatterer!" Janet exclaimed. "But I do appreciate your kindness. Will it take long for this ugly bruise to go away?"

"By this time next week, you'll never know it was there."

"May I ask you a personal question?" Janet prodded.

"You can ask," Layne replied flatly. "But I'm not promising an answer."

"Do you have someone special?"

"Special?"

"Yes. You know, a special woman friend."

"In Texas?"

Janet nodded.

Selina, now listening avidly, waited intently for Layne's answer.

"Well," he drawled, "there's someone but. . . ."

"Who is she?" Janet interrupted.

"Jessie Harte. She and her brother operate Chamberlain's ranch."

"Do you love her?"

"That's my business, little lady," Layne replied, but not unkindly. He could've said no and felt easy with his answer. Although he was deeply fond of Jessie, his feelings had failed to blossom into love.

"Are you going to marry her?" Janet continued.

Layne chuckled pleasantly. "I'm not the marrying kind. And, little one, you ask too many questions."

"Please don't treat me as though I'm a child. I'm

eighteen years old. Doesn't that make me a full-grown woman?"

His gaze swept lazily over her ripe curves. "You're a very beautiful, seductive young lady, but. . . ." He let his words drift.

"But what?" she persisted.

"You have a lot of growing up to do. Your uncle and aunt sheltered you too much for your own good."

Janet was offended, for she considered herself quite grown up. "I don't know where you got the foolish notion that I'm immature." She scooted across the seat, moving as close to him as possible. So Selina couldn't overhear, she whispered in his ear, "Tonight meet me away from camp, and I'll prove that I'm a woman."

Layne quirked a brow. "Don't you want to save yourself for your husband?"

Selina hadn't heard Janet's invitation, but she could well imagine what she had said.

Janet, gasping, declared, "I didn't mean to imply . . . !"

"Then what did you mean?" he questioned, his eyes twinkling.

"I simply meant . . . I wasn't planning to. . . ." Flustered, she withdrew into silence.

"You are still a virgin, aren't you?" Layne queried, grinning wryly.

"Yes . . . I mean . . ." Janet inhaled sharply. "Sir, you go too far!"

"No, young lady, you go too far. Now, I'm going to give you some advice. Don't be a tease, 'cause some-day you might tease the wrong man. I offer you that bit of advice like a concerned brother."

"But I don't want you to think of me as a sister, I want you to think of me as a woman! Who knows? We might even fall in love."

"You might as well get those silly romantic notions out of your pretty little head. I'm not the right man for you, but someday he'll come along, only he's gonna have problems with you. Your uncle and aunt have spoiled you outrageously."

Janet, fuming, remarked heatedly, "Layne Smith, you're not only rude, but you're also a pompous cad!"

With that, she climbed over the seat. Meeting Selina's gaze, she snapped, "I suppose you overheard and agree with him!"

"That you're spoiled?" she questioned. "I agree totally."

Pouting, Janet mumbled, "Well, what if I am spoiled? It's not my fault!"

"No, it isn't," Selina concurred.

"Do you think I'm terrible?"

"No, not really," she answered with a smile.

"You know, I never especially liked you. I thought you were strange and withdrawn."

"And now?"

"Now, I want us to be friends."

"We are." Selina's answer was sincere. Despite Janet's spoiled and somewhat selfish nature, she sensed that she had a lot of goodness in her.

The swirling clouds gathered into one large gray mass, then released torrents of rain. Streaks of lightning zigzagged across the dismal sky, followed by loud claps of thunder. As the dirt road soaked up the pouring rain, mud formed thickly in the deep ruts.

The stalwart wagon that Layne had chosen crossed the muddy furrows easily and with no mishaps; however, the small carriage that Stella Larson had stolen became bogged down in the wet earth. Several times, Hattie was forced to brace her huge frame behind a stuck wheel and push, as Stella urged the lone horse to pull.

The dark clouds finally passed over, leaving a clear, cerulean sky behind. Stella was relieved when the summer storm ended, for the buggy had afforded little protection from the heavy sheets of rain.

Now, as the carriage rolled slowly down the mud encrusted road, Hattied remarked, "Miz Stella, we got to get rid of this-here buggy. It weren't made for this type of travelin'."

"The first town we come to, we'll sell it and get us a sturdy wagon."

Paul, sitting on Hattie's lap, began to fidget. He was sleepy, hungry, and his clothes were damp. During the storm, Stella had covered him with a blanket, but it hadn't kept him as dry as she had hoped.

"This child needs tendin' to," Hattie declared. "Don't you think we should stop for a spell?"

Stella guided the horse to the side of the road, but as she did so, the carriage's right wheel sunk deeply into a heavy mud puddle. The buggy swayed obliquely, placing too much weight on the stuck wheel. The twist resulted in a broken axle.

Stella leapt to the ground and checked the damage. "Oh no!" she uttered gravely. "It's broken!"

"What's broken?" Hattie exclaimed.

Stella moved over and took the child from the woman's lap. As Hattie maneuvered her rotund body from the buggy, Stella moaned, "It looks like a broken axle. Oh, Hattie, what are we going to do?"

"Well, first we's gonna tend to little Paul, then fix some lunch. This child's hungry."

They had spent the night at an inn, and in the morning Stella had ordered fried chicken and biscuits to take with them. Reaching inside the carriage, Hattie gathered up the lunch basket, a blanket, and clothes for Paul. She looked about, then pointed to a nearby oak. "We can spread the blanket under that tree."

Following the woman, Stella mumbled anxiously, "I've got to think of somethin' to do."

Spreading the blanket, Hattie remarked, "While you're a-thinkin', hand me little Paul so I can tend to 'im."

Stella gave her the boy. Then she began to pace back and forth. She had gotten herself and the others in a terrible mess. If only she'd had more time to arrange for their trip. But there hadn't been time! Chamberlain had seemed determined to take her to London!

Stopping her pacing, Stella looked at Hattie. "There's only one thing to do," she said. "After lunch, we'll unhitch the horse. We can take turns ridin' it with Paul. When we come to a town, we'll just get us a wagon and an extra horse to help pull it."

"Have we got enough money without sellin' the carriage?"

"I think so," Stella answered. "But I'm not sure how much a wagon, a horse, and supplies is gonna cost us."

"But what about our clothes and things?"

"We'll carry what we can and leave the rest." Stella smiled encouragingly. "We don't have all that much."

Hattie groaned heavily. "This-here trip is turnin' into a nightmare." She raised her eyes to the sky. "Lord, if you's a listenin', we shore do need your help."

Doug was now driving the team, and Layne was riding horseback. Searching for a good place to stop for lunch, he rode ahead, leaving the others a short distance behind.

As Layne rounded a curve in the road, he spotted the disabled carriage, rode up to it and dismounted. Glancing about for its occupants, he saw them gathered beneath a tall oak.

Stella, holding tightly to Paul, watched the stranger warily. Meanwhile, Hattie stepped in front of them, sheltering her loved ones with her own body. If this man intended her family any harm, he'd have to deal first with her.

Layne checked the broken axle, then he ambled across the grassy field and toward the women. "Looks like you've got a serious problem," he said affably.

"What you want?" Hattie questioned distrustfully.

Layne smiled. "Well, if you don't mind steppin' aside, I'd like to talk to your mistress."

"I do mind, masta, suh!" She refused to budge.

Moving out from behind Hattie's protective stance, Stella asked, "The axle's broken, isn't it?"

"Yes, ma'am. Has your husband gone for help?"

"I have no husband. It's just us. You reckon maybe you could fix the axle? I'd be willin' to pay you."

"It has to be taken to a blacksmith, ma'am." Layne was curious about the stranded threesome. Obviously the white woman wasn't a lady of means, yet her carriage was evidently an expensive one, and the horse was undoubtedly of good stock. He supposed the Negro woman was her slave, even the poor could sometimes afford to own one or two servants. His eyes went to the child, who had his arms wrapped tightly about his mother's neck. The boy smiled bashfully, then turned away.

"Where are you headed?" he asked Stella.

"Texas," she answered.

"In that buggy?" Layne exclaimed incredulously.

"Well . . . no, suh," she stammered. "I was plannin' to sell it in the next town and buy a wagon."

112

"Where exactly in Texas are you headed?"

"Nowhere in particular."

"Did you come from New Orleans?"

Stella grew uneasy under his questioning. "Why do you ask?"

"Ma'am, there's a town of sorts 'bout five miles up the road, but I seriously doubt if you're gonna find a wagon for sale. The place is so small that you can spit from one end to the other. But you might find someone there who can fix that broken axle. Then I suggest you turn around and go back to New Orleans, or wherever you came from. Even if you could get a wagon, a trip to Texas is no undertaking for two lone women. Believe me, you'd never make it."

"How come you know so much 'bout travelin' to Texas?" Stella asked.

"I live in Texas. In fact, that's where I'm headed. I have others travelin' with me. After lunch, I'll give you a lift into town."

At that moment the covered wagon rounded the bend in the road, and Doug brought the team to a halt behind the carriage. Selina and Janet were on the seat with him. He climbed down, then assisted the ladies. As Doug and Selina walked toward Layne, Janet lagged behind, closely scrutinizing the horse and buggy. Then, rushing up to Layne, she exclaimed, "That's William Stratton's horse and buggy!" She looked accusingly at Stella. "What are you doing with them?"

"He . . . he loaned 'em to me," Stella stammered weakly.

"That's a likely story! Mr. Stratton uses that horse and carriage when he races. He'd never loan them to anyone." She turned to Layne. "This woman is obviously a thief!"

Selina was listening, and Janet solicited her sup-

113

port. "Isn't that William Stratton's horse and buggy?"

Selina studied them carefully. "Yes, they belong to William."

Janet placed her hands on her hips, remarking firmly, "Layne, you must locate Sheriff Rawlins and have him arrest this woman!"

Layne spoke gently to Stella, "Ma'am, did you steal that carriage and horse?"

She couldn't answer, for she suddenly broke into uncontrollable sobs. God, this man would turn her over to the law! She'd go to prison, and then what would become of her son and Hattie?

Paul, distressed by his mother's tears, began crying loudly.

Placing an arm about Stella's shoulders, Hattie drew her close. "Don't cry, honey. You just upsettin' little Paul."

Moving to Layne, Selina touched his arm and said quietly, "William Stratton can afford dozens of carriages and horses as good as the ones stolen. Please don't turn her over to the law." Selina looked sympathetically at Paul, then back to Layne. "Think of the child."

Layne studied her with admiration. He wondered why a woman as kind as Selina had married a man like Chamberlain. Looking away from her pleading eyes, he said to Stella, "Ma'am, could I talk to you privately?"

Controlling her tears, she mumbled brokenly, "Yes, suh—I reckon you can." She handed the child to Hattie.

Taking her arm, Layne led her away from the others, and when they were out of earshot, he paused. Studying the young woman thoughtfully, he suggested, "Why don't you tell me why you're runnin' away to Texas in a stolen carriage?"

114

She gazed deeply into his eyes. She could see only concern in their dark depths. She sensed intuitively that it would be best to tell this man the truth.

" 'Fore I tell you why I'm runnin' to Texas, I'd like to tell you 'bout myself. Do you have time Mr. . . . ?"

"Smith. Layne Smith. And I have plenty of time."

"My name's Stella Larson. And I wanna tell you a little about my life."

Layne listened attentively as Stella gave him a full account of her adolescent years, how her father had sold her when she was sixteen for twenty-five dollars. She told him about her oppressive life with Chadwell, and that his death had left her and Paul alone and destitute. She elaborated on her friendship with Hattie, and her accidental meeting with Belle, which had led to her new profession.

It was at this point that Stella grew cautious and paused.

"Go on," Layne prodded gently. "Tell me the rest."

Her heart started pounding anxiously. What if this man was a friend of Chamberlain's? He said his name was Smith. Surely he wasn't the same Smith who owned the other half of Chamberlain's shipping company!

Smith's a common name, she told herself. I'm so scared that I'm imagining things.

Still, she remained cautious. "Is Harold Chamberlain a friend of yours?"

Layne tensed. "A friend? No, he's not."

"But you know him?"

"Yes, I do," he answered. "But, believe me, he's not a friend of mine. I don't even like the man."

Stella was convinced. "Chamberlain is partners with Belle. He saw me one evening, and he decided he wanted me to belong only to him. I didn't have no say in the matter."

She glanced down at her feet, drew a deep breath, then looked back up into Layne's face. "Mr. Chamberlain's a devil. He enjoyed hurting me. I got bruises to prove it. That man 'bout drove me out of my mind. He's mean, and he's evil. I wanted to leave 'im, but he told me if I ever did, he'd find me, then kill me and little Paul. To protect my son, I stayed on and suffered his abuse. Then, night 'fore last, he told me he was going to London, and that I had to make the voyage with him. I just couldn't go through with it. He was drunk, and when he fell asleep, I stole his money and slipped out Belle's back door. I saw this carriage and horse, and I just took 'em. I didn't even know they belonged to William Stratton."

"Let me get this straight," Layne began. "Night before last, Chamberlain was at Belle's?"

"Yes, suh," she answered.

It didn't make sense. Night before last was Chamberlain's wedding night. The man couldn't be in two places at the same time. Maybe the woman was lying. However, Layne felt that she was telling the truth. If Selina and Chamberlain were married, then he doubted if their marriage had been consummated. Their alleged marriage was a puzzle that he aimed to solve, but it would have to wait. Now he had to find a way to help Stella Larson.

"Movin' to Texas won't get you away from Chamberlain," he remarked.

"Of course it will!" Stella argued. "He probably thinks Hattie and me went north."

"Chamberlain owns a ranch 'bout fifty-odd miles west of San Antonio."

"What!" she gasped. "He never told me he had a ranch."

"It would seem he keeps his ranch a secret from a lot of people."

116

Stella's spirits held firm. "Well, he won't be back from London for two or three months. That'll give me time to hole up in Texas for a spell and make a little more money. Then I reckon Hattie, Paul, and me will move on. Maybe we'll go to California, or Oregon."

Layne regarded her warmly. "Travelin' all the way to California or Oregon takes a lot of planning."

"I reckon you're right, but where there's a will, there's a way."

"Well, ma'am, since you've got the will, I'm gonna give you the way. Two months from now, my foreman and some of my ranch hands are due to drive a herd of cattle to Kansas. You can accompany them. Once in Kansas, you can find employment, then next spring when a wagon train comes through, you can join it."

"That's mighty generous of you, suh. But I reckon you'll be expectin' somethin' in return."

Layne smiled. "A simple 'thank you' will be sufficient."

Stella was amazed. "I always knew the Lord made good men like you, but you're the first one I ever met. I sure hope when my son becomes a man, he'll have a heart as good as yours."

"That's quite a compliment, Miss Larson." His eyes sparkled congenially. He liked this courageous young woman.

"Tell me, suh, is Chamberlain's ranch close to yours?"

"Too close," Layne replied.

"Is San Antonio the closest town?"

"No, there's a small town much closer. It's called Passing Through?"

"Does it have a saloon?"

"It does—the Golden Garter. Between ranch hands and drifters, it's a thriving establishment for its size."

117

"Are there any women working there?"

"Rosie's got two women working for her."

"Rosie! You mean the saloon's owned by a woman?"

"Yeah, but Rosie's no ordinary woman. She's as tough as nails."

"You reckon she'd hire me?"

"Miss Larson, she'd hire you in a minute. The two women she employs aren't as young or as pretty as you. But, ma'am, why do you wanna go back to that kind of work?"

"It's all I know, and I gotta make more money. What I stole from Chamberlain won't last forever."

Layne studied her closely. To Stella, prostitution was merely a means of survival. Realizing this, he admired her strong will and her refusal to give up. She was a real fighter. His scrutiny deepened. She was also very lovely. Her long auburn hair, her large gray eyes, and her voluptuous figure were breathtaking.

Layne gazed kindly into her pretty face. "If you don't mind sharing a wagon with two other ladies, then you, Hattie, and the child are welcome to join us."

"Do you really mean that?" she gasped, astonished.

"I wouldn't make the offer if I didn't mean it." Layne felt he had no other choice. He couldn't very well leave two women and a child to fend for themselves.

Stella frowned slightly. "That woman with the blond hair, she ain't gonna like you askin' us to come along."

"Well, I can't abandon you, and I won't turn you over to the law. So Janet will have to make the best of it."

"What about the carriage and the horse?"

"We'll leave the carriage and take the horse with us."

"Don't this make you an accomplice?" she asked, her face visibly serious.

Layne chuckled. "Stratton was my father's attorney, and now he's mine. Don't worry, I'll take care of everything."

"Mr. Smith, Hattie asked the Lord for help, and he sent you!" Her gray eyes twinkled teasingly. "Are you sure you ain't an angel?"

Placing an arm about her shoulders as they headed back to the others, Layne said with a large smile, "Ma'am, I'm a far cry from an angel."

Selina was making friends with Paul when Layne and Stella started back. She noticed Layne's arm draped over the woman's shoulders. The couple were smiling as though they were sharing a special secret. Selina was puzzled by their instant friendship.

Janet, eyeing the pair harshly, declared, "I don't believe what I see! What did that woman do, bewitch Layne?"

Hattie said nothing, but she was just as confused as the others, especially Doug, who was totally perplexed.

Arriving at the wagon, Layne announced calmly, "Miss Larson, Hattie, and Paul will be accompanying us to Texas."

"You can't be serious!" Janet exclaimed. "I refuse to travel with that woman! She's a thief!"

Keeping his arm about Stella's shoulders, Layne said evenly, "Miss Larson, this is Miss Wilkerson." With a gentle nudge, he turned her to Selina. "And this is Mrs. Chamberlain. Mrs. Harold Chamberlain."

He felt Stella stiffen. "Mrs. Chamberlain!" she gasped, astounded.

"Do you know Harold?" Selina asked.

"Yes . . . I mean no . . . What I mean is, everyone in New Orleans has heard of Mr. Chamberlain. But I didn't know he was married."

Layne, his eyes locked on Selina's face, said, "That's because Chamberlain was married very recently. In fact, it was night before last."

Stella froze. "Night before last," she uttered almost inaudibly.

"Yes," Layne continued, still watching Selina like a hawk. "Mrs. Chamberlain is a bride without a groom."

Selina thought she detected a mocking tone in Layne's voice, but she wasn't sure.

Janet butted in, "Layne, I insist that you turn Miss Larson over to the law, or else leave her behind!"

Layne stepped away from Stella and said firmly, "Janet, Miss Larson and the others are coming with us. Now, why don't you and Selina get started on preparing lunch so we can get back on the road?"

Tossing her head angrily, Janet headed in the direction of the wagon. Selina followed hesitantly. She could sense a change in Layne, and she had an uneasy feeling that she was somehow involved.

Meanwhile, Stella grasped Layne's arm and whispered intensely, "That woman's not married to Mr. Chamberlain. He was with me night before last. If he'd gotten married, he wouldn't have come to Belle's."

"Maybe it's a marriage in name only," Layne surmised.

"That woman's too beautiful! If Chamberlain had married her, he'd never have left her on their wedding night. There ain't no way he'd marry a woman as beautiful as her and not demand his husbandly rights."

Stella's grip on Layne's arm tightened. "She ain't married to Harold Chamberlain. I'd be willin' to bet my life on it!"

Nine

"Layne, I need to talk to you," Doug said. When Smith had announced that Stella and the others were joining their party, Doug had remained silent, but now he wanted to speak his mind.

"Sure," Layne agreed. He turned to Stella. "Miss Larson, this is Doug Thompson, my foreman and good friend."

"How do you do?" she said cordially, studying the large man. His dark complexion made her wonder if he was part Indian.

Doug tipped his wide-brimmed hat. "Glad to meet you, ma'am."

Then motioning for Layne to follow, he walked a distance away, turned around, faced his friend, and demanded gruffly, "What the hell are you doin'? We started with one woman, then you agreed to a second one, and now we've got two more, plus a child. I sure hope we don't run into any serious trouble, it'll be hell tryin' to protect four women and a baby."

"Doug, let me explain," Layne replied. As quickly as possible, he gave him an informative account of Stella's life, leading up to her reason for fleeing to

121

Texas. He finished by saying, "What can I do? I can't leave two women and a baby to fend for themselves. Besides, it's about time someone helped that woman."

Doug studied him thoughtfully. "Are you sure you don't have some other motive for invitin' her to join us? Since she's Chamberlain's mistress, she might know if he had a reason to kill your father."

"I admit the idea crossed my mind, but it has nothing to do with my decision to help her."

Doug's brow furrowed. "Do you think Selina's married to Chamberlain?"

"I don't know, but I seriously doubt it."

"Why do you suppose she's pretendin' to be his wife?"

Layne shrugged. "Beats me."

Meanwhile, as the men were conversing, Selina had prepared a cold lunch and was putting the food into a basket. Janet, her arms akimbo, was watching.

"Honestly!" Janet fussed. "I can't believe Layne actually invited that woman to join us! She's not only a thief, but she's obviously poor white trash!"

"Janet, just because she's poor, doesn't mean she's trash."

"Of course she is! She's a thief, isn't she?"

"We don't know why she stole William's horse and carriage. Maybe she was desperate." Selina eyed Janet firmly. "And since we don't know anything about her life, we have no right to judge her."

Picking up the filled basket, Selina stepped away from the wagon.

"Where are you going?" Janet asked. "Surely you don't intend to eat with that woman and—and her Negro servant!"

"Janet, you can either join us, or stay here and go hungry."

122

With that, she walked away. Grudgingly, Janet decided to follow.

Hattie was sitting on the blanket with Stella and Paul, but as the ladies approached, she started to rise.

"Don't get up," Selina said, gesturing for her to stay as she was.

Except for Stella, Hattie had never remained seated in the presence of white folks. A lifetime of servitude dictated that she get respectfully to her feet. She stood up, stepped over to Selina, and took the basket.

"I'll spread out lunch for you ladies and the gentlemen," she said.

Selina sat down on the blanket, looked at Stella and smiled warmly.

Hesitantly, Stella said, "We got lots of chicken and biscuits. Ya'll are welcome to share our food."

"Thank you," Selina answered. "Why don't we put the two lunches together. It'll make quite a feast."

"Yes'm," she whispered, obviously nervous. Stella had never even spoken to a genteel lady, let alone eaten with one.

Smiling at Paul, Selina said to Stella, "You have a beautiful son. How old is he?"

"Eighteen months."

"Do you think he'd let me hold him?"

"He don't take to strangers, but you can try."

She held out her arms and, to Stella's surprise, Paul stood up and toddled over to Selina.

Placing the child in her lap, Selina kissed the top of his golden curls. "Would you like a biscuit with honey?" she asked him.

Stella, astounded, watched as the woman gave Paul a biscuit filled with honey. The boy took a big bite, dropping sticky crumbs on Selina's dress. Stella thought the woman might get upset, but she simply

123

brushed aside the crumbs, laughing merrily as Paul offered her a bite of his food.

"I don't mind if I do," Selina giggled, taking a nibble.

Hattie was as dumbfounded as Stella. An aristocratic young lady fawning over a poor woman's child was a sight she had never encountered.

However, Janet wasn't the least surprised. She was familiar with what she considered Selina's peculiarities. Studying the child, though, she had to admit that he was exceptionally appealing.

Layne and Doug, joining the ladies, sat down and filled their plates.

Layne's eyes were drawn to Selina and Paul. "Mrs. Chamberlain, someday you'll make a wonderful mother. Do you and your husband plan to have a large family?" He watched her keenly.

"I . . . I don't know," she stammered. "Harold and I haven't discussed children." Flustered, she looked away from Smith's steady gaze.

Selina's discomfort was obvious. Layne wondered if she was embarrassed by his question, or was it a guilty conscience that was making her uncomfortable? Was her marriage to Chamberlain a farce? And if so, why? Why was she pretending?

Layne noticed that Hattie was still standing. "Sit down," he told her.

"I cain't do that, masta, suh!"

"Why not?"

"It wouldn't be proper for me to sit with white folks."

"Propriety be damned! Sit down. I need to talk to all of you."

Hesitantly, she eased her heavy frame down beside Stella.

124

"Hattie," Layne began, "hereafter, when we sit down to eat, you'll join us. Is that understood?"

"Yes, suh, masta."

"I'm not your master."

"Yes, suh, Mista Smith."

Janet started to object to Hattie's joining them; but Doug, sitting beside her, nudged her with his elbow. "For once, Miss Wilkerson, keep quiet."

She gave him a dirty look, but kept silent.

Layne's eyes moved back and forth from one woman to the other. "Ladies, I hope we can make this journey without too many disagreements," he said firmly. "I'll expect you to try and get along with each other. I know it won't always be easy, but I'll expect you to make the effort. It'll make the journey more bearable."

He waited, but there were no comments. "I've decided to put a saddle on Stratton's horse. You ladies will take turns riding, except Hattie. Her time will be filled taking care of the boy."

Hattie laughed jovially. "What you mean, Mista Smith, but is too polite to say, is that I's too old and too fat to be ridin' a horse."

Layne actually blushed. Covering his embarrassment, he carried on quickly, "The horse will give you ladies the chance to change your mode of travel and at the same time lighten the wagon. I have an extra saddle, but it's a western one, which means you will have to ride astride."

Selina was pleased. At Cedar Hill, she never used a side-saddle. Stella had never ridden a horse any way other than bareback. Janet, though, was mortified. Ride astride! Heavens above!

"Layne," Janet began angrily. "I do declare! Next you'll be insisting we wear trousers!"

"Not only trousers, but a wide-brimmed hat to protect your face from the sun. There's a town up the road, I want you ladies to buy yourselves trousers, shirts, and hats."

Janet's mouth was agape.

Layne chuckled. "I also want you three to buy sturdy walkin' shoes, unless you brought a pair with you."

"Whatever for?" Janet demanded.

"When you aren't riding, you ladies will need to walk alongside the wagon—it'll lighten the load and keep the team from tiring."

Janet had had enough. Bounding to her feet, she placed her hands on her hips and glared down at Layne. "I want you to take me back to New Orleans—immediately!"

"We aren't turning back."

She raised her chin defiantly. "Very well! However, I must warn you that I intend to give my father a full report. I don't know how much he agreed to pay you, but when I tell him how you treated me, you'll be lucky if he pays you anything!"

Layne spoke calmly. "Sit down, Janet."

When she didn't comply, Doug reached up, grasped her hand, and urged her to sit beside him. "Ma'am," he began, "Layne's takin' you to your father as a favor. Bart isn't payin' him for his trouble." Doug grinned rakishly. "And you are definitely trouble."

"Don't be insolent!" she snapped.

"You know what you need, Miss Wilkerson?" he asked insouciantly.

"No, but I'm sure you're about to tell me."

"You need a sound spankin'. And I'm just the man who's liable to give you one. So if you don't want your bottom too sore to ride horseback, I suggest you stop whinin' and complainin'."

Janet was absolutely furious. No one had ever spoken to her in such a manner. She wanted to lash out at him, but there was a warning look in his eyes that convinced her to remain quiet. The man was insufferable! How dare he threaten her!

Grinning, Layne continued, "Ladies, let's finish lunch so we can get back on the road."

"Will we stop at an inn tonight?" Janet asked.

"Yes," Layne answered. "But once we cross into Texas, don't expect such comfort, for there aren't any inns."

Janet couldn't care less whether there were inns in Texas, for she didn't intend to travel that far. Her only concern lay with tonight. Surely there would be other travelers at the inn, she'd find one who was a gentleman and ask him to escort her back to New Orleans. She knew, however, that she'd have to convince this gentleman to sneak away with her in the middle of the night, for Layne would never grant her permission to leave.

It would be difficult, but she felt she could do it; and as she thought about her plan, Janet smiled secretly.

The travelers arrived at the small, nondescript town. Doug stopped the team in front of the general store, then assisted the women from the wagon.

Layne dismounted and wrapped his horse's reins over the store's hitching rail. "While you ladies are shopping," he began, "Doug and I will go to the blacksmith's." He turned to Stella. "I'll arrange for Stratton's carriage to be repaired and sent back to him."

"What about his horse?"

"The next time I go to New Orleans, I'll return it to him. I'd send it back now, but we need it."

As the men headed toward the blacksmith shop, Selina studied the mercantile. The building was a typical country store, two full grain barrels stood on each side of the open door, and a sleeping hound was curled up across the threshold. Three elderly men, ensconced in cane rocking chairs, were sitting on the porch whittling. They were chewing tobacco and would periodically spit a brownish stream over the railing.

"Does this town have a name?" Janet wondered aloud.

"Brenton," Selina answered.

Glancing about at the small settlement, Stella remarked, "I see what Layne meant when he said you could spit from one end to the other."

"Well," Selina began, "let's hope this store carries what we need."

She stepped up to the porch, the others following. The old men were watching them, and the one sitting in the middle pointed at Hattie, then said to Selina, "Ma'am, Sam don't allow no darkies in his store."

"Sam?" she questioned.

"He's the proprietor, and he ain't gonna want your black mammy in there."

"But she's with me," Selina replied.

"Don't make no nevermind," he drawled, spitting a shot of tobacco juice over the railing.

"Miz Selina," Hattie said, "I's just stay out here with little Paul."

"All right. We won't be long."

Sam, a tall, lanky man, was standing behind a cluttered counter. His eyes traveled appreciatively over his three customers. "If I didn't know better," he said, grinning broadly, "I'd think I done died and went to heaven. A blond, a brunette, and a redhead. And all of you beautiful. What more could a man ask for? Hope you ladies aren't offended. I meant it as a compliment. Now, what can I do for you?"

"We need trousers, shirts, and hats," Selina answered.

The man found her requests peculiar, but didn't say anything. He pointed to a table piled with clothing. "You'll find what you need over there, ma'am."

Stella moved to the table, but Janet held back. Looking at her, Selina asked, "Don't you think you should pick out your clothes?"

Janet saw no reason to purchase any manly attire since she planned to return to New Orleans. "I don't intend to buy anything," she answered defiantly.

"Very well," Selina replied. "Then I'll buy the clothes for you."

"Go ahead, but I won't wear them."

Looking through the stacked clothing, the women found sizes they were sure would fit; then, going over the hats, they discovered three that were suitable.

As they carried their purchases to the counter, Selina asked the others if they had packed sturdy walking shoes. Stella said that she had; Janet managed a terse nod.

"Will this be all, then?" the proprietor asked.

Selina started to say yes, but she spotted a derringer on the back shelf.

"Let me see that," she said, pointing at the weapon.

Sam picked it up and handed it to Selina. "Be careful, ma'am. It's loaded."

"Is it for sale?" she asked.

"Yes, ma'am, and it comes with extra cartridges. A

couple of weeks back, a gambler came through on his way to New Orleans. He was down on his luck and traded that-there derringer for supplies. It's an over-and-under."

"A what?" Selina questioned.

"It's got two barrels, one above the other. Them derringers are favored by gamblers 'cause they're easy to conceal. The gent who traded it kept it hid inside his boot."

Sam turned back to the shelf and picked up a small holster with a leather strap. Showing it to Selina, he said, "He had this-here 'specially made. He kept it strapped above his ankle; that way the derringer was concealed inside his boot."

"Inside his boot?" she repeated. She thought for a moment, then said briskly, "Sir, I'll buy this derringer, plus its holster. I also want to purchase a pair of boots." She glanced at Stella and Janet, then back to Sam. "Make that three pairs of boots."

"I don't want any boots," Janet grumbled.

"When we're wearing trousers and riding horse-back, boots will be more practical than shoes."

"I suppose you plan to hide your gun inside one of your boots." Janet huffed. "Honestly, Selina! You never cease to amaze me."

Ignoring her remarks, Selina asked Stella, "What size shoe do you wear?"

"A seven," she answered.

Selina looked questioningly at Janet. "Your size?"

She lifted her chin stubbornly and refused to answer.

Selina smiled inwardly. Knowing Janet was proud of her dainty hands and feet, she said with a straight face, "I'll just have to guess at your size. Let's see, a nine should fit."

"A nine!" she exclaimed. "I'll have you know that I wear a size six!"

Selina laughed.

"You tricked me!" Janet snapped.

Turning to the proprietor, Selina told him, "We'll take three pairs of boots, two in a size seven and one in a size six."

While the man was seeing to her order, Selina looked her new gun over carefully. A cold, determined look came to her eyes as she recalled her abduction. No man would ever catch her helpless again! She'd keep this small pistol in her possession at all times.

Placing the boots on the counter, Sam nodded toward the derringer, remarking, "At close range that little gun's deadly. Remember, it ain't no toy. It can kill."

"I'll keep that in mind," she answered crisply.

Taking the holster, Selina handed the derringer to Stella. Turning her back to Sam, she lifted her skirt and petticoat and strapped the leather sheathe above her knee. Stella gave her the small pistol, and she slipped it snugly into its cover, then let her skirt and petticoat fall back over the weapon. Her derringer was well concealed.

Sam was thoroughly astounded. He couldn't wait to tell his cronies about this. They'd be shocked.

Stella was smiling, for she admired the young woman's grit.

Janet, however, was so incredulous that, for once, she was actually speechless.

When the women left the store, their arms laden with packages, Smith and Thompson were waiting at the wagon.

Stratton's horse was saddled, and Doug was holding its reins. He looked at Janet and said, "Change clothes inside the wagon. You're ridin' horseback."

"What if I refuse?" she retorted.

"Then I'll dress you myself and place you on the horse."

Janet thought he was bluffing, but she'd detected a seriousness in his voice that made her decide not to chance it.

She went inside the wagon, where she quickly changed into her new clothes. She was glad that Melody Harper couldn't see her in this scandalous outfit.

Climbing over the backboard, Janet stalked angrily over to Doug, jerked the reins from his hand, and mounted the horse without assistance.

"Miss Wilkerson," he began, "this gelding's spirited and kinda skittish, so keep 'im on a firm rein."

"Mr. Thompson," she said haughtily, "I've been riding since I was five years old. I don't need your advice."

She nudged the horse with her knees, expecting it to lope into an easy gallop, but the unexpected jab caused the gelding to bolt. As it broke away recklessly, Doug shook his head and walked over to his own horse.

Mounting slowly, as though he were in no hurry to give pursuit, he looked at Layne and commented calmly, "Before this trip is over, I'm gonna lock horns with that little gal. Just see if I don't."

He cantered out of town, then spurred his mount into a full run. When he caught sight of Janet, she was trying unsuccessfully to control the charging horse. Stratton's gelding was fast, but Doug's cowpony was faster.

Doug caught up and grabbed the horse's bridle,

then slowed the animal down all the way to a stop.

Janet waited for the reprimand. When Doug didn't say anything, she cast him a curious glance. He was simply watching her, his expression inscrutable.

"Well?" she questioned.

"Well, what?"

"Aren't you going to fuss at me?"

"Would it do any good?"

Her chin lifted with a smug tilt. "By the way, I didn't need your help. I was about to get the horse under control when you intervened."

His lips twisted into a skeptical smile.

"Don't you believe me?"

"Does it matter?"

Her green eyes flashed indignantly. "No, it doesn't matter. I don't care what you think, and that goes double for Layne Smith. I've never met two men so overbearing or so inconsiderate! I thought this trip would be a pleasant adventure, but apparently I was wrong! I certainly didn't imagine I'd be crowded into a wagon with four other people! Nor did I think I'd be expected to dress like a man! And if all that isn't bad enough! I'm even expected to walk part way to Texas!"

Janet's flushed cheeks and sparkling eyes were enchanting. "You're a pretty young lady," Doug said indolently. "You remind me of a horse I once owned."

"A horse!" she cried, offended.

"Yes, ma'am. That horse was a real beauty, but it was so damned mean and contrary that I had to shoot it."

"What are you insinuating? How dare you be so insulting!"

"Sorry, ma'am," he apologized lamely, trying vainly not to smile.

"You aren't in the least sorry!" she retorted.

At that moment the others came into sight, and turning her horse about, Janet rode back to the wagon.

Ten

The inn was a two-story clapboard building, and it was a welcoming haven for tired travelers. For a reasonable price, the establishment offered clean beds, hot baths, and nourishing meals.

Layne rented three rooms—one for Hattie, Stella, and Paul, one for Janet and Selina, and he and Doug would share the third.

As the innkeeper showed his guests to their rooms, he let them know that they had time to bathe before supper. The group was eager to wash away the trail dust, and baths were ordered.

The owner, priding himself on quick service, had his two male slaves carry tubs to the ladies' rooms—the men would wash in the public bath at the end of the hall.

After delivering a tub to Janet's and Selina's room, the two servants hurried downstairs, filled four large buckets with hot water, returned upstairs and poured the steaming water into the bathtub. Telling the ladies they'd return soon to empty the tub and refill it, the slaves left to prepare baths for the others.

Janet was anxious to carry out her plan to find a gentleman and solicit his help, so she asked Selina if she could bathe first. Selina had no objections, and Janet undressed and washed quickly. Afterward she slipped into a modestly-cut dress. Although simply made, the garment enhanced her soft, feminine curves. She gave her hair a brisk brushing, leaving the golden tresses unbound, then she departed hastily, telling Selina she'd wait for her and the others downstairs.

Going to the dining room, Janet was disappointed to find it unoccupied. Poised in the entryway, she gave the room a cursory glance. It was small and contained half a dozen tables covered with red-and-white checkered cloths. Although the room was far from elaborate, it was neat and visibly clean.

Janet tapped her foot restlessly. Layne and Doug would be coming downstairs soon, and if she didn't find someone to help her before then, her plans would be ruined. She hated the idea of traveling to her father's ranch under conditions she now considered quite unbearable. The probable possibility put a petulant frown on her pretty face.

A man's voice suddenly intruded on her thoughts, "Is somethin' wrong, ma'am?"

Janet hadn't been aware of another's presence. Startled, she made a half-turn to find a man standing close, watching her intently. She studied him quickly. His casual attire was inexpensive, his boots scuffed and well worn. Apparently, he wasn't an aristocratic gentleman. He was young, not much older than herself. He seemed harmless though, and his clean-shaven face certainly wasn't threatening. Janet decided to ask for his help.

"Sir," she began, smiling charmingly, "are you traveling to New Orleans?"

He wasn't going to New Orleans, but his interest

was so piqued that he decided to lie. "Yes, ma'am, that's where I'm headed."

"Will you please step outside with me for a moment?"

The young man was surprised by her request. What did this beautiful and obviously well-bred lady want from him?

"Please!" she implored, tugging at his arm.

Conceding, he followed her out onto the front porch. As quickly as she could, Janet explained her present circumstances and her wish to return to New Orleans. She assured him that if he escorted her home, her uncle would pay him handsomely for his troubles.

The man, although shocked by Janet's offer, agreed readily.

Janet thanked him warmly, "Tonight, after everyone is asleep, I'll meet you at the stable."

"That'll be fine, ma'am," he replied.

"I must hurry back inside. The others may already be in the dining room. I don't want Layne or Doug to come looking for me and find us together."

She favored him with a pretty smile, then opened the door and went back inside.

The man leaned back against the porch railing and rolled himself a cigarette. He was lighting it when his older brother, who had been at the stable tending to their wagon and team, arrived.

"Jerry," the young man began with a broad grin, "you ain't gonna believe what just happened."

"What's that, Billy?" he asked. Reaching into his pocket, he withdrew a large hunk of chewing tobacco. His brother hastily explained Janet's request. Jerry grinned widely, causing a stream of tobacco juice to dribble down onto his red beard. "Is this woman pretty?"

"Pretty? Hell, she's beautiful!"

"I've always wanted me a real lady. You reckon this rich bitch likes lovin' as much as a whore does?"

Billy shrugged. "I don't know, but I got a hankerin' to find out."

"Hell, Billy! She probably craves lovin' like a bitch dog in heat. Otherwise, she wouldn't have come on to you like she did."

"She didn't exactly come on to me."

"She asked you to take her to New Orleans, didn't she? Just the two of you! That's a proposition, if I ever heard one. She's a-wantin' you between her legs."

Billy grinned lewdly. "I'll sure be glad to oblige her."

"I'm gettin' seconds," Jerry remarked, also grinning. "What are we gonna do with her after we poke her?"

"Hell, we'll just leave her and skitter daddle home. She can find someone else to take her to New Orleans."

"We'd better not let her see us together though. She might change her mind if she knows I ain't travelin' alone."

"You're right," Jerry agreed. "We won't let her know 'bout me 'til she comes to the stable. Hell, the hot little bitch will probably be happy to learn she's gonna get a double dose!"

Janet lay beside Selina in the large double bed. She stared up at the dark ceiling, waiting anxiously for Selina to fall asleep. A pleased smile touched the corners of her lips. She'd soon be home! She had been such a fool to agree to this trip! Why, never in her life had she been treated so outrageously! How dare

Layne and Doug show her such little respect! She wished she could see their faces in the morning when they found her gone.

Growing eager to leave, Janet whispered softly, "Selina? — Selina?"

There was no answer, for the young woman was sleeping soundly.

Carefully, so she wouldn't awaken Selina, Janet left the bed and dressed as quietly as possible. She was thankful that the moon shining through the open window cast enough light for her to see what she was doing. She had brought a small bag into the inn, and she packed it quickly.

As she moved stealthily across the room, she thought about her belongings that were still in the covered wagon. Should she try and take everything with her? No! She must get away from the inn without further delay!

Janet eased open the door, then closed it softly behind her. She moved quietly down the hall, to the stairs and outside.

Meanwhile, Selina had awakened. At first she didn't know what had roused her, then her dream flashed before her with clarity. Her nightmare had revisited her. She had again dreamt that she and Harold were really married and that he was about to take her brutally. A cold shudder ran through her as she sat up and moved to the edge of the bed. Hoping she hadn't disturbed Janet, she glanced over to see if her companion was still asleep.

Finding Janet's side of the bed empty, Selina leapt to her feet and lit the lamp. Looking quickly about the room, she was alarmed to see that Janet's bag was missing.

"Oh no!" Selina moaned. "Janet! You little fool!"

Intending to look for her, Selina dressed hastily. She remembered, however, to strap on her derringer—just in case. For a moment she considered going to Layne and letting him know about Janet, but she quickly dismissed the idea. If she couldn't find Janet, then she'd let Layne know what was happening. She was hopeful, though, that she'd catch Janet before she left, then Layne would never know that Janet had done something so foolish. If possible, she'd save the young woman from Smith's wrath, for Selina didn't doubt that he would be furious.

A lantern was hanging from a beam in the stable, and as Janet approached, she could see her new traveling companion standing beside a buckboard. Two horses were hitched to the wagon.

"Evenin', ma'am," Billy said congenially, his outer politeness concealing his inner lust.

Placing her bag in the rear of the wagon, Janet said briskly, "Let's leave, shall we? By morning, I want to be miles away. I wouldn't put it past Layne and Doug to try and catch up to us. Those two men are impossible!"

Billy assisted Janet up onto the seat, then sat beside her and took the reins into his hands.

When he didn't set the team into motion, she asked testily, "Why are we just sitting here? Let's go!"

The young man grinned slyly. "Ma'am, my brother's travelin' with us."

"What!" Janet exclaimed.

At that moment, Jerry, who had been hidden in the far corner, stepped into the light.

Seeing him, Janet said to Billy, "Sir, you should've told me about your brother!"

Jerry was about to leap into the wagon when, suddenly, he caught sight of Selina coming toward the stable. "Hey, Billy," he said, "look what we got here. There's two of 'em."

Arriving, Selina looked sternly at Janet and demanded, "Get down from there and come back to the inn with me! Have you taken leave of your senses?"

"The lady's goin' with us," Jerry said quietly, edging his way to Selina. Reaching her, he moved speedily and imprisoned her in his strong grasp. "You're comin' with us too," he chuckled, lifting her into his arms.

He carried her into the back of the wagon, placed her on the floorboard, and drew his sheathed knife. Resting the sharp edge against Selina's throat, he uttered gruffly, "If you scream, I'll slit your pretty neck." He turned his cold gaze to Janet. "If you scream, I'll kill this woman and you too. Do you hear me, bitch?"

"Yes," Janet managed to whisper raspingly.

"Make tracks, Billy!" Jerry ordered.

The young man slapped the reins against the team, and the horses took off with a bolt. The buckboard rolled swiftly past the quiet inn and onto the road. The wayside establishment soon faded into the distance.

Stella hurried to Layne's and Doug's room and pounded loudly on their door.

"Just a minute," she heard Layne call.

She waited anxiously, and the moment Smith opened the door, she blurted, "Selina and Janet are gone!"

"What do you mean they're gone?"

141

"Paul woke up, and I had just got 'im back to sleep when I heard a wagon and horses. I looked out the window, and I saw Selina and Janet leavin' with two men. I happened to catch a glimpse of Selina. She was lyin' in the back of the wagon, and I think one of the men had a knife held to her throat. But I ain't sure. I mean, it's dark out and it all happened so fast."

"Dammit!" Layne muttered, his rage surging. "Go back to your room, Stella. Doug and I will catch 'em and bring 'em back."

As he closed the door, Doug was already getting dressed, mumbling crankily, "Those two women are nothin' but trouble!"

"That's puttin' it mildly!" Layne remarked. His tone was furious.

Billy guided the buckboard off the dirt road and into a small clearing in the woods. Bringing the team to a halt, he shoved the brake into place and secured the reins; then he grabbed Janet's arm and jumped to the ground, pulling her behind him.

"Let me go!" she cried, trying vainly to struggle free.

Laughing, he swooped her into his arms and carried her into the surrounding foliage.

As the two disappeared into the dark shadows, Jerry told Selina to get out of the wagon. Pretending submissiveness, she obeyed; but the moment her feet touched the ground, she took off running.

Bolting after her, Jerry's long strides quickly shortened the distance between them. He was close to catching his prey when, suddenly, she stopped, reached beneath her skirt, drew her derringer, and spun about. The gun aimed at his chest brought

Jerry's strides to an abrupt halt.

"Call Billy, and tell him to get out here!" Selina said firmly. "Do it! Or I'll shoot you where you stand!"

Before he could comply, they heard the sounds of horses approaching. As the riders drew into sight, Selina's heart sank with dread. Layne! She had hoped he'd never learn of this terrible incident. Now, like Janet, she'd be forced to face his wrath.

"Where's Janet?" Doug asked, reining in.

Selina nodded toward the foliage. "The other one took her in there."

As Doug dismounted and hurried into the dark thicket, Layne remained on his horse. Selina dared to raise her gaze to his. The fury burning in his dark eyes unnerved her; yet she was helpless to turn away from his heated stare.

Jerry, noticing that the man's pistol was holstered, decided to take advantage of the woman's preoccupation. He lurched toward Selina, intending to grab her weapon; but Layne, seeing his intent, edged his horse forward. As the large stallion blocked Jerry's path, Layne's foot came out of the stirrup. He kicked the man under the chin, and the powerful blow knocked him to the ground.

As Jerry lay moaning, Doug was slipping up to Billy and Janet. The young man had his captive on her back, and while holding her down with one arm, he was trying to lift her skirts. Janet was crying pathetically, begging him to leave her alone.

Doug, moving silently up behind them, drew his pistol, and placed the barrel to the back of Billy's head. "I oughta blow your brains out!" he uttered viciously.

Billy froze, and his heart pounded rapidly.

Doug stepped back. "Get up, you horny bastard!"

He obeyed without question, and when Doug saw that he was unarmed, he slipped his pistol back into its holster.

Awkwardly, Janet got to her feet, but her knees were trembling so bad that she almost fell. Catching her arm, Doug steadied her. "Are you all right?" he asked.

She looked up through her flowing tears into his concerned face. "Yes, I'm all right. Oh thank God, you're here!"

He slid his arm about her waist, and she leaned against him gratefully. She found his strength comforting.

Speaking to Billy, Doug said tersely, "Let's go!"

Layne was dismounting as the others emerged from the foliage. He waited until they had reached him before jerking Jerry to his feet. Eyeing the brothers with hostility, Layne ordered, "Get in your buckboard and get the hell out of my sight — before I decide to string you up from the nearest tree!"

The men wasted no time getting to their wagon and leaving. As they were driving away, Layne said to Doug, "Take Janet back to the inn. Mrs. Chamberlain and I have a few things to discuss."

Selina cringed. Layne had said Mrs. Chamberlain as though it were a curse instead of a name. She dreaded the upcoming confrontation and wished she could miraculously disappear.

"Layne," Janet began hesitantly, "I'm sorry. . . ."

"I don't want to hear an apology from you!" he said, cutting her off sharply. "I don't want anything from you but silence! I promised your uncle that I'd be patient! But young lady, you're driving my patience to the limit!" He looked at Doug. "Get her out of here before I say something I shouldn't!"

144

Thompson assisted Janet onto his horse, then swung up behind her. As he picked up the reins, his muscular arms went about her. Defeated and feeling miserable, Janet relaxed against his wide chest.

She began to feel safe in Doug's presence; and soothed by the horse's smooth gait, she soon fell asleep. His arms tightened about her, holding her supportively close.

A short time later, Doug guided his horse to the front of the inn and stopped. "Wake up, little one," he murmured gently.

Janet awakened slowly, saying with a yawn. "I'm so tired, I'll probably fall back asleep the moment my head hits the pillow."

After dismounting, Doug helped Janet to the ground. Gazing up into his eyes, she said somewhat pertly, "The other night when I was knocked unconscious, I awoke to find you watching over me. Then tonight you came to my rescue. I couldn't feel more protected if I had my own watchdog." She smiled disarmingly. "Please don't misunderstand. I didn't mean that quite the way it sounded."

"Unlike a watchdog, ma'am, I can't be placated with a pat on the head and gentle words."

"What do you want from me?" she asked querulously. "An apology?"

"It might be a good place to start," he retorted. "I've never known a woman so spoiled or so ungrateful."

She lifted her chin arrogantly. "Mr. Thompson, your insolence is intolerable. Furthermore, your manners are sorely lacking." Her eyes, sweeping over him, mirrored her disdain.

"Is it my Indian blood that you find so distasteful?" he asked. "Or is it simply my looks? I know I'm not handsome, but I'm not downright ugly either."

145

"I don't find you ugly," she answered truthfully. "Intimidating, maybe. Are you a half-breed?"

"I'm one-quarter Apache."

"I suppose your Indian heritage is somewhat forbidding. However, as I said before. Your manners are lacking."

"And your behavior deserves a good spankin'."

"How dare you!" she exclaimed in anger. "You're an insolent, pompous brute!" She tossed her head haughtily. "Good night, Mr. Thompson!"

She started to sweep past him, but his arm snaked out and wrapped about her waist. Taking her to the porch steps, he sat down and flung her face down across his lap.

"Let me up!" she demanded, squirming wildly.

Lifting her skirts, he remarked devilishly, "I'm glad to see you're wearin' pantaloons. Otherwise, this spankin' might be embarrassin'."

"Spanking!" she screeched. "You can't be serious!"

"I've never been more serious. I'm gonna give you what your uncle should've given you years ago."

His large hand came down soundly on her rounded buttocks, the sudden whack causing Janet to cry out sharply. Despite her cries, he continued until her bottom was thoroughly spanked. Then, with no warning, he stood up, letting her tumble down the short flight of steps to the ground.

Getting clumsily to her feet and rubbing her sore behind, she raged through her tears, "Oh you beast! You despicable cad! I hate you!"

Ignoring her tirade, Doug went to his horse. Leading the animal toward the stable, he said calmly over his shoulder, "Good night, Miss Wilkerson."

Janet, crying more from anger than pain, fled up the steps and into the inn. She slammed the door so

146

loudly that Doug, now halfway to the stable, heard it
clearly.

Eleven

Layne waited for Doug and Janet to ride away before turning his steely gaze to Selina. His jaw clenched, anger radiating from his dark eyes, he demanded gruffly, "Mrs. Chamberlain, what do you have to say for yourself?"

Stifling her own anger, she answered somewhat collectedly, "What do you want me to say?"

"You can begin by telling me why you and Janet were with those men! I can't believe they came to your room and abducted you, so you two must've made plans to meet them."

"I didn't make any such plans, but Janet apparently did."

"Why did she do that?"

"I don't know. I suppose she wanted them to take her to New Orleans." Selina placed her hands on her hips and eyed him querulously. "If you hadn't dismissed Janet so brusquely, then you could be asking her these questions."

"Why should I ask her, when I can ask you?" he grumbled.

"Because I don't have the answers!" she remarked peevishly. "Janet didn't say anything to me about running away. I happened to wake up and find her gone.

148

I went to the stable looking for her. She was with those two men, and one of them grabbed me and forced me into the wagon. He held a knife to my throat and said he'd kill me if I screamed."

Layne sighed testily. "Dammit, Selina! Are you tel-lin' me that you once again took it upon yourself to go after Janet? Didn't the other time teach you anything? That time, you almost got raped! And this time. . . ."

"Yes?" she snapped archly. "What about this time?" She lifted her chin defiantly. "This time, I was in no danger. I had the incident completely under control."

"With that little toy?" Layne, smiling skeptically, gestured to the derringer she was holding.

"At close range, this so-called toy is a deadly weapon. And if I remember correctly, I had my vic-tim at very close range."

"Would you have shot him? Are you capable of killin' a man?" He awaited her answer with an amused grin.

"I'm perfectly capable of killing a varmint, and men like him are varmints!" Lifting her skirt a bit, she slipped her derringer into its holster.

Layne admired her courage and her dauntlessness. However, he felt that this time she had been lucky. What if there were a next time?

"We aren't even out of Louisiana yet," he warned, "and you and Janet have managed to be abducted twice. Texas, madam, is a lot more dangerous. That little derringer of yours will be useless against outlaws, Mexican bandits, and Indians." His eyes bore into hers. "Once we cross into Texas, if you and Janet continue such defiance, it might very well cost you your lives."

Moving to her side, he placed his hands on her shoulders and turned her so that she was facing him.

"Do I make myself clear, Mrs. Chamberlain?"

"Yes, you've made yourself quite clear," she said irritably. "And will you please stop calling me Mrs. Chamberlain?"

"Why?" he taunted. "It's your name, isn't it?"

She stepped back, saying evasively, "Don't you think we should return to the inn?"

"In due time," he answered quietly. Again, he grasped her shoulders, drawing her close. His eyes searched hers with an intensity.

She tried to move away, but his hold merely tightened. His gaze was now focused on her lips, and she wondered if he was going to kiss her. She knew she wouldn't have the strength to resist. His dark eyes returned to hers, and she sensed that he was now watching her with something more than masculine interest.

Layne didn't believe that Selina was married to Harold Chamberlain. He wanted desperately to kiss her, and he was certain that if he did so, he wouldn't be kissing another man's wife.

Slowly he pulled her to him, and their intimacy sent Selina's heart pounding expectantly. Lowering his head, his lips brushed hers in a tantalizing invitation for more. Then his warm mouth blazed a sensuous path over her neck and down to the hollow of her throat.

Selina trembled as a tingling sensation coursed through her. "Layne," she whispered raspingly, her arms going about him, drawing him even closer.

His lips came down on hers with a sudden force, and his rough, aggressive kiss held her captive. She surrendered urgently, returning his demanding ardor with a passion equal to his.

Suddenly, without warning, Layne relinquished her

so brusquely that she tottered backward. Wondering why he had broken their embrace, she lifted her puzzled gaze to his. The fiery intent smoldering in his brown eyes made her gasp.

"Selina," he said hoarsely, "I've never wanted a woman as bad as I want you."

She was confused. "Then why . . . ?"

"Why did I stop kissing you?"

"Yes," she whispered timorously.

"If the kiss had continued, I would've made love to you — with or without your consent." His voice took on a rasping note of pleading, "You have no idea how badly I want you."

His declaration was thrilling to Selina, for she desired him with every fiber of her being. But I can't give myself to him! her better judgment intervened. It would only lead to more heartache!

She tore her gaze away from his, swallowed heavily, and said evenly, "I think we should return to the inn."

Layne was disappointed. He was hoping that she wanted him as much as he wanted her. Keeping these feelings to himself, he replied, "You're right, Mrs. Chamberlain. We should leave."

"Darn it, Layne!" Selina spat. "I told you to stop calling me that!"

He moved swiftly, grasped her arm, and pulled her close. "Why, dammit? Why don't you want me to call you Mrs. Chamberlain?" He held his breath as he awaited her reply. Would she tell him the truth and admit that her marriage was a hoax?

It was on Selina's lips to confess, but she held back the words. If she told him the truth, what would he think of her? Avoiding a confession, she struggled out of his grasp. "I don't have to explain myself to you."

"No, you don't," he agreed testily. He held out his

hand. "I want you to give me that damned derringer before you get yourself killed with it."

"Killed?"

"You might aim it at someone who will shoot back!" He quirked a brow. "Do you even know how to use it?"

"Of course I know how to use it." She bent down, reached beneath her skirt, and drew the derringer. Aiming it at Layne's chest, she replied calmly, "I simply aim it at a varmint's chest and pull the trigger."

"Are you insinuatin' that I'm a varmint?" he queried, grinning indolently.

"If the name fits . . ." she teased.

Layne's hand shot out, grasped the derringer, and snatched it with incredible ease. "Let this be a valuable lesson, my beauty. The next time you hold a varmint at gun point, shoot first, then ask questions."

Going to his horse, Layne placed the gun inside his saddlebag. He then went over and picked up Janet's bag. Billy had thrown it on the ground before leaving. Layne attached it to his saddle, turned to Selina, and said, "If you're ready, we'll leave."

Selina was fuming. How dare he take her derringer! She stalked angrily to his side. "Give me back my gun!"

"Believe me, madam, I'm keepin' it for your own good."

"I'll decide what's good for me and what isn't," she snapped .

"It's obvious that you have no idea what's good for you! Otherwise, you wouldn't chase after Janet! You'd come to me, like you're supposed to!"

"Go straight to the devil, Layne Smith!" Whirling toward the horse, she started to reach inside the saddlebag, but Layne's hand on her arm impeded her.

She flung off his hold. "It's my gun!"

"But it's in my possession, and it's stayin' there."

Her temper blew. "You arrogant, demanding bully! Oh, if only I were a man!"

Selina's flashing eyes and flushed cheeks were enticing, and Layne struggled against the need to take her back into his arms. Barely controlled desire flickered in the dark depths of his eyes.

Suddenly, becoming aware of his male hunger, Selina's anger dissolved. Her heart began beating rapidly. Her better sense surfaced, warning her to remain aloof; her heart, however, demanded that she surrender unequivocally to this man.

Obeying her heart's desire, she stepped forward into his opening arms. As his lips descended to hers, Selina knew her heart was lost forever. It now belonged to Layne Smith. She wondered if he'd treasure it, or would he break it into little pieces?

"Selina," Layne whispered, "I want to make love to you."

"Yes," she moaned tremulously. "Yes, my darling."

Sweeping her into his arms, he carried her to a high patch of grass that was well sheltered by surrounding bushes. Easing her gently onto nature's bed, he lay over her, his lips pressed demandingly to hers. She could feel his superb hardness, and her hips arched instinctively.

He reached beneath her dress and removed the holster strapped above her knee. Then, whispering her name with deep yearning, his hand moved to her breasts, caressing their fullness. Gently, but passionately, his kisses and petting aroused her deepest passion, and when he knew the moment was right, he lifted her skirts. He wished that he could fully undress her, and see her lying beautifully nude before him,

153

but he didn't consider their place of concealment all that safe.

As his fingers moved tenderly up her legs and to the lace on her pantaloons, he whispered, "Someday, my beauty, we'll make love behind a locked door, then there will be no clothing between us."

Slowly he drew the undergarment down past her thighs, and as the night air touched her bare flesh, Selina tensed. The cool breeze brought her coldly back to her senses. What was she doing? She couldn't make love to Layne! He'd certainly realize she was still a virgin and demand an explanation. She'd be compelled to tell him the truth, then what would he think of her?

Meanwhile, Layne's practiced hands had her pantaloons past her legs. Kneeling, he removed them completely. The moonlight shone down softly, and he could see the tempting triangle between her velvety thighs.

Selina, her better judgment now in control, sat up quickly, squirmed out of Layne's reach, and scrambled to her feet.

"What the hell?" Layne grumbled, standing.

"I changed my mind," Selina managed to choke out. "I want to go back to the inn."

"Why, you teasing little she-devil!" Layne raged quietly, stalking her.

She backed up a couple of steps. "Leave me alone," she whispered feebly.

"Sweetheart, you're gonna finish what you started," he threatened.

Selina turned to flee, but Layne caught her about the waist, sending them both plunging to the ground. Pinning her struggling frame beneath him, Layne muttered, "Tomorrow, I'll probably hate myself for this, but, by God, I'm gonna have you!"

Her mouth was smothered by his demanding kiss, his lips conquering hers savagely. A wild surge of pleasure washed over her, drowning her will to resist; and she parted her lips in surrender.

Layne unbuckled his gun belt, placing it within his reach. Then, releasing his trousers, he positioned himself between her parted legs. He gazed down deeply into her passion-glazed eyes. "Although I'm tempted to do so, I won't force you to submit. Tell me to leave you alone, and I will."

Selina's response was a hand to the nape of his neck, urging his lips down to hers.

"Darlin'," he groaned, his mouth opening over hers, intensifying their kiss.

A mutual shudder coursed through their bodies as Layne's hardness touched between her thighs, seeking entrance. She felt the thundering of his heart against her breasts and heard him whisper her name before, suddenly, he thrust deep within her.

The sharp pain made her cry out as her fingers dug into his strong shoulders. Layne paused, waiting for her discomfort to subside. He smiled inwardly. She had been a virgin.

As Selina relaxed beneath him, Layne's hips began pumping rhythmically, his sensuous movements evoking her response.

Overcome with rapture, Selina twined her arms about his neck and arched her hips, letting him plunge ever deeper.

As his mouth bore down upon hers, she returned his passion, kissing him with an unbridled frenzy. His thrusting hips were now pounding rapidly, his deep strokes fanning a fire within her.

Layne's hands slipped beneath her buttocks, bringing her thighs flush to his. As he shoved his manhood in and out, in and out, Selina's arching hips met his in perfect timing. She clung tightly, letting their love-making totally engulf her. She had never dreamed such pleasure existed.

Layne's aggressive motions soon brought her to a feverish pitch; then with a final demanding thrust, he took her with him to love's ultimate climax.

He kissed her tenderly, then he lay beside her, urging her to snuggle close.

Selina sighed contentedly. "I never imagined making love could be so wonderful."

"I'm glad you enjoyed it, but the next time we make love will be even more pleasurable for you."

"You must be teasing," she murmured. "How can it get any better?"

"It will. Believe me." He paused for a moment, then said softly, "That is, if there is a next time for us."

His words chilled her like a cold splash of water. "Why . . . do . . . you . . . say that?" she stammered. Sitting up, she reached for her pantaloons.

"You have some explaining to do," he remarked. He got to his feet and straightened his trousers. "Stay as you are," he told her. "I'll be right back."

Layne stepped to his horse and got his canteen. Removing his bandanna, he dampened it with water, replaced the canteen, and returned to Selina.

Handing her the wet kerchief, he said, "Here, you need this. There's virginal blood between your beautiful thighs — Mrs. Chamberlain."

As she took the bandanna, she cringed inwardly. Apparently, he was going to be difficult. As she wiped away the proof of her virginity, Layne strapped on his gunbelt.

Selina slipped on her undergarment and refastened

156

her holster. She pitched the soiled scarf into the bushes.

"You and Chamberlain aren't married, are you?" Layne demanded quietly.

"No," she whispered. "But you already knew, didn't you?"

"Let's just say, I had my suspicions. Why are you two pretending to be married?"

"Harold thinks that my marital status will keep men, such as yourself, from taking liberties with me."

"That sounds like Chamberlain's warped reasoning. Are you two even engaged?"

"Yes, we are," she answered, her eyes downcast.

"You obviously don't love him, so why are you marrying him?"

"For his money," she said bluntly. Realizing her answer sounded too cold, too calculating, she was about to explain further; but before she could, Layne lashed out bitterly.

"If I had known you were for sale, I'd have asked your price before sampling your goods!"

Layne almost apologized. His accusation had been too cruel. But, dammit, he had believed Selina above such calculated deceit. He almost felt sorry for Chamberlain, the fool probably thought his fiancée was actually in love with him.

Layne's harsh retort had rendered Selina speechless. She was stunned, his words had hit her like a slap in the face. Her anger flamed slowly, spreading through her with the intensity of a fire burning out of control. She had laid her heart on the line, had given herself to this man unequivocally, with no strings attached. Her need to be with him had been born out of love. Now, damn his cold heart, he had thrown her love back into her face as though it were something

157

cheap and ugly!

Selina's anger blazed fiercely. "Layne, you're an unfeeling bastard! If you ever lay a hand on me again, I'll put a bullet right through your cold heart!" She brushed him aside and went quickly to his horse.

Layne followed. Out of his saddlebag he withdrew her derringer and handed it to her. "Here. If you plan to shoot me, you'll need a gun."

She replaced the derringer into its leather sheath. "I'd like to leave," she said frigidly.

Layne hesitated. Should he offer an apology? Had he treated her too severely? Hell, he thought irritably, why should I give a damn if she marries Chamberlain for his money? The bastard will get what he deserves.

His thoughts raced on curiously. Surely Cedar Hill was making Selina wealthy, so why did she want to become even richer by marrying Chamberlain? He shook his head slightly. How could he have been so wrong about her? Apparently, she wasn't only calculating but also greedy.

Selina, growing impatient, said sternly, "I'd like to return to the inn."

His mouth lifted in a menacing, sarcastic smile. "Yes, ma'am. Whatever you say."

Grasping her arm firmly, he helped her onto his horse, then swung up behind her. To avoid touching him, she sat rigidly.

They had nothing to say to each other, and silence prevailed during the ride back to the inn. The moment Layne reined in, Selina, who refused his assistance, slid from the horse, landing soundly on her feet.

Without glancing back, she darted inside and hastened upstairs. She was surprised to find Stella sitting in the hall.

The young woman was on the floor, leaning back

against the closed door to Selina's room. She asked anxiously, "Are you all right?"

"Yes, I'm fine," Selina answered, wishing her words were true.

"I was so worried," Stella replied. "When Janet returned, she was cryin' somethin' fierce. I tried to get her to talk to me, but she went inside her room and shut the door. I was afraid she was cryin' 'cause somethin' awful had happened to you."

Selina was warmed by the woman's concern. "Thank you for caring, Stella. However, I have no idea why Janet was crying. Have you seen Doug? He brought her here."

"I ain't seen 'im, and I've been out here in the hall the whole time."

"I wonder where he is." Selina murmured.

As Layne led his horse inside the lit stable, he was somewhat surprised to find Doug sitting on a bale of hay.

"Waiting up for me?" Layne asked, grinning wryly.

Doug chuckled. "I ain't no mother hen. I was just sittin' here, doin' some serious thinkin'."

After leading his stallion into an empty stall, Layne began unsaddling. "Is something bothering you, Doug?"

"I think I went a little too far with Janet."

"What do you mean?"

"I gave her a sound spankin'."

Layne laughed. "She's had one comin' to her for years."

Doug moved over to the stall. "Now that my anger has mellowed, I kinda feel badly about hurtin' her."

"I'm sure you hurt her pride more than anything

else." He regarded Doug speculatively. "You aren't falling for her, are you?"

He skirted the question. "Does it matter?"

"Yes, it matters. Janet's spoiled, selfish, and arrogant beyond belief."

"She was raised to be that way. I think deep down inside, there's a lot of good in her."

"Yeah? Well, if what you say is true, then that goodness is buried mighty deep. Forget her, Doug. She'll bring you nothing but trouble, and a helluva lot of pain."

"I know," Doug agreed solemnly. "But I can't help how I feel."

Twelve

Selina skipped breakfast and went straight to the covered wagon that was hitched and parked in front of the inn. She pitched her carpetbag inside and leaned against the raised backboard. It was still early, but she could already feel the sun's intense heat; she knew the day was going to be extremely warm.

Her thoughts went to Layne; she dreaded facing him. She could hardly believe that she had given herself to him. She had been raised to believe a lady saved herself for her husband. That thought, however, made her shudder. She was promised to Harold Chamberlain, and sharing his bed filled her with terrible apprehension.

She tensed, and a thin layer of perspiration beaded her brow. Harold was determined to marry a virgin. When he learned what had happened between Layne and herself, would he withdraw his proposal? The results would be devastating. The bank would forclose, her slaves would be sold, and her mother would be homeless and destitute. Selina moaned; her night of passion might cost her dearly!

She supposed she could marry Harold, then confess her infidelity afterward. She considered it for a moment, then discarded the notion. Deceit went against her grain. She shrugged her shoulders with a calm she was far from feeling. She'd simply tell Harold the truth before marrying him. If he couldn't forgive her, then so be it.

Unexpected tears came to her eyes as she imagined her beloved Cedar Hill belonging to someone else. Her mother's welfare, and that of her slaves, also crossed her somber thoughts.

"What's wrong?" Janet asked.

Selina hadn't heard the woman's approach, and she was startled. "Wrong?" she repeated absently.

"There are tears in your eyes."

"Nothing's wrong," Selina murmured evasively. "I'm just feeling a little melancholy." She wondered if she should question Janet about last night. Stella had said that she had been crying fiercely. She decided not to pry, she had enough problems of her own without becoming involved in Janet's.

Janet lowered the backboard, and while climbing inside, said, "Stella's riding horseback this morning. Layne said you're to ride this afternoon."

"Do you know who's driving the team this morning?"

"Layne, which means, he'll be riding the same time you are." Janet eyed her suspiciously. "Maybe he's planning a romantic interlude?"

I'm sure he is! Selina thought irritably. Well, she knew how to put a stop to his sneaky maneuver! Her thoughts raced on heatedly. The man is so arrogant, so vain, he thinks all he has to do is twitch his little finger, and I'll come running! How dare he be so smug!

Then, seeing Stella leaving the inn, Selina rushed over and met her halfway. "Stella, I must talk to you."

"All right," she said. "You can talk while I change

162

clothes. Layne wants me to ride horseback."

"Yes, I know," Selina hastened to say. "Janet already told me, and she also said that I'm supposed to ride this afternoon. Stella, will you change with me?"

The woman was confused. "What do you mean?"

"I want you to change times with me. I'll ride this morning, and you can ride this afternoon."

Stella paused. "I don't know if we should. I wouldn't want to do anything to anger Layne. He's been so nice to me and all."

"I'll take full responsibility," Selina promised.

Stella was uncertain.

"Please!" Selina pleaded. "It means a lot to me!"

"All right, if it really means that much to you."

"Thank you, Stella!"

Moving quickly, Selina hurried inside the wagon, where she hastily donned her riding clothes. She was climbing outside when Layne and the others came out of the inn.

As he took in Selina's attire, Layne's eyes squinted angrily. "You're supposed to ride this afternoon," he told her.

"I convinced Stella to change times with me." She smiled shrewdly. "Why should you care which one of us rides first?"

Layne cared; he cared a great deal. He had hoped to get Selina alone so he could apologize. Last night he had not only insulted her but had treated her unfairly. Well, so much for an apology, he thought sourly. He supposed he could change places with Doug and still get Selina alone, but he decided against it. Obviously, she wished to avoid him, so he might as well appease her.

Meeting Selina's cunning gaze, he smiled wryly. "Ma'am, if you want to ride this morning, then by all

163

means do so." Taking Hattie's arm, he helped her and Paul into the wagon, then assisted Stella. He latched the backboard, and without giving Selina so much as a desultory glance, he went to the front and climbed up onto the seat.

The weather grew so uncomfortably warm that Layne decided to extend their lunch break a couple of hours. The travelers set up camp beside the river, its banks shaded by oak and cypress trees.

Following lunch, Layne went over to a towering oak, stretched out beneath it and was soon dozing. Meanwhile, Selina and Hattie washed and dried the dishes as Doug had a second cup of coffee.

Stella took Paul down to the river, where she removed his shoes and allowed him to wade in the cool river. The boy laughed gaily as he splashed his hands in the water.

Janet was resting close to the bank, and she watched the child. She had never had anything to do with children and usually considered them a nuisance. Most of her girlfriends fawned over them and could hardly wait to become mothers. Janet never thought about motherhood, though; her thoughts never went beyond romance.

"Miz Stella!" Hattie's blustering voice carried easily to the riverbank.

"What is it, Hattie?" Stella called back.

"Can you come here a moment?"

Stella went to Paul, but as she reached for him he threw a tantrum. He was having fun, and he wanted to stay in the water.

His mother felt badly about cutting his playtime short. She looked over at Janet and asked somewhat hesitantly, "Would you mind watchin' Paul for a moment? I'll be right back."

Janet was resting comfortably beneath a cypress, its branches a canopy against the sun. Heaving a deep sigh, she answered tediously, "Very well, I'll watch him. But do hurry back."

"I will," Stella promised. As she hurried back to camp, Paul returned to splashing in the water, his tiny voice ringing with delightful giggles.

Taking her eyes off the child, Janet's thoughts turned to Doug. The man's brutality still infuriated her. She had every intention of reporting his beastly conduct to her father. In her opinion, Doug Thompson was a barbarian and deserved to be strung up and whipped.

Suddenly, Stella's blood-curdling cry shocked Janet from her thoughts.

"Paul! . . . Paul!" Stella was screaming.

Janet's eyes flew to the river. The boy was nowhere in sight. As she bounded to her feet, she spotted him. He had waded into water that was over his head, and he was going under.

By this time, Layne's and Doug's long strides had surpassed Stella's, and they raced past her and into the river. Reaching the drowning boy, Layne lifted him into his arms.

The youngster coughed several times; then, his face turning beet-red, he bawled at the top of his lungs.

Chuckling with relief, Doug said, "Obviously, he's all right."

Layne carried Paul to the river bank and handed him to Stella.

As his chubby arms went about his mother's neck, his cries quieted somewhat. Fortunately, he hadn't swallowed very much water and was mostly frightened.

Hattie swayed precariously as a feeling of relief relaxed her taut muscles. Standing beside her, Selina placed an arm supportively about her shoulders.

"Thank God, little Paul's safe!" Hattie cried, as grateful tears stung her eyes.

Meanwhile, Janet was silently uttering her own prayer of thanks. She had taken her eyes off the child only for a moment. It hadn't dawned on her that he might wade into deeper water. And so quickly!

Stella, crying happily, rained kisses over her son's face. God, she had come so close to losing her baby! Keeping him held tightly, she stepped over to Janet. Her eyes glared resentfully. "Damn you!" she said angrily. "If you wasn't gonna watch Paul, why didn't you tell me?"

"I meant to watch him," Janet answered shakily. "I only took my eyes off him for a moment. I never thought. . . ."

"That's your problem!" Stella remarked. "You never think! You never think 'bout anyone but yourself!"

Turning away, Stella carried her son to the wagon. Except for Doug, the others followed.

Janet shook as her anguished sobs came on all at once.

Moving to her side, Doug offered her his arms tentatively. She fell into his strong, comforting embrace. He let her cry undisturbed, then as her sobs abated, he moved her so that he could gaze down into her tear-streaked face.

"Oh Doug!" she cried brokenly. "If that baby had drowned! . . . I didn't mean . . . !"

"Shh . . . shh . . ." he whispered soothingly. "It's all right."

"No, it isn't!" she said in sudden anger. She stepped

back, leaving his embrace. "Everyone thinks I purposely allowed that child to wade into deep water! Now, they all hate me!"

"They don't hate you, nor do they think your negligence was deliberate." He leveled her with a stern expression. "But Stella was right, you simply don't think."

"You're just as bad as they are!" she spat. Then recalling the spanking he had given her, she added spitefully, "Stay away from me, Doug Thompson! I despise you!"

With a petulant toss of her head, she wheeled about and headed toward the wagon. Selina met her halfway, blocking her path.

"What do you want?" Janet asked sharply, girding herself for Selina's reprimand.

"I think you should apologize to Stella."

"Aren't you going to lecture me?" Janet asked with surprise.

"No," she replied. "I'm sure you're quite aware that your carelessness almost cost Paul his life. But I do believe you should tell Stella that you're sorry."

Janet tilted her head imperiously. "You want me to apologize to that . . . that thief?"

"She's a mother who nearly lost her child through your negligence. If you can't understand why you owe her an apology, then God help you!" With that, Selina walked away.

Janet's emotions were in turmoil. There was a part of her that wanted to ask Stella for her forgiveness, but there was another part; that part ruled by a lifetime of superiority that couldn't fathom humbling herself before a woman like Stella Larson. Janet's conscience, however, won the battle.

Going to the wagon, she found Stella inside putting

167

Paul down for a nap. Selina was there also. Janet waited for one of them to acknowledge her presence. When it seemed as though they were determined to ignore her, she began haltingly, "Stella . . . I'm sorry. Please believe me."

Stella, sitting beside her son, turned and faced Janet. She studied the woman closely, recognizing only sincerity in her eyes. "I believe you," she murmured.

"Thank you," Janet whispered. "Then you forgive me?"

"Yes, I reckon I do."

Easing the tension, Selina was quick to say, "Well, it's over now, and except for being frightened, Paul's just fine. I think we should put this incident behind us. We still have a long way to travel together, and we don't need any hard feelings festering."

Stella concurred. "I don't harbor no bad feelins'." She moved over and picked up her riding attire. "I need to change clothes, but ya'll stay and talk to me."

Selina, still wearing her trousers, was sitting cross-legged. Placing her elbows on her knees, she cupped her chin in her hands and sighed reflectively. "You'll enjoy riding horseback. Believe me, it's better than traveling in this confining wagon."

Stella had a favor to ask, and as she began to undress she said hesitantly, "I was wonderin' 'bout somethin'."

"What is it?" Selina asked.

"I hope I ain't bein' too forward, but I was wonderin' if ya'll would teach me to read and write."

"You don't know how to read and write?" Janet blurted out.

Stella blushed with shame. "No, I never learned."

"Didn't you go to school?" Janet asked.

Her blush deepened. "Ma and Pa didn't see no reason for me to be educated. A lot of poor folks don't get any schoolin'."

"Of course we'll teach you," Selina answered, speaking for Janet as well. "I brought a few of my favorite books, plus the Bible, and some writing paper."

Stella smiled gratefully. "Thank you kindly." She could barely restrain her excitement.

"You can have your first lesson tonight," Selina told her.

Removing her dress, Stella slipped into her trousers. "I hope I ain't imposin' too much, but I'd sure appreciate it if you could also teach me to talk proper."

"Do you have a special reason for wanting to improve yourself?" Selina asked.

"I wanna become a lady, so my son won't be ashamed of me."

"You're already a lady," Selina assured her.

"Thank you, but you know what I mean."

"Yes, I do. Janet and I will help you." She looked at Janet. "Won't we?"

Janet saw no reason to refuse. She grinned impishly. "I hope I make a better teacher than I did a student. I used to drive my poor tutors' patience to the limits."

"I can well imagine," Selina murmured, smiling.

The remainder of the day passed without further incident. The countryside began to take on a swampy appearance, and swarms of mosquitoes congregated by the water and in the shrubbery. Fortunately, the insects shunned fire, so that evening everyone remained seated about the campfire, even though supper had been eaten and the dishes washed. The heat from the flames was too intense for a summer's night, but the group decided it was better than being eaten by mosquitoes.

Paul had fallen asleep in his mother's lap. "I guess I'd better put little Paul to bed," Stella said.

"Keep the canvas pulled tightly closed," Layne told her. "It'll keep out the mosquitoes."

"It'll sure be hot, though," she replied. "We won't have a breeze."

"By tomorrow we'll be out of this swamp."

"I'm glad to hear that," Stella remarked.

Hattie got to her feet and drew Paul from Stella's lap. "I'll help you put 'im to bed, then I reckon I'll try to get some sleep myself."

As the women headed toward the wagon, Janet, deciding to retire, left the fire and followed.

Muttering an excuse, Doug went to his bedroll.

Everyone left so quickly that Selina suddenly found herself alone with Layne. Still wishing to avoid him, she moved to leave, but was deterred by his hand on her arm.

"Please wait," he said. "We need to talk."

"We have nothing to discuss. I believe you said it all last night, and you made yourself quite clear."

"I didn't mean what I said. I spoke rashly and out of anger." He paused, gazed deeply into her eyes, and continued, "This afternoon I wanted us to ride together so I could tell you that I'm sorry. But you insisted on ridin' with Doug." He turned his eyes from hers, and emitting a heavy sigh, murmured, "I don't blame you for wanting to avoid me. But, Selina, jealousy is a new emotion to me. I don't know how to handle it."

"Jealousy?" she questioned, her hopes soaring. Did this mean that he was falling in love with her? "Are

170

you saying you insulted me because you were jealous?"

"Partly," he answered.

"I don't understand."

"Part of it was jealousy," he replied, remaining totally honest. "The other part was strictly anger."

"Why were you angry?"

"I don't understand how you can coldly marry a man for his money. It's not as though you're desperately poor. I'm sure Cedar Hill's a prosperous plantation. So why the hell are you marrying Chamberlain? Are you that damned greedy? Does wealth mean that much to you?"

Although Selina was hurt by his accusations, she answered evenly, "I don't consider myself a greedy person, nor does wealth mean everything to me. But I find survival very important. Not only my own survival, but my mother's, my slaves', and Cedar Hill itself."

She poured herself a cup of coffee, took a sip, and continued, "My father was a compulsive gambler. To cover his enormous losses, he mortgaged our New Orleans home and Cedar Hill. My mother and I knew nothing about this until after his death. The bank threatened to foreclose. We were about to become homeless when Harold paid us an unexpected visit. He offered to pay our debts, plus an allowance for my mother. All he wanted in return was my hand in matrimony."

"And you agreed to his terms?"

"Yes, I did."

"Has he paid off the mortgages?"

"No, but he gave the bank a promissory note. On the day we are married, he'll pay the mortgages."

She put down her cup; she didn't really want any

coffee. She turned her face to Layne's. He was touched to see a tinge of sadness in her eyes. "I don't want to marry Harold," she said softly. "But I must, for my mother's sake, my slaves', and to save Cedar Hill." She shrugged her shoulders as though resigned to her fate. The courageous gesture went straight to Layne's heart. "A lot of marriages are ones of convenience, and they usually turn out quite well." She added with little conviction, "Maybe mine will too."

Layne withdrew into his own thoughts. He silently cursed himself for thinking the worst of her. He wouldn't blame her if she never forgave him.

Selina continued speaking, "Harold's father and your father were the original partners in the shipping company, so you and Harold must have been boyhood friends."

"We were never friends," Layne replied. "Even as boys, we didn't especially like each other."

"But you must know him fairly well."

"Well enough, I guess. Why?"

"Do you think he'll be a compassionate husband?"

"What do you think?"

"I have a feeling that he's selfish, maybe even a little cruel."

"Then don't marry him," Layne said firmly.

"I can't think only of myself. My mother's welfare, and that of my slaves, are my responsibility. Also, I must save Cedar Hill. It's my home and . . . and I love it. Surely you understand my feelings. You love the Diamond-S, don't you?"

Layne did understand, he understood only too well. However, he wasn't going to let Selina make such a sacrifice. The money he'd received from selling his father's half of the shipping company was still in the bank in New Orleans. It was an enormous amount and would more than cover the mortgages, plus furnish an allowance for Selina's mother. He was sure Selina's pride would prevent her from accepting his money as a gift, but would she accept it as a loan? She might, but if he allowed such a transaction, she'd return to Cedar Hill. He didn't want her to leave. He needed time to win her heart. Layne smiled inwardly as his thoughts continued. Tomorrow they'd pass through the town of Clarksville. He'd stop and send a wire to William Stratton, instructing his lawyer to pay the Beaumonts' mortgages and begin a generous allowance for Mrs. Beaumont. Soon thereafter, he'd let Selina know that she was no longer obligated to Chamberlain. He was hopeful that by then she'd be in love with him.

"Layne?" Selina murmured, bringing him out of his deep thoughts. "You didn't answer my question."

"I'm sorry, but I seem to have forgotten the question."

"Don't you love the Diamond-S as much as I love Cedar Hill?"

"Yes, I suppose. But I wouldn't marry someone I don't love to save it. It's only a piece of land. But I understand that you're marryin' Chamberlain to save your mother and your slaves. That's entirely different."

"Believe me, Layne, as much as I love Cedar Hill, I wouldn't marry to keep. . . ."

"I know," he cut in gently. "I understand, honey."

Selina smiled, "Thank you, Layne."

He arched a brow quizzically.

"Thank you for understanding," she explained. "I was afraid you wouldn't."

"Why didn't you tell me all this last night?"

"I don't know. I guess I was too angry."

173

"And that was my fault. I'm sorry."

"So am I," she murmured. She could hardly believe that she and Layne had finally communicated without hard feelings erupting. She got hesitantly to her feet. "Well, I guess we'd better get some sleep."

Layne replied, "You're right. Tomorrow's another long day."

As she turned to leave, Layne caught her hand and drew her into his arms. She welcomed his embrace, and raising her face to his, she met his kiss halfway. His mouth moved over hers with exquisite tenderness, but slowly the pressure of his lips increased. Then, stilling his passion, he released her with a tearing reluctance.

Smiling a little shakily, he whispered, "Good night, Selina."

"Good night, Layne," she responded. Happiness shone in her brilliant blue eyes. She turned and hurried to the wagon and climbed quietly inside.

Stella was still awake and was sitting close to the lit lantern. A tablet was on her lap, and she was deeply engrossed in writing the alphabet.

"How are you doing with your letters?" Selina asked, her tone hushed, for the others were asleep.

"I'm doin' pretty good," Stella whispered. "Will this light bother you?" she asked, gesturing toward the lantern.

"No, but don't stay up too long. You need your sleep."

"I'll quit soon. Is there any coffee left?"

"Yes, there's still half a pot."

Stella started to rise, but Selina waved her back down. "Keep writing. I'll get you a cup."

Stella barely had time to say thanks before Selina was out of the wagon.

Layne was no longer at the fire, and Selina supposed he had gone to his bedroll, or else was taking the first watch. Going to the pot, she poured Stella a full cup. She was about to return to the wagon when she heard a rustling noise. The sound had come from the shrubbery at her back, and, alarmed, she whirled about. Then, spotting Layne and Doug making their way through the thick bushes, she gave a sigh of relief.

She left before they could see her, and was getting ready to step up into the wagon when she happened to overhear Doug remark to Layne, "You know, if you were a little friendlier to Selina, it'd make it a lot easier to find out if she knows anything about your father's alleged suicide."

Selina, listening, was now riveted.

"You agreed to take her to Chamberlain's ranch so you could pump her for information," Doug went on. "Yet all you've done is argue with her. If you ask me, that's a helluva way to gain her trust. You might try bein' nice."

"I am being nice," Layne answered.

"Since when?" Doug remarked skeptically.

"Tonight, I was very nice to Selina."

"So you finally got smart, eh?"

Layne laughed good-naturedly.

Selina had heard enough. Entering the wagon, she closed the canvas tightly, blocking out the mosquitoes, as well as Layne's laughter. She handed Stella the coffee, then went to her pallet.

Outside, Layne's laughter had ceased. "I wasn't nice to Selina for the reasons you think," he told Doug. "Pumping her for information wasn't even on my mind. Besides, she doesn't know anything about Chamberlain's business, and she certainly wouldn't know if he had a reason to murder my father. Let's have a cup of coffee, and I'll tell you why she's marrying him and how I plan to help her."

Doug regarded him questioningly. "Are you fallin' in love with her?"

"Yeah, I guess I am."

As the men walked to the fire, Selina lay on her pallet, her thoughts racing fiercely. Damn Layne Smith! So he was being nice because he wanted information! Oh, the deceitful cad!

Confusion mingled with her anger, causing her brow to furrow. She knew nothing about his father's death. Why would he even think such a thing?

It doesn't matter! she told herself bitterly. I don't care what he thinks! As far as I'm concerned, Layne can go straight to hades and take his lying heart with him! I hate him! I hate him!

But the pain in her heart denied her words, and she forced back tears. Hate him? If only she could! But she loved him. A few tears trickled free, but she wiped them away. She'd not cry over Layne Smith, for he wasn't worth it!

Thirteen

The next morning, Selina was the last one to leave the wagon. Wishing she could postpone facing Layne indefinitely, she had deliberately lagged behind. She knew he'd greet her with feigned cordiality, pretending to be her friend when, hard as it was to believe, he was really a deceitful, sneaky, low-down scoundrel!

Moving away from the wagon, Selina approached the campfire slowly. The others were gathered about, eating breakfast.

Seeing her, Layne put down his plate and hastened over to meet her halfway. "Good morning," he murmured, smiling warmly. He reached for her hand, but she drew away.

"Don't touch me!" she spat, keeping her voice reasonably low so the others wouldn't hear.

Layne was totally perplexed. "What's wrong?"

"There's nothing wrong that your absence won't cure." She attempted to sweep past him, but his hand snaked out and captured her wrist.

"Dammit, Selina!" he uttered.

"Don't curse me, Layne Smith!" She jerked her arm free. "Stay away from me, or I'll . . . I'll . . ."

"You'll what?" he taunted, his own anger piqued.

"Shoot me with that little derringer of yours?"

"I'd shoot you right through your heart, if I thought the bullet could penetrate stone!" With that, she walked away.

Anger began spreading hotly through Layne as, gritting his teeth, he tried to find a reason for Selina's sudden hostility. He couldn't think of a plausible cause, he'd done nothing to offend her. Damn! He'd never met a woman so ambivalent; friendly one moment, hostile the next!

"We're runnin' late!" he growled testily, getting everyone's attention. "Break camp!"

It was Selina's turn to ride horseback. She was now sitting at the fire drinking coffee. Layne stepped to her side and took the cup from her hand, then pulled her to her feet. "We're riding on ahead. There's a town up the road, and I have some business there." He looked over at Doug. "We'll meet you in town."

Maintaining a firm hold on Selina's hand, Layne led her to the saddled horses. He helped her mount, then swung up onto his stallion.

"I don't want to ride with you," she uttered peevishly.

"We don't always get what we want, do we, Miss Beaumont?" His tone expressed impatience more than anger.

Knowing she had no choice but to tolerate his presence, she asked coolly, "How far away is this town?"

"Less than an hour's ride."

"Good," she remarked, her chin lifted defiantly.

Selina was a skilled rider and, taking Layne unawares, she urged her steed into a loping gallop. Once out of camp, she allowed the beast to break

178

into a full run.

Soon she heard Layne's horse gaining ground, and realizing Stratton's gelding was no match for Layne's stallion, she pulled back on the reins and slowed down.

Layne rode up alongside of her. "Are you in a hurry?" he asked, eyeing Selina somewhat irritably.

"No," she answered haughtily. "I just felt like a brisk ride. It's invigorating. I sometimes do things on a whim."

"When we're travelin' through territory occupied by Comanches, if you should get another such whim, stifle it. 'Cause if you don't, you'll find yourself riding in the wagon for good."

"Oh? Are you afraid that I might get thrown and find myself afoot?"

"Well, actually, I was thinking about the horse." He grinned lazily. "You don't want a winded horse beneath you if you're confronted by a band of hostile Indians. A rested horse can be the difference between living and dying."

"I see," she replied, understanding that his advice, though spoken lightly, should be taken seriously. "Do you think we'll be attacked by Comanches?"

Layne noted no fear in her voice; she had asked the question as calmly as though she were discussing the weather.

"I don't know," he answered. "But there's always a chance that we might run across a roving band. They'd find three young women and a child a big temptation."

"Temptation? What do you mean?"

"The Comanches have lost a lot of their people to disease, war, and the elements. Kidnapping women and children is one way to replenish their dwindling tribes."

"Do they have many white captives?"

"The number would shock you."

"Why doesn't the army do something?"

"Like what?"

"Rescue these white captives!"

"There's more Comanches than soldiers. The army doesn't infiltrate Comanche territory without invitation. It would be suicidal."

"Then these white captives are doomed?"

"The ones who were captured at a young age, don't consider themselves doomed. Quite the opposite. They were raised to be Comanche, and although their skin is white, on the inside they're pure Indian." He turned to Selina, and smiled somewhat ruefully. "Someday the soldiers will outnumber the Indians, more whites will move west. The buffalo will be slaughtered, then the Comanches and all the Plains Indians will be conquered."

"You sound a little sad."

"Maybe I am. I have a lot of respect for the Comanches."

"But you've fought with them."

"An enemy can be respected. Besides, they were here first. We're the intruders."

"Yes, I suppose we are," she answered thoughtfully.

Silence fell between them for a long moment, then Layne decided to ask, "Do you mind telling me what's bothering you?"

"Bothering me?" she toyed.

"Why were you so curt this morning?"

She wasn't about to tell him that she knew of his deceitful ploy, at least not yet. Let him squirm; it was no more than he deserved.

He demanded gruffly, "Are you going to tell or

not?"

"I'd rather not talk about it," she replied in an icy manner.

"All right!" he grumbled. "Have it your way!"

"I intend to," was her riposte.

Layne didn't offer Selina an explanation for stopping at the telegraph office, nor did she ask for one. He simply told her to wait outside; and when he completed his business, they'd go to the general store and buy a few supplies.

Handing her his horse's reins, he dismounted and went inside the small office. Despite Selina's unexplained hostility, he still planned to send a wire to William Stratton.

Selina glanced about curiously. The rural town was impressive, for it was clean, neat, and serene. Obviously, the citizens of Clarksville took pride in their town.

The door to the telegraph office opened, and two middle age ladies stepped outside. Selina was about to smile politely, but when their eyes swept over her with distaste, the smile froze on her lips. The women, whispering to each other, hurried down the wooden sidewalk. They glanced back over their shoulders a couple of times as though making sure their eyes hadn't deceived them.

Selina blushed. She could well imagine what they thought of her manly attire. With her hair tucked up beneath her hat, she thought glumly, they had probably mistaken her for a boy!

The town was busy, and as more citizens walked past Selina, she was confronted by more disdainful stares. By the time Layne left the telegraph office, she was fuming.

The moment he was mounted, she snapped, "Damn you, Layne Smith!"

Dumbstruck, he threw up his hands in despair. "Now what?"

"How dare you bring me to this town!"

"What's wrong with this town?" he asked, totally at a loss.

"Well, obviously it's very respectable!"

"And that's bad?" He was now thoroughly confused.

"Are you blind? Look at me! I'm dressed like a man! People are staring, and I don't blame them!"

Layne laughed heartily.

"It isn't funny! I've never been so embarrassed!"

Catching sight of the covered wagon entering town, Layne told her, "The others are here. You can skip going to the store and hide inside the wagon."

"I will!" she remarked.

She started to dismount, but Layne deterred her. "Selina, for what it's worth," he began, grinning wryly, "I think you look kinda cute."

"Layne, for what it's worth, I don't care what you think!" She dismounted to await the wagon. Her back was turned, and she didn't see the anger smoldering in Layne's eyes.

"It's getting late, and we'll be stopping soon," Selina said to Stella. She reached over and took the tablet from her companion's lap. "After supper, I'll give you a reading lesson."

The two women were alone with Hattie and Paul, for it was Janet's turn to travel horseback. She was riding behind the wagon, Doug was in front. He had tried to ride beside her, but she had vehemently refused his company.

Stretching, Stella said with a yawn, "I didn't know learnin' to read and write could be so tirin'."

"That's because you're trying too hard," Selina replied. "Maybe you shouldn't push yourself."

"I gotta learn as quickly as possible. I ain't gonna be seein' you and Janet much longer. Hattie and me, we're only stayin' in Texas for a couple of months, then we're goin' to Kansas, and from there we're gonna head to California or Oregon."

"I don't understand. Why are you going to Kansas by way of Texas? It doesn't make sense."

Stella shifted uneasily. She didn't know how to answer Selina's query.

Seeing the young woman's uneasiness, Selina replied, "I'm sorry. I shouldn't pry."

"It's all right," she assured her hastily. "But for reasons I can't explain, I ain't free to answer your question."

"I understand," Selina murmured. She paused for a moment, as her eyes flitted back and forth from Stella to Hattie. "There's something I want to tell you both."

"What's that, Miz Selina?" Hattie asked.

Determined to get the truth out in the open, she replied, "I'm not married to Harold Chamberlain. I won't bore you with my reason for pretending to be his wife. However, we are engaged." Her listeners' faces registered no surprise. "Apparently, this isn't news to either of you. Did Janet already tell you?"

"No," Stella answered. "She didn't say nothin'."

At that moment, Layne brought the team to a halt, turned in the seat and told the women, "We're stopping here for the night. It'll be dark soon, so let's

183

hurry and set up camp."

Selina moved to the rear of the wagon and unlatched the backboard. Paul tottered up behind her and held out his arms to be picked up. Selina jumped to the ground, lifted the child and walked away.

Stella started to follow, but was impeded by Hattie's hand on her arm. "You gots to warn Miz Selina 'bout Masta Chamberlain. She cain't marry that man. He's a devil!"

"I can't tell her! I just can't!"

"Of course you can!"

"If I tell Selina 'bout Chamberlain and me, she's gonna know I worked at Belle's."

"When we get to Passin' Through, you's plannin' to work at that Golden Garter. Miz Selina's gonna know you's a prostitute then, ain't she? What's the difference if she knows now or later?"

"I done changed my mind 'bout workin' at the Golden Garter. I'll find some other kind of work. Selina and Janet are ladies, and I'm gonna be one too."

"But you gots to tell Miz Selina that Masta Chamberlain's a monster. You cain't let her marry a man like him!"

"Selina's been real nice to me, but if I tell her I'm a prostitute, she won't have nothin' more to do with me. Selina's a lady, and ladies don't associate with whores."

"Don't call yourself that ugly word!"

"Why not? It's the truth, ain't it? 'Til now, I ain't never been ashamed of what I do." Tears came to Stella's eyes. "But after becomin' friends with a lady like Selina, and Janet too, I know just how cheap and dirty I am. Selina likes me a lot, I just know she does. And Janet's even beginnin' to like me. But if they knew that I worked at Belle's. . . ."

"I understand, honey," Hattie said gently. "But if them ladies is truly your friends, they ain't gonna stop bein' your friends just 'cause you worked at Belle's."

"Maybe you're right," Stella gave in lamely.

Hattie was hopeful. "Then you're gonna tell Miz Selina 'bout Masta Chamberlain?"

Stella sighed sadly. "I guess I ain't got no other choice. I'll tell her, but not right away."

"Exactly when do you plan to do it?"

"Soon," she whispered.

During supper Layne tolerated Selina's cold indifference with a smoldering rage. He cursed himself for loving a woman so damn contrary. Her ambivalence could drive a preacher to drink!

Finally, his patience at an end, his rage blazing, Layne bounded to his feet, glared at Selina, and remarked gruffly, "I want to talk to you! Now!"

All eyes turned to the furious man, but Selina's expression was cool and calm. "Very well, Layne," she agreed.

She had decided it was time to let Layne know that she was onto his ploy. Maybe then he'd stop pretending that her anger upset him. He didn't truly care about her feelings; he merely wanted to inveigle information from her. Well, she knew nothing about his father's death, and she intended to make that fact quite clear.

Layne reached for her arm, but she avoided his touch and started toward the edge of camp. He quickly fell into step beside her. When they were a good distance away from the others, Selina halted and turned so that she was facing him.

Gazing down into her face, Layne studied her in long, silent scrutiny, and she met his steady gaze without flinching. He finally looked away, sighed heavily, then turned his eyes back to hers. She thought she saw a flicker of pleading in their dark depths, but she couldn't be sure.

"Selina," he began evenly, "I want you to tell me why you're being so hostile. Apparently, I've done something to anger you, but I'll be damned if I know what it was. I've racked my brain trying to figure it out."

The man was quite an actor. If she didn't know better, she'd actually believe he cared! Tired of playing games, she began to lead up to the discussion she'd overheard between him and Doug. "Last night, after I went to the wagon, I went back to the campfire to get Stella a cup of coffee."

Before she could say more, the sound of approaching horses arrested their attention. In a flash Layne's pistol was drawn. He took a protective stance in front of Selina.

The four riders, leading an extra horse and two pack horses, came into sight. Recognizing the man in the lead, Layne holstered his pistol. He watched as the men rode into camp.

Selina, looking over Layne's shoulder, inhaled sharply. "Harold!" she exclaimed in astonishment.

"It seems your fiancé didn't go to England," Layne muttered bitterly.

Meanwhile, Stella, her heart pounding erratically, stared at Chamberlain with fear-glazed eyes.

Harold was totally shocked to find Stella. He had believed he'd never see her again; and now, to find her here, traveling with his fiancée! A murderous rage coursed through him. If the little slut had dared to tell Selina about them, he'd kill her!

Keeping his composure, he told his three men to tend to the horses, then he saw Selina and Layne coming toward the fire. His eyes narrowed suspiciously. Why had they been alone? A romantic interlude, perhaps? He was suddenly consumed with jealousy. Had Selina been unfaithful? If so, he'd make her pay dearly!

Concealing his jealous suspicions, he feigned a warm smile as he stepped to Selina and drew her into his arms. "My darling, I missed you," he murmured.

Before Selina could avoid his kiss, his lips swooped down on hers as his embrace tightened to hold her possessively close.

"Let her go!" Layne's deep voice thundered.

Releasing Selina, Harold pivoted smoothly toward Smith. "What did you say?" he asked calmly.

"You heard me," Layne replied.

Chamberlain turned to Selina. "My dear, is there something going on between you two that I should know about?"

Selina's emotions were swirling. She wanted to tell both men to go straight to Hades. But her mother's welfare, and that of her slaves, crossed her turbulent thoughts, quieting them. Harold Chamberlain was their salvation. Layne Smith, however, represented no such haven. Although Harold was undoubtedly smug and imperious, he was at least honest. He hadn't tried to deceive her, whereas Layne had deceitfully used her.

"Selina?" Harold questioned, impatient with her silence. "Answer me. Is something going on between

187

you and Smith?"

"No," she answered firmly. "That is, there's nothing worth mentioning."

Layne now believed that Selina had played him for a fool. With effort, he kept his feelings under control.

Casting Smith a smug expression, Chamberlain brought Selina back into his arms.

She withheld her gaze from Layne. She didn't want to look into his sensual eyes, because she might throw her pride, her mother's future, as well as her slaves', to the wind, and rush into Layne's arms and beg him to love her.

"We'll be leaving in the morning," Harold said to Selina.

"Are we returning to New Orleans?"

"No, we're going to my ranch." He looked at Layne. "Smith, I thank you for taking such good care of my bride. But I now relieve you of your responsibility."

"She's all yours," he uttered flatly.

Selina, still withholding her gaze, heard the cold finality in his tone.

Fourteen

Chamberlain slipped an arm about Selina's waist, then smiled at Layne and asked, "You don't mind if my men and I share your camp tonight, do you?"

"Suit yourself," Layne muttered. He walked away briskly and was soon swallowed by the dark night.

Taking Selina to the fire, Harold sat beside her and helped himself to a cup of coffee. Stella was seated across from them, and her eyes, with a will of their own, kept staring at Chamberlain. She was sure he'd find a way to punish her for stealing his money and running away.

Hattie, seated beside Stella, was just as frightened. She didn't fear for her own life, but for Stella's and Paul's.

Muttering an excuse, Doug left the fire and went in search of Layne. Meanwhile, Janet, unaware of the silent tension hovering over the group, said gaily, "Mr. Chamberlain, it's so good to see you. But why didn't you go to London?"

"I sent an employee in my place. It wasn't until after Selina had left that I realized I couldn't bear our separation. My wife has me totally bewitched."

Selina slipped his mother's wedding ring from her finger and handed it to him, then said dryly, "Janet and the others know I'm not your wife."

"What?" Harold gasped, annoyed more than surprised.

"I told them the truth."

"I see," he answered. He slipped the ring into his pocket. "I suppose you had a good reason for revealing our secret?"

"Yes," she answered calmly. "I don't like living a lie."

He wasn't sure that he believed her. He wondered if Smith had something to do with it. Keeping his suspicions concealed, he said brightly, "It doesn't matter, my dear, in the morning we'll return to Clarksville. It has a church and a reverend. By this time tomorrow night, we'll be married."

A cold chill ran up Selina's spine. "So soon?"

"Why should we wait?" His watchful eyes scanned her face.

She looked away from his keen scrutiny. "There's no . . . no reason to wait, I suppose."

"A wedding!" Janet exclaimed. "I can hardly wait! I've only been to a couple of them." She inhaled dreamily. "Weddings are so romantic."

"I doubt if you'll be attending our marriage," Harold told her gently. "I'm sure Smith won't turn around and go back to Clarksville."

At that moment, Selina stood up abruptly.

"Where are you going, love?" Chamberlain asked.

"If we're leaving in the morning, I need to gather my belongings." Packing was merely a pretext to leave. The man grated on her nerves.

He watched Selina closely as she walked toward the wagon. His jealous suspicions were still simmering. Tomorrow night, if he learned that his bride wasn't a virgin, he'd make her pay severely. He sup-

190

posed he could have their marriage annulled, but why let her off so easily? If she remained his wife, he could mete out his own brand of vengeance. Then, once he had her completely submissive, he might forgive her infidelity. After all, he still wanted sons, and Selina Beaumont came from excellent stock. She was also exceptionally beautiful, and since he himself was handsome, their children would be good-looking, true-blood aristocrats.

"Miz Stella," Hattie murmured, tugging at the woman's arm. "Don't you reckon we oughta go to the wagon and see if little Paul's still asleep?"

Stella merely nodded her head and got to her feet. As she and Hattie moved away, she could feel Chamberlain's eyes following her. The women veered to the far side of the wagon, placing themselves out of Chamberlain's vision.

"Oh God, Hattie!" Stella moaned. "I'm so scared!"

"I know, honey. I's scared too, but maybe we ain't got no reason to be so scared."

"What do you mean?"

"Maybe Masta Chamberlain ain't gonna do nothin'. He knows that you's friends with Mista Smith and Mista Thompson. If he hurts you or little Paul, he'll have to answer to them. He's got to know that!"

Stella was hopeful. "Maybe you're right."

"You go find Mista Smith and let 'im know you's scared. He'll see no harm comes to you or little Paul."

"But he walked off into the darkness. I ain't sure if I can find 'im."

"Just take the same direction he took, you'll run across 'im."

"I cain't do that! Chamberlain will see me!"

"Let that ole devil see ya! Let 'im see that you's good friends with Mista Smith. It'll give 'im somethin' to think about!"

Stella smiled brightly. "You're right, Hattie—as usual."

Stella hurried conspicuously past the campfire, and past Chamberlain's watching eyes. With long, bold strides, she followed the path Layne had taken.

She had walked only a short way when she detected voices. "Layne?" she called softly.

"Doug and I are over here," he replied clearly.

The night was overcast, and without the moon to light her way, Stella had to step cautiously through the surrounding brush. Coming upon the men, she said apologetically, "Excuse me for interruptin'." She looked at Doug. "Do you mind if I speak alone with Layne?"

"No ma'am, I don't mind."

Stella waited until Doug was gone before saying anxiously, "Layne, I'm afraid that Chamberlain might try to hurt me or little Paul."

"I'll have a talk with 'im."

"You reckon he'll listen to you?"

"He'd better." There was a threatening note in his tone.

"Thank you. I don't know how Hattie, Paul, and me would make it without you."

"You're more than welcome, Stella. But I need to ask you for a favor."

"Anything!" she exclaimed at once. "I'll do anything for you. I owe you so much."

"You aren't in my debt," he said gently.

"You might not think so, but I do. What kind of favor do you need?"

"I want you to talk to Selina."

192

"Talk to Selina?" she questioned.

"Yes, and you must do it tonight."

"What do you want me to tell her?"

"I want you to let her know that she's no longer obligated to Chamberlain."

Stella was understandably confused. "I don't understand."

"She's marryin' Chamberlain because her New Orleans home and Cedar Hill are mortgaged. Mr. Beaumont left his wife and daughter heavily in debt. Chamberlain has promised to pay the mortgages in return for Selina's hand in matrimony. When I was in Clarksville, I sent a wire to Stratton, instructing him to withdraw money from my account and pay off the Beaumonts' debts."

"Why don't you tell Selina yourself? Why do you want me to do it?"

"I doubt if she'd agree to talk to me." He frowned testily. Furthermore, I'd just as soon not talk to her."

The moon peeked out from under cloud, and Stella could see Layne plainly. She studied him speculatively. "You're in love with Selina, ain't ya?"

"I thought I was, but now I'm not so sure. But my feelings aren't the issue here. She doesn't deserve a husband like Chamberlain. That's why I want you to tell her that she doesn't have to marry him."

"She might marry 'im anyhow."

"No, I'm sure she won't."

"She might not like you payin' her debts. She's still obligated, only now she's obligated to you."

"There are no strings attached. I want you to make that quite clear. She can consider it a loan and can pay back the money when she's able."

"All right. I'll talk to her."

"I appreciate your help."

193

"I like Selina a lot, and I sure don't want her to marry a monster like Chamberlain."

"Neither do I," Layne replied softly.

Layne preferred to be alone. And Stella had nearly reached the camp area when suddenly Chamberlain stepped out of the shadows, blocking her path. Frightened, she stood as though riveted to the ground.

"Hello, Stella," he said quietly.

"Wh . . . what do you want?" she stammered.

The moon had scurried beneath a dark cloud, and she could barely see Chamberlain. He stepped stealthily closer, so close that she could feel his breath on her face.

"Did you tell Selina about us?" His voice was a rasping whisper.

"No, I didn't tell her."

"I'm warning you, Stella. If you say anything, I'll kill you." His threat was spoken with a deadly calmness.

"I won't say anything," she promised fearfully.

"If Selina doesn't leave with me in the morning, for whatever reason, I'll kill you and your little bastard."

"You cain't mean that! If she changes her mind, it might have nothin' to do with me."

"As long as I have Selina, I don't give a goddamn about you. But if I should lose her, you'll suffer my vengeance."

Stella was about to plead with him when she suddenly thought of Layne. Her fear dwindled somewhat. "If you hurt me or my son, you'll have to answer to Layne Smith. He's my friend, and so is

Doug Thompson. They'll protect me."

Harold laughed cruelly. "Do you really believe Smith and Thompson can protect you and your son every minute of the day? Or indefinitely? Their protection will wane, and when it does, I'll be waiting. I don't forgive, Stella, nor do I forget. Now, if you value your life and your child's, you'd better pray that I don't lose Selina."

His hands lurched incredibly fast and, grasping her shoulders, drew her against him. Leering down into her frightened eyes, he uttered viciously, "Cross me, Stella, and as God is my witness, I'll see you dead!"

He still had the power to intimidate her, and she cowed before him. "I won't cross you," she murmured shakily.

"See that you don't!" he growled, releasing her roughly.

He walked away, leaving her in a paroxysm of fear. Should she tell Layne that Chamberlain had threatened her? No! Chamberlain was right! Layne couldn't protect her indefinitely, and sooner or later he'd find her and Paul and kill them!

"Oh God!" she groaned aloud. "I cain't tell Selina 'bout Layne payin' her debts. If I do, she won't marry Chamberlain!"

Stella was miserable. Layne and Selina were her friends, but she was going to betray them. I have to! she thought wretchedly. Not for my sake, but for Paul's!

Layne found Chamberlain seated at the fire with his three men. Joining them, he poured a cup of coffee, took a drink, then, looking at Harold, said evenly, "I know about you and Stella, and I also know how you treated her."

Chamberlain arched a brow. "How I treated my whore is none of your business."

"I'm makin' it my business."

"Why is Stella traveling with you? Did you meet her in New Orleans and convince her to run away with you to Texas?"

"No. Her buggy broke down on the road. I couldn't leave her, Hattie, and the boy to fend for themselves, so I invited her to travel with us."

"I see," Harold murmured. "Did you know that she's a thief?"

"She told me why she stole your money."

"And you believe whatever cock-and-bull story she told you?"

"I believe her," Layne said firmly.

Harold heaved an impatient sigh. "Smith, what's on your mind?"

"Stella thinks you'll try to harm her and the boy."

He laughed shortly. "Stella has quite an imagination."

Layne finished his coffee and got to his feet. "If you try to harm Stella or her son, I'll come after you."

"Are you threatening me?"

"No, I'm promising you."

Arching his arm through the air, Harold gestured at his three bodyguards. "You try coming after me and you'll find yourself outnumbered."

Layne's hard gaze swept briefly over the three-some, then he turned back to Chamberlain. "If I have to go through them to get to you, I will. I've stepped on cockroaches before."

Before his men could make a move, Chamberlain

motioned for them to remain seated. "Smith," he said, grinning collectedly, "even when we were boys, you were always fighting for the underdog. You haven't changed, have you?"

"No, I guess not."

"You're a fool, you know. Stella's no underdog, she's a two-bit whore."

"And you're a two-bit bastard."

Layne started to leave when the largest of the three men stood up. "Smith!" he uttered. "I'm gonna kill ya for callin' my boss a bastard and for callin' me and my friends cockroaches!" His hand hovered above his holstered pistol. "Draw, damn you!"

"Jack, sit down!" Chamberlain yelled, bounding to his feet. "When I want you to use your gun, I'll tell you!"

Grumbling, the man did as he was told.

A cocky smile flickered across Layne's lips. "Jack, whenever you wanna die drawing against me, just let me know. I'll be glad to oblige."

Turning about, Smith walked away. He wasn't worried that Jack might shoot him in the back; for Doug, his rifle handy, was standing close by, watching the man's every move.

"Miz Stella, honey," Hattie said. "I wanna talk to you outside."

"All right," she murmured uneasily.

The women were inside the wagon, watching Selina pack. Hattie waited for Stella to leave, then she carefully maneuvered her rotund frame over the lowered backboard. Taking Stella's hand, she led her a short distance from the wagon.

"Miz Stella," she began anxiously. "You gots to tell

197

Miz Selina 'bout Masta Chamberlain! You cain't let her ride off with that man! He's mean, through and through!"

"I cain't tell her!" she moaned.

"You gots to!"

"Hattie, listen to me! I talked to Layne, and he was real nice to me. I know he thinks he can keep Chamberlain from killin' me and Paul, but he cain't do it! It just ain't possible!"

Wringing her hands nervously, she began pacing. "Selina's Pa left her and her Ma heavily in debt. She's marryin' Chamberlain 'cause he's supposed to pay off these debts. But Layne's done paid 'em. He wants me to tell Selina that she ain't no longer obligated to Chamberlain."

"Why ain't you told her?"

In a trembling voice, Stella gave Hattie a full account of her meeting with Chamberlain.

"Good Lord!" Hattie cried gravely.

"So you see," Stella continued, "I cain't tell her 'bout Chamberlain's meanness, and I cain't tell her that Layne paid her debts. If she don't marry Chamberlain, he'll kill me and Paul. Believe me, Hattie, I ain't protectin' myself, I'm protectin' my son!"

"I know you is, honey." Her huge frame shuddered as though struck by a bitter wind. "Poor Miz Selina! She don't deserve this! That Masta Chamberlain will make her life a livin' hell!"

Selina couldn't fall asleep; she had lain on her pallet for hours, tossing and turning. Finally, deciding sleep was impossible, she got up quietly, put on her robe and slippers and left the wagon. She knew the men were sleeping about the fire, but she didn't

198

give them so much as a cursory glance.

Hoping a short stroll might relax her, she moved away from the wagon. Having no specific course in mind, she walked aimlessly. She listened with little interest as her common sense reminded her that wandering away from camp was dangerous. She was so dispirited that she didn't really care.

"Selina." Layne's voice, seeming to come out of thin air, brought her steps to a sudden halt.

He was standing behind her; and for a moment, she froze, then whirled about. "Leave me alone," she demanded quietly.

"What are you doing out here?" he asked, his eyes slightly stirred to anger.

"I was taking a walk."

"You were taking a walk," he mocked impatiently. "Late at night, in the middle of nowhere, you decide to take a walk. When God handed out common sense, where in the hell were you?"

She was too angry to think of a retort.

Layne's temper was now at flash point. "You little fool! You're bound and determined to get yourself raped or killed, aren't you?"

"Must you over-dramatize? Look around, Layne! Do you see any rapists or killers lurking about?"

He gritted his teeth. Her defiance was infuriating!

Selina's fury continued, "Furthermore, what are you doing here? Don't you ever sleep?"

"Occasionally," he replied. As an angry silence wedged between them, Layne studied her thoughtfully. Before Stella retired, he asked her if she had talked to Selina. She assured him that she had. He wanted to ask her for details, but after mumbling an excuse, she hurried to the wagon.

Now, as he continued to study Selina, he silently

damned her ungrateful heart. He had saved her from marrying a man she didn't love, and she didn't even have the common courtesy to thank him.

He was about to mention this to Selina; but before he could, she brushed him aside, saying fiercely, "Stay away from me, Layne Smith!"

His hand shot out and captured her wrist, the motion sending her stumbling into his arms. "Why you ungrateful little . . ." he muttered furiously. He pulled her so close against him that she felt crushed by his strength.

Slowly, almost submissively, she raised her gaze to his. She had thought to see anger in his eyes, instead she recognized a hungry male desire simmering in their depths.

His fiery gaze set her own passion aflame, and his overpowering nearness melted her defenses. She wanted desperately to resist him, but she couldn't. She loved him too much. He had heartlessly used her, had played her for a fool; still, she loved him!

Her eyes, staring helplessly into his, mirrored her passion.

For a long moment Layne's dark, piercing eyes probed hers, then with a husky chuckle, he murmured, "You might loathe me with your heart, but not with your body."

Suddenly, his lips seized hers in a savage conquest, his questing tongue ravaging the sweetness of her mouth.

His demanding kiss left her weak and trembling. Sweeping her into his arms, he carried her into the brush nearby.

Fifteen

Layne eased Selina down upon a soft bed of grass, then lay beside her, drawing her against him. His lips suddenly took hers in a kiss so forceful that it was almost brutal.

With her arms about his neck, Selina returned his ardor to the fullest. She couldn't fight her desire for Layne; she loved him too desperately!

Loosening her robe, Layne parted the garment so he could caress her soft breasts. He could feel the nipples harden, then stand erect beneath her thin, cotton gown.

A rush of ecstasy wafted through Selina in heated waves, her passion dancing inside of her like a leaping flame. A moan of intense longing escaped from deep in her throat as, drawing him even closer, she raised her lips to his and kissed him with sweet and total abandon.

Selina's ardent response added fuel to Layne's fiery passion; grasping the hem of her gown, he drew it up to her waist. Slowly, tantalizingly, his hand moved to the womanly softness between her delicate thighs. She parted her legs, for his intimacy was sending a primitive, exciting desire all through her.

"Layne . . . Layne," she whispered. "I need you."

His lips swooped down on hers, and as their tongues met in love's warfare, a wild, uncontrollable surge of passion swept over them.

Anxious now to take her completely, Layne rose to his knees and quickly removed his holster. Then, releasing his trousers, he shoved them past his hips. The sight of his superb maleness sent Selina's heart pounding with anticipation.

As an unfulfilled ache centered itself between her thighs, she held up her arms and beckoned her lover into her embrace.

Lowering his body to hers, he uttered huskily, "Wrap your legs around my waist."

She did, and waited breathlessly for his exciting entry. He pressed his lips tightly to hers, then with one thrust he shoved his hardness into her velvety depths.

Selina moaned with rapturous delight, and surrendering to their passionate union, she wished such ecstasy would never end.

Layne's wondrous love-making spiraled them onward to passion's ultimate peak, and with a final explosion of physical release, they achieved complete satisfaction.

For a long moment Selina basked in the afterglow of their passionate union, then cold reality suddenly hit her with force. Her body grew rigid, and placing her hands on Layne's shoulders, she tried to push him away. "Let me up," she demanded.

Responding to her sudden curtness, Layne stood quickly and drew up his trousers. As he buckled on his holster, Selina got shakily to her feet.

They faced each other in silent combat, each waiting for the other to make the first move.

Selina was angry, but her anger was aimed at herself more than at Layne. She had always considered herself a strong woman, but with Layne she was completely vulnerable. Love, she thought sadly, it strips away your pride and leaves your heart totally exposed. Layne had stolen her pride and her heart. No, she decided, he didn't steal them; I gave them to him. I gambled on love and lost.

Her anger was now supplanted by wistfulness, and as Selina's eyes traveled intently over Layne, she painted a permanent picture of him in her mind. She believed she'd never see him this way again, his blond hair mussed and his eyes still glazed from their love-making. His shirt was tucked haphazardly into his pants, and his breathing was still labored, for their passionate union had been an undeniably wonderful exertion. In perfect detail, she duplicated his image onto the canvas of her mind, where she would treasure it forever.

Layne, studying her intensely, was waiting, hoping she'd give him a sign that she cared.

Believing there was nothing left to be said between them, Selina moved to walk away, but was stopped by Layne's hand on her arm.

His eyes pierced hers. Now that he had paid her father's debts, surely she wasn't going to marry Chamberlain! "After what I've done for you, you aren't still leaving with Chamberlain, are you?" he asked, his tone somewhat gruff.

What had he done for her, except take her innocence and break her heart? Did he think she'd sacrifice her mother and her slaves just to appease his passion? Did he plan to use her for his own enjoyment, then cast her aside? She hadn't forgotten overhearing his conversation with Janet. He'd told Janet that there was someone special in his life, a woman named Jesse Harte.

"Answer me!" Layne grumbled, finding her silence exasperating.

"Yes, of course I'm leaving with Harold!" she snapped, flinging his hand off her arm.

Layne was fuming. She had obviously lied to him! She wasn't marrying Chamberlain to pay her father's debts, but apparently was just as greedy as he had first suspected.

Selina took a step to leave, but she turned back to Layne. She wasn't sure if he deserved a courteous deed, but she'd nonetheless tell him that she knew nothing about his father's death. "Layne . . ." she began.

He cut her off rudely. "Go back to the wagon, Selina! You need your rest. Tomorrow's your wedding day, remember?"

His brush-off brought tears to her eyes, but she held them back. "Goodbye, Layne," she said with quiet dignity.

Despite her dispirited state, she moved with elegant grace as she walked away from the man she loved.

Selina didn't see Layne again, for the next morning he was gone. At breakfast she asked Doug about his absence, and he told her that Layne was scouting the area ahead. She figured that was a likely story; he had probably left to avoid a last meeting between them. Telling herself that she was glad to be spared his presence, she went about coaxing Harold into a hurried departure. If they dallied too long, Layne might return. Seeing him would only be a painful reminder of how much she loved him.

Determined to pick up the pieces of her life, she mentally prepared herself to accept whatever the future might bring.

Selina bid her friends a warm farewell, kissed Paul's chubby cheek, then mounted the gentle mare that Chamberlain had brought for her to ride.

One of Chamberlain's men attached Selina's packed belongings on an extra horse. She had left a lot of her things behind, but Janet had promised to take them to her father's home. Selina could pick them up whenever she wanted.

Waving goodbye to the others, Selina rode out of camp beside Chamberlain. She was wearing her riding clothes, and her fiancé's eyes swept over her attire. Her trousers adhered to her shapely legs and womanly thighs. She was provocative, and he could feel a stirring in his loins. He could hardly wait to make this sensually beautiful woman his own. The thought of ravishing her lovely flesh was arousing, and his erection soon became so uncomfortable that he had to steer his thoughts to a different course.

"Harold," Selina began curiously, "why didn't you go to London?" Before he could reply, she held up a hand to ward off his answer. "Please don't belittle my intelligence by telling me that you couldn't bear our separation. That answer might have satisfied Janet, but I didn't buy it for one moment."

"Why are you so sure that I didn't tell Janet the truth?"

"As I said once before, I think you're too much in love with yourself to love anyone else."

Chamberlain's bodyguards were riding close behind, and he knew they overheard Selina's insolence. Her defiance was infuriating! How dare she be so impertinent in the presence of his employees! He wanted to slap her across the face and put her soundly in her place. But he held himself in check. It was still too soon to show her who was boss; he'd wait until they were married.

"Selina," he said collectedly, "I've decided to sell my half of the shipping company. A friend of William Stratton's has agreed to buy it. Before leaving New Orleans, I gave my lawyer full power of attorney, so he'll handle all the final paperwork. So you see, my love, there was no reason for me to go to London."

Selina was surprised. "But why did you sell such a lucrative business?"

"I plan to become a full-time rancher."

She somehow sensed that he wasn't telling the truth. She couldn't imagine him selling his company on the spur of the moment just to become a rancher. She knew there had to be more to the story; however, she wasn't really interested. Harold's business dealings were of no concern to her. As his future wife, of course, she should care a great deal, but Selina didn't truly believe she and Harold would get married. The man was intent on marrying a virgin, and when she told him she was no longer untouched, he'd certainly break off their engagement. She knew this likely possibility should bother her, and in a way it did. But in another way, it gave her a feeling of relief. Selina had never considered herself a quitter, but now she felt that she was. She had agreed to marry Chamberlain to save her mother, her slaves, and Cedar Hill; but she had failed. Later, she'd speak to Harold privately and let him know that she had been unfaithful; in all probability he'd refuse to marry her. If so, in the morning she'd start back to New Orleans. Her mother would be terribly disappointed; but then, she was always disappointing her mother.

As her thoughts continued to flow, Selina lifted her chin determinedly. Somehow, someway, she and her mother would survive. After all, she wasn't above finding employment. Maybe she could get a job as a tutor. Well, she'd find a way to support herself and her mother. She didn't need Harold Chamberlain or Layne Smith! She'd make it without them!

Cedar Hill and her slaves crossed her mind, sending her spirits tumbling. She was powerless to save them.

She cleared these somber thoughts from her mind. Why dwell on things she could not change? She must concentrate on her own self-preservation and that of her mother's, for their future rested entirely in her hands.

The sun was directly overhead when Layne told the others it was time to stop for lunch. The weather was hot, sultry, the humidity so thick that it hung heavily in the air.

Again, Layne decided to extend the lunch break so they could rest during the hottest time of the day. These delays didn't sit well with him, though. He was anxious to reach his ranch and have this trip behind him.

Selina's absence was felt acutely by everyone, especially by Stella and Layne. Stella, guilt-ridden, withdrew into herself and had little to say. Layne, it seemed, was even more withdrawn than Stella. Losing Selina had wounded him deeply, and he doubted if the pain would ever completely heal.

Following lunch, Layne walked to a tree in the distance and sat down in its shade. Leaning back against the sturdy trunk, he drew the brim of his hat over his eyes. Relaxing, he tried to clear his mind and take a short nap. The effort was futile, for Selina's memory refused to go away.

Lost in thoughts of Selina, he didn't detect Stella's approach until she was almost upon him. Pushing back his hat, he looked up at her.

She paused as she met his affable gaze. She had never known a man as kind as Layne Smith, nor as handsome. She loved him dearly. It wasn't a passionate love; she loved him like a brother. A love of passion was beyond Stella's comprehension.

Smiling hesitantly, she asked, "Do you mind if I join you?"

"Of course not," Layne replied.

She sat beside him. "I've decided not to work at the Golden Garter. I don't wanna be that kind of woman anymore."

Layne smiled. "I'm glad you changed your mind."

"I don't know how I'm gonna support all of us, but I reckon I'll find a way."

"I'll help you work something out. Don't worry."

"Thank you, Layne."

She watched him closely as he looked off into the distance. She knew where his thoughts had wandered. He was thinking of Selina, missing her, and it was all her fault. She could imagine how badly he was hurting. He believed that Selina knew her debts were paid, yet she had left with Chamberlain. He must think the worst of her. Stella longed to tell him the truth, but her fear of Chamberlain was too real. The man was a monster, and he was perfectly capable of killing Paul without blinking an eye.

Stella couldn't stand watching Layne's suffering, so she stood up to leave. Glancing back at him, she asked softly, "Are you gonna be all right?"

"Sure," he answered. "No one ever died of a broken heart, or so I've heard."

"You must love Selina an awful lot. Have you ever been in love before?"

"No, this was my first." Then he added bitterly, "And my last."

She wheeled about quickly so he wouldn't see the tears welling in her eyes. But Layne bounded to his feet and followed, for a rider had ridden into camp.

Doug was taking the reins to the man's horse when Layne and Stella arrived. Recognizing the visitor, Layne asked curiously, "What are you doin' here, Floyd?"

"Bart figured you were on your way, so he sent me to give you a hand. He thought you could use an extra man, and an extra gun, just in case there's trouble. I didn't think you'd still be in Louisiana. I was expectin' to meet up with you days ago."

"I stayed in New Orleans a little longer than I had originally planned." Janet walked up to Layne's side, and he made introductions, "This is Floyd Miller. He works for your father."

Finding the young man excitingly handsome, Janet smiled radiantly. "I'm very happy to meet you."

Doug, looking on, wished Janet would smile at him just once in such a way.

"I'm glad to make your acquaintance, Miss Wilkerson," Floyd replied, pleased to note that Bart's daughter was so attractive.

"Please call me Janet," she remarked pertly, her eyes flirting with his.

Doug could stand no more; pitching the horse's reins to Miller, he moved away.

Layne hurried to catch up with him. "What do you think?" he asked.

"Floyd's a trouble maker, and we sure as hell don't need him ridin' along."

"You're probably right. But I guess we're stuck with him. Besides, he's good with a gun, and if we run across trouble, we'll be glad he's with us."

"Janet's already glad," Doug muttered. He walked off to tend to the horses.

When they broke camp, Floyd offered to drive the team, claiming his horse was tired. As he had suspected, Janet decided to ride beside him. He helped her onto the wagon seat, then climbed up behind her. Taking up the reins, he slapped them against the horses, and the wheels set into motion.

As Janet chattered on in a frivolous manner, Floyd listened half-heartedly. Watching her out of the corner of his eye, he measured her with lustful intent. Before collecting his fortune, he'd sample the goods.

Floyd Miller no longer worked for Bart Wilkerson. He had been fired weeks ago. Knowing that Smith and Thompson were delivering Wilkerson's daughter, he had rounded up a group of men as unsavory as himself. They were waiting for him in a Texas town called Dry River. He knew Layne wouldn't circle the

210

town, but would stop there to buy supplies. Floyd planned to meet secretly with his men and set up an ambush. The others would ride ahead and lie in wait. Since he himself would be traveling with Layne and his party, he hoped to get the drop on Smith and Thompson before his men had to open fire. Then he'd kidnap Janet. Her father was a wealthy man, and he intended to demand a high ransom for her safe return.

Janet grew silent as she examined the young man at her side. Just looking at him sent her heart aflutter. His lean frame was strong, and his hair was as black as coal. His eyes, framed by long lashes, were as blue as the sky.

Feeling her scrutiny, Floyd turned his face to hers and smiled charmingly. Aware of his own good looks and the effect he had on women, he was confident that he'd have no problem seducing her. Of course, if he should fail, which was unlikely, he'd wait until she was his prisoner, then take her against her will. Either way, he was going to have her. He hoped she was still a virgin; there was nothing he enjoyed more than busting a maiden.

Meanwhile, Janet, who was still admiring her handsome companion, was wondering if she was falling in love. Was love at first sight possible? She decided that it was indeed possible. How could any woman help but fall in love with a man as sensual as Floyd Miller! Suddenly, she was struck with a very disturbing thought. What if he was married?

"Floyd," she began anxiously, "you aren't married, are you?"

"No ma'am," he answered.

"My goodness, I should think a man as handsome

211

as you would be married."

"I guess I just haven't met the right woman." He gave her a meaningful smile. "That is, until now."

Janet was thrilled. Floyd Miller was so wonderfully romantic! Taking her eyes from his handsome face, she looked ahead, her gaze coming to rest on Doug's turned back. He and Layne were riding in front of the team.

As though he could feel her perusal, Doug glanced over his shoulder. She hadn't forgiven him for spanking her, and she glared at him resentfully. He quickly looked away, and she didn't see the hurt in his gentle eyes.

Sixteen

Doug silently berated himself for caring about Janet. He felt he couldn't win her love in a million years. Even if he were rich and could support her in the manner in which she was accustomed, she'd still scorn his affections. In her eyes he was probably an unattractive brute, and he knew Janet set a great store by a man's looks. From the moment she saw Floyd Miller's handsome face, her eyes had lit up with feminine interest. He couldn't compete with men as good-looking as Floyd Miller, and a woman as pretty as Janet drew them like moths to a flame. He resigned himself to loving her from afar.

At that moment Layne, riding beside him, remarked suddenly, "Selina wouldn't marry Chamberlain strictly for his money!"

Doug regarded his friend dubiously. "What brought on that outburst?"

"A few nights ago, when Selina told me that she didn't want to marry Chamberlain, she meant it! Thinking back, I remember the sadness in her eyes, her look of sorrow. It was too real, she couldn't have faked it."

"If that's true, then why is she marrying him? Stella told her that you paid her debts. She knows she doesn't have to marry Chamberlain."

"I don't know why she's going through with it," Layne replied. "But the puzzle doesn't fit. There's a missing piece somewhere." He withdrew into deep thought for a short time, then, his eyes alight, he remarked, "I'll be damned!"

Doug looked at him quizzically.

"I think I found the missing piece to the puzzle, and I bet Stella's holdin' it."

Turning his horse about, he rode back to the wagon, telling Floyd to pull up the team. Dismounting, he called impatiently, "Stella! I need to talk to you."

She climbed outside, and Layne took her arm and led her a short distance away.

Stella's heart was pounding, and nervous perspiration began to accumulate on her brow and in the palms of her hands. She sensed that somehow Layne had caught on to the truth. He knew she hadn't talked to Selina!

She regarded him hesitantly through half-lowered eyes. He was watching her intently.

Gently, Layne placed a hand under her chin, tilting her face up to his. "Stella, you didn't tell Selina that I paid her father's debts, did you?" His tone was devoid of anger.

"Yes, of course . . . of course I did," she stammered, her eyes again downcast.

"Look at me, Stella. Look me straight in the eyes and tell me you talked to Selina."

God, she couldn't look this wonderful man in the eyes and lie to him! As heart-rending sobs tore from her throat, Layne brought her into his arms. Resting her head on his shoulder, she said between broken sobs, "I didn't tell her! . . . Please forgive me! . . . Chamberlain told me if Selina didn't marry 'im, he'd kill me and little Paul! . . . I didn't lie to you for my sake, but for my son's!"

All at once, she pushed out of his arms, crying desperately, "He'll do it too, Layne! If Selina don't marry 'im, he'll kill my baby!"

"No, he won't," he assured her.

"God, Layne!" she declared frantically. "You cain't protect me and Paul every minute of the day! Somehow, someway, Chamberlain will get us!"

"Stella, do you expect me to just stand aside and let Selina marry that bastard?"

She didn't answer right away, she waited for a bit of calm to come over her. "Layne, what I expect don't matter none. You love Selina, and there's no way you're gonna let her marry Chamberlain. I don't blame you. What kind of man would you be if you didn't save her?"

He smiled tenderly. "Stella, Chamberlain's threat to kill Paul is probably just that; a threat, and nothing more."

"But you don't know that for sure," she argued.

"No, I don't," he admitted. "But your safety and Paul's are my responsibility. I promise you, if Chamberlain even looks as though he's thinkin' of harmin' either one of you, I'll send his soul to hell where it belongs."

Stella smiled feebly. "I reckon you'd better high-tail it to Clarksville, if you're gonna get there in time to stop that weddin'."

"I'm gone!" he remarked, walking away swiftly.

"Layne!" she called after him.

He glanced over his shoulder.

"Thanks for not hatin' me."

His answer came in the form of a friendly nod.

At the hotel in Clarksville, Chamberlain rented a room for himself and Selina. He saw no reason to get her a room of her own; by tonight they'd be man and wife.

He allowed Selina to go upstairs alone, telling her that he'd join her later. He located the preacher, set up a time for the wedding, then visited the saloon and had a couple of drinks before returning to the hotel.

When he knocked on the door of their room, Selina told him to come in.

As he entered he was surprised to see that she was still wearing her riding attire. "I thought by now you would have bathed and changed clothes. I talked to the minister, and he'll marry us tonight at eight. That's only two hours from now. Don't you think you should start getting ready? Surely you don't plan to get married in trousers."

"Of course not," she replied. She gestured to a chair placed beside the bed. "Harold, sit down. I must talk to you."

He complied, watching her carefully.

Selina was uneasy. She dreaded telling Chamberlain that she had been unfaithful. She wasn't sure how he would take her candid confession. However, she wouldn't marry him under false pretenses.

Stepping to the bed, she sat on the edge and faced him. "Harold," she began with difficulty, "I have something to tell you. I know your feelings on marrying a virgin, and when you asked me to marry

216

you, I had never been with a man."

Chamberlain listened intently, his jaw clenched tightly.

Deciding not to mince words, Selina said outright, "I'm no longer a virgin."

It took great effort for Chamberlain to hold his temper in check. "Smith?" he asked hoarsely.

"Yes," she whispered.

He rose from his chair and moved to the open window, his back turned so she couldn't see the raging fury in his eyes. So she had spread her legs for Smith! Goddamn her! Well, he'd get even with the little slut!

A kind of calm washed over him. He had prepared himself for this moment; her infidelity came as no real surprise. He had rightfully suspected her and Smith. His vengeance was already planned. It was now a simple matter of carrying it out.

Feigning compassion, he turned, met Selina's gaze, and said gently, "I won't try to deny that I'm disappointed. It's only natural for a man to want his bride to be a virgin. But what's done is done." He brushed his fingers through his hair, then with a heavy sigh, murmured, "I suppose what happened is my fault. I shouldn't have trusted you in Smith's care. I know the man's a womanizer. That's why I wanted you to pretend we were married. Smith enjoys his women, but he usually avoids married ones."

"He's a womanizer?" Selina repeated. She didn't quite believe him.

"His reputation is well known." He forced a forgiving smile. "An innocent like yourself was putty in his hands. I can understand why you gave in to him. He's not only charming but also quite handsome.

217

Well, we'll just have to find a way to put this behind us. Don't fret, my love, I intend to forgive and forget. I'll leave, so you can take a short rest. Later, I'll have the desk clerk send up a bath."

He gave her a chaste kiss on the cheek, then hastened out of the room. As he stepped into the hall, his face reddened with rage, and violence flickered in his eyes. His hand moved intentionally to his belt. A cruel sneer curled his lips as he envisioned himself lashing Selina's bare buttocks. When he was finished with her, she'd wish she had never laid eyes on Layne Smith!

Meanwhile, Selina was pacing back and forth, her thoughts confused. Harold's forgiveness had come as a complete surprise. She wondered if she had judged the man too rashly. After all, she didn't really know him. Her opinion of him had been based on nothing but speculation.

She laid her head down on the pillow. Tears came to her eyes, and giving in to her despair, she wept uncontrollably. Her tears finally ended, and she drifted into a restless slumber. Repose brought no peace, for Layne filled her dreams.

Layne's horse, winded and sweating profusely, galloped wearily into the quiet town. Layne felt badly about pushing the stallion so relentlessly, but time was of the essence. He hoped that he wasn't too late to stop Selina from marrying Chamberlain.

The small, steepled church was located at the edge of town, and deciding to try it first, Layne guided his horse to the hitching rail and dismounted.

Inside, Selina and Harold were at the altar, facing

218

the preacher. Chamberlain's men were standing behind them. Opening his Bible, the preacher was about to begin the ceremony when the front door flew open with a bang.

Selina and the others stared with disbelief as Layne strode down the narrow aisle. Her heart thumping like a drum, Selina didn't dare hope that he had come to whisk her away from Harold. But why else would he be here? He loved her! He must love her!

Pausing, Layne looked at Selina and said calmly, "Come on. Let's go."

"Smith!" Chamberlain bellowed. "What's the meaning of this! How dare you intrude!"

Ignoring him, Layne told Selina, "You don't have to marry this bastard. I took care of your father's debts and started an allowance for your mother."

"What?" she gasped. "When?"

"When we were here in Clarksville, I sent a wire to Stratton."

"But why didn't you tell me?"

"I asked Stella to tell you." Layne pointed an accusing finger at Chamberlain. "He told Stella if you didn't marry him, he'd kill her and Paul. So she was afraid to tell you."

"That's a lie!" Harold remarked.

"Shut up, Chamberlain! If you open your mouth again, I'm gonna shove my fist in it!"

Turning to his men, Harold was about to give them the order to draw; but having read his intent, Layne already had his pistol drawn and aimed at Chamberlain.

"Selina's leaving with me, and if you or your gorillas try to stop us, you'll find yourselves dead!"

Grabbing Selina's arm, he kept her at his side as he backed down the aisle, then outside. Holstering his pistol, he said quickly, "Let's go get your things, then get the hell out of this town."

"Layne . . ." she began.

He held up a quieting hand. "Not now, Selina. We'll talk later."

As they headed toward the hotel, Harold was shouting at the preacher. Talking with wide sweeps of his arms, he carried on convincingly, "Reverend, that man held you and the rest of us at gun point! You can't let him get away with that! Drawing a gun in God's house! Threatening you!"

The preacher was uncertain. "I don't think he was threatening me, but you and your friends."

"Believe me, he was threatening us all! I know that man! He's a killer! You must go to the sheriff and demand that he arrest him! Now! Before he leaves town!"

The preacher brushed his fingers through his graying hair, thought a moment, then relented, "Very well, Mr. Chamberlain, if you think I should."

"I'll go with you to the sheriff's office," Harold said, smiling inwardly.

"Should I change clothes?" Selina asked Layne, gesturing toward her riding attire. Earlier, when she had undressed to bathe, she had pitched the garments on the bed.

"No, we don't have time," he answered. "Just get your belongings together, and let's go before Chamberlain tries something."

At that moment a loud knock sounded on the

door, followed by a man's blustering voice, "Open up! This is the sheriff!"

"Damn!" Layne groaned. "What the hell does he want?" Crossing the room, he unlocked the door and opened it. He was confronted by the sheriff's pistol aimed at his chest.

"You're under arrest," the man said gruffly.

"Arrest?" Layne exclaimed. "For what?" As he stepped across the threshold, he saw Chamberlain, his men, and the preacher standing down the hall.

"Give me your gun," the law officer ordered. "And hand it over real easy, butt first."

Complying, Layne demanded, "Why the hell are you arresting me?" He indicated Chamberlain with a jerk of his head. "If he told you I kidnapped the lady, he's lying. She's with me of her own free will."

"That's true!" Selina declared, appearing in the open doorway.

"Mr. Chamberlain ain't pressin' charges, he's only a witness. Reverend White's bringin' charges against you." The sheriff drew Layne's arms behind his back and locked handcuffs about his prisoner's wrists. "I run a peaceful town," the man grumbled. "I won't tolerate no stranger comin' here and threatenin' the reverend."

"But he didn't threaten the reverend!" Selina cried.

Sheriff Cullins, his huge body verging on obesity, turned his rotund frame toward Selina. His eyes traveled over her appreciatively. He could see why the stranger had stolen her from Chamberlain. She was a rare beauty.

"Sheriff, you must believe me!" Selina continued. "Layne meant the reverend no harm!"

"That's for the judge to decide," he replied. Grasping Smith's elbow, the officer ushered him down the hall and toward the stairs.

Chamberlain smiled smugly as Layne was escorted past him.

"Reverend White," the sheriff called over his shoulder, "you need to come to the jail and fill out a complaint. Bring Mr. Chamberlain with you."

"You go ahead," Harold told the preacher. "I'll be there shortly." As the man moved away, Chamberlain spoke to his men. "Jack, you come with me. The rest of you go downstairs and wait."

Selina's eyes flared as Chamberlain and Jack came toward her. "Harold," she began angrily, "you convinced the reverend to press charges, didn't you?"

"Shut up!" he raged, shoving her roughly into the room.

His rough treatment made her stumble and come close to falling, before regaining her balance.

Pointing a finger at her, Harold promised gruffly, "I'll tend to you later!" He turned to Jack. "Stay with her. I'm going to the jail; afterwards, I plan to stop for a couple of drinks. I'll be back in an hour." He left, closing the door soundly.

"Gettin' the boss mad at you wasn't too smart," Jack told Selina, a cold smile on his lips.

"Oh?" she questioned, sounding unconcerned. With a provocative sway to her hips, she stepped closer to him. "I can handle Harold." She smiled suggestively. "I know how to turn a man's anger into passion."

"I just bet you do," he agreed, ogling her hungrily.

"Do you like what you see?" she asked, her voice sensually husky.

"Of course I do. I'm a man, ain't I?"

"Yes, and a very attractive one," she murmured, leading him on. She could hardly believe inveigling him was so easy. "Jack, would you like to see more?"

"Do you wanna get me killed? You're the boss's woman, and I ain't touchin' you."

"But there's no harm in looking, is there?"

He was weakening. "No, I reckon there ain't." He wondered just how far she was willing to go.

She reached down and lifted the hem of her skirt. "I'll remove my undergarment." Her hands slipped beneath her dress.

Jack, now eager, uttered, "Hurry up! Show it to me, baby doll!"

"Take a gander at this!" she remarked as she drew her derringer and aimed it at his chest.

"Why, you little bitch!" Jack growled. "Give me that gun or I'll take it away from you!"

"Don't try it! Now, unbuckle your gun belt."

Certain he could grab the derringer, he lurched forward. Selina fired, and the bullet slammed into his shoulder, sending him stumbling backward.

"This derringer is an over-and-under," she said calmly. "Which means there's still a bullet in the second barrel, and I'll send it right through your heart if you don't unbuckle your holster. Let it drop to the floor then, very carefully, kick it over to me."

His wound was hurting fiercely. Grimacing with pain, he did as he was told.

"Now turn around," she ordered.

Holding onto his bleeding shoulder, he turned his back.

Moving quickly, Selina reached down and took his pistol. She slipped her derringer back into its sheath, then stepping up behind Jack, she hit him over the

223

head with his own gun. He fell heavily to the floor. She stared at him for a moment, her heart pounding rapidly. She prayed he wasn't dead.

Then, getting rid of his pistol, she darted to the bed, grabbed her riding clothes and boots, and rushed out of the room. She fled down the stairs and through the lobby and got outside. Layne's horse was still tied in front of the hotel, and she crammed her belongings into Layne's saddlebags. Untying the stallion, she led him down the street.

Hoping, praying, she wouldn't run into Chamberlain and his men, she headed in the direction of the jail. Spotting an alley between the general store and the telegraph office, she decided it was an ideal place to wait because it was directly across from the jail.

Keeping a firm hold on the stallion's reins, she led him into the dark passageway. She didn't have long to wait before Chamberlain, his men, and the Reverend White came outside. The preacher walked toward his church as Harold and the others headed for the saloon.

Selina, forcing herself to be patient, gave the men ample time to be off the street before she ventured out. The town was fairly crowded, and she walked at a leisurely pace so she wouldn't draw unnecessary attention. Going to the jail, she draped the horse's reins over the hitching rail.

Quelling her anxieties, she opened the door and stepped inside. The sheriff was seated at his desk. A large smile crossed his face; the lady was a beautiful sight to behold.

"Good evening, sheriff," she said affably.

"Evenin', ma'am. If you're lookin' for Mr. Chamberlain, he just left."

The small jail contained only two cells, which were adjacent to the sheriff's office. Layne, his hands grasping the bars, watched Selina as she went into action.

"I didn't come here to see Mr. Chamberlain," she said, her tone sugar sweet. "I'm here to see you."

"Me?" he questioned, heaving his heavy frame out of the chair.

Stepping to his desk, she waved a dainty hand. "Sheriff, please sit down."

"Wh . . . what can I do for you, ma'am?" he asked, returning to his chair. He suddenly became cautious. "I hope you ain't gonna try to break your boyfriend out of jail. You try anything, and I'll lock you up too."

"Honestly, sheriff!" she remarked saucily. "Look at me. Do you see any weapons? Now, how could I break anyone out of jail? Unless you think little ole me can physically overcome a big, strong man like you."

He chuckled heartily. "Sorry to be so distrustful, ma'am."

She sat on the edge of his desk and leaned forward. Her dress had a deep-cut neck, and the sheriff's eyes were drawn immediately to her tempting cleavage. He didn't see Selina lift her skirt stealthily, nor did he see her draw her derringer.

Still unable to tear his eyes away from her lovely bosom, he uttered, "What can I do for you?"

"You can unlock that cell!" she demanded. Holding him at gun point, she moved off the desk. "Do it now!" she ordered sharply.

Getting to his feet and raising his hands in a don't-shoot pose, he said shakily, "Don't get excited, ma'am." He knew at close range a derringer could be fatal. "Be careful, now, or that gun's liable to go off."

"It's gonna go off right between your eyes if you don't unlock that cell!" She hoped he wouldn't realize that she was bluffing.

He took the keys and unlocked the cell. Layne lurched quickly and drew the sheriff's holstered pistol. Removing the bandanna from his neck, he used it to gag the man. Then he pushed him into the cell and locked the door.

Moving swiftly, Layne placed the sheriff's pistol and keys on the desk, then located his own gun. He turned to Selina and, with a disarming, one-sided grin, remarked, "You're quite a woman, Miss Beaumont." Then, sobering, he took her arm and said urgently, "Darlin', let's get out of here!"

Seventeen

"How long are we gonna stay holed-up here, waitin' for Smith?" Floyd asked Doug.

The two men, along with the women, were seated at the campfire. Supper had been eaten, the dishes washed and put away.

Doug took a sip of his coffee and looked at Miller, and answered, "Layne said to give him twenty-four hours. If he hasn't returned by then, we're supposed to move on, and he'll catch up to us."

Miller was annoyed. He didn't know how much longer his men would stay in Dry River, waiting for him to show up. They were liable to figure something had gone wrong and pull out of town. Certain that Smith and the others were already in Texas, he had told his men it wouldn't take more than a few days for him to meet up with them. He hadn't taken into account that Smith wouldn't leave New Orleans on schedule.

Finishing his coffee, Doug got to his feet. "Miller, you can take the first watch." His eyes swept over the women. "You ladies had better go on to the wagon and get some sleep." He walked away and went to his bedroll.

As Stella and Hattie headed toward the wagon,

Floyd detained Janet. Speaking quietly, he asked, "Are you sleepy?"

"Not especially," she answered, interest growing.

"Why don't you give the others time to fall asleep, then come keep me company?"

The light from the fire defined his handsome face, and the sensual invitation in his brown eyes was irresistible. "I'll be back," she said, smiling warmly. "You can count on it."

She hurried to the wagon and undressed for bed. Hattie extinguished the lantern; and Janet, lying on her pallet, waited eagerly for everyone to fall asleep. The time seemed to drag, and she was tempted to leave. But her better judgment advised her to wait a little longer. She wasn't too concerned about Stella and Hattie, but she wanted to give Doug time to fall soundly asleep. She had no doubt that if he knew, he'd be furious with her for talking to Floyd, who was supposed to be standing guard.

Doug Thompson! she thought angrily. I've never known a man so overbearing! It must be his Indian blood that makes him that way. Warriors probably boss their squaws around something terrible. They probably snap their fingers and expect their women to jump. Well, Doug Thompson isn't going to boss me around!

Deciding enough time had elapsed, she wiped Doug from her mind, slipped on her robe, and crept stealthily out of the wagon. Floyd was waiting for her a short distance from the dying fire, and taking her hand, he led her through the surrounding brush. They came to a clearing, where he propped his rifle against a tree, then turned to look at her.

Janet was lovely in the saffron moonlight. Its

228

golden glow, shining through her thin sleepwear, accentuated her young, ripe curves. Her long blond hair fell past her shoulders in silky softness, and her eyes sparkled with vitality. She was a fetching sight, and Floyd had to struggle against the urge to lay her on the ground and ravish her.

"What are you thinking about?" she asked.

"I was thinking about how beautiful you are. I've always had a weakness for green-eyed blonds, but you're the prettiest one I've ever seen."

She blushed becomingly. "Why Floyd Miller, you're such a flirtatious rogue! My uncle warned me about men like you."

He hid his annoyance. She was the typical Southern belle. She expected him to court her, woo her, and remain chivalrous through the entire event, while she sportively held off his advances. Well, he didn't have the time or the patience to play her silly game. Furthermore, he was sure Janet was just as hot as the hottest whore; all he had to do was stick it to her once, and after that she'd spread her legs willingly.

He stepped closer and drew her carefully into his arms. He didn't want to make any fast moves and frighten her away. Once he awakened her passion, though, she'd be his to take as he pleased.

Floyd had every confidence in his ability to seduce a woman, and as his lips came down on Janet's, he didn't doubt that she'd soon give in to him.

Lacing her arms about his neck, Janet allowed his kiss to continue. She waited expectantly for the touch of his lips to spark a fiery longing. Although his mouth on hers was a pleasant sensation, it didn't evoke a fervent response. Janet was confused, as well as disappointed. Floyd was so excitingly handsome, so why wasn't his kiss igniting an uncontrollable fire?

"My beautiful darlin'," Floyd whispered hoarsely, raining butterfly kisses over her neck and down to the hollow of her throat. His arm, tightening about her tiny waist, brought her thighs flush to his. His mouth took hers again, this time in a wild, hungry caress.

Janet encouraged him by moving her hand to the nape of his neck, hoping this time his kiss would leave her breathless with wonder.

"Miller!" Doug's thundering voice disrupted their embrace.

Floyd released her at once, and backing up a couple of steps, he watched guardedly as Thompson emerged from the dark shadows.

Janet, her heart skipping a beat, stared wide-eyed as Doug's huge, brawny frame crossed over into the moonlight. His expression was furious, and dreading his rage, she swallowed with a gulp.

"When I tell you to stand guard," he said to Floyd, "that's what I expect you to do! Try something like this again and I'll kick your butt so hard you'll fly all the way back to Bart's ranch!"

Enraged, Miller's hand hovered over his holstered pistol, poised in a shooting stance as his eyes dared Doug to draw.

Thompson's large fist shot out so fast that Floyd never saw it coming. His knuckles smashed against Miller's jaw, the vicious blow knocking him to the ground. Standing over him, Doug uttered threateningly, "Miller, don't even look like you're gonna draw on me! Next time, I'll break that gunhand of yours in so many pieces it'll be permanently out of commission."

Getting up clumsily, Floyd considered whipping out his pistol and blowing the man to hell. His better sense, however, held steadfast. The ransom he planned to collect for Janet was too important. Shooting Thompson would ruin everything. He'd be patient; killing Thompson would come about in due time.

Rubbing a hand over his throbbing jaw, he feigned a lame apology, "Sorry, Thompson." Grabbing his rifle, he headed back to camp with murder raging in his heart.

Fearing a confrontation, Janet started to leave, but Doug grasped her arm and swung her about so that she was facing him. "You've been nothing but trouble since this trip began. I oughta take to tyin' you up at night."

Her anger overcoming her fear, she wrested free and lashed out, "Don't manhandle me! You pompous bully! How dare you strike Floyd! He's half your size! Why don't you pick on someone as big as you are!"

"If he ever threatens to draw on me again, I'll do more than hit 'im!"

"Draw on you!" she spat. "What makes you think Floyd was going to do something so ruthless?"

"What makes you think he wasn't?"

"Because he's a gentleman."

"If you think he's a gentleman, then you're a bigger fool than I thought you were."

"You aren't only insulting but utterly impossible! And I have nothing more to say to you!"

"Well, I have a lot to say to you."

"I suppose if I try to leave you'll hold me here by

force!"

"If necessary."

Folding her arms and stamping her foot angrily, she said peevishly, "Well, go ahead! Speak your piece!"

"I'm gonna give you some advice, even though I'm probably wastin' my breath."

"Your advice will make no impression on me whatsoever!" she spat. Oh how she abhorred this demanding, ill-mannered brute!

"Stay away from Miller. He's trouble."

She laughed harshly. "And why, pray tell, is he trouble?"

"I know his type. He'd cheat his own mother."

"Do you have facts to back up such an accusation?"

"No, I don't."

"That figures!" she said testily.

"He's been in jail a couple of times. Once, for starting a fight. He lost at cards and was a poor loser. He took his anger out on the winner, a man old enough to be his grandfather."

"And why was he jailed a second time?"

"He got too rough with one of Rosie's girls."

"Who is Rosie?"

"She owns the Golden Garter. It's a saloon."

"Surely you don't expect me to shun Floyd because he got into a fight over a game of cards, or because he had some trouble with a harlot! I understand that fights often erupt during cards, and as far as that . . . that harlot . . . well, doesn't that kind of woman expect rough treatment? She probably enjoys it."

"I don't think she enjoyed gettin' her nose broken."

"I refuse to believe Floyd abused that harlot!" she

232

remarked stubbornly.

Doug turned away from Janet's glaring eyes. Why did he even try to help her. She despised him too much to believe anything he told her. A picture of her in Miller's embrace flashed across his mind. It pained him to the core of his heart.

"May I leave now?" she asked crossly.

Compelled by an emotion too powerful to control, Doug stepped forward and drew her into his arms so quickly that she didn't have time to resist.

His lips seized hers so aggressively that a small sound of wonder came from her throat. There was not only passion in his kiss but also anger, and his fiery, demanding assault set fire to every nerve in her body. She fell trembling against his muscular frame for support, and his sinewy arms brought her so close that their bodies seemed inseparable.

Parting her lips, she let him possess her mouth fully, and his questing tongue sent the sweet ache of longing right through her. The feeling was staggering, and it almost overpowered her; but suddenly her senses returned, jolting her back to reason.

She tore her mouth away from his, and pushing against his chest, she demanded, "Let me go!"

He released her at once. Although he was somewhat angry at himself for having forced her into his embrace, he was nonetheless pleased that, for a moment, she had actually responded. He tried to hold his emotions in check. Her response might not mean anything. It was probably nothing more than a weak moment.

As Doug was keeping his emotions controlled, Janet's thoughts were in turmoil. She was shocked, even abashed, that she had responded to this man's forceful kiss. She despised Doug Thompson, was not attracted to him, and considered him barbaric! Searching for an explanation, she convinced herself that Floyd's kisses had aroused her passion, which had made her vulnerable to Doug's kiss.

Doug looked on as Janet's eyes, hardening with anger, shattered his hopes.

She wiped a hand across her mouth as though his kiss had left a bitter taste on her lips. "Don't ever take liberties with me again, Doug Thompson! Don't you realize how much I detest you?"

"The feeling's becomin' mutual," he replied dryly.

Whirling about, she stormed off. Floyd was waiting for her at camp; but when he approached, she waved him back and hurried inside the wagon.

Meanwhile Doug, walking slowly back to camp, was wondering if it was possible to love a woman and detest her at the same time. He supposed it was possible, for when he told Janet the feeling was mutual, he had meant it. Feeling miserable, crushed, he hoped his love for Janet wasn't enduring; that in time it would diminish and die out altogether.

Selina's arms were locked tightly about Layne's waist as he guided the large stallion through the dark night. Afraid the sheriff would give chase, she kept glancing over her shoulder, hoping she wouldn't see a posse in pursuit.

When they were miles away from Clarksville, Layne decided it was safe to stop. After dismounting, he reached up and grasped Selina about the waist, and drew her from the horse.

They were in an area well sheltered by trees and

brush. The shrill chirping of crickets sounded from every direction, their music filling the air.

"Layne, why are we stopping?" Selina asked.

"The horse has to rest."

"But what if the sheriff is chasing us?"

"We've been out of his jurisdiction for the past five miles or so."

"Then we're safe?" she asked hopefully.

He smiled wryly. "Your jailbreak is now officially successful. We're free, my little partner in crime."

"Layne, don't tease. I'm serious. If that sheriff catches us, he'll put us both in jail."

His hands spanned her waist, drawing her against him. "Don't worry, darlin'. He doesn't want us bad enough to chase us into another county. We aren't exactly hardened criminals." He lowered his lips to hers, kissing her tenderly. Then taking a rolled blanket from behind his saddle, he told her to spread it out under a tree while he gave the horse some water.

She put down the blanket under a tall oak, then sat back against the tree's trunk. A weary sigh was released as she became aware of how tired she was. The long, exhausting day had sapped her strength. A loving smile, however, shone on her face as she watched Layne coming toward her. Just looking at him sent her heart racing. She wondered if he would always have this wonderful effect on her. With a dreamy sigh, she decided that he would indeed.

Joining her, Layne said, "We'll give the horse about an hour's rest, then leave. We should reach camp by dawn."

"Layne, why did Harold threaten Stella? Did he know her in New Orleans?"

He told her some details about Stella's life and

explained the relationship with Chamberlain.

"I always sensed Harold had a sadistic streak in him. Apparently my feelings were right." Turning to face Layne, she reached over and slipped her hand into his. "The other night I happened to overhear your conversation with Doug. I know the only reason you agreed to take me to Texas was to get information from me."

"Not really," he replied. "That was the excuse I gave myself. I believed you were married, and I didn't want to admit that I was falling in love with another man's wife. Selina, did you listen to everything Doug and I said to each other?"

"No," she answered. "But I heard enough to know you were being nice to me because you wanted information. I was too hurt to listen to any more."

"Now I understand why you turned on me. Darlin', you should have listened a little longer. I told Doug that getting information from you wasn't on my mind. The only thing on my mind was loving you."

She smiled radiantly. "Layne, do you truly love me?"

"From the bottom of my heart," he murmured.

"I love you too!" she declared, falling gracefully into his arms. Then recalling Jessie Harte, she asked hesitantly, "Layne, how do you feel about Jessie?"

"How did you know about her?" he asked.

She told him about overhearing his conversation with Janet.

"Jessie's a fine woman and a good friend. That's all."

"Are you sure?"

"I'm positive. Selina, you're the only woman for

236

me."

When he bent his head, she met his lips halfway, their kiss full of passion and need. "I love you, Selina Beaumont," he whispered, holding her close.

Nestling her head on his shoulder, she cuddled against him. "Layne," she said softly, "I know nothing about your father's death."

"I know," he murmured.

"Don't you believe he committed suicide?"

"I think Chamberlain might have killed him, then made it look like suicide."

"Why do you think that?"

"Just a gut feeling, I guess. My father wasn't the kind of man to take his own life. He liked living too much."

"But why would Harold murder him?"

"I don't know."

"Have you questioned Stella? She might know something."

"I doubt it."

"It's worth a try, isn't it?"

"I suppose, but I wouldn't want her to think that I had an ulterior motive for helping her. When I invited her to travel with us, it crossed my mind to ask her if she knew anything about Chamberlain and my father. Besides, she's so terrified of Chamberlain that even if she knew something she'd be too scared to tell me."

"All the same, I think you should ask her."

"I'll think about it," he replied.

"Stella's life has been terribly oppressive. I certainly hope her future will be a lot better. Maybe Texas will be a good turning point in her life. She might even find the right man and fall in love."

Layne chuckled softly. "Quite a romantic, aren't you?"

"Yes, but that's because I'm head over heels in love."

"Well, I also hope that Stella's life will improve, but I doubt if she'll find Texas a turning point. She won't stay."

"Because of Harold?"

He nodded. "She won't live that close to him."

Selina frowned. "Damn Harold! He should be shot for browbeating that poor, helpless woman!"

"You could always shoot him with your little derringer," Layne said, smiling amusedly.

"I will, if he tries to harm Stella or Paul!"

"I don't doubt it. You once told me you could shoot a varmint."

"I already shot one."

Layne was astounded. "What?"

"I shot one of Harold's men. The one called Jack. Harold left him to guard me. I had to get out of the room so I could go to the jail and break you out. I drew my derringer, and Jack tried to take it away from me. I shot him in the shoulder. Then I hit him over the head with his own pistol and knocked him unconscious."

"Selina," Layne began, smiling, "did you wear your derringer to your wedding?"

"I certainly did!" she remarked. "I always have my derringer handy—just in case. And it's a good thing I do, because if it weren't for this little gun you'd still be in jail."

Chuckling, Layne hugged her tightly. "You're quite a gal, Selina."

Stifling a yawn, she snuggled close. Comfortable,

contented, she closed her eyes; and surrendering to her fatigue, she came close to falling asleep.

Layne placed a light kiss on her forehead, then easing her down on the blanket, he lay beside her, drawing her close. She was soon sound asleep. Needing rest himself, he dozed lightly. His senses, though, remained attuned to his surroundings. In case of danger he'd be wide awake, ready to draw his gun in a trice.

Eighteen

"Wake up, Selina," Layne whispered. Leaning over her, he lightly kissed the tip of her nose. "Open your eyes, sleepy-head. It's time to leave."

Her long lashes fluttered open, and she regarded him through half-lowered lids. Slowly she laced her arms about his neck, whispering provocatively, "Let's stay here a little longer."

He grinned expectantly. "Are you seducing me?"

"Well, I'm certainly trying," she answered pertly. "You won't be difficult, will you?"

Taking her hand from about his neck, he moved it down to his aroused maleness. "Does this feel like I'll be difficult?"

"My goodness, Mr. Smith," she murmured saucily. "I think I should take care of your problem immediately."

"You will be tender, won't you?" he asked, his dark eyes twinkling.

"Yes, trust me," she purred, raising her lips to his.

He smiled against her mouth, then kissed her demandingly, urgently, as he pressed every inch of his body to hers.

"Selina . . . Selina," Layne whispered, his warm

240

lips traveling to her neck, covering her throat with feather-light kisses.

Responding with total abandon, she arched against him, and his hardness was so powerful that her skirt and petticoat didn't prevent her from feeling his throbbing desire.

He removed his shirt, and Selina's eyes roamed adoringly over his naked chest. Strong muscles rippled through his arms as he unbuckled his holster, then released his trousers.

Anxious to make them as one, he drew the long folds of her dress and petticoat up to her waist. An amused smile flickered across his lips as he removed the holster strapped above her knee. Then when he reached for her pantalets, she lifted her hips, making it easier for him to slide the garment past her thighs and down her legs.

Layne's eyes raked her passionately, his fingers skimming over the smooth textures of her stomach, then downward to caress her fully. His lips soon followed the path his fingers had taken, his intimacy causing Selina to shudder with pleasure as waves of ecstasy washed over her.

His passion growing to fever pitch, Layne moved over her, and as his mouth descended to hers, he plunged deeply into her enveloping heat.

Surrendering to their all-consuming joining, they made love blissfully, giving and taking all the other had to offer. As they climbed gloriously to the peak of excitement, their thrusting became aggressive, wonderfully demanding.

Together they crested love's apex, finding breathless, rapturous fulfillment.

Layne kissed her sweetly, and moving to lie at

her side, he murmured, "I could make love to you for a hundred years and still want more."

She laughed softly. "Greedy, aren't you?"

"Where you're concerned, I am," he said, hugging her tightly.

Caressing the smooth, muscled flesh of his back, she said wistfully, "I wish we didn't have to leave."

"So do I," he replied. "But we need to catch up to the others."

"I suppose you're right," she agreed reluctantly. Sitting up, she put on her undergarment, then went over to Layne's horse and removed her riding attire from the saddlebags. Turning and meeting Layne's questioning gaze, she said, "If I'm going to travel horseback, I might as well travel in comfort."

She felt completely at ease with this man she loved, and she undressed without hesitation. As she donned her riding clothes, she wondered if Layne would ask her to marry him. He had professed his love; surely a marriage proposal would follow. Her anticipations were high, but as she suddenly recalled Layne's telling her that he wasn't the marrying kind, her elations wavered.

Layne handed her the holstered derringer, then gathered her discarded apparel and put them in the saddlebags. It was a tight fit, and he had to stuff them inside. "Are you ready to leave?" he asked, offering Selina his hand.

He helped her mount, then swung up behind her. As his arms encircled her, he whispered in her ear, "I love you, Selina."

His word were music to her heart. "I love you too," she murmured. "I always will."

Hattie was starting breakfast when Layne and Selina rode into camp. Delighted that Selina had returned, she hurried to greet the young woman; and the moment Selina's feet touched ground, Hattie clasped her in her warm embrace.

"Miz Selina, I'm so glad you's back! You didn't marry Masta Chamberlain, did you?"

"No, I didn't. Layne arrived in time to stop the wedding."

At that moment Stella, carrying Paul, left the wagon and walked haltingly toward Selina. On the verge of tears, she said softly, "I reckon you're awfully mad at me, and I don't blame you."

"I'm not angry," Selina assured her.

Paul was happy to see Selina, and he held out his arms, wanting her to hold him.

She hugged him fondly. "I missed you," she said, kissing his rosy cheek.

"You mean, you don't hate me?" Stella asked. She could hardly believe that Selina could be so forgiving.

"Of course not," she answered. "In your place, I'd have done the same thing."

"I don't know about that," Layne spoke up, grinning at Selina. "Knowing you, if Chamberlain was to threaten you, you'd probably draw your little derringer and shoot him."

Hattie cackled. "And I know where she oughta shoot that ole devil. Right where his brains is located, and I ain't talkin' 'bout his head. That man thinks between his legs!"

Laughing, Layne remarked, "Why, Hattie, I didn't know you were so malicious."

Lumbering back to the fire, she said over her shoulder, "Don't know what that word 'malicious' means, but it'd do my heart good to see that man get what's comin' to 'im!"

Layne, glancing about the area and not seeing his friend, called to Hattie, "Where's Doug?"

"I don't know," she answered. "I ain't seen 'im. His horse is here, though, so I reckon he's around somewhere."

Floyd, still in his bedroll, threw back the cover, put on his boots, and got up. His eyes traveled furtively over Selina as he ambled over to meet her. She was a real beauty, and he didn't blame Smith for going after her.

Layne had told Selina about Miller; and as he approached her she said with a friendly smile, "You must be Floyd Miller. I'm pleased to meet you. I'm Selina."

"Howdy, ma'am," he replied, as though shy.

Layne touched Selina's hand. "I'm gonna look for Doug." Then he asked Miller, "Would you mind unsaddlin' my horse? I'll drive the wagon this mornin'."

Although Floyd resented Smith treating him like hired help, he hid his annoyance and led the stallion away.

Layne went in search of Doug, and Selina asked Stella, "Is Janet awake?"

"She's gettin' dressed." Stella hesitated before asking, "Did Layne tell you 'bout my past?"

"Yes, he did."

"You won't say nothin' to Janet, will you?"

"Not if you don't want me to."

"I'd rather she didn't know. Janet ain't quite as

244

understandin' as you are."

"Stella, your past is a part of your life. Instead of running away from it, you should stand and face it."

"I suppose you're right, but all the same I don't want Janet to know."

Selina handed Paul back to his mother and climbed inside the wagon.

Janet had finished dressing and was about to leave. "Selina!" she exclaimed. "I'm glad you're back! But, tell me, why didn't you marry Harold Chamberlain? He's so handsome and such a gentleman!"

"He might be handsome, but he's no gentleman. Furthermore, I don't love him. I'm in love with Layne."

"Layne!" Janet was astounded.

Laughing at Janet's startled expression, Selina replied, "Hattie's cooking breakfast, shall we go help?"

Placing her hands on her hips, Janet remarked impatiently, "Selina Beaumont, you can't make such an astounding announcement and not give me the details!"

"There are no details. Layne and I simply fell in love."

Janet studied her for a moment. "Selina," she began uncertainly, "when Layne kisses you, how does it make you feel?"

"Janet, what a strange question! Why do you ask?"

She went on, "Do you think it's possible to be attracted to a man you despise?"

"I suppose it's possible. Janet, do you want to tell me what's going on?"

"Have you met Floyd Miller yet?"

"Yes, I have."

Janet sighed dreamily. "Isn't he handsome?"

Selina agreed that he was.

"Last night he kissed me twice."

When she said no more, Selina asked, "Are you saying that you despise Floyd Miller, yet you responded to his kiss?"

"Heavens no! I think Floyd is wonderful! I responded to Doug's kiss!"

Selina was now even more confused. "Would you mind clarifying all this?"

Janet told her exactly what had happened, summing it up by saying peevishly, "I can't believe that I actually enjoyed Doug's kiss!"

"Why not?"

"I detest him, and I don't find him attractive."

"Doug might not be classically handsome, but there's a rugged aura about him that's very appealing."

"I suppose," Janet admitted reluctantly.

Walking up to the back of the wagon, Stella announced, "Hattie's got breakfast done." Her eyes flitted from one woman to the other. "You two look mighty serious. Did I interrupt something important?"

"We were discussing matters of the heart," Selina answered.

"Love?" Stella questioned. "Well, I cain't be no help to you. I ain't never been in love, and I don't reckon I ever will be." She motioned for her friends to follow, "Come on. Hattie's fixed a big breakfast, and if we don't get over there and start eatin', she's gonna skin us alive!"

* * *

Doug was heading back to camp when Layne came upon him.

"Glad to see you made it back," Doug remarked. "Is Selina with you?"

Falling into stride beside his friend, Layne answered, "Yeah, she's with me."

"That's good. Is everything straightened out between you two?"

"Everything's fine."

"Selina's a good woman. You're a lucky man."

"I know." Layne could sense Doug's depression; hoping to cheer him up, he said enthusiastically, "Hattie's cookin' breakfast, and it sure smells good."

"I'm not very hungry," Doug mumbled.

"What's bothering you?"

"I've been thinkin'. I know you need me to take your herd to Kansas. That's only a couple of months away, so I'll stick around that long and deliver the herd. But when the drive's over, I'm headin' to Oregon."

Grasping Doug's arm, Layne brought their steps to a halt. "You can't be serious!"

"I'm dead serious."

Layne's eyes narrowed testily. "It's because of Janet, isn't it?"

"Yeah, she's part of it."

"And the rest?"

"I'm twenty-eight years old, and I've never done anything but work for someone else. I think it's time I started workin' for myself. I've got some money saved. When I get to Oregon, maybe I can buy a few acres of land and farm."

"You aren't a farmer!"

"Maybe not, but I can learn."

"Doug, if it's land you want, I'll sell you top grazing pasture. Hell, you're a rancher, not a farmer!"

"I can't afford to build a ranch."

"Then I'll loan you what you need."

"For God's sake, Layne!" he bellowed. "I don't want charity!"

Layne, knowing Doug was a proud man, let the matter drop. "All right, if you're determined to leave, then all I can do is wish you luck."

Doug smiled. "You're a good friend and a good boss. But you know how it is. I gotta move on."

The travelers had been on the road only a short time when Miller, riding flank, became aware of three horsemen approaching. Urging his horse to the front of the wagon, he yelled to Layne, "Three riders are comin' this way!"

Selina, sitting beside Layne, grasped his arm. "Do you think it's Chamberlain?"

Pulling up the team, he answered, "I wouldn't doubt it."

Doug was riding in the lead, and he turned his horse about. Reining in, he drew his rifle from its sheath and rested it across his folded arms.

The approaching riders brought their horses to a stop.

Wondering what was happening, Stella peeked over the back of the seat, and the sight of Chamberlain sent her heart pounding.

"What do you want?" Layne asked Chamberlain calmly.

"Nothing," he answered. "I merely stopped to return Selina's belongings. She left the hotel so suddenly that she forgot her things." He nodded to one of his men, who dismounted and detached Selina's bag from the pack horse. He pitched it into the wagon.

With a cockeyed grin, Layne looked at Harold and said, "By the way, I see you're short one bodyguard. Where's Jack?"

Chamberlain laughed harshly. "I had to leave him behind. He's disabled."

"That's a real shame," Layne replied, still smiling.

Harold turned his gaze to Selina. "I underestimated you. I certainly didn't imagine that a wellbred lady was capable of shooting a man, knocking him cold, then breaking her lover out of jail."

With that, he spurred his horse into a fast trot, his two men following.

"We haven't seen the last of him," Selina murmured, a note of worry in her voice.

"We can't very well avoid him. His ranch borders on mine."

As Layne slapped the reins against the team, setting the wagon back into motion, Selina asked hesitantly, "Where am I supposed to live?"

He looked at her quizzically.

"Layne," she began impatiently, "I was going to Texas to live on Harold's ranch. Remember?"

"So?" he queried.

"So, now where do I live?"

"With me, of course."

Her blue eyes flashed petulantly. "Layne, I love you, but I'll not be your mistress!"

He laughed heartily. "Selina, you delightful little minx, do you really think I want you as a mistress?"

"You once told me that you aren't the marrying kind."

"But that was before I fell in love with you."

Her face brightened. "Layne, are you saying . . . ?"

"No, I'm asking. Will you marry me?"

"Oh yes!" she cried happily, throwing her arms about him.

Holding the multiple reins in one hand, he wrapped an arm about her waist to draw her closer. His lips met hers in a long, love-filled kiss.

From the back of the wagon, they heard Hattie say, "Well, I's shore glad they's gonna get married, but if Mista Smith don't keep an eye on the road, them horses is liable to take this wagon right into a ditch."

Breaking their kiss, Layne called back to her, "I'll keep my eye on the road, Hattie. I promise."

"You just do that, Mista Smith," she said with a laugh. "That way, we'll all make it to your weddin' in one piece."

Part Two
Texas

Nineteen

The travelers crossed the Sabine River, entered Texas, and left Louisiana behind. As the days passed, Selina became more and more anxious for the journey to end. She and Layne planned to get married at his ranch, and she could hardly wait to become Mrs. Layne Smith. The small town of Passing Through had no church or preacher, so Layne intended to send to San Antonio for one.

Now, as they stopped for the noon break, Selina walked over to study a strange-looking tree. It wasn't very tall and had a short trunk with deep V-forks. Its heavy branches came low to the ground, and the closely knitted twigs were full of catkin-like flowers.

"It's a mesquite," Layne said, coming up behind her. "They grow all over the southwest. Indians use the bean pods for food, and the gum as an adhesive."

Moving closer, he drew her into his arms. "You'll find Texas different from Louisiana. Not only is the terrain different, but so is life in general." He made a sweeping gesture with one arm. "This land gets into a man's blood. He'll fight for it, even die to keep it. White man as well as Indian. But this land can be merciless to those who love it. Furious dust storms, or drought, can wipe out everything a man has worked for. Also, hostility breeds here. There's the whites against the Indians, plus bandits who cross over from Mexico. Texas seems to draw unsavory characters from all parts of the country."

Layne moved his hands to Selina's shoulders, and gazing down into her eyes, he asked seriously, "Are you sure you're willing to give up the comforts and securities of Cedar Hill to live in Texas?"

"Darling," she replied, her eyes shining, "you are my comfort and my security. I love Cedar Hill, but you're my heart. I want only to be with you. I'd follow you to the ends of the earth just to be at your side."

He embraced her tightly. "Selina, I love you."

"The feeling is quite mutual," she murmured, raising her lips to his. Their kiss was tender and filled with devotion.

As Layne was leading her back toward the wagon, the distant plodding of horses' hooves carried across the vast plains.

"Indians?" Selina gasped.

Layne listened more closely. "No, they don't sound like Indian ponies."

"How can you tell?"

"Indian ponies aren't shod."

They hurried to the others. Doug had his rifle in hand, and Floyd had his pistol drawn. The group looked on as the riders came into sight. There were four of them, and as they rode in closer, the men aimed their weapons, ready to fire if necessary.

"If I tell you women to take cover under the wagon," Layne began, "I want you to do it at once.

No questions and no hesitations." He cast Selina warning glance. "That goes for you too." He grinned wryly, adding, "And keep that little derringer holstered."

Selina came close to telling him to give her a rifle; she could shoot as well as a man. She kept silent, though; she knew Layne would still insist that she take cover. Besides, he didn't know that her father had taught her to use a rifle, and there wasn't time to explain.

The four horsemen slowed their mounts and advanced at an unthreatening pace. One man, urging his horse ahead of the others, said cordially, "Good afternoon folks. My name's Phil Watts."

Layne walked out to greet him and his men. "State your business."

"I'm a government agent," Mr. Watts replied. "These men are my deputies." He handed Layne his credentials.

After reading the man's official paper, Layne invited Watts and his deputies to stay for lunch.

Following introductions, the women began preparing the meal, and Watts asked Layne if they could talk privately. Layne agreed and led him to the lone mesquite.

Watts reached into his shirt pocket and drew out two cheroots. He offered one to Layne, but he declined. The agent lit his own smoke, then asked, "Are you the same Layne Smith whose father owned half of the Smith and Chamberlain Shipping Company?"

"Yes, I am."

"You sold your father's half of the business, correct?"

"Why are you so interested?"

"I'm looking for Harold Chamberlain. I have reason to believe he's heading for his ranch. Have you seen him?"

"Mr. Watts, if you're smart enough to work for the government, then you're smart enough to stop at towns and ask questions. I'm sure you stopped at Clarksville and had a long talk with the sheriff."

The man couldn't help but smile. "Yes, I did. The sheriff had a lot to say about you, Miss Beaumont, and Mr. Chamberlain."

"I'm sure he did," Layne replied. "Do you mind telling me why you're after Chamberlain?"

"He's wanted for questioning. The government has reason to believe that Mr. Chamberlain has been illegally transporting slaves into the country. His ships deliver cotton to England, then we believe they return with illegal cargo."

Layne was taken aback. "I never thought . . . ! Knowing Chamberlain, though, I shouldn't be surprised." He eyed Watts sternly. "I hope you don't think my father was involved."

"I don't know whether he was or not."

"My father would never have done anything that was against the law, and if he had learned that Chamberlain was doing something illegal, he would have tried to stop him." He thought for a moment, then remarked, "I never believed my father committed suicide, I suspected Chamberlain of murdering him. But I couldn't find a motive — until now."

"Do you think your father found out what Chamberlain was doing and threatened to expose him?"

"Yes, I do. That's why Chamberlain killed him."

"What you suspect may be true, but proving it

won't be easy."

"Chamberlain and his men can't be that far ahead of us. If you have no objections, I'll ride with you. When we catch up to that bastard, I'll get a confession out of him."

"You're more than welcome to ride along."

"Did Chamberlain know about you? Is that why he left New Orleans so suddenly?"

Watts shrugged his shoulders. He was a nice-looking man, his lean, muscled frame belying his forty-odd years. "I don't know if he realized he was under investigation. He might have suspected, which would explain his hasty departure."

Layne turned his gaze back toward camp and centered on Selina. She was sitting beside the fire, tending to Paul. Sensing his scrutiny, she glanced over her shoulder and met his eyes. She somehow felt that he was troubled.

Handing the child to Hattie, Selina went to Layne and asked, "Is something wrong?"

He told her why Watts was pursuing Chamberlain, and that he had decided to accompany him.

Selina didn't want Layne to leave. She knew he didn't plan to be away for very long, but even a short separation seemed unbearable. "I wish you wouldn't go," she murmured.

A tender smile crossed his lips. "Darlin', Chamberlain can't be more than a day, maybe even less, ahead of us. I'll be back before you have time to miss me."

"I already miss you, and you haven't even left."

Sliding an arm about her waist, Layne drew her to his side. Speaking to Watts, he explained, "Selina and I plan to be married very soon."

The man's eyes measured Selina appreciatively. "You're a very lucky man, Mr. Smith."

"Don't I know it," Layne replied.

The shadows of dusk were casting a grayish mist over the landscape as Layne, deep in thought, rode beside Phil Watts. The agent's deputies were trailing close behind.

Layne had spotted fresh tracks he assumed belonged to Chamberlain and his men, and he knew that he and the others would soon catch up to them. He wasn't sure how he'd get a confession out of Chamberlain, but he was now certain that Harold had killed his father. Somehow, someway, he'd make the man tell the truth. Chamberlain had committed cold-blooded murder, and Layne wouldn't rest until the man paid for his crime.

Layne was the first to notice a flock of vultures circling the sky. The carrion-eating birds sent a cold chill up his spine. Bringing them to Watts's attention, he said, "They've found something, and whatever it is, you can be sure it's either dead or dying."

The vultures were a distance away. Watts started to spur his horse into a gallop, but Layne detained him.

"Wait," he said. "We'd better approach cautiously." The agent nodded. "You're right, of course."

Holding their horses at any easy canter, the men proceeded toward the area. As they drew closer the smell of blood assailed their horses' nostrils, the pungent odor caused the animals to tremble.

Death waited on the other side of a small hill, and as the men ascended the grassy incline, they drew their rifles. Reining in, they looked down at the ghastly sight below. The vultures, aware of the mens' presence, squawked, flapped their wings, and soared into the air. Reluctant to leave their find, the birds circled overhead.

Layne slipped his rifle back into its sheath. There was no danger here; danger had already struck, carried out its vengeance, and left.

Watts, unable to tear his eyes away from the three bodies sprawled below, asked Layne, "Do you suppose they're Chamberlain and his men?"

"Probably," he answered, urging his horse forward. The others followed him down the hillside.

The men dismounted, and Watts stepped over to the nearest body. There was little left to recognize for the dead man had been horribly mutilated. Watts's stomach churned, and as bile rose in his throat, he turned about and vomitted onto the ground.

"My God!" he groaned, heaving. "What kind of savages would cut a man up like that?"

"Comanches," Layne answered. He went to the other two bodies, and as he gazed down at the bloody corpses, he came close to being sick. It wasn't the first time Layne had come across mutilated bodies, but such butchery was a sight he was never truly prepared to face.

Watts came to Layne's side. "Why?" he moaned. "Why did those savages do this?"

"They sometimes mutilate their slain victims for religious reasons; enemies with crippled bodies can't be a threat in the spirit world. They usually don't become this riled, though, without good reason. Something has happened to anger them, and they're out for blood. Every white person this side of the Brazo River is in danger. Let's get these bodies buried and get back to the wagon. If the Comanches who did this are still in the area, they're liable to spot Selina and the others."

Watts wasn't ready to leave. First, he hoped to make a positive identification. He couldn't return to his superiors and tell them that Chamberlain was supposedly dead; he needed substantial proof.

"I've only seen Chamberlain once," he said to Layne. "And I'm not sure if one of these bodies is his. Are you?"

Layne shook his head. "No, I can't be sure. All the bodies are too badly butchered."

"If only the Indians hadn't taken the horses and the mens' belongings. There's nothing left to identify these bodies. The savages even stripped them of their clothing." Hesitant, he cleared his throat, then continued, "Mr. Smith, I hate asking you this, but will you please take a closer look back at the bodies? You might be able to recognize at least one of them."

Layne stepped to one of the bodies, knelt, and examined what was left of the man's face. Unable to recognize him, he stood, shook his head, and went to the next one. He caught sight of a gold watch partially hidden beneath the dead man's body. Pulling it free, Layne turned the timepiece over and read the inscription on the back.

"What does it say?" Watts asked.

"To my son Harold on his twenty-first birthday." Layne handed the watch to Watts. "It's Chamberlain's. I've seen it before."

"Now we have the proof we need," the agent remarked, slipping the watch into his pocket.

Layne forced himself to look back at the mutilated corpse. It was Chamberlain's weight and size. The man had been scalped, his face disfigured. Stepping away from the body, Layne mumbled, "The poor bastard. What a helluva way to die."

"Your sympathy surprises me, considering the man murdered your father."

Layne didn't want to waste time discussing Chamberlain or his father. "Watts, let's get the hell out of here. My fiancée and my friends might be in danger."

The agent told his men to get the two shovels off the pack horse and start digging the graves. Then turning to Layne, he said, "Mr. Smith, it's a long ride back to the wagon. Our horses won't make it without rest. Also, we need rest ourselves, and food and coffee. We'll set up camp a good distance from this place, then after sufficient rest, we'll be on our way."

Layne's jaw clenched tightly, and his dark eyes narrowed. "You're right on one account, the horses need rest. But Watts, you can forget a hot supper and coffee. You light a fire, and you might as well send those Comanches a written invitation to dinner. We'll rest the horses for an hour, eat cold jerky, then be on our way."

"Whatever you say, Mr. Smith. You know more about these matters than I do. You seem quite worried. Do you think there's a chance the Comanches will attack your friends?"

"Your guess is as good as mine," Layne mumbled.

"The . . . the women," Watts began haltingly, "will the Comanches kill them . . . mutilate them?"

"I don't know, dammit!" Layne raged, his fear getting the best of him. "They might, but then again they might decide to abduct 'em!" He walked to his horse, grabbed its reins, and led it to the top of the hill. His thoughts were filled with Selina and the others, and he watched vaguely as Watts and his deputies dug the shallow graves.

Layne silently berated himself for leaving with Watts. His place was with Selina and the others and, dammit, that's where he should be!

"Selina!" he moaned. "If anything happens to you, I'll never forgive myself!" His deep voice breaking with emotion, he uttered desperately, "Oh God, I shouldn't have left her! . . . I shouldn't have left!"

The roving band of Comanches, having wreaked vengeance across the territory, were now ready to return to the Great Plains. Their last massacre had sated their thirst for blood and evened the score.

Chief Sleeping Wolf, his face streaked with warpaint, rode in front of his warriors. Revenge had brought him a measure of satisfaction, and his expression was somewhat content. But as his thoughts wandered back, intense hatred flickered in his black eyes. In vivid detail he relived the day the white soldiers had invaded his village. Most of his warriors had been away on a hunting trip, and the village had been vulnerable. The soldiers had killed at will, even murdering women and children. Some of his people, himself included, had managed to flee to the hills and escape.

Now, as he looked at the young man riding at his side, worry replaced the hate in his eyes. His son,

Lone Elk, had lost his wife during the massacre, and his taste for revenge was still not sated.

"Father," Lone Elk said, "I have decided to ride alone."

"It is too dangerous. The spirits have shown us signs which tell us that the bluecoats are close by. They are looking for us."

"Let them look!" the young man grunted. "They will not find me!"

Sleeping Wolf was reluctant to let his son leave, but he knew he couldn't dissuade him. Once Lone Elk's mind was made up, there was no changing it. "You will be careful, my son?"

"Yes, Father."

"When can I expect to see you again?"

"The white-eyes have taken my woman, now I will take one of theirs. I will not come home until I have her."

"You would take a white woman as a wife!" his father exclaimed.

A murderous rage distorted Lone Elk's face. "No, I do not want her as a wife!"

"Then why do you want the woman?"

"I will bring her to our village, and there I will kill her for all to see. I will avenge my wife's death by taking the white woman's life. I want our people and the spirits to watch as I carry out my vengeance."

"Then, my son, will your revenge be complete?"

"It will be complete, my Father."

"That is good. Go, Lone Elk, and may the spirits keep you safe."

He bellowed a furious war cry, then turning his pony about, he galloped past the other warriors.

263

The Comanches watched as Lone Elk faded farther and farther into the distance. When he had ridden out of sight, Sleeping Wolf asked the spirits to watch over his son.

The chief and his braves urged their horses onward. Dusk had fallen, and the landscape was growing so dark that Sleeping Wolf decided to stop for the night.

Knowing it was too risky to light a fire, the Indians ate a cold meal, then went to sleep in their blankets. The two warriors standing guard, dozing from utter fatigue, never heard the two army scouts who slipped up behind them and slit their throats. The scouts then returned to their commander, telling him it was safe to attack the Indians' camp.

Sleeping Wolf and his warriors were awakened by the thundering of charging horses. The chief barely had time to leap to his feet before a bullet slammed into his chest, killing him instantly. The soldiers, ordered to take no captives, continued firing until every warrior was dead.

Meanwhile, Lone Elk, now miles away, had decided to ride through the night. He wondered how long he would search before finding a white woman. He hoped it wouldn't take too long, for he was anxious to avenge his wife. He longed for retribution.

Twenty

Janet wasn't sure what had awakened her, and sitting up on her pallet, she looked about the moon-lit wagon. Everyone seemed to be sleeping soundly. Deciding she had awakened for no apparent reason, she was about to lie back down when a coyote's eerie howl sounded across the plains. She supposed the animal's wailing had disturbed her.

Now fully awake, Janet wondered what time it was. She knew that Floyd had the second watch, and she was tempted to sneak outside and see if he was standing guard. Since that night when Floyd had kissed her, she hadn't been alone with him. They talked often, and when he drove the wagon, she always sat beside him. But Janet was becoming bored with just talking, and she longed to be in Floyd's embrace again. That she had responded passionately to Doug's kiss was a fact that she had managed to bury far in the recesses of her mind. She considered him far beneath her, and quite plain looking. Janet couldn't imagine becoming romantically involved with Doug Thompson.

Leaving her bed, she put on her robe and slippers. She would check and see if Floyd was standing guard. She moved slowly toward the fire that by now had burned down to glowing embers. The full moon, effulgent in the cloudless sky, afforded Janet light to scan the area.

She saw Floyd standing a short distance from camp. She glanced over her shoulder, checking Doug's whereabouts; he was asleep in his bedroll, close to the wagon. She stepped stealthily toward Floyd.

Miller, hearing footsteps, swiftly drew his pistol and spun about. Seeing Janet, he holstered his gun as a large smile spread across his face. He was sure he knew her reason for coming to him. The little bitch was ready to spread her legs. Well, it was about time!

Janet was about to speak, but he lifted his hand in a silencing gesture. He was perfectly aware that Thompson was a light sleeper. Motioning for her to follow, he led her farther away from camp, and coming upon an isolated boulder, he leaned against it and folded his arms across his chest.

Janet's desirable curves were silhouetted beneath her flimsy nightdress, and Floyd's eyes raked over her boldly.

He grinned confidently. "I knew that one of these nights you'd come to me."

He moved away from the boulder, reached for her and pulled her into his arms. Holding her flush against his hard frame, he murmured huskily, "I'm on fire for you, darlin'. Don't you realize how badly I want you? You've totally bewitched me."

Janet slipped her arms about his neck. "You wouldn't trifle with my affections, would you?"

Miller, gritting his teeth, held back a snapping retort. He had no patience with Janet's coquetry and was tempted to order her back to the wagon. Why waste time playing her silly game? After he kidnapped her, she would be his for the taking. Her closeness, however, had him sexually aroused, and he didn't relish being left unfulfilled. He'd kiss her a few times, whisper sweet nonsense in her ear; but if that didn't work, then to hell with her! She could damn well return to the wagon with her virtue still intact!

"Floyd?" she whispered, finding his silence confusing. "Is something wrong?"

"No," he replied. "I was just thinking of how much I love you."

"Love me?" she asked with pleasure. "Floyd, I had no idea you felt this way."

"I adore you," he declared throatily. His lips descended to hers, his kiss well practiced and full of passion.

Janet steeled herself for the tide of pleasure she was sure would carry her away; to her disappointment, Floyd's kiss evoked only a lukewarm response.

Frustrated, she was about to push out of his arms when all at once there was a thudding sound. Floyd's body grew lax, and he pulled her down as he fell to the ground. She landed on top of him; but before she had time to realize what was happening, a large hand grasped her hair, jerking her to her feet.

Pressing her back against his naked chest, Lone Elk threatened gruffly, "Scream, white woman, and I cut out your tongue!"

He roughly turned her around so that she was facing him. Staring frightfully up into his hideously painted face, Janet gasped weakly. Her knees buckled, and as she fainted, the warrior caught her in his arms. Slinging her limp body over his shoulder, he carried her past the boulder and to his waiting pony. Throwing her face down across the animal's back, he leapt up behind her, turned his horse, and urged it into a loping run. The quiet campsite was soon far behind.

He had successfully stolen his white woman. Soon now, he would fully avenge his wife's death. This woman would die, and he'd take great pleasure in killing her!

Above the horizon rose a blurred, red-fire sun, its dazzling rays bringing Doug instantly awake. Why the hell had Floyd let him sleep so late? Dammit! He had told Miller to wake him at first light.

Throwing off the top blanket, Doug slipped on his boots, then bounded to his feet in a rage, grabbed his rifle, and went in search of Miller. Finding footprints left in the dust, Doug quickly figured out what had happened. During the night Janet had obviously come to Floyd, and they had slipped away from camp.

His rage now at fever pitch, Doug charged forward. When he told Miller to stand guard, that's what he expected him to do! Didn't the man have enough sense to realize that clandestine meetings with Janet placed them all in danger?

Doug was working himself into a furious frenzy when he spotted Miller's prone body beside the small boulder. He knelt beside Floyd. The man was breathing evenly, and Doug drew him into a sitting position.

Floyd grimaced with pain as his hand went to the back of his head. He felt a large knot, surrounded by dried, sticky blood. "Wh . . . what happened?" he moaned.

"Why don't you tell me?" Doug growled.

Floyd, his head throbbing, tried to search his memory. His mind was hazy, though, and it took a moment for him to remember. "Last night Janet and I came here to be alone. While I was kissin' her, someone must've knocked me over the head."

Doug jumped up, and moving with desperate speed, he rushed back to the wagon and called loudly. Janet! Selina, is Janet in there?"

Selina had been sleeping soundly, but Doug's blustering voice woke her with a start.

"Is Janet in there?" he called again.

"No!" Selina cried, finding Janet's pallet empty. The others were now awake. They dressed quickly and hurried from the wagon.

"What's happening?" Selina asked Doug.

"Ask him," Thompson remarked tersely. He nodded at Floyd, who was coming toward them.

Doug brushed past Miller and returned to the spot where Janet had been abducted. Examining the site and a short way beyond, he read the tracks Lone Elk and his pony had left behind. Fear for Janet's life had his heart pounding as he hastened back to camp.

Floyd was asking Selina to wash the clotted blood from his hair when Doug, his strides long and angry, reached his side.

Grasping Miller's arm, he swung him around. Doug's fist, moving with a blurring speed, delivered a plow-driving blow to the man's jaw. The powerful impact sent Miller sprawling to the ground. Bending over him, Doug clutched his shirt collar and jerked him back to his feet. He was about to hit him again, but Selina's hand on his arm impeded him.

"Doug, no!" she shouted. "Beating Floyd isn't going to help Janet!"

"Maybe not, but it'll sure give me a lot of pleasure!" Stifling his rage, he simply shoved Miller; but the unexpected push took the man off balance, and he fell awkwardly to the ground.

Turning to Selina and the others, Doug said with a calm he was far from feeling, "Janet's been kidnapped by a Comanche warrior."

"Oh God!" Selina cried. "Doug, are you sure?"

"I know a Comanche's tracks when I see 'em. I've trailed 'em too many times."

"Listen!" Stella interrupted. "Someone's coming!"

The sounds of approaching horses drew closer, and as the riders came into sight, Selina ran forth to greet the man riding in the lead.

Dismounting swiftly, Layne swept her into his arms and hugged her as though he never intended to let her go.

"Layne," Selina began anxiously, leaving his embrace with reluctance, "Janet's been abducted!"

Layne looked over at Doug, his gaze questioning, then noticed Floyd getting clumsily to his feet. "What the hell's goin' on?"

Indicating Floyd with a jerk of his head, Doug answered angrily, "This stupid ass was supposed to be standin' guard last night, but instead he was seducin' Janet! A Comanche warrior slipped up on 'em, knocked Miller unconscious, and took off with

Janet!"

"Damn!" Layne cursed grimly.

Watts and his men were still mounted, and the agent said loudly, "Mr. Smith, I hate to interrupt."

"Then don't!" Layne grumbled.

Deciding to ignore his curt remark, Watts proceeded, "I must continue on to New Orleans. I'm sure you understand that my superiors are anxiously awaiting my report."

You aren't goin' anywhere, except to Dry River," Layne remarked flatly.

Watts was annoyed. "I don't take orders from you, Mr. Smith!"

"There's a good possibility that we're surrounded by hostile Comanches. Our best chance for survival is to stay together. I'm sure you're aware that there's safety in numbers."

"I suppose you're right," Watts relented, somewhat sheepishly. "How far away is Dry River?"

"Two day's ride."

"Very well," the agent replied, getting down from his horse. "My men and I will accompany you."

Dismissing Watts, Layne turned back to Doug. "When you and the others get to Dry River, wait five days. If I'm not back by then, leave without me."

Selina grasped Layne's arm, exclaiming, "Are you going after Janet?"

It was Doug who answered, "No, he's not. I am."

"She's my responsibility," Layne argued.

"But she was abducted while under my care," Doug countered. "It's my place to go after her." He cast Floyd a shrewd glance. "Unless, of course, Miller wants to volunteer."

271

Floyd had been rubbing his bruised jaw, but at Thompson's remark, he quickly shifted his hand to the back of his head. Massaging it gently, he said hesitantly, "I'd sure like to look for Janet but . . . but I think that Comanche gave me . . . I mean I'm kinda dizzy and . . . and my vision's even blurred." He wasn't about to get himself killed rescuing Janet.

Floyd stalked to the fire and poured a cup of coffee. Damn it to hell! Now with Janet gone, there would be no ransom! As his gaze went to Doug, a sudden smile curled his lips. Surely the crazy son of a bitch didn't think he could rescue Janet! His mission was suicidal! Miller laughed under his breath. He didn't have to worry about killing Thompson; the Comanches would do it for him!

Doug asked Selina to pack provisions, and some clothes for Janet. As she was complying, Layne accompanied Doug to his horse.

"How many hours headstart does the warrior have?" Layne asked.

"Four, maybe five."

"If he and Janet are riding double, it'll slow 'em down."

"I checked his tracks; there's only one horse."

"We found Chamberlain and his men. They were massacred by Comanches. If this warrior is with that band, and if he catches up to them, rescuing Janet will be impossible. We'll have to ask the army for assistance."

Doug heaved a deep, distressful sigh. "God, I keep tryin' not to think of what Janet's goin' through. She must be scared to death." His eyes bore meaningfully into Layne's. "I've got to catch up to her before that warrior does anything!"

Layne placed a consoling hand on Thompson's shoulder. "I still think it's my duty to go after Janet, but I'm not arguing with you. I know how you feel about her. If it was Selina. . . ."

"I know," Doug answered softly.

At that moment Selina and Stella walked up to them. Handing Doug his supplies, she asked, "Aren't you taking a horse for Janet?"

"Leading another horse will slow me down. I've got to move fast."

Stella gave Doug a small carpetbag. "Janet's clothes are inside." She watched as he attached the bag to his saddle, then she stepped forward and hugged him. "We'll all be praying for you."

His smile, though weak, was encouraging. "I'll be back, and I'll have Janet with me."

"We'll wait for you in Dry River," Layne said.

"Don't wait longer than five days," Doug replied. "If I don't show up by then — well, you may as well move on."

Layne shook his friend's hand firmly, his strong grasp reluctant to let go. "See ya," he mumbled quietly, hoping that he would indeed see him again.

Selina then embraced Doug tightly. "May God keep you and Janet safe," she murmured tearfully.

The three watched silently as Thompson mounted, waved, then rode out of camp. When he was no longer in sight, Selina asked Layne, "What are his chances?"

"It all depends. If that warrior's alone, Doug's chances are better than average. But if the warrior's riding with others, then it doesn't look good."

Stella started to move away, but Layne stopped

273

her. "Wait. I have something to tell you both. We found Chamberlain and his men. They were killed by Comanches."

"Harold's dead?" Selina gasped in shock.

Layne nodded.

At first Stella was too stunned to respond. Then as tears burned her eyes, she said weakly, "I can hardly believe it."

"I didn't think you'd actually grieve for the no-account bastard," Layne remarked, his tone somewhat hard.

"Oh, these ain't tears of sorrow, they're tears of relief! My son's safe! That monster can't threaten Paul ever again!" She grasped Selina's hands, saying joyfully, "Now, I don't have to go to Kansas! I can get a job and stay in Passing Through. I don't have to leave my two best friends, you and. . . ." Thinking of Janet, her jubilation plunged.

"Doug will save Janet!" Selina said strongly. "I just know he will!"

"You know," Stella murmured sadly, "I already miss her. Janet can be exasperating at times, but I can't help but like her. I like her a lot."

"So do I," Selina replied.

"I best go tell Hattie 'bout Chamberlain. I know it ain't . . . I mean, I know it isn't right to rejoice over a person's death, but all the same, Hattie's gonna be mighty glad."

Layne smiled warmly as he watched her hurrying away. "I've noticed considerable improvement in Stella. You and Janet must be good teachers."

"Stella's an excellent student. She really wants to learn."

Drawing her close, he lowered his lips to hers and

kissed her. "I was so worried about you," he whispered. "There's a band of Comanches somewhere in the vicinity, and they're out for blood. I have a feelin' they don't care whose blood is spilled, as long as it's white man's blood. We'd better eat breakfast, break camp, and get moving. I won't rest easy until we reach Dry River."

He tugged at her arm, but she drew back.

"Layne, if we're attacked, I want you to give me a rifle."

He grinned amusedly. "Sweetheart, you and the other women will be busy reloading guns. Besides, shootin' a rifle takes more skill then shootin' that little derringer of yours.

"But Layne . . ." she began, intending to explain that she was an accurate shot with a rifle.

"Not now, darlin'," he said, cutting her off. "Let's get breakfast over with so we can get out of here." He draped an arm about her shoulders.

As he ushered her to the campfire, she was bristling inwardly. If they were attacked by Indians, she'd be damned if she'd reload! She was about to make this point quite clear to Layne, but then decided to let the matter rest for now.

Selina was confident that she could shoot a rifle as well as any man present; Layne Smith included!

Twenty-one

Lone Elk's spirits were high as he swung down from his pony. His captive was still draped facedown across his horse; and he reached up and slung her to the ground. The impact was so hard that it almost forced the breath from Janet's lungs. She lay crumpled, too frightened to move.

The warrior's moccasined foot jabbed into her ribs. "Get up, white woman!" When his demand wasn't immediately obeyed, he clutched a handful of her long blond hair and drew her painfully to her feet. Entangling his fingers into her thick tresses, he jerked her head backward and leered down into her fear-glazed eyes. "Do as I say, or I kill you!"

Janet wanted to look away from him, but her eyes seemed to have a will of their own. He was too hideous, too frightening to gaze upon, yet she was helpless to turn away. Red paint was streaked across his dark face, and his long hair was an unruly black mane falling to his shoulders. A bow and quiver were slung across his naked chest, and a sheathed knife and tomahawk were tied about his waist. His short, muscular legs were encased in fringed leather leggings.

Janet's eyes widened as the warrior unfastened his leggings and whipped out his manhood. For a fleeting moment she feared rape, but when he began instead to empty his bladder, she quickly turned her back. Facing the pony, she rested her arm on its side and pillowed her head. Heaving sobs shook her body, but she was too terrified to cry.

"Oh Doug!" she moaned, her voice rasping. "Please! Please find me!"

"Your man not find you," Lone Elk remarked.

Janet, unaware that she had spoken aloud, whirled about with surprise.

The warrior continued, "From this point on I cover our tracks. No white man can trail." He spit onto the ground, emphasizing his hatred for white people. "White man too . . ." he paused as he tried to think of the right word, "he too stupid to track Comanche warrior."

Janet thought otherwise. Doug was no ordinary white man, he was part Apache. But would he come for her? Why should he? She'd made her feelings quite clear, she had spurned him at every opportunity, had even refused his friendship. A terrible foreboding washed over her, drowning all hopes of rescue. More than likely, Doug felt that she had gotten what she deserved. If she had been inside the wagon where she belonged, this couldn't have happened.

Janet's thoughts raced onward to Floyd Miller. He had said that he loved her! Her hopes suddenly resurfaced. She didn't need Doug; Floyd would rescue her!

As Janet was hoping for Miller's rescue, Lone

Elk's feral eyes were measuring his captive. The woman's flimsy nightwear did little to conceal her ripe, desirable curves, and for an instant, Lone Elk was tempted to throw her to the ground and take her forcefully. With great effort he managed to resist such temptation. This woman was not for pleasure but was a means for revenge. Through her he'd seek retribution; his wife's death would be fully avenged, and the score would be evened. Hereafter, the bluecoats would not be so hasty to attack a Comanche village, for they would know that the consequences were too severe.

"We must leave," Lone Elk grumbled. "When I cover tracks, nothing can be left for white man to find. You need to go now, or you hold it till sun far in sky."

Janet pointed to a clump of sagebrush. "I'll step over there for privacy."

Lone Elk laughed derisively. "You lift gown and go here!"

"No!" Janet cried, her cheeks reddening.

Ready to leave, Lone Elk said harshly, "Then get on pony. You ride, I walk. When I finish covering tracks, I then ride and you walk. It is many days' ride to my village, you walk the whole way. You fall, I drag you behind pony."

Janet glanced down at her dainty slippers. They wouldn't last two hours, let alone days.

"Get on pony!" he barked, stepping toward her.

She turned to the horse. There was no saddle, and how was she to mount without stirrups? She didn't have long to ponder the query, for Lone Elk's large hands suddenly were around her waist. The strength in his sinewy arms lifted her easily onto the pony's back.

Janet's hands were trembling as she laced the braided reins through her fingers, and her heart was pounding. She could hardly believe the warrior was making escape so easy. The savage must be a complete fool! Did he think she was too incompetent to handle a horse? Or did he think she was too scared to make a run for it? Well, he was wrong on both accounts!

Her small feet thrust strongly into the pony's sides, the unexpected jab causing the beast to break with a bolt. The horse's fast-moving legs had taken only a couple of strides when Lone Elk's sharp whistle sounded clearly.

Hearing its master's command, the pony stopped so abruptly that it reared up on its back legs. Janet, having nothing to hold onto, slid off the animal's back and fell heavily to the ground.

Lone Elk trotted to her side, grasped her arm, and drew her up onto her feet. He struck her face with the flat of his hand, the hard blow sending her stumbling backward.

"Try to escape again, white woman, and I kill you now!" Grabbing her roughly, he lifted her back onto the pony.

Janet's cheek stung from his vicious slap, and as she rubbed it gingerly, she dared to ask, "What do you mean, kill me now? Is it your plan to kill me later?" She was almost too terrified to listen to his response.

"I kill you in my village where my father, Sleeping Wolf, my people, and the spirits will gather to

279

watch."

"But why?" she cried wretchedly. "I've never done anything to you! Why do you want to kill me?"

"The soldiers kill my wife, now I kill you!" he answered ruthlessly.

Janet, numb with fear, watched as he hastened to the sagebrush, broke off a large portion, and returned. He slapped his hand against the pony's flank, and it moved out at a steady, unhurried pace. Trailing, Lone Elk brushed the full-leafed shrub back and forth across the ground, the sweeping motion destroying all tell-tale signs of their passing.

Tracking the warrior and Janet was childsplay for Doug. The signs were easy to find, too easy. He knew that the Comanche, more concerned with distance, was deliberately leaving a discernible trail. Doug was sure that as soon as the warrior had decided it was safe to travel at a slower pace, he'd start covering his tracks.

When Doug rode up to the area where Lone Elk and Janet had stopped, the sun was directly overhead and its intense rays were scorching the landscape.

He rubbed a hand over his brow; it was dripping with perspiration. He dismounted and then uncapped his canteen to take a long drink. He filled his hat with water, then stepped to his horse and offered it a drink.

As the animal quenched its thirst, Doug wondered how Janet was holding up. Traveling in this intense heat was difficult for a toughened veteran;

for a delicate woman like Janet it had to be exhausting. Shading his eyes, he glanced upward, hoping to spot an approaching cloud coverage. The sky, however, was clear as far as the eye could see. The horse had finished drinking, and as Doug replaced his hat, he imagined Janet riding bareheaded across the sun-bathed land. Would she succumb to a heatstroke? A wave of worry came over him, for he knew the possibility was very likely.

Stepping away from the horse, Doug moved slowly, carefully, over the area, his experienced eye missing nothing. Kneeling beside the sagebrush, he noticed immediately that a portion of it was gone. He brushed his fingers lightly across the broken stem, then he gazed toward the north. Distant foothills rose above the far horizon; over and beyond them lay Comanche territory.

Doug returned to his horse and mounted. Following Janet and the warrior was no longer easy. He knew the Comanche had taken the broken shrub to sweep away their tracks. Hereafter, he'd have to search keenly for signs. He knew they would be few and far between, and for the most part, he'd have to follow on instinct alone.

Urging his horse forward, he started north. The warrior was undoubtedly heading for Comanche territory; however, the plains leading to the distant hills were vast, and there was no direct route. That Doug could lose Janet and the Comanche in the widespread land was a distinct possibility. Also, if he didn't catch them before they reached the hills, Janet might be lost forever, for there were too many passages across the hills and into the Comanche lands.

Janet tripped and fell, and as her body hit the ground, she cried out with pain. Her hands were tied in front of her, and there had been no way for her to break her fall.

Lone Elk, mounted on his pony, heard her cry. Reining in, he turned and looked down at her. He was holding the long end of the rope that was tied about her wrists, and jerking on it, he grumbled, "Get up, white woman! Now—or I drag you!"

Clumsily, her tired body aching, Janet managed to stand. She stared hopelessly down at her shoes. The fragile slippers were torn, ragged, and afforded her feet little protection.

Lone Elk sent his pony into a loping walk, and Janet had to run to keep up. The hot sun shone down on her mercilessly, its blazing rays reddening her exposed flesh.

She had been afoot now for over an hour, and as she labored to keep from falling, she knew she'd soon succumb to the unbearable heat and the exhausting pace. Her strength and endurance were failing rapidly, and as tears ran down her dirt-smudged face, she prayed that Floyd would soon find her.

Lone Elk brought his horse to a halt so suddenly that Janet's momentum sent her crashing against the animal's flank. The unexpected impact caused her to lose her balance, and she dropped to the ground. Afraid that the Indian would urge his pony onward and drag her behind, she forced herself to get back up. Her tired legs could barely support her, and as she looked up at Lone Elk, her body swayed unsteadily. The warrior was sitting rigidly, his feral eyes darting over the quiet landscape.

Watching him, she sensed that he was listening intently. But listening to what? There were no sounds.

Lone Elk, knowing something was amiss, grew cautious as he nudged his horse into a slow walk. Why was the land so still? Not even a bird's chirping could be heard. A summer's breeze suddenly stirred, its gentle force carrying the smell of blood to Lone Elk's nostrils. Had there been a battle, and had its violence frightened away the surrounding wildlife?

Keeping his pony moving in a straight path, Lone Elk's acute vision suddenly spotted bodies in the distance. Pulling up, he told Janet to mount up behind him. The instant she had done so, he broke his horse into a fast gallop.

A hard fist of fear grew in the warrior's stomach as he drew closer to the bodies he had recognized as those of his own people. Reaching the death-ridden area, he brought his horse to a sudden stop, then slid off its back, his moccasined feet touching the ground soundlessly.

Janet, her stomach queasy, stared wide-eyed at the dead Indians. There were at least a dozen of them, their bullet-riddled bodies sprawled beside their blankets.

Apparently, they had been asleep when attacked and were killed before they had time to defend themselves. Janet wondered if soldiers were responsible and, if so, were they still in the vicinity? If she were to escape, could she possibly find them?

She turned her gaze discreetly to Lone Elk. He was seated and was embracing one of the dead Indians. Cradling the body as though it were still alive, he was rocking back and forth, moaning woefully.

Lone Elk's grief seemed to have his full concentration, and deciding to take advantage of the moment, Janet took the pony's reins into her hands. She turned the horse around and was about to sneak away when, thunderously, Lone Elk shouted, "Stop, white woman!"

Janet considered slapping the reins against the pony's neck and making a run for it. But she knew the gesture would prove futile. The warrior would simply whistle, and his horse would stop dead in its tracks.

She didn't wait for Lone Elk to jerk her off the horse. Instead, sparing herself his brutality, she dismounted and watched as he came to her side.

Grabbing the rope restraining her wrists, Lone Elk pulled her to a cottonwood. He freed one of her hands, then wrapped her arms about the tree's trunk. He then tied her securely embracing the cottonwood. The rough bark scraped her face, and she tried to move back a little, but he had her tied flush to the trunk. She couldn't budge so much as an inch.

The warrior was in her line of vision, and she watched as he returned to the dead Indian and took him back into his arms.

Holding dearly to Sleeping Wolf, Lone Elk expressed his sorrow with deep, mournful sobs. He blamed himself for his father's death. He should never have left him. If he had been present, he would have known the bluecoats were close by. He was a much better warrior than Sleeping Wolf and the others. The soldiers could never have slipped up on him! If he hadn't been so intent on taking a white woman to his father's village, then Sleeping Wolf would still be alive! Had his plan to spill the woman's blood on Comanche grounds angered the spirits?

He hugged his father's lifeless form even closer. He knew that he must pacify the spirits and kill the white woman, but for now he was too racked with grief to do anything but mourn his father.

The cottonwood's full, sweeping branches afforded Janet protection against the sun's burning rays. Although the tree's shade was a comfort, its bark-roughened trunk chafed her face and irritated her eyes. She longed to sit down, but the way she was tied made sitting impossible. Her shoulders ached from having her arms wrapped about the cotton-wood, and a dull pain was pinpointed in her lower back.

Hours passed as Janet waited wearily for the warrior to untie her. She wondered if the dead Indian he was mourning was his father and, if so, would he take her life to appease his grief? He had said that he would kill her in his village, but had he now changed his mind?

She felt so fatigued and dejected that she almost

wished he would kill her now and get it over with. However, there was still a spark of hope flickering in her heart; maybe Floyd would soon find her! Surely this delay had given him time to catch up to them.

Lone Elk decided it was time to kill the white woman. He left his dead father and got to his feet in anger. His hatred for white people had now climbed to a raging apex. They had destroyed his family and were intent on destroying his way of life. From this moment on he would dedicate himself to killing not only soldiers but any white person who crossed his path. He'd show no mercy, and gather many scalps and hang them proudly in his tepee for all to see and admire. His ruthless killings would make him famous, and his name would be feared by the whites; praised by the Comanches!

Bolstered by his dreams of recognition, Lone Elk walked briskly to Janet and untied her.

A pain shot through her strained shoulders as she lowered her arms to her sides. Her legs were wobbly and could barely support her weight. Afraid she might collapse, she leaned back against the tree's trunk. Wishing to avoid the warrior's hideous face, she kept her eyes downcast.

"White woman, look at me!" he snapped harshly.

She raised her gaze and met his cold stare unwaveringly. An icy chill ran up her spine as she read her own death reflected in the black depths of his hate-filled eyes.

"Oh God!" she moaned pathetically. "God, please help me!"

Janet looked on as Lone Elk unsheathed his

knife. His fingers stroked the weapon's sharp blade, the movement a gentle caress.

He turned his eyes back to Janet, and as his gaze admired her long, golden tresses, he uttered huskily, "White woman's hair the color of sun. I not hang scalp in tepee, but carry it on my knife."

"Please!" she cried tearfully. "Kill me quickly! Don't . . . don't make me suffer!"

"You die slowly!" he growled. Moving as quick as a striking snake, he grasped a handful of her hair, swung her around, and threw her to the ground. Standing over her, knife in hand, he said in a stoical, determined manner, "I make many cuts, you bleed much, then I watch as life leaves your body."

A scream rose in her throat, but she was too numb with terror to release it. Fear, like a hot torch burning into her stomach, doubled her over, and rolling to her side, she curled up into a fetal position. Too frightened to move, she waited with heart-stopping horror for the knife's first plunge into her flesh.

Suddenly a thunderous explosion resounded, but Janet's paralyzed mind failed to recognize it as a rifle shot. When Lone Elk's lifeless body fell over hers, she was too dazed to push it away.

The warrior's dead weight was jerked from her as though it were feather-light, and a pair of strong arms lifted her from the ground. Gazing into her rescuer's familiar face, she cried weakly, "Doug!"

Keeping her in his powerful embrace, he carried her past the dead Indians to his horse. As her arms wrapped tightly about his neck, he murmured soothingly, "You're safe, little one. Don't cry, sweetheart," he whispered, cradling her tenderly. He kissed her tear-streaked cheek. "I'm here now, and I'll never let anyone hurt you."

Twenty-two

Doug and Janet were miles away from the death-ridden scene before Thompson pulled up his horse. Janet had fallen asleep cradled against his chest, and he nudged her gently. "Wake up, little one."

Her eyes popped open immediately, and for a moment she was disoriented. She sat up stiffly, her face pale with an expression of stark terror.

"It's all right," Doug murmured soothingly. "You're safe, remember?"

"Oh Doug!" she cried, snuggling back against his wide, comforting chest. "For a moment I thought . . . !"

"I know," he whispered.

Relaxing, she asked, "Why are we stopping?"

"It'll be dark soon, and this looks like a good place to spend the night."

She gave their surroundings a cursory glance. The verdant landscape was interspersed with cottonwoods and mesquites, and nestled among the trees were clumps of sagebrush and wild barberry bushes.

Doug dismounted, then lifted Janet from the horse. He carried her to an area bordered on all sides by dense brush and trees. He put her down beneath a cottonwood. "Selina and Stella packed some clothes for you. I'll get 'em."

He started to leave, but Janet grasped his arm. "Doug, is Floyd all right?"

"Miller's fine," he muttered tersely.

"Then why isn't he with you?"

Doug didn't answer; he simply moved away, returned to his horse, grabbed Janet's bag and brought it to her. "Here. You can step into the bushes and change clothes while I start a fire."

"Isn't a fire dangerous? There might be more Indians lurking about."

"They're all dead," he mumbled flatly. With that, he walked off.

Janet noticed that he moved with unusual grace for a man so tall and muscularly built. He was strong; and yes, she admitted, Doug Thompson was impressive indeed! She supposed a man didn't have to be classically handsome to be attractive. There was a rugged quality about him that was savagely sensual, an aura inherited no doubt from his Apache ancestors.

She wondered why Doug had reacted so curtly when she'd mentioned Floyd. Was he hiding something? Was Floyd seriously injured, dead perhaps? No, she decided quickly. Doug was just being stubborn; he wasn't about to discuss someone he didn't like.

Taking her bag, she stepped into the brush and removed her torn, soiled nightwear, then slipped into her trousers and shirt. Carrying her socks and boots, she emerged from the bushes and went to the small fire, where Doug was fixing a pot of coffee.

She sat down and took off her ragged slippers.

The bottoms had worn through in places, and her feet were bruised and cut. She moved a hand to her face. Sunburn! she thought glumly. Continuing her examination, she ran her fingers through her tangled, unruly tresses. Emitting a deep, wretched sigh, she groaned, "I must look a sight! I'm certainly glad Melody Harper can't see me." She slipped the socks over her aching feet.

Doug moved over and sat beside her. "Who's Melody Harper?"

"We've been good friends since we were children. She's married now." Janet eased her feet into the boots, then continued, "Before I left, Melody asked me if I wasn't scared that I might be captured by Indians."

"What did you say?"

"I told her that it might be exciting." Without forethought, she slipped her small hand into Doug's large one, squeezed tightly and remarked, "Oh Doug, I was so foolish!"

"You've changed a lot since we left New Orleans."

"Maybe I'm starting to grow up." She smiled timidly, and her sweet vulnerability touched Doug's heart. "You know," she went on, "I haven't even thanked you for saving my life. It seems every time I'm in trouble, you're there to rescue me."

"Like a faithful watchdog?"

"I should never have called you that. I've said a lot of things to you that I wish I could take back, but I can't. All I can do is ask you to forgive me."

He placed a hand under her chin, tilting her face up to his. Gazing down into her emerald-green eyes, he murmured, "Janet Wilkerson, you're beautiful."

"How can you say I'm beautiful? My face is sun-burned and dirty and my hair is a mess. I know I must look. . . ."

He put a finger to her lips, silencing her. "I said, you're beautiful. Don't argue with me, little one." He wanted to kiss her, but fearing rejection, he held himself in check.

Mesmerized by his dark, gentle eyes, Janet wondered if she was about to be kissed. When Doug turned his face away, she was surprised to find that she was disappointed. She was also confused. She harbored no romantic feelings for Doug, he was merely — well, he was merely a friend. So why had she desired his kiss?

"I guess I'd better start supper," Doug remarked, interrupting her puzzled thoughts.

"I'll cook supper," she offered.

Her willingness impressed him. She certainly wasn't the same lazy, spoiled, selfish girl who had left New Orleans. He grinned warmly. "Why don't we both cook supper?"

Her green eyes sparkled mischievously. "A marvelous suggestion, Mr. Thompson. What, pray tell, is on the menu?"

"Bacon and beans." He stood, bowed from the waist, then offered her a hand. "Madam?"

Accepting his assistance, she got gracefully to her feet. "If you'll be so kind as to fry the bacon, I'll heat the beans. Then following dinner, we can relax over a glass of sherry."

He pretended great consternation. "I'm sorry, my dear, but I forgot to replenish our sherry supply.

But we do have some whiskey."

"Whiskey? My goodness, I suppose it'll have to do." She giggled merrily.

Doug thought he detected a warm intimacy in her humor, and it added fuel to his simmering love, fanning it into a blazing flame.

"Riders are coming!" Watts's deputy announced, hurrying into camp. He had been standing guard a short way from the campsite.

Everyone was gathered about the fire, and as Watts and Layne leaped up simultaneously, the agent asked his man, "Comanches?"

"No, sir."

"How many riders?" Layne wanted to know.

"Around eight, maybe ten."

Taking his rifle with him, Layne moved away from the fire and to the edge of camp. Watts followed close behind. As the horsemen came into sight, Layne handed his rifle to Watts and stepped forward to greet the man riding in the lead. As he watched the visitor dismount, his body grew taut, and anxiety gnawed at his stomach. Dreading telling this man about his daughter, he swallowed heavily.

Grabbing Layne's hand and shaking it firmly, Bart Wilkerson said heartily, "I'm sure glad to find you safe and sound. There's a hostile band of Comanches wreaking havoc. That's why I decided to ride out and look for you."

Before Smith could reply, a soft, sultry voice called his name, "Layne?"

He was astounded to see Jessie Harte getting down from her horse. Layne's full concentration had been centered on Bart, causing him to miss seeing Jessie.

Selina was walking over to join Layne when the young woman moved away from her horse and flung herself into Layne's arms. Taken aback, Selina paused, her eyes glued to the embracing couple.

"Oh Layne!" Jessie exclaimed, clinging to him. "I was so worried about you! Those Comanches have killed so many people!"

As Layne was managing to free himself from the woman's tenacious grip, Bart explained, "When Jessie learned that I was planning to ride out and meet you, she insisted on coming along."

Meanwhile, as Selina was studying Jessie, the woman slipped her arm about Layne's waist and leaned familiarly against his tall frame. Jessie Harte was seductively beautiful. Her hair, as black as a raven's, cascaded past her shoulders in full, silky waves. Her voluptuous curves filled out her western-style riding clothes superbly. Selina's eyes scanned the woman's attire. She was wearing a black velvet skirt with a matching vest. The set was trimmed in red, which was the exact shade of her long sleeved blouse. Her tasteful outfit was in stark contrast to Selina's own manly attire. She compared herself to Jessie Harte and found herself sorely lacking. Turning about, she went back to camp and sat down beside Stella.

Bart told his men to tend to the horses, then he and Watts followed Layne and Jessie to the fire. Layne knew that he should make introductions, but

294

manners could wait. First, he had to let Bart know about Janet. However, before he had the chance to do so, Bart caught sight of Floyd. The young man was standing back in the shadows.

"Miller!" Bart yelled. "What are you doing here?"

Floyd, moving into the firelight, quickly conjured up an explanation, "Mr. Wilkerson, I thought if I helped Smith escort your daughter safely to your ranch, you might give me back my job."

"Your job!" Layne exclaimed. He turned to Bart. "He told me he was here on your orders."

"I fired him weeks ago."

Miller cursed inwardly. Damn it to hell! All his plans had gone awry! First Janet's abduction, and now Wilkerson's arrival!

"Miller, I have no intentions of rehiring you. But with those Comanches on the warpath, we need every gun. I'll pay you to ride with us, but you can forget permanent employment." Bart, looking about for his daughter, asked, "Where's Janet?"

Layne shifted uneasily. "Bart," he began, troubled by his sense of inadequacy—this man had trusted Janet in his care, and he had failed him—"Janet isn't here. Last night, she slipped out of the wagon to meet Miller. They sneaked away from camp, and from what I understand, while they were kissing, a Comanche warrior knocked Miller unconscious, then abducted Janet."

For a frozen moment Bart was too numb to respond. Then his deep voice breaking, he moaned, "Dear God! My little girl kidnapped by a Comanche warrior!"

"Doug's looking for her," Layne said hastily, knowing the information would elevate his hopes.

"Then she's got the best man in these parts tracking her. If anyone can save her, he can." Bart, his eyes hardening, glared at Floyd. "If anything happens to my daughter, I'll kill you!"

"Mr. Wilkerson, I'm just as worried about Janet as you are," Miller hastened to say, hoping the lie would mellow Wilkerson somewhat. "I would've gone with Thompson, but I got a slight concussion."

"Mr. Wilkerson," Selina spoke up. "Please, sit down and have a cup of coffee."

Layne, stepping away from Jessie, went to Selina, drew her to her feet, and said, "Darlin', I'd like you to meet Bart Wilkerson and Jessie Harte."

"How do you do, ma'am?" Bart said politely, tipping his wide-brim hat.

Jessie, consumed with jealousy, said nothing.

Layne continued, "This beautiful young lady is Selina Beaumont, my fiancée."

Despite his concern for Janet, Wilkerson was able to summon a smile. "Congratulations, Layne." He stepped to Selina, took her hand, and kissed it lightly. "Miss Beaumont, it's a pleasure to meet you."

"Call me Selina, please."

Feigning a warm smile, Jessie looked at Selina and said cordially, "Welcome to Texas, Miss Beaumont. And I wish you and Layne all the happiness in the world."

"Thank you," Selina murmured. For some reason she didn't believe her.

Layne, gesturing to Stella, continued the introductions, "And this beautiful young lady is Stella

Larson."

Stella started to rise, but Bart motioned for her to remain seated. Deciding to have a cup of coffee, he sat down beside Stella, saying warmly, "I'm pleased to meet you, Miss Larson."

Stella, uneasy in the presence of gentry, withdrew into silence. She watched as Bart removed his hat and placed it at his side. He was a strikingly distinguished gentleman, and as her scrutiny deepened, she guessed him to be in his early forties. His frame was tall, slender, and lithe. His dark hair was streaked with silver, and a thin, carefully clipped moustache grew above his finely-shaped lips.

Bart turned his head and looked at her, and she found herself gazing into a pair of eyes as green as Janet's. She saw a flicker of anxiety behind those clear emerald eyes, and knowing he was worrying about Janet, her heart went out to him. She admired his courage.

He smiled and was about to speak to Stella when Hattie, carrying Paul, walked up to the fire. She had been inside the wagon, dressing the boy for bed.

Layne quickly introduced Hattie, then taking Paul from her arms, he said, "And this little fella is Paul Larson."

"Your son?" Bart asked Stella.

"Yes, sir," she murmured.

"Please pardon my blunder, ma'am. When we were introduced, I called you Miss Larson. Is your husband traveling with you?"

Stella's cheeks reddened. Too ashamed to admit that she wasn't married, had never been married, she said softly, "I'm a widow." Her eyes, flying to the others, pleaded for their silence.

"I'm sorry," Bart murmured. Smiling, he glanced at Paul. "You have a very handsome son."

No one noticed as Jessie caught Floyd's attention and motioned stealthily for him to follow her. Moving quietly away from the fire, she hurried across the campsite and into the night's dark shadows.

She didn't have long to wait before Miller found her. Handling her as if he owned her, he drew her body tightly to his, bent his head, and kissed her feverishly.

She almost surrendered to his passion, but as Layne's image flashed in her mind, she pushed out of his arms, saying angrily, "Don't touch me!"

"That's a helluva way to talk to your lover," he retorted.

"Ex-lover!" she corrected.

"Since when?" he questioned archly.

"Since Layne's return."

He sighed testily. "Don't tell me you're still hopin' to get him to put a ring on your finger. That Selina gal's got him hogtied and ready for the altar."

"Maybe so," she replied. "But he hasn't married her yet. I don't know how, but I'll find a way to get rid of that little piece of fluff. But I didn't bring you out here to discuss Layne and his slut. I want you to tell me what you're up to."

"What do you mean?"

"Don't play dumb with me! You didn't join up with Layne to get on Bart's good side. You don't want your job back."

Miller grinned, but there was no humor in it. "I

guess I can tell you. I know you won't run to Wilkerson." As quickly as possible, he relayed his foiled plan to kidnap Janet. He finished by grumbling, "Even if Thompson finds her, I can't kidnap her, not with Wilkerson and his ranch hands ridin' along."

Placing her hands on her hips, Jessie frowned impatiently. "Floyd, you don't have the sense God gave a goat!"

He was offended. "You don't have no right to talk to me like that!"

"Well, someone needs to talk some sense into you. Just for the sake of argument, let's say you do kidnap Janet and collect your ransom. Knowing you, you'd have the money spent before you had time to turn around. Then what would you do? You'd probably get caught by the law and spend the rest of your life in prison."

"I suppose you have a better plan?" he asked skeptically.

"Yes, I do. Marry the girl."

"What?" he exclaimed.

"She's Bart's only heir. She's due to inherit everything."

"Wilkerson doesn't like me. He'd never give Janet permission to marry me."

"True, but he could always have a fatal accident."

Interest sparked in Floyd's eyes. "I see what you mean. All I gotta do is knock off her old man, then marry her."

"Yes, but you must use caution. Don't make any rash plans, or else you'll find yourself hanging from the end of a rope."

"Don't worry, I'll be careful." He studied her suspiciously. "Why are you so willin' to give me advice? What's in it for you?"

"When it's time to get rid of Selina Beaumont, I might need your services." She smiled wickedly. "One favor deserves another. Don't you agree?"

"Yeah, I sure do," he replied, returning her smile.

"Are you sure you want a drink of whiskey?" Doug asked Janet, showing her the capped bottle. He grinned wryly, adding, "I thought ladies didn't partake of hard liquor."

They had finished eating and were sitting close together beside the fire. Taking the bottle from his hand, she replied, "I need something to help me sleep. I hope to get so inebriated that I fall into a drunken stupor. Maybe then I won't dream about that horrible warrior." She twisted off the cap, tilted the bottle to her lips, and took a big swallow. The potent liquor seared her throat, and for a moment she thought she might be sick. When she was fairly certain that the whiskey was going to stay down, she helped herself to another swig, relieved that this swallow burned a little less.

Watching with amusement, Doug warned her, "I'd take it easy if I were you."

"Well, you aren't me," she remarked defiantly, quaffing down another deep swallow.

Pouring himself a cup of coffee, Doug said with a grin, "In the mornin', you're gonna have one helluva hangover."

"I'd rather suffer a hangover than dream about

that hideous warrior!"

"That's 'cause you ain't never had a hangover," Doug chuckled.

Refusing to take him seriously, Janet continued her drinking. The potent liquor soon had her under its influence, and as her whiskey-clouded thoughts went to Miller, she said thickly, "Doug, I think I'm in love."

His hopes soared. Could her feelings possibly be the same as his? "Who do you love?" he asked quietly, waiting intensely for her answer.

"Floyd Miller," she replied. Clumsily, she managed to put the bottle to her lips and take a large drink.

"Then you're a fool," he muttered, his hopes dashed.

"Don't be an ole grouch," she said, her words beginning to slur. "Can't you be happy for me?"

He grabbed the half-empty bottle from her hand and capped it. "You've had enough of this."

Her eyelids growing heavy, she murmured sleepily, "Yes, I suppose I have." She swayed against him. Slipping an arm about her shoulders, he drew her close.

"I feel so light-headed," she murmured sluggishly. "And the ground seems to be rocking back and forth."

"You're drunk," Doug replied tersely.

"Yes, I know. Doug?"

"What?"

"I've always wished that I had an older brother, and now I have you. I love you like a brother. You don't mind, do you?"

He did mind. If she couldn't love him like a

301

man, he'd rather she didn't love him at all. "Janet, why don't you try and get some sleep? We'll be leaving at daybreak."

"Why so early?"

"I want to reach Dry River by nightfall."

"Will the others be there?"

"I hope so."

"Then this time tomorrow night, I'll be with Floyd."

Doug offered no reply; instead, he stared at the fire, watching its darting flames. He silently cursed himself for falling in love with Janet. He felt he had no chance to win her love — not now, or ever!

Her head, resting on his shoulder, grew heavy. Glancing down into her face, he saw that she was asleep. Gently, he picked her up and carried her to a spread blanket. He laid her down tenderly, then covered her with a second blanket. "Good night, little one," he whispered, as he bent down so that his lips touched hers in a feather-soft kiss.

Twenty-three

Leaving Floyd to follow later, Jessie headed back toward camp. She hoped Layne didn't suspect that she had been alone with Miller. A petulant frown creased her brow. He probably hadn't even missed her! Earlier, she had gotten the distinct impression that Selina Beaumont had him totally mesmerized! A look of determination crossed her face. Well, she'd not stand idly by and let that little Southern tart marry Layne Smith!

Jessie and her brother, Larry, had been working for Chamberlain for over a year. Larry ran the ranch, and she took care of Chamberlain's home. She had been living in San Antonio when Larry was offered the position. He had accepted it gratefully and asked Chamberlain if his sister could also be employed. Harold had had no objections, so Larry sent for Jessie. In San Antonio, Jessie had been slinging hash for a living, barely making enough money to live on. She had been more than happy to move to the Circle-C.

From the first moment that Jessie had set eyes on the handsome Layne Smith, she had wanted him. She had never doubted that she could win him as a lover, but she wanted him on a permanent basis.

She'd not settle for anything less than marriage. She would be Mrs. Layne Smith, one way or another! Believing Layne would propose if she withheld her favors, she kept her passion in check. She allowed his kisses and fondling, but would let him go no further. These encounters, however, had always left her with her inflamed desires unsatisfied. Needing appeasement, she had taken Floyd Miller as a lover. Not wanting Layne to know that she was seeing another man, she had kept her affair with Miller well guarded. As time passed without Layne's proposal, Jessie had begun to worry that he might never ask her to marry him. Finally, frustrated and desperate, she had decided to make love to him, and if that didn't result in a promise of marriage, she'd use the oldest trick in the book; she'd tell him she was pregnant then, after they were married, pretend that she had been mistaken. But before she could put her scheme into action, Layne had been called to New Orleans.

Now, as Jessie neared the campsite, anger flickered in her dark eyes. How dare Layne return from New Orleans with a fiancée! For over a year she had been trying to snag him, and then Selina Beaumont comes along and traps him in record time! A violent, malicious hate for Selina filled her heart! The woman would regret the day she had met Layne Smith! Jessie would see to it personally.

Seeing Layne coming toward her, she cast thoughts of Selina aside and pasted a bright smile on her lips.

"Jessie," he said, reaching her. "I was looking for you. I need to talk to you."

Slipping her arm into his, she suggested, "Let's take a walk, shall we? You can talk to me while we stroll."

"All right," he agreed. "But we'd better stay close to camp. There could be hostile Comanches in the vicinity."

Tightening her grip on his arm, she fell into step beside him. "I suppose you want to talk about your fiancée."

"Yes, I do. But I also need to talk to you about Chamberlain."

She looked at him questioningly.

As simply as possible, he let her know that Harold and his men had been killed by Comanches.

Pausing, Jessie gazed up into Layne's eyes, saying anxiously, "This is terrible! If Mr. Chamberlain is dead, then what will happen to Larry and me?" Realizing she sounded unfeeling, she continued quickly, "I don't mean to sound so cold, but my brother and I are wholly dependent on our jobs. Naturally, I'm very sorry about Mr. Chamberlain."

"Larry's told me more than once that he wants to buy his own ranch. Chamberlain's only kin is an uncle who lives in St. Louis. He's a prosperous physician, and I doubt if he'll want to give up his practice to become a rancher. I'm fairly sure he'll put the Circle-C up for sale. If Larry wants to buy it, tell him to come talk to me. I'll gladly loan him the money he needs. Your brother's a good rancher, and I consider him a safe investment."

"Thank you, Layne. I'm sure Larry will take you up on your generous offer."

Layne hesitated a moment, then said uncertainly,

"Jessie, about Selina. . . ."

"You owe me no explanations, Layne," she murmured sweetly, "believe me, I'm very happy for you."

He was relieved, for he had been worried that his engagement to Selina might hurt Jessie.

She carried on in a cheerful manner, "I hope Selina and I will become good friends."

Placing his hands on her shoulders, his eyes met hers and he smiled affectionately. "Someday, the right man will come into your life, and when he does. . . ."

"I know," she whispered, fighting the urge to fling herself into his arms. His virile maleness was overwhelming, and his nearness was staggering. Right man? he had said. He was the only one for her! No man could be the equal of Layne Smith!

Dropping her eyes from the power of his gaze, she glimpsed Selina moving away from the campfire. She was heading to the wagon, which brought her directly in Jessie's line of vision. Knowing Selina couldn't help but see her and Layne, she returned her gaze to Layne and asked irresistibly, "May I kiss you one last time?" Reading his indecision, she added quickly, "It means a lot to me."

He conceded. "Well, I suppose there's no harm."

Layne bent his head and placed his lips softly on hers. He'd intended to keep their kiss polite, but Jessie, catching him off guard, locked her hands tightly about his neck. Pressing her voluptuous body against his, she tried to turn their kiss into one of passion.

Extricating himself from her clinging hold, Layne

306

held her at arms' length. "Jessie . . ." he began.

"I'm sorry," she cut in, checking cautiously on Selina. The sight of her rival hurrying inside the wagon gave her reason to gloat. Obviously Selina had seen their intimate embrace. Appearing embarrassed and somewhat ashamed, she said softly, "Please forgiven me, Layne. It won't happen again, I promise. But you do mean a great deal to me, and I wanted to tell you goodbye with emotion."

He grinned wryly. "Well, you certainly did that."

She returned his smile. "Friends?" she asked, offering to shake on it.

"We'll always be friends," he answered, accepting her extended hand.

Meanwhile, inside the wagon Selina was close to tears. She could hardly believe that Layne had kissed Jessie Harte; he had been holding her as though he never intended to let her go!

Hattie, putting Paul to bed, glanced over at Selina. Noticing her distress, she asked, "Is somethin' wrong?"

"I just saw Layne kissing Miss Harte," she answered sharply. Her hurt was quickly turning into anger.

"Miz Selina, don't you go gettin' all upset. Mista Smith loves you."

"Then why was he kissing another woman?"

"I don't know, but if I was you, I'd ask 'im."

"I think I will!" she decided.

The words had no sooner passed her lips when Layne, approaching the wagon, called softly, "Selina?"

She moved to the lowered backboard, and as

307

Layne assisted her to the ground, she asked icily, "What do you want?"

Layne was puzzled by her frigid tone. "I simply want to tell you good night."

"Oh?" she questioned querulously. "Is that why you were kissing Jessie Harte? Were you bidding her good night? Or do you plan to meet her later?"

Layne sighed heavily. "Selina, that kiss was completely harmless."

"Harmless!" she spat, her blue eyes flaring.

Grasping her wrist, Layne led her a short way from the wagon. Jerking free, she folded her arms beneath her breasts, tapped her foot angrily, and waited for an explanation.

Layne was in no danger of losing his patience. He didn't blame Selina for being upset. "Darlin'," he began evenly, "Jessie asked me if she could kiss me." He shrugged. "I guess she wanted it to be a good-bye kiss. I saw no reason to refuse, and certainly meant the kiss to be one between friends. But apparently that wasn't what she had in mind. Afterward, she was sorry and apologized."

"And you believed her?"

"Yes, I did." Stepping forward, he rested his hands on her shoulders, drawing her close. "I love you, Selina. I don't want any woman but you."

Her jealousy mellowing, she murmured, "I love you too, Layne. But I don't trust Jessie Harte, and I don't like her."

"How can you say that? You barely know her."

"I know her type," she asserted firmly.

"When you get to know her better, I think you'll change your opinion. Jessie's a fine person. And, darlin', she's no threat to us. No woman on the face of this earth could take me away from you."

"Do you really mean that, Layne?"

"With all my heart," he murmured, bringing his lips down to hers.

A mutual, passionate shudder ran the lengths of their bodies as their heart-stopping kiss professed their deep, undying love.

Selina's spirits were high when, a few minutes later, she re-entered the wagon. Layne loved her totally, unequivocally; she believed it with all her heart! However, the sight of Jessie sitting on Janet's pallet put a damper on Selina's gay mood.

Jessie had seen Selina's happy expression. Dammit! Apparently she had forgiven Layne! It would take more than a kiss for her to get Layne away from this determined woman! Then, meeting Selina's questioning gaze, Jessie explained her presence, "I prefer not to sleep outdoors, so Mrs. Larson suggested that I sleep in here. After all, Janet's pallet isn't being used."

Selina said nothing. Although she didn't like the woman, she certainly didn't begrudge her a place to sleep. Going to her own place, she sat down and removed her boots.

Jessie said in a concerned manner, "I'm sure all of you must be worried sick about Janet. I know poor Bart is beside himself. He's putting on a brave front for everyone, but deep inside, he's terribly worried."

"I'm sure he is," Selina mumbled. Undressing

309

quickly, she took off her shirt and trousers, then slipped her cotton nightgown over her head.

Jessie's eyes had been on her the entire time, measuring her competition. Selina Beaumont was exceptionally beautiful, and she knew, depressingly, that whisking Layne away from this lovely young woman was probably impossible. That she could inveigle Layne back into her arms, and into her bed, was highly unlikely. He'd never succumb to her charms as long as he had Selina.

Removing her own clothes, Jessie put on her gown, then stretching out on her bed, she turned her back to Selina and drew up the top blanket. She was determined to find a way to get rid of Miss Beaumont—permanently!

Layne and Floyd had taken the first watch, and because Bart's men were wrapped up in their bedrolls, Stella found herself alone at the fire with Janet's father. She hadn't planned to be left with him, but she was so engrossed in his pleasant company that the others' whereabouts had escaped her notice. Suddenly realizing that she and Mr. Wilkerson were quite alone, she said hastily, "I'm sorry if I've kept you from retirin'. I reckon . . . I mean, I guess I'll bid you good night."

She started to stand, but Bart placed a hand on her arm, saying quickly, "Please, don't leave—not yet. Stay a moment longer."

Stella was obviously hesitant. "We both need our sleep."

"Sleep!" he groaned. "How can I possibly sleep

knowing my daughter is out there somewhere at a Comanche warrior's mercy?" He rubbed a hand over his face. "Dear God!"

Instantly sympathetic, Stella tried to soothe his worry, "Maybe Doug has found her by now."

"I pray that he has!" Bart replied, his deep voice strained. He studied the young woman watching him with concern. He thought she was strikingly lovely, and gazing into her gray eyes, he felt as if he were losing himself in their charcoal depths.

Stella was finding his scrutiny strangely unnerving, for it was stirring an alien longing in her; a feeling she had never experienced before. For some inexplicable reason, she had an overwhelming desire to reach out and touch him.

Bart tore his eyes away from hers. "Mrs. Larson, forgive me for monopolizing your time. I'm sure you're sleepy and wish to retire. It's just. . . ."

"Just what?" she prodded him.

"I don't want to be alone with my worries—my grief."

"Mr. Wilkerson," she hastened to say, "I'm sure Janet is all right!"

He smiled warmly. "No. You aren't sure, but it's kind of you to say that you are." He took her hand into his, clasping it gently. "Won't you please call me Bart?"

"If you'll call me Stella," she replied, wondering why his touch was making her heart flutter. Confused and ill-at-ease, she withdrew her hand and placed it in her lap.

"I'm sorry," he said softly. "I didn't mean to be forward."

Her cheeks reddened.

"You seem very shy for a woman who has been married and has a child. How long have you been a widow?"

"A few months," she mumbled, uncomfortable with the lie.

"Tell me about yourself, Stella."

Her eyes widened. "Wh . . . what do you want to know?"

"Anything you're willing to tell me."

"There ain't . . . There isn't much to tell. I was married at sixteen, and my husband was killed by runaway slaves. Paul and I were left alone and destitute. It was at that time that I met Hattie. She took care of Paul, and I went to work."

"What kind of work did you do?"

Stella swallowed heavily. Why was she so opposed to telling this man the truth? Because if he knew she was a whore, he wouldn't like her! she admitted. Looking away from his fixed gaze, she stammered, "I . . . I worked as a maid."

"You sound as though you're ashamed. You shouldn't be, you know. You're a very strong young lady, and you should be proud of yourself. It's not easy for a woman to survive on her own. You not only supported yourself but Paul and Hattie as well. What do you plan to do in Passing Through?"

"I don't know," she replied quietly.

"Why did you leave New Orleans?"

"I just wanted to get away."

"I think there's more to it than that."

"There is, but I don't wanna talk about it."

"I understand. And forgive my prying." He smiled

gently. "I won't keep you up any longer, Stella. Please, go to bed."

She rose hesitantly, looking sympathetically down into his worried face, and murmured, "I'll pray for Janet's safe return."

"So will I," he whispered, his voice choked.

She walked swiftly to the wagon. Bart's eyes remained on her until she disappeared inside, then he poured himself a cup of coffee. His thoughts on Stella, he stared vacantly into the flickering flames. There was something about the young woman that touched his heart. He couldn't quite put his finger on what it was. She was very lovely, true, but it wasn't her beauty that drew him to her. It was something more, something intangible.

Clearing Stella from his mind, he returned to thinking about his daughter. "Janet!" he groaned aloud. "God, I pray you're all right!"

Detecting footsteps, he glanced up to find Layne approaching. Reaching the fire, Smith knelt and poured a cup of coffee. He took a drink then, turning his gaze to Wilkerson, said contritely, "Bart, I can't tell you how sorry I am about Janet. I feel that it's all my fault. You trusted her in my care, and I let you down." Putting the cup to his lips, he took another swallow. A frown furrowed his brow. "Dammit! If only she hadn't left the wagon!"

"Don't blame yourself, Layne. My daughter is very head-strong and disobedient. I'm sure she tried your patience on several occasions." He exhaled deeply. "I'm afraid I've failed my daughter terribly. I should never have left her upbringing to my brother and his wife. I knew they would spoil her unreason-

313

ably. Quite a few times I considered raising her myself, and would go to New Orleans with the intention of bringing her back with me. But she seemed so happy where she was — surrounded by luxuries, servants, and comforts. It didn't seem right to take her away from all that. Then, as time passed, we grew further and further apart, and when I'd go to visit her, we were almost like strangers. When she wrote and told me that she wanted to come to the ranch, I was overjoyed."

"Doug will find her and bring her to you safe and sound."

"You don't really believe that, do you?" He watched Layne raptly.

"I believe if any man can do it, Doug can."

"So do I," Bart said in a low voice. A hopeful smile touched his lips.

Twenty-four

In Dry River the hotel, which was a two-story clapboard building, had more than enough rooms to accommodate the large group of travelers that had arrived quite unexpectedly. The proprietor, delighted to receive so many paying guests, assigned rooms expeditiously, helped the porter show everyone to their quarters, then rushed to the kitchen to inform the cook to expect a good-size dinner crowd.

Selina, sharing a room with Stella, stood at the open window and gazed down at the dusty street below. She found Dry River the typical western town, unimpressive and nondescript. Sitting on the wide window seat, she looked over at Stella. Her companion was settled comfortably in an overstuffed chair; she seemed engrossed in the open book resting on her lap. Studying Stella more closely, though, Selina had a feeling that her friend's concentration wasn't on the printed pages.

Stella glanced up. Smiling sheepishly, as though she'd been caught wool-gathering in class, she closed the book and said quietly, "I can't concentrate."

"Are you too worried about Janet?"

"That's part of it," Stella replied.

Selina arched a brow. "Oh?"

315

As a warm blush colored her cheeks, Stella asked, "What do you think of Bart Wilkerson?"

"Why do you ask? Are you taken with him?"

Stella's blush deepened. "No, of course not. 'Sides, Mr. Wilkerson's gentry, and I'm nothin' but poor white trash."

"You aren't trash!" Selina asserted.

"Yes, I am," she disagreed. "I had a baby out of wedlock. I became a whore and then a mistress. If that don't make me trash, then what does?" She sounded bitter.

"I don't intend to argue with you, Stella. However, I don't like the term 'trash,' and I hope you won't use it again. Furthermore, you must stop thinking about your past and think about the present and the future."

"I suppose you're right," Stella relented. "But all the same, I ain't . . . I mean, I'm not in Mr. Wilkerson's class. And if he knew the truth, he wouldn't be so nice."

"You don't know that," Selina pointed out.

It was on the tip of her tongue to advise Stella to be perfectly honest with Bart when Hattie, opening the door adjacent to their room, peeked inside their room and said, "Miz Stella, honey, little Paul's a-wantin' his supper."

"I'll go downstairs and order a tray," she said as she stood up.

As Stella left the room, Selina returned to gazing out the window. Stella's obvious interest in Bart had come as a complete surprise to Selina. But now, deep in thought, she skimmed over the day, recalling that Bart Wilkerson had been very attentive to

Stella. A slight smile curled her lips. Bart and Stella? An unlikely pair, perhaps, but love wasn't always rational; it had a mind of its own!

As Selina's musing drifted to Janet, a worried sigh escaped her lips. Dear God, she prayed silently, please let her be safe!

Then, as though on cue, she spied Doug and Janet riding into town. Selina leapt from the window seat, darted out of the room, and ran down the hall to Bart's door. Knocking loudly, she exclaimed, "Janet's here! . . . Janet's here!"

Not waiting for an answer, she sped to the stairs and descended quickly. Reaching the lobby, she slowed her steps somewhat as she made a beeline out the front door.

"Janet!" Selina cried happily, as she hurried into the street.

Doug reined in. Janet was seated behind him, and he reached back an arm and lowered her to the ground. On flying feet she rushed into Selina's outstretched arms.

Hugging her friend tightly, Selina asked anxiously, "Are you all right?"

"Yes, I'm fine," she assured her.

At that moment, Janet was suddenly drawn out of Selina's embrace and into her father's. Holding his daughter close, Bart uttered raspingly, "Janet, my baby! Thank God, you're safe!"

"Papa, what are you doing here?" she asked, finding his presence a total surprise.

"I'll explain later," he replied, holding her before him and examining her intently. "You look remarkably fine," he observed.

317

Janet smiled brightly. "Thanks to Doug. Papa, he saved my life. That warrior was about to kill me when. . . ." The remembrance sent a shudder coursing through her. "Doug found me just in the nick of time."

Thompson was still astride his horse, and Bart turned and looked up at him. "Doug," he began emotionally, "I don't know how to thank you."

"A handshake will be good enough," he answered, grinning.

Doug was about to dismount when Miller, coming out of the saloon, caught sight of Janet and called her name. At the sound of his rival's voice, Doug froze. Motionless, he looked on as Janet hurried away from her father and into Miller's arms. The couple's clinging embrace tore painfully at Doug's heart, but keeping his feelings well masked, he turned to Selina and asked, "Where's Layne?"

"He took the horses and the wagon to the livery."

He nodded his thanks, and urged his horse forward.

Taking note of Doug's departure, Janet moved out of Floyd's embrace and called to him. "Where are you going?"

"To the livery," he said over his shoulder, before kneeing his horse into a trot that quickly put distance between himself and Janet.

Janet had an overpowering urge to run after him; although the feeling made no sense whatsoever, she took a step forward. However, she was deterred by Miller's hand on her arm. The strange sensation passed, and dismissing it, she turned to Floyd and smiled radiantly.

318

Bart, his eyes locked on the pair, frowned with stern disapproval.

"I don't want you to have anything to do with Floyd Miller!" Bart told his daughter. They were in his hotel room, and his thunderous voice filled the small space.

Placing her hands on her hips, Janet fixed her father with a rebellious gaze. "I will not stop seeing him!"

"I forbid it!" Bart snapped.

"Very well, Papa," she retorted. "But if I can't see him with your permission, then you're forcing me to take drastic measures."

"Drastic?" he quizzed. "Like what?"

"Like elopement." Her chin was lifted stubbornly.

Scowling furiously, he turned away from his daughter's defiant eyes. As he cooled his rage, he sunk into deep thought. Then reaching a decision, he faced her again and said in a controlled manner, "All right, Janet, let's compromise, shall we? If you promise you won't run off and marry that no-account drifter, I'll give you permission to see him."

She gave her promise freely, for she wasn't sure if she really wanted to marry Floyd, at least not in the near future. She eyed her father dubiously. "Why did you give in so easily?"

Bart smiled somewhat confidently. "I think when you become better acquainted with Miller, you'll lose interest in him."

"Why do you dislike him so much?"

"I don't especially dislike him. I just don't think

319

he's trustworthy. Furthermore, he's hot-headed, selfish, and lazy. That's why I fired him."

"Fired him?" she questioned. "When?"

"Weeks ago."

"Then why did he tell Layne he was still working for you?"

"He claims he was trying to get on my good side. He figured if he helped deliver you safely to the ranch, in return I'd give him back his job."

"Will you?"

"Is that what you want?"

"Yes, Papa! Please!" Her tone was imploring.

"He can have a job," Bart said, conceding.

She hugged her father briefly then, smiling up at him, said sincerely, "I promise I won't consider marriage until I know Floyd better. You have my word on it, Papa."

Jessie was entering the hotel as Floyd was descending the stairs. He met her halfway across the lobby, and noticing a smug expression on her face, he asked curiously, "Why do you look so pleased?"

"I just paid a visit to Dry River's physician, Doctor Harrison." She patted her skirt pocket. "He gave me a powder to help me sleep. I told him that I have insomnia."

Floyd was perplexed. "So?"

"So, I now have the means to carry out my plan." She smiled complacently.

"What plan?"

"This powder is quite potent, and the doctor cautioned me to take it in carefully measured doses."

Floyd gasped incredulously. "Damn! Are you plannin' to kill Selina by givin' her an overdose?"

Jessie glowered at him. "Floyd, sometimes I think you must be a halfwit!"

He reached over and angrily clutched her wrist, his grip painful. "Jessie, I'm a-warnin' you. Insult me one more time and I'll knock the livin' daylights out of you! You understand me, woman?"

Knowing he would carry out his threat, she decided to smooth over the incident. "I'm sorry, Floyd. It's just that my nerves are on edge."

Accepting her apology, he released her wrist somewhat brusquely.

"I don't plan to give this powder to Selina," Jessie explained. "I intend to give it to Layne. It's a very effective drug when mixed with alcohol."

"Once you have him drugged, then what?"

"I intend to get him in bed and have his fiancée find us there."

"Don't you reckon Layne will know that you sedated him?"

"No, not if he's drinking heavily. Besides, this powder leaves no noticeable after-effects. If he feels sick when he wakes up, he'll figure he's suffering from a hangover."

"Just how do you plan to work all this? First you gotta get him drinkin', then get him in bed, and last, but most important, you gotta make sure Selina finds you two together."

Jessie sighed deeply. "I don't know how I'm going to succeed, but I will. I might need your help, though. If I should, you'll cooperate, won't you?" She smiled at him sweetly.

"Sure," he agreed, meaning it. "By the way, Janet's here. She and Doug showed up 'bout an hour ago."

"That's wonderful!" Jessie exclaimed. But she didn't mean it. She couldn't have cared less if Janet were alive or dead.

"Her old man just sent for me. It seems Janet must be real persuasive, 'cause he told me that I have his permission to see her. He also gave me back my job. The job don't mean beans to me, of course. But it'll give me the opportunity to see Janet whenever I want to. As soon as I get her promise to marry me, I'll make sure her old man ain't around no more."

"The men who were going to help you kidnap Janet, are they still in town?"

"No. It was like I figured. They must've got tired of waitin' and moved on." He smiled expansively. "Which is all right with me. Marryin' Janet is gonna make me a lot richer than kidnappin' her."

"It's getting late," Jessie said hastily. "I need to dress for dinner."

She brushed past him and hurried upstairs to her room. Since she had packed lightly for the trip, she hadn't bothered to bring an evening dress. Luckily, the mercantile in town had one that fit her perfectly—a lovely red silk gown, with a low decolletage that would temptingly reveal her ample bosom. It was in a package on the bed, where she had left it earlier.

She envisioned herself entering the dining room, and Layne, seated at a table, looking up, seeing her, and being completely mesmerized by her stunning beauty. She would see in his eyes how desperately he desired her!

Bringing herself back to reality, Jessie decided it was time to get dressed. She patted the packet in her pocket. If she failed to seduce Layne through her beauty, she still had the sedative to fall back on.

Jessie was the last one to come to the dining room, for she wanted Layne to see her grand entrance. As she had suspected, all eyes turned in her direction. The men, pushing back their chairs, stood and waited for her to reach the table. Jessie, her eyes going to Layne's, hoped to see desire smoldering in their depths. She was, however, sorely disappointed. His expression, though congenial, was impartial.

Layne was standing at one end of the table, Bart at the other. Selina was occupying the chair on Layne's left, but the one on his right was empty. Jessie went to it and waited for Layne to help her be seated.

Layne complied politely, telling Jessie that she looked very lovely. Then his attention returned to Selina.

Jessie glowered at her rival. The woman's exquisite beauty infuriated her. She bitterly berated herself for thinking she could tempt Layne away from this beautiful Southern belle. If she wanted Layne Smith, then she would have to resort to trickery. She thought about the sleeping drug hidden in her room; she hoped to use it tonight.

Selina's beauty, enhanced by her powder-blue

evening gown, was captivating; and Layne, totally enchanted, could barely take his eyes off her.

"Layne?" Bart said.

Tearing his eyes away from his fiancée, Layne gave Wilkerson his full attention.

"I've decided to ride to the fort with you," Bart continued.

Selina asked with confusion, "Layne, what's going on?"

"I'm sorry, honey. I haven't had a chance to tell you. There's an army fort a few hours' ride from here. Tomorrow I need to go to the fort and let the officer in charge know about Chamberlain and his men."

"May I go with you?" she asked.

"Of course," he answered.

"Do you think that's wise?" Bart questioned. "Those Comanches might still be in these parts."

"They're dead," Layne replied. He then explained that Doug had found the guilty Indians, all of them dead from gunshot wounds.

Janet overheard the conversation and cringed. She knew she'd never forget the gruesome sight. Then turning her thoughts elsewhere, she glanced anxiously at the open doorway.

"The army?" Bart asked Layne.

He nodded. "Doug's pretty certain they were killed by soldiers."

"Good!" Floyd spoke up. "Now we can travel to Passing Through without worryin' about an Indian attack." He smiled at Janet, who was sitting beside him. "I wouldn't want anything to happen to this beautiful young lady."

Janet didn't return his smile, and Miller got the impression that she wasn't paying attention to him. His gaze traveled over her briefly. She was strikingly lovely in her pale-yellow gown. Floyd could feel an awakening in his loins. In an effort to cool his passion, he looked away from her and took a large drink of his champagne.

Miller's suspicion was correct. Janet wasn't aware that he had spoken, for she had become too deeply buried in thoughts of Doug. Wondering why he was so late, she kept her eyes glued to the doorway, hoping to see him.

When the waiter came to their table to receive their orders, Janet looked at Layne and asked, "Shouldn't we wait for Doug?"

"He's not coming," Smith answered.

Janet tried to hide her disappointment; but Bart, watching her, saw his daughter's spirits plunge. A puzzled frown furrowed his brow. Why should Doug's absence depress her?

Bart waited until everyone had ordered their dinner, then asked Layne, "Where is Doug?"

"Across the street at the saloon," he answered with an undertone of worry. Layne was concerned about his good friend. Doug wasn't a heavy drinker, but tonight he was quaffing down whiskey.

"Didn't you ask him to join us?" Wilkerson inquired.

"I asked him," Layne replied. "He said he'd rather drink. After dinner I'll go to the saloon and check on him."

"Mind if I join you?" Bart asked.

"No, I don't mind."

325

Wilkerson cast his daughter a glance. She was listening intently. He turned his gaze back to Layne. "Why do you suppose Doug's drinking? I know him quite well, and I've never known him to drink to excess."

"He's got problems," Smith mumbled. Bart, paying close attention, saw the furtive glance Layne cast in Janet's direction.

Leaning back in his chair, Wilkerson picked up his goblet and took a long, thoughtful drink of champagne. Could Doug be in love with Janet? The possibility met with his complete approval. He liked and respected Doug Thompson and would wholehearteldy welcome him as a son-in-law. Wilkerson's ranch was huge, and he had a large portion of good grazing land set aside for Janet and her future husband. As his gaze went to Miller, he scowled deeply. If his daughter chose this sorry excuse of a man over Thompson, then she was an utter fool!

Stella, sitting on Bart's right, noticed his frown. "Is something wrong?" she asked.

His scowl was quickly replaced with a warm smile. "No, nothing's wrong. I was just thinking."

She knew it had to be an unpleasant thought, but she decided not to pry. Stella folded her hands in her lap and toyed nervously with her napkin. She was uneasy but also elated. Moving her fingers from the wadded napkin, she brushed them lightly over her sea-green gown. She had never imagined that someday she would wear a dress so beautiful. It wasn't hers, of course—she had borrowed it from Selina—but that didn't make it any less enchanting.

"You seem nervous," Bart told her, his tone quiet so no one else could hear.

She smiled timidly. "I am nervous. I . . . I don't belong here."

"Why do you say that?"

"I've never dined formally, and I don't know nothin' . . . I mean I don't know anything 'bout proper manners."

Although Bart was warmly amused, he didn't let on. "Don't worry, Stella. We may all be attired in finery, but this hotel is not the Hotel St. Louis. You're in the West now, where etiquette is almost obsolete. Most formal occasions occur in homes, not in towns like this one."

"Do you give many parties?" she asked.

"Not many, but now that Janet's living with me I'm sure that will change."

"Is your ranch very large?"

"Immense," he answered, but not boastfully.

"I suppose you have a real nice home?"

"Well, it meets with my approval. But I'm glad you brought up my home. My housekeeper quit a couple of weeks ago to get married. So far I haven't replaced her. Stella, I'd like to offer you the position."

She was genuinely surprised. "But what about Hattie and Paul?"

"My housekeeper was also my cook, so I figure Hattie can do the cooking. And as for Paul, I'd love to have him in my home. However, I must warn you that I'll spoil him."

Stella could hardly believe her good fortune. "Mr. Wilkerson . . ."

"Bart," he reminded her.

"I mean Bart, I don't know what to say."

"I hope you'll say yes," he remarked encouragingly.

With joyful tears she answered, "Yes! And thank you!"

Meanwhile, at the other end of the table, Selina was saying quietly to Layne, "Darling, you seem preoccupied. I have the feeling your mind is miles away."

"Not miles," he answered. "Only as far as across the street."

"The saloon?"

He nodded. "I'm worried about Doug. I've never seen him so deeply down."

"I don't understand. Why is he depressed?"

"He's hopelessly in love with Janet."

For a moment, Selina was too astounded to reply. Then remembering, she said to Layne, "It might not be as hopeless as you think. Janet told me that Doug kissed her. It was back when you and I were in Clarksville."

Layne quirked a brow. "And?"

"And Janet responded."

"That doesn't mean anything," he mumbled dryly.

Selina wasn't so sure.

In the meantime, Jessie was watching them with disguised jealousy. They were speaking in hushed tones, and she couldn't hear what was being said. However, their intimate discussion didn't really interest her. She lowered her gaze to her glass of champagne and absently rubbed her fingers up and down its stem. She knew it was vital for her to keep a close surveillance on Layne, because an opportunity to set her wicked plan into motion might present itself at any moment. Somehow she knew it would happen tonight; she felt it, sensed it with every fiber of her being!

Twenty-five

"Selina," Layne said, putting down his empty coffee cup, "I'm going to check on Doug. It's late, so why don't you go on to bed. It's a long ride to the fort, and we'll be leaving early. I'll wake you at daybreak."

Selina took her napkin from her lap and placed it on the table. Dinner had been delicious and filling, and sighing uncomfortably, she told Layne secretly, "I'll be glad to get out of this corset."

He grinned wryly. "I told you once before that you don't need to wear those dadblasted things."

"Yes, I know," she whispered quietly.

"Your body is perfect the way it is," he whispered. "And I adore every inch of it."

She leaned over, kissed his cheek, and murmured, "I love you, darling."

He squeezed her hand, then stepped to the back of her chair and helped her rise. He glanced at Bart. "I'm heading across the street. Are you coming with me?"

"Yes, I am," he answered, getting to his feet.

They quickly bid the ladies good night, then crossed the dining room and left the hotel.

"Stella and I are going upstairs," Selina said to

Janet. "Are you coming with us?"

Janet sighed. "Yes, I think I will. I'm utterly fatigued."

Floyd touched her arm, saying pleadingly, "Don't you want to take a walk? I'd sure like for us to be alone for a while."

"I'm sorry, Floyd. But I'm too tired." She favored him with a sweet smile. "You don't mind, do you?"

"No, of course not," he assured her. However, he did mind! He sensed a change in Janet, a change that had come about since her abduction. Something was definitely different about her, but he couldn't quite pinpoint it.

Janet's thoughts were as puzzling as Miller's. She couldn't understand why she had refused his invitation. But her refusal had escaped her lips naturally, and without forethought. She told herself she was simply too fatigued for romance, and shrugged it off.

Stella smiled politely at Jessie. "Miss Harte, are you comin' upstairs?"

"No, I think I'll have another cup of coffee."

Jessie watched as the three women left the dining room, and the moment they were gone she stood and said to Miller, "Floyd, I want you to go to the saloon and watch Layne. If he starts drinking, report back to me. I'll be in my room."

Miller balked. "Hey, where do you get off tellin' me what to do? Don't you know how to ask?"

Concealing her anger, Jessie said congenially, "I'm sorry, Floyd. Will you please watch Layne for me?"

A cocky grin crossed his lips.

Jessie fumed. The man was exasperating, and she

longed to slap that smug grin off his face!

Watching her closely, Floyd asked with a leer, "If I help you, what do I get in return?"

Her impatience was now evident. "What do you want?" she snapped.

"The pleasure of your company in my bed."

She swallowed back a retort. "Very well."

"Tonight," he insisted.

"All right, dammit!" she raged quietly. "But not until I've carried out my plan."

"That's okay with me. I ain't in that big of a hurry." His face sobering, he wrapped his fingers tightly about her wrist. "But don't stand me up, Jessie. 'Cause if you do, I'll get mad, and when I get mad, I get even!" With that, he walked away.

Jessie, confident that she could handle Floyd, dismissed his threat and went in search of the waiter. She intended to order a bottle of brandy and two glasses.

As Layne and Bart entered the crowded, noisy saloon, they looked about trying to locate Doug.

Two prostitutes, spotting the handsome strangers, hurried over, eager to sell their favors. Slipping their hands about the men's arms, they tried to steer them to the bar.

They drew away gently. Layne smiled at the women and said, "Not tonight, ladies. We're looking for a friend. He's a big guy, wearing buckskins and probably drinking heavily."

One of the women pointed toward a corner of the room. "He's over there sittin' at a table."

"Thanks," Layne replied. With Bart following, they made their way through the crowd, past numerous tables where men were gambling at cards.

Doug drained the bottle as he filled his glass. Then, as he quaffed the whiskey down neatly, he saw Layne and Bart coming toward him. Two empty chairs were at his table, and he kicked them out a way, mumbling, "Sit down and join me."

As the men were seated, Doug beckoned to the waiter and ordered another bottle.

"How was dinner?" he asked, his glassy eyes flitting from one man to the other.

"Dinner was fine," Bart answered. "However, we missed your presence." His gaze zeroed in on Doug as he added carefully, "I think my daughter was very disappointed that you didn't join us."

Thompson's brow furrowed. "Don't hand me that crap."

Bart started to say more, but Layne, touching his arm to catch his attention, gave him a look that warned Wilkerson to let it rest.

However, he didn't take the warning. He had to know if Doug was in love with Janet; for if he was, he intended to do everything within his power to persuade his daughter to marry this man.

The waiter brought the order. As Layne reached into his pocket, Bart insisted, "No, I'll buy." He quickly handed over the money, then uncorking the bottle, he said to Doug, "I don't know how to thank you for saving my daughter."

"I already told you, a handshake is good enough."

Bart shook the man's hand firmly. "I'll always be in your debt."

Pointing to his empty glass, Doug responded, "In that case, fill it up, will ya?"

Wilkerson complied, and as Doug was downing the whiskey, he said, "I'm sure Janet is also very grateful."

Thompson banged his empty glass on the table top. His dark eyes glared into Bart's. "Wilkerson, if you're gonna keep talkin' 'bout Janet, then I'm gonna ask you to leave. You're a good friend, and I wouldn't wanna offend you, but that's just what I'm gonna do if you don't shut the hell up!"

"Doug," Layne cut in. "Cool down, will you?"

"It's all right, Layne," Wilkerson said hastily. "I'm not offended." He turned back to Doug. "I'm glad you consider me a friend, for I certainly consider you one. I only have one more thing to say about Janet, then that's it. Do you mind?"

"Go ahead, say it."

"I know how you feel about her, and I wish she shared your feelings."

"Well, she doesn't." Doug smirked bitterly, picked up the bottle, filled the three glasses, then lifted his and toasted, "Here's to good whiskey."

As the three men proceeded to drain the bottle, they didn't notice Miller standing at the bar. Due to the crowd, he could barely see them, but he could make them out well enough to know that Layne was drinking. He finished his own whiskey, then he left the saloon and returned to the hotel.

He hurried up the stairs and went to Jessie's room, where he knocked softly.

The door was opened almost immediately, and she asked anxiously, "Well? Is Layne drinking?"

"Like a fish," he answered, a large grin on his face.

Jessie was pleased. "Good! Now here's what I want you to do. Wait in the lobby, and when Layne returns, follow him upstairs. But don't let him see you. When I get him in my room, give me plenty of time to sedate him, get him undressed and into bed. Then bring Selina."

"How am I gonna get Selina here to your room?"

"I have a plan, and if you do as I say, everything will run smoothly." She smiled smugly. "Listen closely. Here's what I want you to do. . . ."

By the time Layne convinced Doug to call it a night, the man was obviously feeling his drinks. His steps were unsteady, so Smith and Wilkerson assisted him across the street and into the hotel. As they moved through the lobby and up the stairs, Floyd followed stealthily and undetected. Reaching Doug's room, Layne tried the door, which was unlocked, and he and Bart ushered their drunken friend inside. Then Bart left, telling Layne that he'd see him in the morning.

Layne lit the bedside lamp and, as he was adjusting the wick, suggested, "Don't you think you should get some sleep?"

Thompson didn't heed his friend's advice. He was staring at the mirror, seemingly absorbed with his reflection.

"Doug?" Layne called uncertainly.

He didn't hear Smith, for he was too engrossed in thought; and stepping to the dresser, he peered

335

more closely at his image. For a tense moment in his mind he compared his face to Miller's and, finding himself sorely lacking, doubled his large hand into a fist and sent it smashing into the glass. He laughed bitterly as his reflection shattered, then fell to the floor in jagged pieces.

"Doug, what the hell!" Layne grumbled. He moved to Doug quickly and checked his hand. Ironically, it was free of cuts.

Jerking his hand away, Doug complained gruffly, "Aw, leave me alone, dammit! I'm all right."

"Why did you break the mirror?"

"I don't wanna look at my ugly puss, do ya mind?" Thompson's words were slurred drunkenly. Lumbering to the bed, he fell across it. "Go away, Layne. Just leave me alone and let me sleep."

"Doug, Janet's not worth you torturing yourself like this."

"I know," he whispered, his tone rasping. "But I love her, Layne! I love her so damned much!" He rolled to his side, and within minutes his deep, methodical breathing told Layne that he was deeply asleep.

Smith left, closing the door quietly behind him. He was surprised to see Jessie standing in the hall. She was wearing a sheer, frilly dressing gown, and as she came to his side, he wondered if something were wrong.

"Layne," she began urgently, "I must talk to you."

"Is everything all right?" he asked.

"Yes, but . . . but we need to talk."

"Can't it wait? I'm tired."

She grasped his hand, urging him to follow.

336

"Please, Layne. It's very important."

Conceding reluctantly, he allowed Jessie to lead him farther down the hall to her open door. She stood back for him to precede her, and he stepped inside the room. She cast a secret glance down the corridor and, seeing Floyd standing in the shadows, smiled inwardly. Everything was going like clockwork.

Leaving the door ajar, she stepped to the dresser, where she had placed the brandy and glasses. The sleeping powder was already inside the glass she planned to give to Layne. She poured the drinks and handed Layne the drug-laced brandy.

He took the proffered liquor, even though he didn't really want it. He'd had enough to drink for one night. He took a big swig. The sooner he finished it, the sooner he could be on his way.

Jessie watched him warily. When he didn't question the taste, she sighed with relief. Apparently, the powder wasn't detectable.

"What do you want to talk about?" he asked, his voice tinged with impatience.

She lowered her gaze, pretending reluctance. "Layne, I don't know exactly how to tell you this but. . . ." Playing for time, she let her words fade away.

"But what?" he encouraged. Putting the glass to his lips, he swallowed a liberal amount.

Lifting her eyes to his, she said as though she had made a firm decision, "As soon as I finish my drink, I'll tell you. But first I need to build up my courage." She raised her glass in a toast. "Bottoms up!" she said daringly.

Layne drained his brandy, then handed her his empty glass. "Jessie," he began testily, "I don't have time for you to hedge with me. Please, just tell me what's on your mind." He wiped a hand over his perspiring brow. Damn, the room was hot! "Would you mind opening the window a little more?"

"Are you all right?" she asked. "You don't look well."

"I . . . I feel kinda light-headed. . . . Probably drank that brandy too fast." The floor beneath his feet seemed to be rocking, and he stumbled to the bed and sat on the edge.

Jessie watched him closely. The drug was beginning to take effect; he'd soon be out cold.

Layne, perspiring heavily, groaned, "I don't know what's wrong with me."

Placing her hands on his shoulders, Jessie eased him back onto the bed. "Rest for a moment, Layne. I'm sure you'll be fine."

He sank back onto the mattress gratefully. The whole room was spinning, making him nauseous. Afraid he was about to be sick, he closed his eyes. As blackness surrounded him, he felt as though he were falling into a never-ending void. Falling . . . Falling . . . Falling.

"Layne?" Jessie called softly.

Trying to fight his way out of the darkness, Layne murmured faintly, "Selina?"

Jessie smiled with pleasure. She hadn't counted on Layne mistaking her for Selina. This unexpected turn of events should make her task easier.

"Layne, darling," she urged, "help me undress you. Sit up, so I can slip off your suit jacket."

He did so groggily, and she removed his jacket and dropped it to the floor. She then slipped off his boots and was reaching for his shirt when his arms suddenly went about her shoulders, drawing her down beside him.

"Selina . . . Selina," he moaned.

Struggling free, she said persuasively, "Layne, darling, we must get you undressed." She began unbuttoning his shirt.

Layne, too drugged to separate dream from reality, put up no resistance, and Jessie took off his shirt with relative ease. She then moved her hands down to his trousers. Her fingers anxiously fumbled as they unbuckled his belt. She must hurry! Floyd and Selina would be here any moment!

Meanwhile, Miller, still standing at the far end of the hall, decided ample time had passed. Surely by now Jessie had Smith drugged and in her bed. A cunning gleam shone in his eyes as he headed toward the room Selina was sharing with Stella. He walked with an aura of confidence, for he was certain that Jessie's plan was fool-proof. He didn't doubt that Selina would leave her room with him, nor did he doubt that she'd find her fiancé in bed with another woman.

Reaching Selina's door, Floyd slipped his hand into his pocket and withdrew the key to his own room. Taking a deep breath, he mentally prepared himself to play his role. He acted as though he were trying to unlock the door to his own room.

Inside the room, Stella was in bed reading, and Selina was sitting on the window seat, brushing her hair a hundred strokes when she heard a noise at the door. It sounded as though someone were trying to unlock it. Putting down the brush, she hurried over and asked clearly, "Who's there?"

Miller, his confidence steadfast, answered in a drunken mumble, "Whatcha doin' in my room? . . . How come my key don't work?"

"Floyd?" Selina questioned, recognizing his voice.

"Yes'm, it's me. How come I can't get my key to work?"

Selina frowned irritably. "Floyd, you're drunk! This isn't your room. Your room is down the hall."

"It is?" he asked, as though dumbfounded. "Where exactly is it?"

Selina opened the door and said firmly, "Floyd, your room is next to Miss Harte's."

As he pretended to sway precariously, his eyes swept over Selina surreptitiously. She was wearing a soft, flowing dressing gown, and its azure shade enhanced her sky-blue eyes. Her freshly brushed chestnut tresses cascaded past her shoulders in full, silky curls. For a moment Miller was mesmerized by her breathtaking beauty. Then returning to the matter-at-hand, he said in a slur, "Miss Selina, ma'am, I think maybe . . . I had too much to . . . to drink. Would you . . . show me where my room is?" He faked a sheepish smile. "And, ma'am, would you unlock my door for me? I don't think I can see good enough to find the keyhole."

Selina couldn't help but smile. "Floyd, you shouldn't drink so much."

"Yes, ma'am," he mumbled, looking thoroughly chastised.

Selina turned her head toward the inside of her

room and called out, "Stella, I'll be right back." Closing the door, she motioned for Floyd to follow her.

Miller's room was on the other side of Jessie's, and to reach it they had to pass by Jessie's partially opened door.

Floyd kept his strides even with Selina's, then as they came to Jessie's room, he acted as though he were about to fall. He appeared to lose his balance, and his arms flailed wildly as his hands clutched at thin air.

Selina, hoping to keep him from falling, reached for him; but as she did, he pretended to collapse against Jessie's door, and it swung open wide.

Selina heard Jessie gasp with surprise. Intending to apologize for Floyd's clumsiness, Selina looked inside the room. However, what she saw there rendered her totally speechless. She could only stare with shocked disbelief.

Jessie, disentangling her nude body from Layne's, drew the sheet up over both of them. Turning her triumphant gaze to Selina, she said smugly, "Now, you know who he truly loves and desires."

She snuggled closer, and Layne, believing she was Selina, moved his hand to her breast, murmuring, "I love you, sweetheart." He was still struggling vainly to escape the deep depths of the black void imprisoning him.

"Layne!" Selina cried, confused and furious. When she received no response, she glanced quickly about the room and, spotting the brandy bottle and used glasses, supposed Layne was too drunk to answer. His condition, however, didn't lessen her anger, nor his guilt!

Her fiery gaze went to Jessie, and lifting her chin proudly, she remarked icily, "He's all yours, Miss Harte! I give him to you with my blessings!"

Whirling about, Selina rushed blindly down the hall and to her room.

The moment the door closed behind her, Floyd turned to Jessie and said firmly, "I'm goin' to my room. I'll expect you to join me in a few minutes. Don't keep me waitin'." Without further ado he left.

Jessie, gloating over her victory, wrapped her arms about Layne, holding him possessively close. His nude body pressed to hers was stimulating, and she wished Layne wasn't so heavily drugged. She knew he would sleep deeply for hours, and that rousing him was impossible. She sighed disappointedly, threw back the sheet, and got out of bed. If she couldn't have Layne to appease her passion, then Floyd was the next best thing.

She slipped into her dressing gown, then gazing down at Layne, she said with a crafty smile, "I'll be back before morning. When you wake up, you'll find me wrapped in your arms." She blew him a kiss. "Sleep well, my darling."

Taking her key with her, she left and locked the door securely. As she stepped to Floyd's room, her inner laugh was wickedly exultant.

Twenty-six

Stella looked up from her book as Selina entered the room. "My goodness," she observed. "You look as pale as a ghost." Her eyes narrowed angrily. "Did Floyd make advances toward you? He sounded awfully drunk."

Selina laughed bitterly, irrationally. "No, he didn't try anything."

Setting her book aside, Stella got out of her chair and approached Selina. "Something's wrong, I can tell. What is it?"

Trying unsuccessfully to hold back tears, Selina answered brokenly "It's Layne!" Anger mixing with her grief, she continued harshly, "He's a two-timing cad! I hate him!"

At a total loss, Stella questioned, "What in the world happened?"

"I just found Layne in bed with Jessie Harte!"

Selina swept past her and went to the bed. For a moment Stella was too taken aback to respond. Then, in hesitant steps she moved to Selina, who had fallen across the bed. Sitting beside her, Stella murmured, "I don't understand. Layne loves you."

"He doesn't love me!" she raged. "If he did, he wouldn't be in bed with another woman! Harold told me he was a womanizer, but I didn't believe him. Well, apparently he was telling the truth!"

Stella was thoroughly perplexed. "I just can't imagine Layne doin' something like this." She admired Layne and had set him above reproach.

Selina dejectedly arose from the bed and went to the window seat, where she sat and gazed blankly outside. Her emotions were still in shock, and what she had witnessed in Jessie's room hadn't yet fully sunk in. Her chin quivering, she whispered hoarsely, "I thought he loved me. I believed it with all my heart." Anguished sobs hitting her all at once, she covered her face with her hands, moaning, "He lied to me! He doesn't love me! He just wanted to use me! Oh, I was such a fool to believe him!"

Rushing to her friend, Stella sat beside her and drew her into her arms.

Crying uncontrollably, Selina sobbed, "He's in there with her right now! They . . . they are making love! Oh Stella, I actually heard him tell her that he loved her. And . . . and . . . he called her sweetheart!"

Stella, her heart breaking for Selina, held her tighter. "I'm so sorry," she whispered caringly.

Selina's tears continued to flow, and she cried until finally her sobs abated. Then she sat up stiffly, her posture ramrod straight. Her eyes, strangely cold, looked resolutely into Stella's. "I'm through crying over that heartless scoundrel. He isn't worth it."

She rose and began pacing the room. "He made a fool of me. I can accept that, and I'll simply chalk it up to a lesson bitterly learned. I was a complete innocent, and he wrapped me about his finger with incredible ease." She paused, turned to Stella, and remarked harshly, "Well, after tonight I'll never be vulnerable again! I am now a much wiser person. I learned my lesson well."

"Don't sound so cold and unfeeling," Stella pleaded. "It worries me to hear you talk like this."

"I'm sorry," Selina remarked crisply. "But that's how I feel." Layne's unfaithfulness had been such a severe blow that Selina knew her only recourse was to build an impregnable shield about her heart; otherwise, losing him would certainly throw her into a bottomless pit of depression.

"What are you gonna do?" Stella asked. "I mean, you can't go to Layne's ranch."

Selina, her chin raised willfully, answered decisively, "I'm going home. To Cedar Hill." She had never needed her haven as much as she needed it now. Surely the plantation that she loved so completely would give her the strength to carry on. There, surrounded by tranquility, she'd pick up the pieces of her shattered life, mend her broken heart, and find a way to go on living without Layne.

Stella didn't want Selina to go away, but she understood her reason for leaving. "I'll miss you," she murmured sadly.

Selina smiled timorously. "We'll stay in touch. Now that you can write, I'll expect letters from you."

"When are you leavin'?"

"I'll talk to Bart in the morning and ask him to make traveling arrangements for me."

Stella moaned wretchedly, "I can't believe this is happenin'. I'd been willin' to bet my life that Layne loved you more than anything on the face of this earth. I really thought he did!"

"I thought so too," Selina whispered hopelessly.

The next morning the sun had barely crested the horizon when Selina went down the hall to Bart's room. She knew he'd be awake, for he planned to ride to the army fort with Layne. She knocked lightly on the closed door.

Bart opened it and, gesturing her inside, asked, "Where's Layne?" He had thought they would arrive together. Then noticing she wasn't wearing riding clothes, he continued, "Aren't you going to the fort with us?"

"No, I changed my mind."

"You look tired," he said, studying her keenly. He had a feeling that something was wrong. "Didn't you sleep well?"

"I didn't sleep at all," she muttered flatly.

"Where's Layne?" he asked again. "I thought he'd be here by now. I'm ready to leave."

"Layne will most likely be late," she remarked with an undertone of anger. "He had a little too much to drink last night, and I'm sure he'll sleep in late."

"Then I'll go to his room and awaken him."

"You probably won't find him in his room."

Bart's brow furrowed with puzzlement.

"He's most likely in Miss Harte's room," she explained bitterly. "I'm sure they spent the night together."

Astonished, Bart gasped, "What?"

"You heard me," she said testily.

He took a step toward her, then hesitated. He felt as though he should do or say something consoling, but he was at a loss. "Would you like a cup of coffee?" he asked in lieu of anything better to say. "I had a tray sent up."

"Yes, thank you," she replied.

Bart led Selina to a chair, and her steady composure amazed him. He knew she had to be extremely upset, yet she was holding up remarkably well. His heart went out to her along with his admiration.

Stepping to the serving tray, he poured two cups of coffee. He was totally baffled by Layne's dalliance with Jessie. He could have sworn that Layne truly loved Selina, and he wondered if Selina could be mistaken.

Handing her a cup of coffee, he asked tentatively, "Are you absolutely sure that Layne and Jessie . . . ?"

"Oh yes, I'm sure," she intervened. "I saw them together."

"You actually saw them?" he asked, sitting in the chair across from hers.

Although it pained her enormously to do so, she told him exactly what had taken place.

Bart shook his head with disbelief. "I'm completely shocked."

Selina, steering the discussion away from Layne and Jessie, said, "Bart, I need your help."

"Of course," he agreed quickly.

"Will you please make traveling arrangements for

347

me? I want to return home."

"Are you sure?" he pressed her.

"Yes, I am."

He quirked a brow. "So you're going to let Jessie have him without a fight, eh?"

Selina's eyes hardened resentfully. "Bart, I no longer want him. She can damned well have the lying skunk!"

He nodded with understanding. "Very well, my dear. I'll make the arrangements for you. From Passing Through you'll have to take a stage to San Antonio, then from there a stage to Port's Landing in Louisiana. Then you can book passage on a ferry boat that will take you to New Orleans."

"Must I leave from Passing Through? Can't I take a stage from here?"

"Since we're leaving in the morning, I don't have time to arrange your trip. Besides, you should rest before attempting the long journey back to New Orleans."

"But I don't have a place to stay in Passing Through."

"You're more than welcome to stay with Janet and me."

"I wouldn't want to intrude."

He smiled warmly. "You'll not be an intrusion, but rather a most welcomed guest."

Selina knew he was right. She should rest before starting for home. But she was hesitant. "Bart," she began, stammering, "I don't . . . don't want to see Layne. I know I don't have the right to make such a request, but if I stay at your ranch, will you keep him away from me?"

"If that's what you want."

"It is! I don't want to come into contact with him or Miss Harte!"

"But you'll have to see them for the next couple of days. We're still two days away from Passing Through."

"I know," she replied evenly. A look of hard determination came over her face. "I'll just have to find a way to bear their presence." She wished she felt as confident as she sounded, and she knew that getting through the next two days would be terribly painful.

Jessie's room faced the east, and the morning sun shone through the open window. Its warm rays slanting across Layne's face woke him. Still half asleep and his mind muddled, he started to stretch his cramped muscles when suddenly he became aware of a soft, nude body cuddled against his. Quickly he raised up on an elbow and gazed down at the woman lying beside him. Why in the hell was he in bed with Jessie? Bewildered, he glanced about and, seeing that he was in her room, wondered what he was doing there. He searched his memory frantically, but as hard as he tried to remember, he drew a blank.

Shaking Jessie's shoulder insistently, he said gruffly, "Wake up, dammit!"

She roused herself reluctantly. She was exhausted, for she had spent the night making love to Floyd. He was a demanding, relentless lover, and her passion had been as persistent as his. She hadn't returned to her own room until moments before daybreak.

"Wake up, Jessie!" Layne ordered impatiently.

As Layne's voice penetrated her subconscious, she came fully awake with a start. Opening her eyes, she found him leaning over her, his face mere inches from hers. She smiled inwardly.

"What the hell's goin' on?" he demanded.

She looked at him innocently. "What do you mean?"

"Don't hedge with me, Jessie! Why are we in bed together?"

She forced an impatient frown. "Don't pretend that you don't know!"

Flinging off the sheet, he looked for his clothes. Finding them in a crumpled heap on the floor, he began to dress. "Jessie, I don't remember one damned thing about last night!"

"I don't believe you!" she replied, pretending anger. Her inward smile was still glowing.

Slipping into his trousers, Layne told her, "I remember coming to your room and having a glass of brandy. But after that my mind's a total blank."

Leaving the bed, Jessie drew on her dressing gown. She moved to Layne's side. "Darling, are you sure you don't remember?"

"Hell, yes, I'm sure!" he grumbled.

"You drank your brandy very quickly, and it made you feel lightheaded. You stepped to the bed and sat down."

Layne nodded. "I can remember that much."

"I told you to lie down and rest for a moment. That's when you took me into your arms and drew me down beside you. I tried to resist, but you were

350

determined. You told me that you loved me."

"I did what?" he yelled angrily.

She conjured up tears. "Please don't yell at me! None of this is my fault! I didn't seduce you, you seduced me!"

Layne sunk to the edge of the bed. "God!" he groaned.

She knelt at his feet, gazing imploringly into his ravaged face. "Layne, I asked you to my room last night to tell you that I'm madly in love with you. When you confessed that you felt the same way about me, I was ecstatic. Oh my dearest darling, please tell me you remember how passionately we made love! It was so wonderful, so heavenly!"

"Stop it!" he raved. He couldn't bear to hear anymore. Placing his elbows on his knees, he leaned over and rested his head in his hands. God, how could he have done such a thing? He loved Selina, not Jessie! Selina meant the world to him!

"Layne, are you all right?" she asked, touching his arm gingerly.

"No, I'm not all right!" he snapped. He grabbed his shirt and donned it quickly. He had to get out of there!

Jessie wasn't dissuaded by his abrupt manner; she had been expecting it. Getting to her feet, she stepped in front of him and once again gazed pleadingly into his face. "Layne, you owe me an explanation. You can't just rush out of my room as though nothing happened. Last night you told me you loved me and wanted to marry me. Was it all a lie?"

He sighed miserably. "I don't remember what I

told you but, yes, if I claimed that I loved you and wanted to marry you, then it was a lie. I love Selina, and she's the woman I intend to marry."

Playing the role of the scorned lover, she drew back her hand and slapped him across the cheek. "You bastard!"

He didn't blame her for striking him. He deserved it. "I'm sorry," he murmured, his voice so quiet that she barely heard him. "Nothing like this has ever happened to me before. I've been drunk more times than I can count, but I never had amnesia the next day. I've always been able to remember exactly what I did or said."

Draping his coat jacket and holster across his arm, he swept past her, heading for the door.

"Layne, wait!" she called.

He turned back to face her.

"There's something else you should know."

"What's that?"

Jessie swallowed nervously. This was the most perilous part of her ploy. She hoped he wouldn't react violently. "Selina saw us in bed together."

A look of abject misery fell across Layne's face. "God! How? Why?"

"When I brought you to my room, I left the door ajar. When we started making love, I completely forgot to close it. For some reason Selina and Floyd were in the hall together. All at once the door swung open. I looked up and saw Selina and Floyd gaping at us. Darling, don't you remember?"

Desperate to find Selina, to explain, to beg her forgiveness, Layne rushed out of the room. As he stepped into the hall, he saw her leaving Bart's quarters.

She started down the corridor and had taken a couple of steps before spotting Layne. She halted abruptly.

"Selina," he said huskily, his eyes pleading with hers.

"Stay away from me!" she demanded, her tone furious.

He reached her side in two long strides. "Selina, you've got to let me explain."

"Explain?" she questioned harshly. "What kind of fool do you think I am?" Her eyes raked him disdainfully. He had dressed haphazardly, his shirt halfway tucked into his trousers. His hair was mussed, and he needed a shave. Noticing his jacket and holster draped over his arm, she said caustically, "You're pathetic, Layne Smith! Sneaking into Jessie's room, and now sneaking out of it! You lowdown, despicable worm!"

His free hand shot out, capturing her wrist. "Dammit, Selina! You're gonna listen to me!"

"Let me go!" she yelled, trying to break his hold.

"Not until you hear what I have to say!" he yelled back.

Their loud voices brought both Bart and Stella into the hall.

Aware of their presence, Layne released Selina reluctantly. She brushed past him and retreated into her room. Stella followed, slamming the door closed.

"Layne," Bart said evenly, "there's coffee in my room. Come in and have a cup."

He accepted readily. He needed a cup of coffee.

Maybe it'd help clear his head.

Going to the chair Selina had occupied earlier, Layne dropped into it heavily. Placing his coat and holster on the floor, he mumbled with a grimace, "I didn't realize it until now, but I have one helluva headache."

Handing him a full cup, Bart replied, "Hangovers can be mean. I've had my share." He sat down in the other chair.

Layne drank his coffee in silence. It hit the spot; just what he needed. He set the empty cup on the small table beside his chair. Leaning back and stretching out his long legs, he asked Bart calmly, "Did Selina tell you what happened?"

"Yes, she did."

"Then you know I spent the night with Jessie?"

"Layne, this is really none of my business. Please don't feel as though you owe me an explanation."

Layne laughed shortly, bitterly. "Bart, I couldn't give you an explanation even if I wanted to. I don't remember one damned thing about last night."

"What?"

"Well, let me rephrase that. I can remember up to a point, and that's it. Last night when I left Doug's room, Jessie was waiting for me. She said she needed to talk to me. I went to her room. She poured me a brandy. I drank it a little too quickly, and it made me feel woozy. I stepped to her bed and sat down. After that I don't remember anything. I swear it's the God's truth! When I woke up this morning to find myself in bed with Jessie, it was the shock of my life."

"Whiskey-induced amnesia?" Wilkerson suggested.

"Aw hell, Bart! I've been drunk before, but it never caused me to lose my memory. In fact I've been a lot drunker than I was last night. I don't think I was all that drunk. I'd had quite a few drinks, true, but I wasn't really feeling them."

"Then why do you suppose . . . ?"

Layne shrugged heavily. "I don't know." Picking up his cup, he went and poured himself more coffee. Turning back to Bart, he asked, "Why was Selina here? I can't believe she visited you this early in the morning just to tell you about Jessie and me."

"She asked me to make traveling arrangements for her. She wants to go home."

"To Cedar Hill, no doubt."

"I convinced her to stay at my ranch for a few days, then after she's rested, I'll arrange her passage home."

Layne finished his coffee, then remarked firmly, "She isn't going anywhere, except to my ranch!"

As Layne took a step forward, Bart leapt to his feet, blocking his way.

"I'm goin' to Selina, and don't try to stop me!" Layne uttered inflexibly. "I love her, and I don't intend to lose her!" His eyes were unyielding, and his expression verged on savage fury.

"If you go charging after her like a wild caveman, intending to grab a handful of hair and drag her to your cave, then you'll most certainly lose her! She's a lady, and a very proud one."

Layne conceded to reason. Moving to the chair, he slumped into it. "What the hell am I gonna do? How do I get her back?"

Wilkerson sighed sympathetically. "You might not get her back. The sooner you accept that possibility, the better off you're going to be."

Twenty-seven

Standing at the window in his room, Doug smiled with relief when he caught sight of Layne and Bart. They had just returned from the army fort and had left their horses at the livery. They were now walking toward the hotel. It was late, the sun had set hours ago, and Doug had begun to worry about his friends. He stepped to the door and opened it. When he heard the men climbing the stairs, he crossed the threshold as they were entering the corridor. "I was beginnin' to wonder if you two got lost," he said lightly.

"It's a long ride to the fort," Layne said.

"I have a bottle in my room, if you two want a drink."

"Sounds good to me," Bart replied.

The men stepped inside, and Doug poured three glasses of whiskey. "How did it go?" he asked.

"We talked to Major Winters," Layne said. "He was in command of the troops who killed the Comanches you came across. They confiscated the Indians' horses, and their plunder. The major gave me permission to examine the stolen merchandise, and I found Chamberlain's horse and his belongings."

"Then that's proof that he's dead," Doug remarked.

"Not necessarily," Layne replied. "Chamberlain would never travel without a large sum of money, but no money was found."

"Maybe one of the soldiers found it and stuck it in his pocket."

"That thought crossed my mind too. I mentioned it to the major. He disagreed firmly. He's certain that none of his men kept the money."

"What do you think?"

"I don't think we can completely disregard the possibility. Nor can we be sure that Chamberlain is dead. I have a feelin' he might be wherever his money is."

Doug's brow furrowed. "But if he's alive, how did he get away, and with his money no less?"

"He usually wears a money belt strapped about his waist. So if he was able to escape, the money was on him. I guess I should tell Watts about this."

"He and his men left town shortly after you and Bart left. I suppose he was in a hurry to get back to New Orleans."

Bart, finishing his drink, asked Doug, "Have you had dinner yet?"

"No, I haven't."

"Well, Layne and I are going to clean up, then go to the dining room. Why don't you join us?"

"Thanks. I think I will."

"Have the others already eaten?" Bart asked.

He nodded. " 'Bout an hour ago."

"I'll see you two later," Bart replied and left.

Doug turned to Layne and demanded bluntly, "What's goin' on between you and Jessie?"

Layne poured himself another drink. "Apparently, bad news travels fast. Who told you?"

"Stella. Selina's been closed up in her room all day; when I asked Stella what was wrong, she told me what happened." Doug scowled irritably. "Damn Layne! Why did you do something so stupid?"

"I wish to hell I knew why," he mumbled, downing his drink.

"Would you like to explain that?"

Layne gave Doug an account of last night's activities. He summed it up by saying, "If only I could remember!"

"None of this makes any sense, Layne. I've seen you drunk more than once, but the next day you never had trouble remembering anything."

"I know," he replied heavily. "That's what makes last night so strange." He put down his empty glass and, heading for the door, said, "I'm gonna wash up. I'll meet you in the dinin' room."

Doug helped himself to a liberal drink. He moved to the dresser and gazed into the new mirror. The shattered pieces of the previous one had been removed and another mirror hung. He studied his reflection for a moment and, disappointed with his image, was tempted to once again smash his fist into the new looking-glass. He turned away brusquely and returned to peering vacantly out the window.

Selina lay in bed, wishing repose would take over. If she could fall soundly asleep, then maybe in slumber she could find peace. But her mind remained wide awake. Finally, deciding a brisk walk and fresh air might help her relax, she threw off the cover and got out of bed.

Stella was sitting in a chair, reading intently. Glancing up, she asked, "Can't you sleep?"

"No," Selina answered, stepping to the wardrobe. She began to dress.

"Surely you aren't plannin' to go outside!" Stella remarked.

"I need a breath of fresh air."

"But, Selina, it could be dangerous. It's late, and this town is kinda rowdy."

"I'll be all right," she replied, strapping on her derringer.

"I'll go with you," Stella decided.

"No, please," Selina answered, slipping into a powder-blue gown. "I'd rather be alone."

Stella conceded with reservations. "Well, if you're sure."

Selina dressed quickly. "I won't be gone long," she assured her friend, then left.

She was hurrying down the dimly lit hall when she detected heavy footsteps ascending the stairs. She hesitated. The far end of the corridor was somewhat dark, and she watched warily as a tall figure came into view. As his shadowy form came closer, she saw that it was Layne. She drew a sharp intake of breath, and her heart felt as if it had slammed against her rib cage.

Seeing Selina, Layne's jaw tightened, and his muscles grew rigid as he moved toward her with the stealth of a stalking predator.

She turned to flee, but Layne, moving lithely,

grasped her from behind. Wrapping an arm about her waist, he whirled her around and lifted her smoothly.

"Put me down!" she cried furiously.

His dark eyes bore into hers. "We need to talk, dammit!"

She smelled liquor on his breath. "Drunk again, are you?" she remarked tartly. "If you don't put me down, I'll scream!"

When he didn't comply, she opened her mouth to carry out her threat, but his lips were suddenly on hers, smothering her cry for help.

Despite her struggles, Layne, without interrupting his demanding kiss, carried her to his door, opened it, and took her inside. Then he lowered her to her feet. His fingers latched onto her wrist, and he went to the lamp, taking her with him, lit it, and adjusted the wick down to a low-burning light. He then released her and returned to the door, pushing in the bolt.

"What do you think you're doing?" Selina asked harshly.

Layne's expression was promising. "I once told you that someday we'd make love behind a locked door."

"You contemptible, low-down snake! Do you think I want you after . . . after what I saw last night? If you're so determined to make love, then I suggest you visit Jessie Harte! Why aren't you with her now? Did she turn you out of her bed?"

He dismissed her angry accusations. "Where the hell were you goin'?"

"Outside for a breath of fresh air."

His eyes narrowed. "You'll never learn, will you? When are you going to realize that it's not safe for a woman to come and go as she pleases?"

"I'd rather take my chances in the streets of this town than be here with you."

"Well, that choice isn't yours to make."

"Are you saying that you intend to keep me here by force?"

"Yes, until we settle a couple of things."

"I refuse to talk to you. You're drunk!"

Although Layne had gone to the saloon after dinner, he wasn't drunk. "Believe me, I'm in full control of my faculties."

"Yes, I'm sure you are!" she replied bitingly. "Just like you were in control last night!"

He took a tentative step toward her, but she backed away. Pausing, he said with a note of pleading, "Selina, about last night. . . ."

"I don't want to hear it!" she cut in sharply. Mustering a semblance of composure, she continued, "You said we have a couple of things to discuss. I'm sure one of them is last night. However, I won't talk about it. Now what is the second thing we need to settle?"

An indolent smile crossed his sensual lips. "I intend to remove all your clothes and make love to you in a bed."

"Oh you do, do you?" she spat, fuming. Moving swiftly, she reached beneath her skirt and drew her derringer. Aiming it at him, she ordered, "I'm leaving this room, Mr. Smith, and if you try to stop me, I'll shoot you right through your cheating heart!"

He stepped aside, made a sweeping gesture toward the door, and said, "In that case, Miss Beaumont, you're free to leave. I never argue with a loaded gun."

With the weapon pointed in his direction, she moved cautiously to the locked door. Keeping her eyes on him, she fumbled for the bolt, found it, and tried to release it. But it was stuck and refused to budge. Frustrated, she took her eyes off Layne to check the bolt. He then pounced with lightning speed and had the derringer wrested from her hand before she had time to react.

Pitching the gun into a chair, he once again swept her into his arms. Carrying her to the bed, he laid her down gently, lowering his body over hers.

"So help me, Layne!" she threatened. "If you don't let me up, I'll scream as loudly as I can!"

"Try it, and I'll not only stop you, but I'll also gag your beautiful mouth."

Layne's closeness was very exciting, and Selina could feel her body weakening, betraying her. Fighting her desire, as well as the man evoking it, she pushed against him while struggling wildly.

Seizing her wrists with one hand, Layne pinned her arms over her head. As his lips descended to hers, she tried to turn her face away, but his mouth captured hers forcefully. Demandingly he pried her lips apart, compelling her to accept his aggressive kiss.

"Darlin'," he whispered hoarsely, "I want you! God, how much I want you!"

Selina, her body now completely ignoring her

better judgment, relaxed beneath Layne's weight. Even through their clothes, she could feel his male hardness pressed against her. She felt a sweet ache building between her thighs, an ache she knew only Layne could appease.

He was a lying scoundrel! A cheat! If only she could truly despise him, but her heart had a will of its own. Surrendering to her heart's command, Selina gazed defeatedly into Layne's watching eyes. "I can't fight you," she murmured. "I want you too, Layne."

Carefully he released her imprisoned wrists. Joy swept through him as her arms went about his neck, urging his lips down to hers. Had she forgiven him? Surely she had; otherwise, she wouldn't submit so sweetly.

As his mouth, warm and demanding, moved over hers, she arched her hips suggestively. Burying her pride in the far recesses of her mind, she was conscious only of Layne's nearness and his lips sending fire through every nerve in her body.

Layne's desire was kindled by her response, and his kisses grew more demanding. His passion was so breathtakingly aggressive that Selina was soon yearning for him to conquer her completely.

"Layne," she whispered raspingly. "Now! Take me now. I must have you now!"

"Sweetheart!" he groaned. Eager to admire her bared beauty, he stripped away her clothes with controlled speed.

His dark eyes, raking her fervently, adored her full breasts, tiny waist, and long, shapely legs. As his gaze came to rest on the soft, curling hair between her ivory thighs, his need to consummate their love overwhelmed him.

Lifting her into his arms, he placed her back on the bed, then he quickly shed his own clothes.

Watching him disrobe, Selina was mesmerized by his strong, masculine physique. He was so handsome, so irresistible!

She held out her arms, and he went eagerly into her embrace. He stretched out at her side, and she rolled toward him, pressing her naked thighs to his.

He ran his hand up and down the furrow of her spine as she slid her hand down his back to his firm buttocks. She gazed deeply into his eyes, and her lips opened in mute invitation. He kissed her passionately, his tongue moving into her mouth with a fiery urgency. She clung to him, wanting the kiss to go on and on!

Gently he eased her onto her back, and taking his lips from hers, he rained feather-light kisses over her neck, then down to her breasts. Steadily his warm lips ventured lower, claiming her totally.

A feeling of ecstasy rose and flared in her, and arching her hips, she surrendered ardently. His intimacy worked magic on her senses, and she was soon writhing and moaning with glorious rapture.

Layne's passion was now at fever pitch, and he moved over her, anxious to make them as one. "Put your legs about my waist," he urged huskily.

Locking her ankles firmly, she waited expectantly for his exciting entry. He shoved his hips forward, and a starburst of ecstasy shot through her as his hardness was thrust deeply within her.

They made love with a fiery intensity, and their

hips pumped rapidly, their kisses wet, aggressively amorous. Each deepening thrust brought the lovers closer to the brink of climax, and abandoning themselves to their ultimate fulfillment, they spiraled upward to passion's peak.

Sated, Layne moved to lay at her side. An uneasy silence hovered between them, and their labored breathing was the only sound in the quiet room.

Layne, hoping she would listen to his explanation, broke the silence. "Selina, about last night. . . ."

"Don't!" she interrupted sharply. Leaving the bed, she stepped to her clothes and began to dress.

Sitting up, Layne insisted, "Dammit, Selina! You've got to listen to me!"

"No, I don't have to listen!" she retorted. He started to speak, but she held up her hand, her expression pleading for his silence. She slipped hurriedly into her clothes, then moved to the edge of the bed. Sitting beside him, she put on her shoes. Drawing a deep breath, she then turned to him and said with a composure she didn't truly feel, "Layne, I cannot resist your advances. I won't pretend that I can. But don't make the mistake of thinking that what happened tonight has changed anything. For it hasn't. I can't forgive your infidelity."

Her tone was so coldly final that it chilled Layne to the core. "Selina, I love you," he said, his voice pleading.

She stood glaring into his eyes. "I don't believe you! If you loved me, you wouldn't have gone to bed with Jessie Harte!"

"Selina, I swear that I don't remember taking Jessie to bed. I don't know why, but for some reason my memory is totally blank. I can remember going to her room and having a drink, but after that I can't recall anything."

She laughed bitterly. "That excuse is so pitiful that it's ludicrous! You must think I'm an utter fool!"

"It's the truth!" he asserted, bounding to his feet. He reached for her, but she stepped back. "Layne," she began, her composure precarious, "if you have a shred of decency in you, you'll leave me alone. I'm asking you to stay out of my life." Tears welled up in her eyes, and her voice broke pathetically. "Must I beg you?"

Layne's jaw clenched tightly, and a hard determination burned in the depths of his eyes. "I won't let you go that easily," he said firmly. "I love you, Selina. You're mine, and I'll hold onto you one way or another."

To Selina, his words were a declaration of war. "You can't make me love you!" she cried, flashing into sudden fury.

"You already love me!" was his riposte.

"No, I don't!" she denied angrily. "I might desire you, but I no longer love you!"

He stepped forward to grasp her arm, but she turned on him with a defiant frenzy. She slapped him soundly across the cheek, the force so powerful that it sounded throughout the room.

Whirling about, she rushed to her derringer, turned, and pointed it at him. "Layne, I'm warning you to leave me alone!" she blazed tightly. "Just stay

367

the hell out of my life!"

A blood-chilling anger raced through his veins as he watched her release the bolt, open the door, then rush out of the room.

He walked over and shoved the door closed with a solid bang. Damn the stubborn little vixen! Why couldn't she believe him? He didn't remember last night! Dammit! He didn't remember!

He moved back to the bed and sat down. As his anger began to cool, he found himself recalling Selina's pathetic plea to leave her alone. He wondered if perhaps he should do just that. She'd never forgive him. He had lost her. He might as well admit it, then learn to live with it. Not remembering going to bed with Jessie didn't make him any less guilty. Selina wanted nothing more to do with him, and he had no one to blame but himself. He supposed that sometimes loving was knowing when to let go. Did he love her enough to set her free? He shrugged as though suddenly resigned.

He dressed quickly, stuffed his belongings in his carpetbag then, leaving the room, went down the hall and knocked on Doug's door.

Thompson was in bed. Slipping into his trousers, he stepped to the door and opened it.

Layne entered and told him, "I'm leaving. Now that Bart and his men are here, they can take care of the women. There's no reason for me to go along."

"Or me," Doug replied. I'll get packed and leave with you."

"While you do that, I'll go tell Bart we've decided to move on."

Layne left, and Doug began putting on the rest of his clothes. He didn't doubt that Layne's decision to leave was inspired by his estrangement from Selina. Well, his own reason for pulling out was closely related to Layne's. He wanted to put distance between himself and Janet. Watching her blossoming romance with Floyd was a pain he could do without.

Twenty-eight

As the wagon moved slowly across the Texas plains, white fluffy clouds scudded across the azure sky, affording intermittent relief from the dazzling sun. A summer breeze, stroking the limitless landscape, sent yellow dust drifting from under the omnipresent mesquites and cottonwoods.

Bart was driving the team; and due to the hot weather, he kept the horses at a plodding pace. He had asked Stella to ride beside him, and she had agreed readily, for she found Bart very attractive and was becoming quite infatuated with him.

Janet and Selina rode inside the wagon with Hattie and Paul. Jessie, preferring to avoid Selina, was riding horseback.

Now, as Hattie studied the two sullen women sitting across from her, she clucked her tongue, saying crankily, "You two ain't said more than two words since we left Dry River." She looked tenderly at Selina. Stella had told her about Layne and Jessie. "I's sorry, honey," she said softly. "I know why you is so sad." Then turning her gaze to Janet, she remarked, "But I don't know why you look like someone who just lost her best friend."

Janet sighed glumly. "But I do feel like I lost my

best friend."

"Mista Doug?" Hattie questioned knowingly.

"It just doesn't seem right to be traveling without Doug and Layne. I mean, we all came so far together. And now I miss them—especially Doug." A trace of tears came to her eyes. "I wish he hadn't left. He didn't even bother to tell me goodbye."

Impatience rose in Selina as she wondered if Janet was really as unperceiving as she sounded. Was she truly too blind to see that Doug was hopelessly in love with her? She suppressed the urge to reach over and shake some sense into the young woman. In Selina's opinion, Janet was fortunate to have a man like Doug in love with her. He wasn't a two-timing snake like Layne! He was the kind of man a woman could trust.

"Janet," she began somewhat testily, "I find it hard to believe that you don't know why Doug left without saying goodbye."

Janet was sincerely baffled.

"He's in love with you," Selina said bluntly.

"What?" Janet gasped, thoroughly surprised.

Hattie chuckled. "Miz Janet, honey, if you don't know how much that man loves you, then you is the only one who don't. It's written all over his face everytime he looks at you."

Janet disagreed with her companions. "Doug doesn't feel that way about me. If he did, he'd have said something. He merely thinks of me as a friend."

Hattie decided not to press the issue; instead, she used a different approach. "Miz Janet, exactly how do you feel 'bout Mista Doug?"

"I like him a lot."

"Do you find 'im attractive?"

Janet smiled reflectively. "When I first met him, I thought he was attractive in a savage, forbidding way. But now I don't think of him in that manner. I see him as a very rugged, but irresistible man. He isn't typically handsome, but there's a virile aura about him that is not only charming, but also fascinating."

"Yes,'m," Hattie concurred. "That's a good description of Mista Doug. But don't forget that he's not only a gentle man, but a brave one." She smiled broadly. "That Mista Doug, someday he'll make some woman a wonderful husband. He'll treat her real good, and she'll feel safe and protected."

"Yes, I suppose she will," Janet murmured, wondering why Hattie's prediction had caused her dour spirits to submerge even deeper.

At that moment Bart announced that it was time to stop for the noon break. Anxious to leave the wagon and stretch her cramped legs, Janet dismissed Doug from her thoughts.

Floyd dismounted, stepped to the backboard, and unlatched it. Janet offered him her hand, and he assisted her down to the ground.

"Let's take a walk," he whispered in her ear. "There's something I wanna ask you."

She smiled up into his handsome face. "All right," she agreed.

Watching the pair walk away, Hattie mumbled disapprovingly, "You'd think Miz Janet would have enough sense to know that Mista Floyd ain't worth two cents."

Selina, drawing Paul into her arms, answered, "Janet's a fool. I just hope she'll wise up before it's too late." Hugging the child close, she rested her cheek against his soft golden curls. Fighting back tears, she continued solemnly, "I have no right to call Janet a fool. I'm a bigger one than she is."

"Miz Selina," Hattie said firmly. "I don't believe Mista Layne gives a hoot 'bout Miz Harte. That man's in love with you."

Leaving the wagon with Paul in her arms, Selina said bitterly, "If Layne loves me, then he has a warped way of showing it." She turned back to Hattie, her eyes glaring. "Layne's kind of love I can live without!"

When Floyd and Janet had strolled a good distance from the campsite, Floyd turned to her and took her into his embrace. Feigning devotion, he murmured, "Janet, I love you so much."

As his lips descended to hers, she met his kiss halfway. Entwining her arms about his neck, she surrendered expectantly to his fervent ardor. She waited for their intimacy to send her heart pounding, and her head spinning with ecstasy. The wonderous feelings failed to materialize, and, disappointed, Janet pushed out of his embrace.

"What's wrong?" he asked pressingly. Damn! What was her problem? He'd never encountered a woman so difficult to seduce. Was the little bitch frigid?

"I'm sorry, Floyd," she said quietly. Janet's thoughts were running along the same lines as Mill-

373

er's. In New Orleans she'd had several suitors, and when she could escape her uncle's and aunt's watchful eyes, she had allowed these beaux to kiss her. But, like Floyd, their kisses had failed to awaken her passion. She wondered if perhaps she was frigid. She had heard that some women were naturally that way, and there was nothing they could do about it. Janet didn't want to be like those women, she longed for love, for romance. She wanted to experience breathtaking passion, the kind that comes with true love. Were her dreams in vain? Was she incapable of feeling such primitive, heart-stopping desire?

Janet, certain that she was hopelessly frigid, was on the verge of sinking into a state of despair when suddenly a memory flashed before her. A memory she had pushed to a remote corner of her mind. Now freed, it came to her with clarity. A strange, almost imperceptible tremor ran through her as she recalled the way in which she had responded to Doug's kiss. His lips on hers had evoked a hungry, breathless response.

Floyd's voice nudged into her thoughts, "Janet, you seem miles away. What's on your mind?"

"I was just thinking," she replied evasively. She tried to cast the memory of Doug's kiss from her mind and give Floyd her undivided attention. But the memory was stubborn; it held steadfast.

Placing his hands on her shoulders, Miller's gaze searched her face. He had a feeling that her thoughts were still elsewhere. Well, he knew how to bring her happily back to reality. He'd ask her to marry him.

Meanwhile, Janet was now completely lost in her reverie. Lord, how could she have been such a fool! The proof of her love had been there all the time, but she had been too blind to see it! Was her love returned? she wondered desperately. Recalling her earlier discussion with Selina and Hattie, she hoped that their speculation had been right.

"Janet," Floyd began, pretending deep feeling, "I adore you with all my heart. Darlin', will you marry me?"

Janet brought herself out of her musings reluctantly. "I'm sorry, I wasn't listening. What did you say?"

Miller was annoyed. "I asked you to marry me."

"You did?" she exclaimed with surprise.

"I love you," he said, his tone now almost a whine. "Don't you love me? Don't you wanna get married?"

Oh yes, she wanted to get married! But not to Floyd Miller! She gazed at Floyd tenderly. She liked him and wished that she didn't have to hurt him. "I can't marry you," she said softly.

He was astounded. It had never occurred to him that she might turn down his proposal. "Why?" he demanded. "Why can't you marry me?"

A smile he couldn't discern played across her lips. "I'm in love with someone else."

"What!" he raged. "I don't believe it!"

"Floyd, I'm more shocked than you are. But it's the truth. I've never been more certain of anything in my life."

"Who the hell do you love?"

"Doug Thompson," she replied.

"Thompson!" he shouted, his anger apparent.

Ignoring his agitation, she murmured dreamily, "I love him, Floyd. And I can't wait to tell him." A warm, love-filled smile brightened her face.

Enraged, Floyd mumbled spitefully, "You damned teasing little bitch!" He drew up an arm as though he were about to strike her. "I oughta . . ."

"You should what?" she questioned, her own anger surfacing.

Wisely, Miller cooled his temper. Bart Wilkerson would string him up to the nearest tree if he struck Janet. Afraid she might tell her father that he had come close to hitting her, he faked an apology. "I'm sorry, Janet. I'd never hurt you. You believe me, don't you?"

"Yes, I guess so," she replied uncertainly. Wanting him to go away and leave her alone, she said, "Floyd, please go back to camp. I'll follow later."

He was more than ready to leave. He despised the little tease! Damn her to hell! Her and Thompson both! Whirling about, he walked away swiftly.

Janet, moving as though in a dreamlike trance, walked over to a patch of shade cast by a tall cottonwood. Believing herself totally alone, she hiked her long skirt, crossed her legs, and sat down Indian-fashion. Placing her elbows on her knees, she cupped her chin in her hands and became pleasantly engrossed in thoughts of Doug.

Janet, however, wasn't alone. The three men Floyd had solicited to help kidnap her were hidden in the nearby brush. They had been in Dry River when the travelers had arrived, but had intentionally eluded Miller. They hadn't discarded their plan

376

to abduct Janet, but they had decided not to include Floyd. Why split the money four ways, when they could narrow it down to three? They had been sorely disappointed to find that Wilkerson, along with his drovers, were now escorting Janet. Disillusioned, certain their plan was foiled, they had almost dismissed their project; but reluctant to give up quite so easily, they had decided to follow the travelers. The men were hopeful that a chance to abduct Janet would present itself. And now it had happened! She was alone, and snatching her would be incredibly easy.

A twig snapped, attracting Janet's attention. Glancing up, she was startled to see three men coming toward her. The largest of the three had his pistol drawn and aimed at her. "Scream," he threatened gruffly, "and I'll blow your brains out!"

Janet got shakily to her feet. "What . . . what do you want?" she asked, her heart gripped with fear.

Reaching her, the large man drew her close, clamping a hand over her mouth. He spoke to one of his comrades, "Stick the note on that tree trunk."

The man removed a sheet of paper from his pocket then, unsheathing his knife, used the sharp blade to pin the note to the rough bark. The paper hung securely.

Keeping his hand over Janet's mouth, her captor forced her to leave with him and his partners.

Bart had been so busy helping the others set up a temporary camp that Floyd's return escaped his notice. The young man had been back several minutes before Bart became aware of his presence.

Now, glancing about and failing to spot his daughter, he went over to Miller and asked, "Where's Janet?"

He gestured in the general direction. "She's out there."

"Why did you leave her?" Wilkerson was irritated.

"She said she wanted to be alone," he answered glumly.

Perturbed, Bart wheeled about sharply and headed away from camp to find his daughter.

Looking on, Jessie walked up to Floyd and asked, "What's going on?"

"Wilkerson's mad 'cause I didn't bring Janet back with me."

"Why didn't you?"

Scowling, he grumbled, "I asked her to marry me, but the damned bitch turned me down!"

Jessie was genuinely surprised. "Did she give you a reason for refusing?"

"Yeah!" he uttered between gritted teeth. "She's in love with Thompson."

"Doug?" Jessie exclaimed. Bringing the man's image to mind, she didn't blame Janet for wanting him. In her opinion, Doug Thompson was powerfully masculine.

They talked a few more minutes, and Jessie was sympathizing with Floyd half-heartedly when suddenly they were interrupted by Bart's blustering voice.

"Miller!" he raged, coming toward them with a piece of paper clutched in his hand.

Floyd, certain something had happened to Janet,

378

braced himself for the man's tirade.

"Read this!" Bart ordered, shoving the note at him.

Miller's eyes scanned it hastily. He was certain that he knew the men responsible for kidnapping Janet. His blood began to boil! The dirty bastards had double-crossed him! Concealing his rage, he pasted a contrite expression on his face, handed back the note, and said, "I'm sorry, Mr. Wilkerson. But you gotta understand that Janet insisted that I leave her alone."

"No!" he raved furiously. "I don't have to understand anything you say! Miller, if I get my daughter out of this alive, and if you try to see her, I'll knock the living hell out of you! Now, do you understand me?"

Miller's hands were balled into fists, and he longed to send them plowing into Wilkerson's face. But his better sense held him in check. "You don't have to worry, I won't be tryin' to see her."

"Good!" Bart remarked. He turned about to walk away, but whirling back around, he barked, "Furthermore, you're fired! Get the hell out of my sight!"

As Wilkerson left to tell the others what had happened, Jessie grasped Miller's arm and said, "Floyd, I'm leaving with you." She frowned irritably, explaining, "I don't want to travel another day with these people. They keep looking at me as though I'm Jezebel reincarnated. They're all so pious, so damned loyal to Selina!"

"What did you expect?" Floyd asked. "You should've known it'd be like this."

379

"Yes, but I thought Layne would be traveling with us. His presence would've made it all bearable. I can't believe he didn't even bother to tell me he was leaving."

"Pack us some provisions," Miller ordered tersely. "So we can get the hell out of here."

She started to comply but hesitated, and asked, "Floyd, the men who kidnapped Janet, do you suppose they're the . . ."

He interrupted, "Yeah, they're the same ones. I guess they didn't leave Dry River, but have been watchin' us the whole time. The damned bastards planned to double-cross me from the beginning."

"Well, if they're caught, you better hope they don't involve you."

A stab of fear shot through him. "Damn! I hadn't thought of that!"

As Jessie left to pack the provisions, Miller didn't bother to wipe away the nervous perspiration that was now beading heavily on his brow.

Meanwhile, at the campfire Bart was saying to the women, "I can't go after Janet. In the note the kidnappers said that if I pursue them, they'll kill her. I'm supposed to go to my ranch and wait for one of them to contact me."

Stella was standing beside him, and placing a hand gently on his arm, she asked, "Are you goin' to do as they instructed?"

Heaving a deep sigh, he murmured, "I don't see where I have any other choice. I'm sure they'll keep Janet safe until they collect the ransom. That will give me time to come up with a plan—a way to save her." He groaned heavily. "God, help me!"

Selina turned away from Bart's grief-stricken face. Her eyes meeting Hattie's she whispered wretchedly, "This time, Doug isn't here to save her."

Layne and Doug sat beneath the shade of a cottonwood. The surrounding tableau was fertile, pastoral. Their horses, unsaddled, grazed nearby. Layne, watching his stallion, grimaced as he saw the animal favor his bruised hoof.

The men had been holed-up in the area for hours, but they were hoping to move on in the morning. Layne's horse had stepped on a sharp stone, and the small rock had become embedded in the animal's hoof. Layne wasn't sure how far they had traveled before the stallion pulled up lame. Although he had removed the rock, he wanted to give the horse's bruised hoof time to heal.

The sun descending over the horizon cast a golden radiance across the turquoise sky. Watching the day draw to an end, Doug mumbled lazily, "Well, I guess we oughta start a fire and cook some grub."

"Yeah, I could use a cup of coffee," Layne replied.

They were about to get slowly to their feet when they detected the distant sound of advancing horses. Reacting alertly, they grabbed their rifles and stood quickly.

"There they are," Layne said, pointing in the distance. "They aren't headed this way."

There were three horses, but four riders; one horse was being ridden double. Doug, his gaze centering on the pair riding double, noticed that one of them was a woman. Even from a far distance, he could see that her long hair was golden blond.

"Layne," he began, "look at the woman. Her hair's the same color as Janet's. Do you think they saw us?"

"I doubt it. As fast as they're travelin', they aren't takin' time to view the countryside."

The riders, moving swiftly, were now a blur across the horizon.

"I'm gonna follow 'em," Doug remarked.

Layne looked over at his lame stallion. "I wish I could go with you."

"Don't worry, I'll be all right." Doug grinned confidently. "After all, there's only three of 'em."

Twenty-nine

Layne had the campfire burning and was getting ready to fix a pot of coffee when he heard riders approaching. He recognized Jessie and Floyd, although they were still in the distance.

Jessie was pleased to find Layne. She had thought that he and Doug would be miles away. After all, they had left Dry River hours ahead of her and the others.

Riding into Smith's camp, the pair reined in and dismounted. Jessie hurried to Layne, and sitting beside him, she remarked, "Finding you is certainly a surprise."

"My horse pulled up lame, and Doug and I have been holed up for most of the day." He studied her curiously. "Why aren't you and Miller with the others?"

"Bart fired Floyd and ordered him to leave. I decided to ride with him."

Taking a seat across from them, Floyd said, "Janet's been kidnapped, and Wilkerson blames me for it."

Layne arched a brow. "Why did he blame you?"

"Janet and I took a walk. She didn't want to return to camp with me. She wanted to be alone. I left her, and that's when she was abducted."

Looking about, Jessie asked, "Where's Doug?"

"He left," Layne replied, his thoughts now racing. Apparently the woman he and Doug had seen was Janet. He hoped Thompson would get her back without getting himself killed or hurt. Turning his thoughts back to the matter at hand, he looked at Floyd and asked, "Do you mind takin' a walk? I need to talk alone with Jessie."

Complying with a shrug of his shoulders, Miller stood and ambled off away from the fire.

Meanwhile, Jessie was thrilled. Layne wanted them to be alone! She took it as a good sign, and her hopes began to soar.

When Miller was out of earshot, Layne said calmly but with an undertone of anger, "Jessie, I've been givin' the other night a lot of thought. I know damned well that I didn't drink enough to cause amnesia." His eyes penetrated hers, their expression incriminating. "You drugged my brandy, didn't you?"

"No!" she hastened to deny. "You're talking nonsense!"

"Am I?" he grumbled. "I don't think so!"

Deciding her best defense was to pretend anger, she leapt to her feet. Placing her hands on her hips, she declared peevishly, "How dare you accuse me of such an underhanded trick!"

Layne got to his feet slowly. His tall frame towered over Jessie, and she looked up warily into his heated gaze. His anger, coiled tightly, was on the verge of striking with the quickness of a rattlesnake. "Why did you do it, Jessie?" he demanded, rage creeping into his voice.

His barely controlled fury sent a pang of apprehension through Jessie. Nevertheless, she met his unwavering gaze and replied as though greatly offended, "I can't believe you actually think I'm capable of something so deceitful. Have I ever given you a reason to judge me so unfairly?"

"No," Layne admitted.

Moving closer to him, she declared softly, "I swear everything happened just the way I said it did. You told me that you've always been in love with me, then you showed me how much you care."

Jessie was taken aback when Layne suddenly chuckled coldly. "I think you're lying through your teeth. I could drink a barrel of brandy, and I still wouldn't tell you that I love you."

"Why do you say that?" she questioned sharply.

"Because I'm in love with Selina. I don't give a damn how drunk I might be, I'd still be in love with Selina. I wouldn't tell you or any other woman that I loved her."

Suddenly he grasped Jessie's shoulders, and pulling her close, he leered down into her face. "You conniving little fool! Did you really think that if I lost Selina I'd turn to you? Do you honestly believe I can just turn my love off and on at will? Selina's the only woman I want, and I'll win back her love if it takes me a lifetime!"

"You'll never win her back!" Jessie cried desperately. "She hates you! But, darling, I love you!"

His hands were still on her shoulders, and shoving her aside, he raged, "Love? You don't even know the meaning of the word."

"Considering the passion we shared, how can you say something so cruel?"

"I doubt very seriously if we shared any passion!" he mumbled angrily.

"You woke up in my bed without a stitch of clothing on, didn't you? What do you think happened?"

"I think I passed out and slept through the night."

She started to say more, but Layne cut her off by yelling, "Miller! Miller!"

Returning to camp, Floyd asked, "Yeah, what do you want?"

Smith gestured tersely to Jessie. "Take her and get the hell out of my camp."

"But, Layne," Jessie complained, "it's getting dark. Can't we stay here with you?" Surely if she had more time she could inveigle herself back into his good graces.

He denied her request curtly. "Go somewhere and make your own camp."

"Layne, you don't mean that! Please don't turn me away so coldly!"

"Stay the hell away from me, Jessie! I'll never forgive you for what you did!"

"Surely there's someway I can change your mind."

He interrupted testily, "You can tell Selina the truth!"

"But I've been telling the truth!"

Holding back an urge to slap her lying mouth, Layne looked at Floyd and uttered, "Miller, get her the hell away from me!"

Floyd took a step toward Jessie, but she held up a hand to deter him. Despite the pain of losing

Layne, his icy rejection had her fuming. She now knew that she'd never win his love. He wouldn't come to her, even if Selina never forgave him. Her inward fuming turned into revenge. As a spiteful smile crossed her lips, she said coolly, "Very well, Layne, have it your way. I'll never bother you again." Moving to him, she stood on tiptoe and whispered secretly into his ear, "But just between the two of us, I did drug your brandy. However, don't make the mistake of thinking I'll tell Selina the truth. Because I won't!"

Layne turned on her with a fury. "Damn you! I should . . ."

"You should what?" she dared. "Strike me? Go ahead if it'll make you feel more like a man."

Afraid that he might indeed physically lash out at her, Layne turned away from her taunting eyes and drew a tight rein on his temper. He had never struck a woman, and he wasn't about to let himself stoop so low now.

Jessie had seen his rage before he had turned away, and she now waited for him to whirl back around and unleash his fury. When it became apparent that he wasn't going to do so, she was actually disappointed. She had always felt that she'd find a man's brutality arousing.

"Goodbye, Layne," she said, her tone huskily provocative. "If you should change your mind about us, you know where to find me." With that, she went to her horse, mounted, and rode quickly out of camp.

Hurrying to his own horse, Floyd swung up into the saddle. As he caught up to Jessie, he asked, "What did you whisper in Smith's ear?"

"I confessed the truth. I whispered it to him because I didn't want him to know that you're aware of what really happened. He'd take you to Selina and beat a confession out of you."

"Tellin' 'im the truth was stupid. Now you'll never get 'im to marry you."

She held back tears. "It doesn't matter. I already lost him. He guessed the truth, and convincing him he was wrong was hopeless."

"So now what are you gonna do?"

She shrugged wistfully. "I don't know. Maybe someone else will come along to take Layne's place."

Miller grinned suggestively. "What about me?"

"What about you?"

"You lost Smith, and I lost Janet. All we've got is each other."

"Don't be absurd!" she spat. "There can never be anything between us." She enjoyed bedding Miller, but that was as far as her feelings went. She'd certainly not marry scum like him. Jessie had her cap set for a man who was wealthy and aristocratic, and she'd not settle for anyone less.

Her haughty manner rankled Miller, and although he was tempted to literally slap her off her horse, he managed somehow to keep his rage in check.

The kidnappers drew up their horses. The man riding with Janet dismounted, then reached up and drew her from the saddle. He led her to a cottonwood and shoved her to the ground.

"Stay here!" he ordered harshly. "If you get up,

I'll beat that pretty face of yours so it ain't so pretty no more!"

He wheeled about and returned to his comrades. "We'll stay here for a couple of hours and rest the horses," he told the others. "Then we'll move on. We should reach our hideout by noon tomorrow."

Janet, listening, wondered exactly where they were taking her. She peered into the distance. Was her father following and, if so, would he find her? Desperately her eyes scanned the countryside. Dusk had fallen, blanketing the land with gray shadows. She hoped to catch sight of a rescue party, but only drifting dust and rolling clumps of tumbleweed moved over the vast plains.

She leaned back against the tree's trunk and tried to rest her tired body. The effort was futile, for she was too frightened to relax. Her thoughts flew to Doug. She knew that this time he wouldn't save her. Before, he had always come to her rescue, saving her gallantly, and she had always thanked him. This time, however, it would be different, for she'd thank him with all her heart, then pledge her love forever.

She sighed with exasperation. Why was she thinking about something that wasn't going to happen? Doug wouldn't be rescuing her, he was miles away. Despair washed over her as she wondered if she'd ever see him again. Would these men kill her? Was she destined to die without telling Doug that she loved him? Would he never know that he was loved so desperately, so completely? Tears welled up in her eyes, and she was about to surrender to her sorrow when, all at once, her abductors' discussion captured her interest.

"I think we oughta enjoy the woman while the horses are restin'," one of them was saying.

The man who had ridden with Janet grumbled, "Damn Gabe! Is pokin' women the only thing you ever think about?"

"That and money," he replied, a large grin spreading across his bearded face. "What do you say, Kyle? Let's all get a piece of her."

"What the hell." Kyle remarked calmly. "We might as well have a little fun." He turned his beady eyes in Janet's direction. "She sure is a pretty gal." He licked his lips with lustful anticipation. "I bet she's pretty all over."

Janet trembled with fear as the three men approached, their lewd smiles revealing their forceful intentions. She got to her feet, but her legs were so weak that they barely supported her. Her terrified gaze swept wildly over the threesome. They were a foul group, their unwashed bodies clothed in dirty, dust-covered togs, and all three sported ungroomed, tobacco-stained beards. Janet grew sick, and her stomach knotted as bile rose in her throat. She felt she'd rather die than suffer their assault.

Her heart started hammering, and her head began to swim. She wondered if she was on the verge of fainting. She hoped she'd sink mercifully into black oblivion and stay there until these men were finished with her!

The men unbuckled their gun belts and placed them on the ground. The one called Gabe grabbed her arm and threw her down roughly. His hand was groping for the bodice of her dress when the sudden thundering of a horse's hoofs sent him whirling about.

Moving quickly, the three men reached to the ground and drew their pistols. The lone rider was advancing swiftly; and Gabe took careful aim, but was a trice too slow pulling the trigger. While his horse was still charging, Doug fired his rifle; the bullet slammed into Gabe's chest, sending him sprawling backward before he fell lifelessly to the ground.

Meanwhile, Kyle had gotten off a missed shot, as his remaining partner dropped to the ground to take aim. Deciding to flee, Kyle made a mad dash for his horse. As he was mounting, he heard the rifle fire again and, glancing back, saw that his friend had been shot. Quickly he slapped the reins against his horse's neck, sending the animal into a loping run.

Doug was aware of Kyle's flight. He considered going after him, but he didn't want to leave Janet alone. Deciding to let the man escape, he pulled up and dismounted.

Janet had taken cover behind the tree during the chaos, and crouching behind the sturdy trunk, she hadn't dared to peek at the action. Now, certain that it was safe for her to move away from her shelter, she got to her feet and stepped around the cottonwood. She had no way of knowing that only one man had come to her rescue, and she was expecting to see her father and his drovers. She was shocked to find Doug Thompson instead of a rescue party.

"Are you all right?" Doug asked, wishing he had the right to take her into his arms, hold her close, and never let her go!

"Yes," Janet managed to whisper.

Doug took her hand and led her away from the two bodies. Then moving back to Gabe and his partner, he checked and saw that they were both dead.

He returned to Janet. "I'll leave the bodies here. Bart can send a couple of his men to get 'em and take 'em to the sheriff in Passing Through. But we'll take the horses with us."

As he walked away to get the two horses, Janet watched anxiously. Had Selina and Hattie been wrong about Doug's feelings? He certainly wasn't behaving as though he were in love with her. He seemed strangely detached, and there was a cold reserve about him that was almost chilling.

Janet's eyes remained rooted on Doug as he brought back the horses and then lent a hand to help her mount. Accepting, she swung up onto Gabe's horse. As Doug moved to his own mount, she asked, "How did you know I was kidnapped?"

"Layne and I are camped close to here. We saw you and the men ride by. You were too far away for me to recognize, but I thought it might be you. That blond hair of yours is easy to spot, even from a long way off." He studied her curiously. "Why did these men abduct you?"

"I'm not sure, but I think they kidnapped me for ransom. They left a note behind for my father."

"How did they manage to grab you?"

"I was away from camp."

"Alone?" he questioned, his tone somewhat reproving.

392

"I was with Floyd. . . ."

"That figures!" Doug interrupted gruffly, not giving her a chance to finish. "Let's go," he said tersely. He didn't want to hear anymore about Miller. Grabbing the reins to the extra horse, he urged his mount into a brisk gallop.

Following, Janet was perplexed by his brusque manner, but only for a moment. As she grasped the reason behind Doug's curtness, a delighted smile crossed her face. He was jealous of Floyd! Doug was riding ahead, and she gazed adoringly at his turned back. A tingling thrill coursed through her as she admired the wide width of his shoulders and his strong presence. She longed desperately to be held in his powerful arms, to feel his tough, masculine frame pressed close to her body. She desired Doug Thompson with every fiber of her young being.

As the horses plodded along, taking them closer to her father and the others, Janet grew anxious. She must let Doug know how she felt before reaching Bart's camp. Night had fallen, destroying the shadows of dusk, and a full moon was shining down upon the quiet land; its soft glow making the scenario a romantic background.

"Doug," she called softly. "May we please stop for a while?"

"Sure," he said, reining in. He dismounted then, stepping to Janet, assisted her from the horse. He started to move away, but she deterred him.

"Doug, I must talk to you."

"All right," he answered.

She could see his face clearly in the moonlight,

and gazing up into his dark eyes, she suddenly felt somewhat shy. She wasn't sure how to tell this powerful, rugged man that she was wholeheartedly in love with him.

Impatient with her silence, Doug said testily, "What do you wanna talk about?"

His distrustful expression wasn't very encouraging. She wondered if he would even believe that she loved him. Drawing a deep breath, she began, "Earlier today Floyd asked me to marry him. . . ."

"Good!" Doug intruded gruffly. "I'm happy for both of you!"

"Will you please refrain from interrupting?" she spat, irritated. "This is hard enough for me to say without you making it harder!" She swallowed uneasily. "Allow me to rephrase that. It's not exactly hard to say, but difficult. I'm afraid you won't believe me."

He frowned. "Janet, you aren't makin' any sense."

"I'm sorry," she murmured. "As I was saying, Floyd asked me to marry him, but I refused because I'm in love with someone else." Gazing sincerely into his watching eyes, she said softly, "Doug, I love you. I love you with all my heart."

Thirty

"Janet, what kind of game are you playin'?" Doug asked gruffly.

"It's no game!" she said quickly. "I truly love you!"

Although he smiled wryly, there was no humor in his eyes. "Is this a ploy to make Miller jealous?"

Janet was frustrated and cried pleadingly, "Doug, please believe me! I love you!"

"Sure you do," he mumbled caustically. "You consider me far below your aristocratic status, you find my Apache blood forbidding, and you don't find me one bit attractive. Yet you're in love with me." He snickered bitterly. "You must think I'm awfully damned stupid. I don't know what you're up to, but, little darlin', I'm not gonna be the pawn in your game. If you're tryin' to arouse Miller's jealousy, then . . ."

"Doug!" she interrupted desperately. "Please listen to me!"

"I don't have time for your foolishness," he grumbled. "I think we'd better move on before I lose my patience." He reached for her arm to help her mount, but she shoved his hand aside.

Moving with incredible speed, she drew his holstered pistol and pointed it at his chest. "Now, damn you, you're going to listen to me, or I'll . . ."

"You'll what?" he taunted, grinning.

Stamping her foot angrily, she shouted, "I'm warning you, Doug Thompson, you'll listen to me if I have to hold you at gun point all night!"

Taking Janet unawares, his hand whipped out and grasped the pistol. "Give me that before it goes off!" he ordered gruffly. Taking the gun, he reholstered it. Then folding his arms across his wide chest, he eyed her tolerantly. "All right, I'll listen to what you have to say. But make it fast, will you?"

Janet drew a nervous breath. "I'm not trying to make Floyd jealous. He means nothing to me. At one time I thought I wanted to be in love with him. I judged a man simply by his looks, and Floyd Miller is exceptionally handsome. I thought I would fall in love with him simply because he was good-looking. However, I was dead wrong. Every time Floyd kissed me I began to realize more and more how wrong I was. His kisses left me cold, unresponsive. Not only Floyd's kisses, but those of the beaux I had in New Orleans. I've only responded to one man's kiss. That night when you kissed me. . . ." A warm blush colored her cheeks. "Your kiss left me breathless and . . . and it caused my heart to pound madly and . . . and . . ." Too shy to continue, she fell silent.

"Go on," he encouraged, his eyes searching hers deeply.

"Your kiss made me feel like a woman, and it stirred a longing in me. I'm not sure, but I think the longing was passion."

As she waited anxiously for a response to her confession, her gaze swept over him intently. He was wearing buckskins, and the soft, pliable, snugly-fitting leather emphasized his powerful frame and his bulging muscles. She raised her gaze to his clean-shaven face. His western hat was pushed back from his forehead, and strands of coal black hair fell sensually over his brow. His eyes, seemingly as black as his hair, were watching her with a penetrating force. Looking away from their mysterious depths, she studied his full lips and high cheekbones. His Indian heritage, starkly apparent, added to his rugged yet thrilling appeal. Her intense physical examination awakened a passionate hunger in her, and sensations that were new and compelling coursed through her fervently. Waiting, hoping desperately, that he'd take her into his arms, she tried vainly to still the wild pounding of her heart.

Doug, his emotions reeling, wanted to believe that she truly loved him, but her confession was so unexpected that he was having a difficult time dealing with it. It was almost too wonderful to be true. He had come to believe that his love was in vain.

Janet, mustering her courage, dared to make the first move. She longed for his embrace, wanted desperately to be in his strong arms. Stepping closer, she slid her hands about his neck and urged his lips down to hers.

He wrapped an arm about her waist as, drawing her thighs flush to his, he turned their kiss into one of heated, breathtaking passion.

Responding ardently, Janet pressed the contours of her body to his, and when his brawny arms tightened about her, she felt wonderfully imprisoned in his powerful embrace.

"Janet," he whispered huskily, "I want you, and if we don't stop now, I'm liable to forget that you're an innocent little tease."

She moved out of his arms so that she could look into his eyes. Smiling timorously, she murmured, "Doug, I might be innocent, but I'm not a tease. I'll never again tease any man, because from this moment on I belong only to you." Her green eyes sparkled saucily. "And whether or not I remain innocent is entirely in your hands. I love you, and I'm yours for the taking. So, my darling, why don't you take me?"

His grin askew, Doug replied softly, "Your wish is my command." His lips once again captured hers in a heart-stopping caress, then leaving her with reluctance, he moved to his horse and removed his rolled up blanket. Taking it to a secluded patch of grass, he spread it over the tall blades.

Returning to Janet, he lifted her into his arms and carried her to the blanket, where he laid her down with tender care. Stretching out beside her, he brought her snugly into his embrace.

"Little one," he whispered with deep feeling, "I love you. I've always loved you."

"And I've always loved you. I was just too blind to see it."

"I'm sure glad you finally opened your beautiful eyes," he murmured, leaning over her. His mouth swooped down on hers, kissing her with wild passion.

As she surrendered rapturously to the strong and

vivid desires conquering her senses, she parted her lips and welcomed his probing tongue.

Slow but tantalizing, Doug's passionate kisses and roving hands awakened Janet's deepest passion; and when she felt she could no longer stand such sweet, aching torment, he drew her to her feet. Quickly, his patience waning, he removed her clothes, and as she stood nude before him, his eyes raked her with a fiery intent.

"You're so beautiful," he moaned, admiring her soft breasts, small waist, and slender legs. As his eyes centered on the golden triangle between her ivory thighs, his passion flamed so furiously that he hurriedly stripped away his own clothes.

Watching intently, Janet marveled at his stunningly masculine body. Boldly she lowered her gaze to his aroused manhood. A stab of apprehension shot through her.

Reading her thoughts, Doug asked tenderly, "Is this the first time you've seen a man in my condition?"

She smiled shyly. "Yes, and I'm a little afraid."

"Don't be," he murmured, moving to her and taking her into his arms. Holding her close, he bent his head and kissed her endearingly. Gently he pressed her naked thighs to his.

The feel of his hardness sent an exquisite longing through her, and lacing her arms about him tightly, she arched against his manhood.

With extreme care Doug eased her back onto the blanket, and moving over her, he positioned himself between her parted legs. "Janet," he warned gently, "there will be a moment of pain."

"Yes, I know," she whispered, her voice quivering slightly. "Oh Doug, please hurry. I'm no longer afraid. I want you to take me completely. I want to truly belong to you."

"My darlin'," he murmured hoarsely. Lifting her legs to his waist, he plunged deeply into her moist depths. The sharp pain caused Janet to cry out softly, and he waited a moment for her discomfort to pass. Then with slow and measured strokes, he began to move inside her.

Janet, drifting into glorious ecstasy, surrendered sweetly and passionately to the man she loved.

Doug and Janet were reluctant to leave their secluded paradise. Reveling in their new-found love, they wanted to stay and spend the night in each other's arms. But knowing Bart must be worried, they decided not to linger.

They hadn't traveled very far before spotting the campfire burning in the distance. Doug reined in, gesturing for Janet to do likewise. Turning to her, he said with a grin, "Darlin', before we ride into camp, there's something I want to ask you."

"What's that?" she inquired, returning his smile radiantly. Janet had never been so happy.

"Will you marry me?" he asked. His dark eyes, searching hers, mirrored his deep love.

"Oh yes!" she sighed exultantly. She leaned toward him and he met her halfway, confirming their engagement with a long, loving kiss.

"Janet," Doug began somewhat hesitantly. "I'm not rich like Bart and your uncle. I know you're used to everything money can buy, but . . ."

"Doug," she interrupted. "I don't care if you're as poor as a pauper. You're right, all my life I've had everything money can buy. But what I want now, and what I will want for a lifetime, money can't buy. All I want, darling, is your love. And I want to spend the rest of my life with you. I don't think it's quite dawned on you yet just how much I love you." She reached over and grasped his hand tightly. "Doug, I think I'd die without you!"

Lifting her hand to his lips, he turned it over and placed a kiss on her palm. "You're more precious to me than anything on this earth. I love you more than life itself."

"Let's make love again," she said suddenly.

He arched a brow. "Here? Within sight of your father's camp?"

"Why not? No one will know!"

"You wanton little vixen," he teased.

She smiled invitingly. "I want you, Doug Thompson. I want you right now, this very minute."

"Is this the way our married life's gonna be? Are you gonna get these urges at anytime and anyplace?"

"I certainly will," she replied pertly.

"Then sharing a marriage with you is gonna be pure heaven." Dismounting readily, he went over and drew her from her horse. Holding her in his arms, he carried her into the dark shadows and, kneeling, placed her gently on the grass.

Eagerly, passionately, they became wonderfully absorbed in their love-making.

Bart was sitting at the campfire between Stella and Selina. The threesome, their thoughts on Janet, were unusually quiet.

Stella wished she could say something to boost Bart's spirits, to give him hope, but she was at a loss for words. What could she possibly say to lighten his worry?

Meanwhile, Selina's feelings were the same as Stella's. She longed to help Bart, but she didn't know what to say.

Suddenly the silence was broken by a drover calling loudly, "Riders' comin'!" The man was standing guard and had taken a stance a short distance from camp. Hurrying to his boss, he repeated excitedly, "Riders' comin'!" A large grin spread across his face. "There's two of 'em, and I think one of 'em is your daughter!"

Elated, Bart leapt to his feet, followed by Stella and Selina. They watched anxiously as the two riders came closer, then recognizing Janet, they ran over to greet her.

Dismounting quickly, Janet flung herself into her father's arms and hugged him tightly before embracing her two good friends.

As Thompson got down from his horse, Bart stammered incredulously, "Doug, how the . . . how the hell . . . ?"

He explained how he had learned of Janet's abduction, and then he told Bart about the shootout. "In the mornin'," he concluded, "you need to send a couple of your men for the bodies. I'll draw you a quick map, so they won't have any trouble findin' the area."

Grabbing Doug's hand and shaking it firmly, Bart said heartily, "It seems that once again I'm beholding to you for saving my daughter." He smiled expansively. "I hope this doesn't become a habit. Janet's abductions are turning me gray-haired before my time."

Moving to her father, Janet snuggled into his arms. "I'm sorry, Papa. Both times I was abducted it was my own fault. I shouldn't wander away from camp."

"Thank God, we'll be home tomorrow!" Bart remarked. He smiled lovingly at his daughter. "I'm tempted not to let you out of my sight until I have you safely home."

At that moment Hattie emerged from the wagon and, seeing Janet, hurried over. Leaving her father's embrace, Janet went happily into Hattie's welcoming arms.

"I's so glad you's back safe and sound!" the woman exclaimed. Then turning to Doug and embracing him in a tight grip, she declared, "Mista Doug, I don't know how you found Miz Janet, but I's sure glad you did!" Releasing him, she continued briskly, "I reckon you two is hungry. There's lots of food. I'll heat you up some supper." Lumbering toward the fire, she said over her shoulder, "It'll be done in a whistle."

"Is there any coffee made?" Doug asked to no one in particular.

"A full pot," Selina answered. She and Stella left with Doug, and Janet started to follow but was deterred by her father's hand on her arm.

"Wait," he said. "I want to talk to you."

"Papa, if you're going to scold me, please don't. I've learned my lesson."

"I didn't detain you to give you a lecture."

She looked at him quizzically.

"What I have to say is going to upset you." He paused a moment, then proceeded, "I fired Miller, and I also sent him packing. Furthermore, I forbade him ever to see you again."

"Papa, there's something you should know."

Before she could say more, Bart intruded, "Janet, I know I can't tell you who to love, but, honey, will you take some advice from someone who's a lot older and wiser than you are?"

"I might," she answered, wondering what was on his mind.

"Have you ever considered Doug Thompson as a suitor?"

Janet smiled. "Why Doug?"

"I realize he isn't a handsome rogue like Miller, but still, he's a superb figure of a man. Also, he's mature, honest, and worthy of admiration."

"Papa, I'm surprised. I thought you'd want me to marry a man who's wealthy and aristocratic. And what about Doug's Indian blood? Don't you find his Apache heritage distasteful?"

"No, of course not. There's no man I admire more than Doug Thompson. And whether or not a man's wealthy and aristocratic isn't important. A man's character is all that matters. And in my opinion Doug's character is above reproach."

Janet's smile broadened. "I'm glad you feel this way." A bright sparkle shone in her green eyes.

"Papa, Doug asked me to marry him, and I accepted."

He looked deeply into her eyes. "Janet, do you love him?"

"Yes, Papa! I love him from the bottom of my heart."

Drawing her into his arms, he said warmly, "Janet, I've never been happier."

She hugged him fondly then, stepping back, said eagerly, "I want a nice wedding, Papa. Do you mind?"

"No, of course not. If you like, you can wear your mother's wedding gown. It's packed in her cedar chest."

Slipping an arm about her shoulders, he began leading her to the fire where the others were gathered.

Janet giggled merrily. "Uncle Fred and Aunt Effie certainly wouldn't approve of Doug."

"I love my brother and sister-in-law dearly, but we're as different as night and day."

"Well, I'm sure when they meet Doug he'll win them over."

"Are you inviting them to your wedding?"

"No, it would take too long for them to get here. And I want to get married as quickly as possible. I love Doug too much to wait patiently."

Bart smiled reflectively. "I understand. I felt the same way about your mother."

Doug, catching sight of Bart and Janet, got to his feet. Smiling happily, Janet went to him, slipped her hand into his, and said, "I told father that we want to get married."

405

Thompson turned a questioning gaze to Wilkerson. He wasn't sure how the man felt.

Discerning Doug's expression, Bart remarked, "You not only have my permission but also my blessings."

Then the two men stood back grinning amusedly as the women congratulated Janet with hugs and kisses.

Layne, ensconced in his bedroll, was dozing lightly when he detected an approaching horse. He sat up swiftly and as he reached for his rifle, Doug's strong voice called out, "Don't get trigger-happy, Layne!"

Throwing off the top blanket, Layne got up and stepped to the fire. He was pouring two cups of coffee as Doug rode into camp.

"Well, it's about time," Smith grumbled. "I was getting worried."

Dismounting, Doug unsaddled his horse before joining Layne. Accepting the proffered cup of coffee, he said tiredly, "I'm sorry you were worried, but it's been a full night."

"Did you find Janet?"

"Yeah, I sure did," he answered. Explaining the rescue, he gave Layne an accurate version. "I took her back to Bart," he continued. "He and the others are camped a couple of miles from here."

"I had visitors while you were gone."

"Jessie and Miller?" Doug guessed.

Layne nodded. "Jessie admitted that she drugged my brandy."

406

"The damn conniving little witch!" Thompson muttered.

"If she was a man, I'd take her to Selina and beat a confession out of her."

"You know, that's not a bad idea."

"Hell, Doug! I can't do that to a woman!"

"I don't mean beat the hell out of Jessie. I'm referrin' to Miller."

"He didn't hear Jessie admit the truth."

"Layne, the bastard was probably in on it. Do you really think he was too drunk to find his own room? And isn't it kinda fishy the way he happened to fall against Jessie's partially opened door?"

"I didn't know exactly how everything came about."

"Well, Stella gave me a full account."

Doubling his hands into fists, Layne uttered angrily, "Dammit! I had that sorry sonofabitch within my grasp, and I let him get away!"

"Don't worry about it. Miller won't be hard to find. You can still beat the truth out of him."

"He'll talk or lose his teeth!" Smith grumbled.

"Layne," Doug began somewhat hesitantly, "I know you're dependin' on me to take your herd to Kansas, but do you think you can find someone else for the job?"

"Sure, I can send Pete. He's my best drover. Why did you change your mind? Are you planning to leave for Oregon? I was hoping you had decided against leaving."

"I'm not goin' anywhere. In fact I need my job more now than I ever did." Doug smiled broadly. "Janet and I are gettin' married. That's why I'd rather not go to Kansas. I'd hate to leave my bride."

"You and Janet?" Layne exclaimed. "Well, I'll be damned!" He turned a serious gaze to Doug. "Are you sure she loves you?"

"I've never been more sure of anything."

"In that case I congratulate you," Layne replied, shaking his friend's hand.

Silence wedged between them for a long moment, then Doug said firmly, "Things will work out between you and Selina. All you gotta do is find Miller."

"I'll find that damned weasel. You can count on it!"

Thirty-one

Janet slept late and, dreaming about Doug, awoke with a smile.

Selina, entering the wagon, took note of her friend's happy expression. "Love certainly agrees with you," she said cheerfully.

Sitting up and stretching her arms overhead, Janet replied, "I can hardly wait to become Mrs. Doug Thompson."

A rueful wave washed over Selina. Janet's happiness made her own loneliness more acute. "Well, you'd better get up and get dressed. We'll be leaving soon. Hattie saved you some breakfast."

"Good," Janet remarked. "Love has given me a ravenous appetite."

"Is Doug planning to travel with us today?"

"No. He's riding with Layne. He said they'd reach Layne's ranch late this afternoon. He's supposed to come see me tomorrow. Papa told me that we'd be home before nightfall. Aren't you glad this trip is over?"

"Yes, I suppose," Selina murmured sullenly. "However, I have to turn around and make the trip again."

"No, you can't!" Janet objected, bounding from

her bed. "Selina, you must stay for my wedding!" Please!"

She was hesitant. "I don't think I should. I mean . . ."

"I won't take no for an answer!" Janet insisted. "Don't you realize how much your presence will mean to me? My wedding day will be the happiest day of my life, and I want to share it with my best friends — you and Stella."

"Do you really mean that?" Selina asked softly. "Are Stella and I truly your best friends?"

"Yes, of course. Don't you believe me?"

"It's not that I don't believe you. I was just thinking of how much you have changed. Remember how you felt about Stella at the beginning?"

"Of course I remember, and I'm totally ashamed of myself. I also treated Hattie unfairly."

Taking her hands, Selina squeezed them gently. "That's all in the past. Don't worry about it. Hattie and Stella understand."

Janet grasped Selina's hands tightly. "You will stay for my wedding, won't you?"

"Yes, of course," she replied, embracing her friend. Delaying her departure, however, was somewhat unnerving. She had hoped to leave Texas without coming into contact with Layne. But he would certainly attend Doug's wedding.

As Janet began dressing and chattering endlessly, she was too preoccupied to notice the trace of tears in her friend's eyes.

A dark, depressing shadow had fallen over Selina. She had dreamed so often of her own wedding, and now she and Layne would indeed be attending a wedding; but it wouldn't be theirs!

Determined not to cry, Selina rushed from the wagon, leaving Janet gaping at her sudden departure. She went to the fire, sat down, and poured a cup of coffee. She was afraid to cry, for if she gave in to her heartache, the pain might be more than she could bear. She would wait until she was back at Cedar Hill before surrendering to her grief. There, on the plantation she loved so dearly, she hoped to find the strength to go on without Layne.

The Circle-C was a welcoming sight to Jessie as she and Floyd rode up to the ranch house. Dismounting wearily, she told Miller, "Take the horses to the stables, unsaddle them, and give them some grain."

"Where do you get off givin' me orders?" he grumbled resentfully.

Jessie stifled her anger. The man was a nuisance! Furthermore, he was becoming impossible. As soon as she found another lover, she'd send Floyd packing.

Keeping her patience under control, she forced a sugar-sweet smile. "Will you please tend to the horses?"

"That's better!" he remarked.

"I'm exhausted," Jessie said listlessly. "I intend to retire early. If you want, you can stay in the bunkhouse."

"I'd rather join you," he replied, grinning suggestively.

"I don't think we should take the risk." Certain

her brother was working on the range with the drovers, she continued, "Larry could come home at any minute. I wouldn't want him to find us together." She was merely using her brother's chance arrival as an excuse. She simply wasn't in the mood for Floyd's fondling.

"All right," he relented. "I reckon I'm too tired anyhow."

She cast him a false smile, then hurried into the house. She was wearing a wide-brim hat and, removing it, hung it on a peg beside the door. Needing a glass of sherry, she headed straight for the study.

The door was closed, and she opened it widely. As she stepped across the threshold, she froze. A man she had never seen was sitting behind her brother's desk, and as her eyes swept over him warily, she stammered, "Who . . . who are you? And what are you doing here?"

The stranger smiled rakishly. "You must be Larry's sister. Jessie? Is that your name?"

"Yes," she answered, somewhat vaguely. The man was starkly handsome, and the woman in her was responding to him.

"I'm Harold Chamberlain," he explained, getting to his feet. "Your employer."

"You can't be!" she exclaimed. "Mr. Chamberlain is dead!"

"As you can see, I'm very much alive."

Jessie had never met Chamberlain. He had visited the Circle-C only once since she had moved to the ranch, but that time she had been enjoying an extended shopping spree in San Antonio. By the time she returned home, Chamberlain was on his way back to New Orleans.

Harold gestured to the chair facing the desk. "Sit down, Miss Harte, and tell me why you thought I was dead."

Going to the liquor cabinet, he poured a sherry for Jessie and a bourbon for himself. He handed her the drink, then leaned his tall frame back against the desk, waiting for her answer.

Chamberlain was standing close to Jessie's chair, and the man's closeness overwhelmed her. As she gazed up into his handsome face, she had to hold back an urge to go to him and kiss him boldly, passionately.

Harold was finding her equally attractive. Her tight-fitting riding apparel outlined her voluptuous curves, and her long dark hair fell provocatively about her shoulders. He could see her desire for him reflected in her inviting gaze. His manhood responded readily, but exerting self-control, he curtailed his rising passion. First things first. He had to know why she believed he was dead.

"Who told you I was dead?" he asked.

"Layne Smith," she answered. "I was traveling with him and the others."

Harold was confused. "I was with them for a while, and I certainly didn't see you."

"I didn't join Layne until a couple of days out of Dry River. Bart Wilkerson decided to ride out and meet them, and I accompanied him." She took a sip of her sherry, then met his eyes questioningly. "Layne, along with a government agent, came upon three butchered bodies. Layne was certain that they

413

were you and your men."

"Two of them were my men. The third one was a thief. My men and I had stopped for a short rest. The man came upon us on foot, saying his horse had thrown him and had run off. I suppose we should have been suspicious, but he seemed friendly enough and harmless. Taking us off guard, he drew a gun with intentions of robbing us. I was handing him my watch when this band of Comanches came charging over the hillside. Well, during the chaos it was every man for himself. I made a dash for the distant brush. Somehow, God only knows how, I managed to reach the shelter without being shot. I have to assume that the Indians didn't realize there were four of us; otherwise they certainly would have come looking for me. There were only three saddled horses, so there was no reason for them to suspect a fourth man. I stayed hidden and watched as the savages scalped and mutilated their victims. When they rode away, I decided to stay where I was until after dark. I figured it'd be safer to travel at night, especially since I was on foot. I was still in the brush when Smith and the others showed up. I wasn't about to reveal myself. I recognized the agent, and I knew he wanted to take me back to New Orleans for questioning. I figured he and Smith would mistake the third man for me. I'm sure Watts is on his way back to New Orleans to inform his superiors that Harold Chamberlain is dead."

He lifted his glass to his lips and drained it. "As soon as it was dark, I took off walking and had only gone a short way when I came upon a tethered horse. Apparently it belonged to the thief. I suppose he claimed his horse threw him because approaching us on foot made him seem less threatening. I took his horse"—he smiled charmingly—"and here I am."

"When are you going to let Layne know you're alive?"

Harold shrugged indifferently. "In due time." Stepping to the liquor cabinet, he poured himself a second drink. "I'm waiting for my man Jack to join me. Then my plans are to return to New Orleans and take one of my ships to England."

"How long do you plan to stay in England?"

"Indefinitely," he replied, leaning back against the desk. "In case you don't know it, Miss Harte, war between the North and the South is inevitable. When it finally draws to an end, the North will be victorious. That's when I'll return home. By then no one will give a damn if I illegally imported slaves. What a man did before the war will be of no importance. I don't plan to live in New Orleans, I intend to return here to my ranch. I already talked to your brother, and to guarantee that I have a prosperous ranch to come back to, I signed an official paper that states that if I die, or stay absent for ten years, this ranch automatically becomes his. Knowing there's a chance that he'll get the Circle-C will give your brother the initiative to keep it a flourishing business."

"Your proposition seems risky. If there is a war, it could be years in the future. If it were to drag on for a long time, you might be away for more than ten years. If that happens, you'll lose your ranch."

He chuckled arrogantly. "Then I'll buy another one. I have a fortune in the bank in London. It's enough to live comfortably for the rest of my life."

Interest sparked in Jessie's eyes.

He smiled shrewdly. "Money interests you, doesn't it, Miss Harte?"

"Of course it does," she answered. "And please call me Jessie."

Taking her glass, he placed it on the desk beside his own. Then putting his hand beneath her chin, he tilted her face up to his. "You're a very attractive woman, Jessie Harte. If I were to ask you to come to London with me, what would you say?"

His sudden invitation was astounding. "But . . . but you barely know me," she sputtered.

"I think I do know you, for I have a feeling that we're two of a kind." Placing his hands on her shoulders, he drew her to her feet. Slowly his lips descended to hers.

Leaning into his embrace, Jessie looped her arms about his neck and, as their kiss grew urgent, pressed her thighs against his.

Harold, his passion blazing, thrust his tongue inside her mouth, tasting her kiss fully. Jessie's tongue responded in passionate warfare.

Taking his lips from hers, Harold sent wet, tingling kisses down her neck. "Jessie," he moaned huskily. "I want you!"

"Oh yes . . . yes," she whispered throatily. She was on fire for him.

"Take your clothes off," he ordered.

"Don't you want to go to my room?"

"No. I plan to take you right here." Impatience

radiated in his eyes. "Undress, dammit!"

Jessie was thrilled. "You are a very demanding lover."

"I'm also a very rough one. Do you mind?"

She smiled radiantly. "No, I don't mind."

Chamberlain was pleased. "Why, you hot little bitch. You like being roughed up, don't you?"

"I'm not sure. My lovers have always been gentle. But I think what I really crave is a man like you."

"Then take off your clothes."

She did so quickly, anxiously. She had never been so aroused and could hardly wait to be taken forcefully and with brutality.

Harold's eyes traveled ravenously over her delicious curves, and jerking her into his arms, he kissed her aggressively. His searching hands moved over her soft body, his rough caresses painful, yet evoking Jessie's passion to its zenith.

Unbuckling his belt, he let his clothes fall about his ankles. Grasping Jessie's shoulders, he forced her to her knees. "You know what I want," he groaned raspingly. "Do it!"

She wrapped her fingers about his throbbing erection, then using her mouth and tongue with practiced expertise, she aroused Harold to a point of lustful rage.

He shoved her to the floor then, kneeling behind her, drew her up so that she rested on her hands and knees. Jessie had never been taken in this fashion, and when his manhood plunged deeply into her womanly heat, she cried out with unexpected ecstasy.

He pounded into her madly, his hips pumping

rapidly. Then without warning he suddenly withdrew.

"Don't stop," Jessie pleaded.

"I'll continue in a moment," he replied gruffly. A cruel, calculated grin spread across his face as he reached for his belt. "But first I'm gonna give you what you really want."

Stepping from Bart's house onto the front porch, Stella went to a pine rocker and sat down. Dusk had fallen but the land wasn't yet fully dark, and she could make out the sun's descending light fading over the distant horizon.

She rocked in the chair gently. Stella had never been more content. Harold Chamberlain was dead, and he could never again threaten her or Paul. The corners of her lips lifted in a small, gratifying smile. Her life had certainly taken a change for the better. Her hasty decision to leave New Orleans and run away to Texas had indeed turned out wonderfully. She knew she owed her good fortune to her friends, especially to Layne. Thinking of Layne, however, caused her smile to disappear. Her heart ached for him and for Selina. If only Jessie Harte hadn't interfered in their relationship. She still found it hard to believe that Layne was capable of such deceit. He loved Selina; she was certain that he did.

She turned her musings to Janet and Doug. She was happy that everything had worked out so splendidly. It was obvious to Stella that Janet simply adored her future husband. In a way, she envied Janet's freedom to express her love. For Stella was also in love, but due to her past she felt she didn't have the right to reveal her feelings.

Closing her eyes, she conjured up Bart Wilkerson's image. The mental picture alone had the power to send her heart racing.

"Stella?" Bart's pleasant voice suddenly intruded.

She opened her eyes quickly, and as a blush colored her cheeks, she stammered, "I . . . I didn't hear you come outside."

"You seemed totally absorbed. What were you thinking about?" He smiled tenderly. "Or were you perhaps thinking about someone special?"

"You mean a man?" she blurted impetuously.

Moving to the porch railing, he leaned back against it and folded his arms across his chest. "Is there a special man in your life?"

She lowered her gaze from his, answering almost inaudibly, "No, there's no one."

"You sound very sad. Are you still grieving for your husband?"

Husband? she thought bitterly. Ben Chadwell was the closest she'd ever come to having a husband, and she had despised him. Keeping her eyes downcast, she replied quietly, "No, I'm not grievin' for my husband."

Bart was puzzled by the aura of sadness that always seemed to surround Stella. He cared very deeply for the young woman and wished there were some way he could help her. Deciding not to pry, he steered their discussion to a different course. "What do you think of my ranch?" he asked.

"I'm very impressed. I've never been inside so grand a house."

419

He chuckled congenially. "Well, this is now your home, to run as you please. As my housekeeper I give you full rein."

Unsure of herself, Stella said hesitantly, "I just hope I can do a good job. I mean, I've never done anything like this."

"I'm sure you'll do a marvelous job." Moving away from the railing, he reached down, took Stella's hands into his, and drew her from the rocker. "I came out looking for you because Hattie said supper will be done in a few minutes."

His hands, wrapped about hers, were causing a tingling delight to flow through her. She gazed up into his face. He was smiling, and his askew grin lent him a boyish appeal that was irresistible.

Bart, now physically aware of Stella, wanted to kiss her, to relish the sweetness of her lips. However, considering himself too old for her, he kept his feelings under control.

Tearing her eyes from his, Stella turned to go into the house, but her foot tripped over the chair's rocker, sending her tottering into Bart's embrace.

As his arms tightened about her, she raised her face to his. Her trembling lips so close to his was a temptation he couldn't resist. His mouth came down on hers, his kiss warm and urgent. With a soft sigh of pleasure, she leaned against him as her hand went to the nape of his neck.

Somewhat shaken, Bart released her gently. Her kiss had been intoxicating. Mustering a semblance of composure, he apologized, "Forgive me, Stella. For a moment I forgot that I'm old enough to be your father."

"In years I'm still quite young, but in experience I'm older than you realize."

"A short, tragic marriage doesn't make you older than your years." He spoke almost paternally.

It was on Stella's lips to blurt out the truth, to tell him that she had been a man's chattel, a prostitute and a mistress; but before she could, Hattie's blustering voice called out from inside the house. "Supper's on! Come and get it!"

Bart laughed heartily. "Maybe I should get Hattie a dinner bell. It'll save on her lungs."

Taking Stella's arm, he ushered her to the front door. As he stepped aside for her to precede him, she met his gaze directly and said, "Bart, if you only knew, you'd understand that I'm much older than my years." But if he knew the truth, her thoughts added solemnly, he would probably think she was nothing but trash.

"If I only knew what?" he asked, perplexed.

"Never mind," she mumbled. Turning away from him, she walked quickly inside. She couldn't tell him about her life. She couldn't! She felt that she'd rather die than lose his respect.

Thirty-two

Bart was alone at the breakfast table when Selina entered the dining room. Pushing back his chair and getting to his feet, he said blithely, "You're up early. It's barely past dawn."

"I couldn't sleep," she replied. Hoping to catch Bart before he rode out to the range, she hadn't taken time to change out of her robe. She continued, "Please forgive my state of dress, but I wanted to talk to you before you left."

He drew out a chair for her, and when she was seated, he returned to his own chair and poured two cups of coffee. "What do you need to talk about?" he asked, handing her a cup.

"Layne," she said softly.

Bart quirked a brow. "Go on."

"I've decided to pay him a visit, and I want you to give me directions to his ranch."

"Selina, I can't allow you to ride to Layne's ranch alone. It's too dangerous. You've got to realize that this land can be perilous."

"I can take care of myself," she remarked, her chin lifted.

Bart smiled tolerantly. "Nonetheless, I'll accompany you. First I need to take care of some business, but I'll be ready to leave in a couple of hours. Will that be all right?"

"Yes, that'll be fine," she answered.

"Do you prefer a buggy?"

"No, I'd rather ride horseback."

As Wilkerson took a drink of coffee, he studied Selina over the rim of his cup. Her reason for visiting Layne had his curiosity aroused. In Dry River she had seemed determined to avoid contact with Smith, even going so far as to ask him to keep Layne away from her.

Discerning his thoughts, Selina said somewhat hesitantly, "I know what you're thinking. But I've been giving what happened between Layne and Jessie a lot of thought and . . . and . . ." Her words drifted.

"Yes?" he encouraged.

"I never really gave Layne a chance to explain." A petulant frown wrinkled her brow. "I don't suppose there is an excuse for what he did, but all the same, I owe him the courtesy of listening."

"Selina, stop deceiving yourself."

"What do you mean?" she questioned, thoroughly confused.

"Regardless of the reason Layne gives you, you've already decided to forgive him."

"No . . . No, I haven't," she stammered.

"Of course you have. You love him."

Sudden tears smarted her eyes. "Oh Bart, you're right! I do love him! But his affair with Jessie hurt me so deeply! I don't think the hurt will ever go away!"

He reached over and clasped her hand consol-

423

ingly. "I guess you have to decide between your pride and your heart."

"My pride demands that I return to Cedar Hill, but my heart . . . ? I think Layne had it captured from the first moment I looked into his eyes."

Squeezing her hand, Bart said firmly, "Layne loves you very much."

"Then why . . . ?" she cried desperately.

"I don't know. But Layne told me that he doesn't remember seducing Jessie, and I believe him."

"He said the same thing to me."

"But you don't believe him?"

"Bart, when I saw them together, I actually heard Layne tell Jessie that he loved her!"

"Well, apparently, he doesn't. If he did, he'd be with her now."

"How do you know he isn't?"

"Because he's in love with you. He told me how he feels, and I know Layne well enough to believe that he wouldn't lie." Releasing her hand, he finished his coffee, then got to his feet. Gazing tenderly down at Selina, he said, "Returning to Cedar Hill or remaining isn't a decision you have to make right away. Give yourself plenty of time—it might be the most important decision you'll ever make."

She smiled faintly. "I'll heed your advice, I promise."

"Good," he replied. "I'll be back soon, and then we'll go see Layne."

As Bart left the dining room, Selina stared blankly down at her cup of coffee. Was she doing the right thing? Was her decision to visit Layne a mistake? Should she change her mind and hold tenaciously to her pride? Was her pride more important than her heart?

There were no firm answers to these questions; and as tears ran down her cheeks, Selina tried to ease her aching heart, but the effort was useless. She loved Layne too desperately! He was a part of her, and she was a part of him! He was the center of her life, and her reason for living!

Jessie was in the kitchen preparing a large breakfast for Chamberlain when Floyd swung open the back door and intruded.

Turning away from the stove, Jessie remarked testily, "Don't you know how to knock? How dare you barge in here as though this is your house!"

"Don't be so damned bitchy!" he grumbled. A cunning grin crossed his face. "I saw your brother and the drovers ride out. I thought you might be cravin' a little lovin'."

Removing the skillet from the fire, she turned back to Floyd and eyed him sternly. "Floyd, I don't want to see you anymore. Mr. Chamberlain has returned and . . ."

"I thought he was dead!" Miller butted in.

"Well, he isn't!" she snapped, impatient with his interruption. "As I was saying, Mr. Chamberlain is here. He asked me to go to London with him, and I told him that I would."

"I get it," Floyd muttered sourly. "He's your new lover, which means I've been booted out of your bed."

"That's right!" a man's voice suddenly cut in.

Miller whirled about. Chamberlain, his gun in hand, stood in the doorway leading from the kitchen into the dining room.

"You heard the lady. She doesn't want to see you anymore," Harold remarked authoritatively. "Now get the hell out of my home and off my property. If I catch you anywhere near the Circle-C, I'll have you shot on sight."

"Aw hell!" Floyd mumbled, gesturing toward Jessie. "You can have the damned slut! And you don't have to worry about seein' me on your property. I'm headin' for Mexico." He turned and looked coldly at Jessie. "Goodbye, bitch! I'd wish you a pleasant voyage, but I'm a-hopin' the ship sinks to the bottom of the ocean with you on it." With that, he stomped outside, the door slamming shut behind him.

Placing his gun on the table, Harold moved over to Jessie and took her into his arms. "Your boyfriend is pitifully crude. I should think you'd have better taste."

"In these parts a woman can't be too choosy. True gentlemen are very scarce."

"Yes, I suppose they are," he replied vacantly, his eyes studying her intently. Against his will, he found himself comparing her to Selina. By comparison, Jessie was sorely lacking. Rage began building inside him as he was reminded that he had lost Selina, would never experience the pleasure of ravishing her beautiful flesh and forcing her to bow to his will. He had wanted Selina Beaumont! Damn, how badly he had wanted her!

His rage was now in full swing, and taking his

anger out on Jessie, he suddenly bent her face down across the kitchen table. His rough, terse treatment excited Jessie, and passion mounted within her.

Moving swiftly, Chamberlain drew her long skirt up to her waist, then he shoved her flimsy undergarment down past her smooth buttocks. Loosening his trousers, he freed his protruding member. Then grasping her bared thighs, he penetrated deeply into her womanly core. Imagining it was Selina taking his sexual abuse, his fervor grew to a wild frenzy, causing his hips to pound vigorously.

Pain mixed with ecstasy shot powerfully through Jessie, and loving Chamberlain's brutality, she writhed and moaned with passion.

Harold had returned to bed for more sleep, and Jessie was washing the breakfast dishes when Layne rode up to the ranch house. Dismounting, he strode across the front porch and entered the house without bothering to knock. Searching for Jessie, he moved quickly through the parlor and the dining room.

As Layne stepped into the kitchen, Jessie was standing at the counter with a soapy plate in her hand. Sensing another's presence, she wheeled about. The dish fell from her hand to the floor. As it shattered, she gasped, "What do you want?" She was wary of the smoldering fury burning in his dark eyes.

"Floyd Miller," he replied flatly. "Where is he?"

"I don't know."

"Damn you, Jessie!" he uttered fiercely, taking a step toward her.

"I'm telling the truth!" she remarked quickly. "He was here earlier, but he left. And he's not coming back."

"Did he say where he's going?"

"To Mexico."

"What?" he raged. He couldn't let Miller get away!

"Layne, I swear I'm not lying. He told me he was heading for Mexico."

"So help me God, Jessie, if I find out you're covering for him . . ."

"I'm not!" she cried.

"You better hope you aren't!" he grumbled, his tone unmistakably threatening. Then he left as quickly as he had arrived.

Floyd, feeling sorry for himself, was riding across the plains at a pace as sluggish as his mood, when he detected a horse advancing from the rear. Drawing his pistol in a flash, he turned his mount around and waited vigilantly for the lone rider to draw closer. As recognition set in, he was tempted to take aim and shoot the man without waiting to see what he wanted.

"Miller!" the man called, his horse steadily shortening the distance between them. "Put away your gun. I just wanna talk to you."

A bitter smirk distorted Miller's otherwise handsome face. "Sure you do," he mumbled disagreeably. Nevertheless, he holstered his pistol. As the man rode up alongside him, he said furiously, "You god-damn double-crossing bastard, what the hell do you want?"

"Don't be so touchy," the man said, his tone cranky.

"Kyle, you sorry, no-account sonofabitch, you double-crossed me!"

"But it wasn't my idea," he claimed untruthfully. "It was Gabe's idea."

"Where is that no-good bastard and his partner? And what did you do with Janet? Has Wilkerson already paid the ransom?"

Glumly, Kyle explained how the kidnapping had been foiled. "If I ever see that big sonofabitch who killed my friends and grabbed the woman, I'll shoot him dead on the spot!"

"What did this man look like?" Floyd asked.

He gave him an adequate description.

"Sounds like Doug Thompson."

Kyle feigned a penitent smile. "You ain't holdin' no grudge against me, are you?"

Floyd shrugged. "I guess not. What you did doesn't matter anymore. It's all water under the bridge."

"Where are you headed?" Kyle asked.

"I thought I might ride down into Mexico." He gave Kyle a warning glance. "You know, it's danger-ous for you to be in these parts. Janet Wilkerson can identify you. You stick around here, and you'll find yourself behind bars."

"Yeah, I know," he replied. "Mind if I ride to Mexico with you?"

"Naw, of course not. I can use the company. We'll

find you a good place to hole up, then I'll ride into town and buy us some provisions." He smiled largely. "Then it's Mexico here we come! Señoritas, start spreadin' your legs!"

"Them señoritas are always hot to trot," Kyle remarked, and was about to elaborate further when Floyd suddenly held up a silencing hand.

"Listen. Someone's comin'."

A steep, grassy hill was behind them. "Whoever's comin', he's about to ride over the top of that hill," Kyle said, drawing his gun.

Floyd unsheathed his rifle, and he had it aimed and cocked to fire as the lone horseman crested the hilltop. "Hold it right there!" Miller warned, grinning sadistically. "Make a move and I'll blow a hole straight through you!" He could hardly believe his good luck. Before going to Mexico, he'd savor a sweet taste of revenge. Killing this man was a treat he hadn't counted on.

Meanwhile, Kyle's thought were running parallel to Floyd's.

"Get down off your horse, Thompson!" Miller ordered. "Do it now, you half-breed bastard, or I'll shoot the horse out from under you!"

Dismounting, Doug cursed his own carelessness, and berated himself harshly for letting these two dim-witted bastards waylay him. He knew better than to ride over a hill without exercising caution, but his thoughts had been on Layne. Earlier, as he was getting ready to ride to Bart's ranch to see Janet, one of the drovers had mentioned that Layne had gone to the Circle-C. Doug was certain that Layne was hoping to find Miller, and worried that

430

trouble might erupt; and so he decided to follow.

"Step away from your horse," Floyd ordered. "Then real careful-like, unbuckle your gun belt and let it drop to the ground."

As Doug complied, Miller told Kyle to get Thompson's rifle. The man hurried over to Doug's horse and slipped the weapon from its leather encasement.

Gesturing with his pistol, Miller continued, "Thompson, move away from your gun belt."

Doug stepped to the side.

A crazed, raving glare radiated from the depths of Floyd's eyes, and as a hateful sneer curled his lips, he uttered gruffly, "You goddamned, smug-assed half-breed!" Remembering the times Doug had struck him and had made him look like a fool added fuel to Miller's rage. Also, it had been Thompson who interfered with his plans to marry Janet.

"If you don't kill that bastard, I will!" Kyle told Miller.

"Don't be so damned anxious!" Floyd snapped. "He's gonna die, but it ain't gonna be no fast death. We're gonna let 'im think about it as we stretch a rope over a tree branch, then wrap the noose around his neck."

Selina and Bart rode at an unhurried pace. Since leaving the ranch, their conversation had been minimal and sporadic. Wilkerson, knowing Selina's thoughts were on Layne, hadn't tried to engage her in a lengthy discussion.

He was hoping, however, to talk to Selina about Stella. He cleared his throat, then asked, "How well do you know Stella?"

She had been thinking deeply about Layne, and it took a moment for her to clear her mind. "I know Stella quite well. Why do you ask?"

"I'm concerned about her. She seems very sad."

Selina didn't agree. "Stella's never been happier."

"I don't think so. Something is bothering her, and I suspect it's related to her past."

Selina didn't say anything. She knew that Stella hadn't told Bart about her life. She as well as Hattie had advised Stella to be completely truthful with Bart. Selina decided to have another talk with Stella and this time convince her to tell Bart everything.

Hoping to discourage further talk of Stella, Selina urged her horse into a fast trot. She knew Bart was sincerely worried about Stella, and she was uncomfortable giving him evasive answers.

Wilkerson kept his horse abreast of Selina's. It was apparent to him that she didn't want to discuss Stella. He wondered why.

Selina was wearing the same riding togs that she had worn on the journey from New Orleans. The day was growing extremely warm, and as she loosened the two top buttons on her shirt, she pondered buying some material and making herself more attractive riding clothes. Her current apparel, though serviceable, was certainly not suitable garb for a woman. She frowned testily. Why was she planning on improving her wardrobe? She wasn't even sure yet if she was going to stay in Texas long enough to wear new riding attire. Did her heart have that much control over her pride? Had she already decided to forgive Layne? Had Bart's speculation this morning been right? Was she merely deceiving herself? Had she never really planned to return to Cedar Hill? Did she love Layne that desperately?

Thrusting these confusing questions aside, Selina drew her wide-brimmed hat forward to shade her eyes from the sun's dazzling rays. She glanced thoughtfully at the verdant countryside. The pastoral tableau was unblemished, and as far as the eye could see, blades of grass covered the earth like a green carpet. The land was undoubtedly a rancher's paradise.

Changing their course, Bart turned his horse to the right, and Selina followed. "The Diamond-S is about an hour's ride straight ahead," he called over his shoulder.

A grassy hill loomed in the distance, and keeping their horses at a steady gallop, they reached it quickly. Bart, riding in front, was about halfway to the top when, suddenly, he reined in.

Coming to a stop behind him, Selina asked, "Is something wrong?"

"I don't know," he replied. "I think I heard something." He got down from his horse. "Stay here while I have a look."

Selina waited as Bart strode to the top of the hill, then when she saw him drop stealthily to the ground, she dismounted swiftly. Stepping to Bart's horse, she drew his rifle.

Bart motioned for her to join him, gesturing for her to stay low to the ground.

She crept up to him, handed over the rifle, and

asked, "What's wrong?"

Grasping her arm, he drew her to a crouching position. On their hands and knees they crawled forward until they could see over and beyond the hilltop.

The scene below caused Selina's heart to lurch. "Dear God!" she whispered.

Floyd, carrying out his threat, had Doug on his horse with his hands tied behind him. A rope was slung over a tree's branch, and a noose was looped about Doug's neck.

"Bart, do something!" Selina cried, keeping her voice low.

Nervous perspiration was beading on Wilkerson's forehead. "If I shoot Miller or the other man, the gunshot will cause Doug's horse to bolt. The fall could break Doug's neck. If I tell the men to throw down their weapons, they'll open fire"—he groaned deeply—"which will send Doug's horse charging."

"Then what can we do?"

"I'll have to try and shoot the rope."

"But you might shoot Doug instead. There's not much rope between that branch and his head."

"I know," he said gravely. "But what other choice do I have? It's Doug's best chance."

As Bart cocked his weapon, Selina noticed that his hands were trembling. "How good are you with a rifle?" she asked, beginning to doubt his ability to make such a shot.

He summoned a shaky smile. "There's room for improvement." Lying flat to the ground, he shifted the rifle butt to his shoulder and took careful aim.

Bart was a fairly good shot, but he knew he

434

wasn't a marksman. Praying he'd make the best shot of his life, he tried to still his pounding heart and his trembling hands. Heavy perspiration dripped from his brow and into his eyes.

Selina was now almost certain that he'd miss his target. He was too nervous and too unsure of himself. Moving decisively, she reached over, grasped the weapon, and said firmly, "Give me that rifle! I won't miss!"

He was obviously hesitant.

"Give it to me!" she insisted. "Now!"

Thirty-three

Layne was riding at a steady pace when he spotted Doug and the men who were about to hang him. They were quite a distance away, and although Layne knew they were still out of rifle range, he nonetheless drew his weapon and cocked it. Urging his horse into a loping run, he began to gain ground.

Miller wasn't aware of Layne's approach. With a cruel grin on his lips, he pointed his rifle into the air, smiled at Doug, and said coldly, "When I shoot this gun, it's gonna send your horse chargin'. Only it ain't gonna have a rider, 'cause you're gonna still be here hangin' around!" He laughed outrageously at his own pun.

Kyle was growing impatient. "Get on with it, Miller! Let's hang this big half-breed, then get the hell out of here!"

Floyd's finger was curling about the trigger when suddenly a rifle shot rang out. The rope, now severed, dropped to Doug's shoulders. His horse, frightened by the shot, bolted wildly. Although it was difficult for Thompson to remain in the saddle with his hands tied behind him, he managed to do so.

In the meantime Selina had given Bart back his rifle, mounted her horse, and was in pursuit of Doug.

Floyd and Kyle, deciding to flee, made a mad dash for their horses. Wilkerson fired two warning shots, yelling for them to halt. By this time Layne was drawing close, and as Kyle spotted him, he cocked his rifle and took aim. Before he could pull the trigger, Layne fired, sending a slug into the man's shoulder. As Kyle fell to the ground, Miller wisely threw down his weapon and raised his arms in a gesture of surrender.

Selina caught up to Doug and brought his horse to a stop. Untying Thompson's hands, she asked anxiously, "Are you all right?"

"Yeah, I'm fine." He rubbed his sore wrists where the rope had cut into his flesh. Smiling somewhat shakily, he looked at Selina and said uneasily, "You know, I've flirted with death more times than I'd care to remember, but this is the first time it really mattered."

"I'm not sure I understand."

"Life has never been as precious to me as it is now."

Her eyes sparkled. "Because of Janet?"

"Love is what makes it all worth while, isn't it?"

"Yes, I suppose it is," she murmured. Looking back to see if Bart had the men covered, she was astounded to find that Layne was with him. She hadn't been aware of his arrival.

Following her gaze, Doug said with a smile, "Layne's been lookin' for Miller."

"Well, he's found him," she replied, her even tone belying her suspicions. Why was Layne looking for Floyd? Was he planning to order him to stay away from Jessie Harte?

Selina kept her horse abreast of Doug's as they galloped back to the others. Reining in, she withheld her gaze from Layne, dismounted, and stepped to Bart's side.

Layne had disarmed Miller and left him standing beneath the cottonwood. Floyd's eyes were glazed with fear as he watched Thompson swing down from his horse. He wondered if the man was going to kill him, and if Wilkerson and Smith would stand by and let him do it! Surely they'd stop the half-breed from committing cold-blooded murder!

Miller's fright wasn't completely unfounded. Thompson's eyes were blazing with the viciousness of a stalking predator as he stepped menacingly toward Floyd.

Moving alertly, Layne stepped forward and blocked Doug's path. "Don't do it," he said calmly. "Let the law deal with Miller."

Conceding to reason, Doug mumbled, "Aw hell, you're right. Besides, he ain't worth killin'." He nodded toward Kyle. "How bad is his wound?"

"It's just a shoulder wound. He'll live to stand trial with Miller."

Turning to Wilkerson, Thompson said heartily, "Bart, shootin' that rope was one helluva shot."

"I didn't know you were that good," Layne

added.

"I'm not," Bart answered. "I didn't make that shot. Selina did!"

"What!" Layne exclaimed, looking at her with astonishment. "Why didn't you tell me you could shoot like that?"

"You never asked," she retorted.

"That isn't something I'd ask just out of the clear!" he grumbled, waving his arms in an exasperating gesture.

"Hereafter, Layne Smith, maybe you should start asking instead of taking things for granted!" Her blue eyes were flaring, and her temper rising.

Suddenly a wry grin spread over Layne's lips. "Selina, that was a great shot. I don't know if I could've made it."

Doug moved to Selina. He was hugging her gratefully when Layne interrupted.

"Excuse me," he said firmly, taking Selina's hand and drawing her aside. "I need to talk to you."

"All right," she replied.

He led them a little farther away. "Selina, where are you and Bart headed?"

"To your ranch."

"Why?"

"I've decided to listen to your explanation." She lifted her chin proudly. "I don't think there is an excuse for what you did, but . . . but . . ." Words failed her, and she suddenly found herself gazing at him helplessly. She tried to quell the desire his closeness was awakening within her. The effort was futile, for she loved him too deeply to control her feelings. Her eyes, with a will of their own, studied him adoringly. He was hatless, and she couldn't help but smile when she saw that his sandy-blond hair was falling boyishly across his brow. As she resisted the urge to reach up and brush the curls aside, her gaze rested on his full lips. Then stepping back, she studied his tall, muscular frame. His buckskin shirt was tucked inside his black trousers. The western clothes fit him superbly; the tight-fitting shirt emphasized his strong build, and the trousers hugged his masculine thighs and long legs.

Meanwhile, Layne's scrutiny was just as intent. Her thick, chestnut-brown tresses cascaded past her shoulders. Her high cheekbones accentuated her sky-blue eyes and her beautifully shaped lips. As his gaze raked her soft, desirable curves, Layne could feel a stirring in his loins.

"Layne," Selina murmured. Her voice was even, despite her inner trembling. "I love you. And . . . and I'd rather be miserable with you than miserable without you."

He smiled disarmingly. "Sweetheart, there's no reason for you to be miserable. But knowing that you love me enough to forgive . . ."

"I didn't say anything about forgiving," she interrupted. "To be perfectly honest, I don't know if I'll ever truly forgive you, but I'm willing to try."

He took her hand. "Come with me, darlin'."

"Where are we going?"

"We're gonna have a little talk with Miller."

Although Selina was confused, she didn't question Layne as she allowed him to lead her back to the others.

"Wait here," Layne told her.

Doug and Bart had Kyle on his horse, but Floyd was still standing beneath the cottonwood. Layne went to Miller, and grabbing the man's arm, he forced him to move over to Selina.

"All right, Miller!" Smith demanded harshly. "If you wanna keep your teeth, you'd better tell Selina about the game you and Jessie played in Dry River!"

"I don't know what you're talkin' about," he mumbled.

"This is my last warning," Layne threatened. "Start talking, or you're gonna be gummin' your food!"

Floyd yielded. "What the hell. I don't have no reason to protect Jessie. Besides, she already told you what happened."

"But Selina doesn't know. So why don't you tell her?"

He looked at Selina. "Jessie got a sleeping powder from the doctor in Dry River. The doc told her it was real potent mixed with alcohol. She put it in Smith's brandy. I gave her time to get him drugged and in her bed, then I went to your room and pretended I was drunk. She left her door open on purpose so I could fall against it. When we found her and Smith in bed, he was totally drugged. He was so damned out of it that he actually thought Jessie was you. He wasn't tellin' Jessie that he loved her; he was sayin' it to you. I know because after you left she came to my room and told me that Smith had her confused for you. She was really pleased about that. Furthermore, the bitch spent the night with me and didn't return to her room until dawn. Jessie Harte's a conniving little slut. Now she really thinks she's hot stuff. She's too good for me 'cause Cham . . ."

"Layne!" Selina intruded, her gaze flying to his. "I don't know what to say! You swore that you didn't remember, and I wouldn't believe you!" Tears came to her eyes. "Can you ever forgive me?"

He brought her into his arms. "We'll talk later," he whispered in her ear.

"Doug," Bart began, "let's take Miller and his buddy to the sheriff." He turned and said to Layne, "Why don't you and Selina leave? Doug and I will take care of everything."

Agreeing, Layne helped Selina onto her horse. As he was mounting his stallion, Bart asked, "Can you come to dinner tonight?"

Layne accepted, then he and Selina rode quickly away from the area.

"I saved the best for last," Layne said to Selina as he opened the door to his bedroom.

After leaving Doug and Bart, they had ridden to the Diamond-S; and Layne, showing Selina his home, had intentionally avoided his bedroom. Now sweeping her into his arms, he carried her across the threshold. Taking her to his large four-poster bed, he laid her down gently. Moving decisively, he closed and locked the door, then returned to Selina and stretched out beside her.

Snuggling contentedly into his arms, she murmured, "Layne, let's promise to always trust each

442

other."

"You have my promise," he replied, hugging her tightly.

They sealed their promise with a long, love-filled kiss. Placing her head on his shoulder and cuddling intimately, Selina said softly, "I'm very impressed with your home."

"It's now our home," he corrected.

The two-story ranch house, made of adobe, resembled a Spanish hacienda. Layne had furnished it with large, ornately carved furniture, and the glossy polished floors were covered with brightly colored throw rugs. The house was decorated expensively but elegantly, and Selina had loved it at first sight.

Layne, raising up on an elbow, gazed down into Selina's face and murmured, "Darlin', let's get married as soon as possible."

She smiled warmly. "You'll get no argument from me."

"As you know, there's no reverend in Passing Through, so in the morning I'll come to Bart's ranch, pick you up, and take you to San Antonio. We can be married there."

"Sounds like a marvelous idea," she purred, sliding her arms about his neck.

As his lips seized hers in a deep, emotional kiss, he deftly unbuttoned her shirt. Then he quickly removed her boots and trousers. Slowly, for he was enjoying the view, he stripped off her shirt and undergarments. He hastily doffed his own clothes.

As he went eagerly into her embrace, his lips conquered hers in an aggressive, questing kiss. Responding fervently, she welcomed his exploring tongue, letting hers entwine with his.

Lowering his mouth to her soft breasts, Layne kissed one taut nipple before moving to the other. A gentle moan of passion came from deep within her throat as an exultant sensation wafted through her in heated waves.

Glorying in the feel of her silken flesh, Layne's hand, descending with slow inevitability, moved down to stroke the womanly softness between her thighs. His probing finger sent her senses reeling with pleasure.

Layne, his need soaring, wrapped an arm about Selina's waist and placed her on top of him.

Wanting him deep inside her, she lowered herself onto his stiff manhood. His arching hips encouraged her to ride him with unbridled passion.

Moments later Layne, his fulfillment building, eased her onto her back, moved between her parted legs, and penetrated her swiftly. His demanding, steady thrusting brought them to the brink of climax; then with a burst of exploding ecstasy, they achieved love's total rapture.

"I love you, Selina," Layne whispered, moving to lie at her side.

Curling up against him, she murmured, "I love you too."

He kissed her deeply, then leaning up and gazing into her face, he said with a grin, "Now, my little vixen, why don't you tell me how you learned to shoot a rifle so well. That was one helluva shot you made."

"Impressed, are you?" she asked pertly.

"Impressed is an understatement." His eyes twinkled with amusement. "Have you ever considered joining the Texas Rangers?"

She laughed merrily. "Not hardly! Besides, I plan to be too busy having your children to ride with the rangers."

"In that case," he said with a wink, "I think we'd better stop wasting time talking and start making a baby."

She smiled saucily as her arms went about his neck. "But I thought you wanted me to tell you how I learned to shoot."

"Later," he whispered, then his lips came down on hers with a demanding urgency.

Doug was standing on Bart's front porch as Selina and Layne rode up to the house. Hurrying down the steps, he met them at the hitching rail.

Dismounting, Layne asked, "We aren't late for dinner, are we?"

"No, in fact you're early."

Layne helped Selina down from her horse.

"Chamberlain's alive and he's back," Doug announced quietly.

"He isn't dead!" Selina cried in shock.

"Did you see him?" Layne asked.

"No," he replied. "But Miller told me Chamberlain's at his ranch."

"Damn!" Layne cursed softly. He turned to Selina. "Honey, will you find Stella and tell her I need to talk to her? I'll wait on the porch."

"Layne, you don't think Harold will try to harm

Stella or Paul, do you?"

"No, I don't think so."

Hoping he was right, Selina went into the house to look for Stella. Doug offered to tend to the horses, and he was leading them to the stables when Stella opened the front door and stepped onto the porch.

"Do you want to see me, Layne?"

"Yes, I do," he replied.

She studied his grave expression. "Is something wrong?"

"Stella," he began carefully, "Chamberlain isn't dead."

"No!" she gasped, her face paling.

"Miller told Doug that he's at the Circle-C."

She felt a frightful chill. "Oh God! What if he tries to harm Paul?"

Layne spoke firmly, "Stella, Chamberlain's no fool. He won't try to hurt you or Paul. He knows he wouldn't get away with it."

Her anxiety quieted somewhat.

Silence prevailed for a moment, then Layne emphasized intensely, "He won't physically hurt you but, Stella, he might hurt you in another way."

"I don't understand."

"Have you told Bart about your past and your relationship with Chamberlain?"

"No, not yet," she murmured, lowering her gaze guiltily.

"You must tell him before Chamberlain does."

She was confused. "But why would he tell Bart?" she questioned, her eyes now staring into his.

"Are you really that blind to Bart's feelings?" he

446

asked kindly. "Chamberlain will tell Bart about your life just to spite you. Don't you realize that Bart's falling in love with you?"

Happiness rose inside her. "Bart in love with me?" she asked hopefully. "Layne, are you sure?"

"I'm reasonably sure." He smiled. "I can see you feel the same way about him."

"I think Bart is wonderful!" she admitted, blushing becomingly.

"Tell him the truth," Layne advised firmly. "He should hear it from you, not from Chamberlain. Also, just in case Chamberlain's stupid enough to try and harm you and Paul, Bart can't protect you two if he doesn't know you could be in danger."

Before Stella could reply, the front door opened and Wilkerson stepped outside. "Layne," he remarked warmly, "I just talked to Selina, and she told me why you two are going to San Antonio." He shook Layne's hand. "Congratulations!"

Stella was perplexed. "Why are you and Selina leaving?"

"We're getting married in San Antonio."

"I'm so happy for both of you!" she exclaimed.

Giving Stella an opportunity to talk alone with Bart, Layne conjured up an excuse to join Doug at the stables and left quickly.

Watching him leave, Bart said cheerfully, "I'm glad Layne and Selina are back together." He emitted a deep sigh. "I can't help but envy Layne and Doug."

"Why?" Stella asked.

He smiled ruefully. "They're happily in love." He turned to Stella, and as his eyes searched hers, he

447

murmured with feeling, "If you were older . . ."

When his words faded away, she coaxed anxiously, "If I were older, then what?"

"Then I could fall in love with you."

"Oh Bart!" she cried. "Why must I be older for you to love me?"

"Stella, you're so young and beautiful that you can have your choice of young men, so why would you want a man my age?"

"Why do you place so much importance on age? Besides, I already told you that I'm older than my years."

He studied her thoughtfully. "Yes, I suppose you are. Although you're young enough to be my daughter, you're a lot more mature than Janet." An amused grin touched his lips. "Doug's going to have his hands full with her."

"Doug can handle Janet," she replied with a confident smile.

"Yes, I know," Bart murmured.

An uneasy silence suddenly wedged between them. Stella, filled with apprehension, was trying to gather courage to confess her past. Meanwhile, Bart was barely controlling the urge to draw Stella into his arms.

He remembered vividly their kiss and her fervent response. Was he a fool for allowing their age difference to keep them apart? If he continued to adhere to his resolve, would he live to regret it? Was Stella right? Did he place too much importance on age?

He placed his hands gently on Stella's shoulders. "You're a very sweet young lady. I know your life has been difficult, perhaps even oppressive; yet, despite your hardships there is an aura of innocence about you." His eyes softened with devotion. "I find your innocence very touching."

Her innocence? Stella's heart sank.

Unaware of her despair, Bart brought her tenderly into his embrace. He pressed his lips lightly to hers, and as she shifted closer to him, their kiss intensified into one of breathless passion.

"Stella," he whispered huskily, "I love you very much, and although I'm tempted to carry you to my bed, I won't rush you. I want you to be sure of your feelings. I'll not take advantage of you."

She pushed gently out of his arms. "You have me on a pedestal, and I don't belong there."

"In my eyes you do."

Drawing a deep breath, Stella was about to remove his blinders, but at that moment Janet came onto the porch looking for Doug.

Stella swallowed back her confession. She knew she had to tell Bart the truth, but she decided to wait until tomorrow. Tonight was so pleasant, why spoil it?

"Stella's living at Wilkerson's!" Chamberlain exclaimed.

He and Jessie were in bed. Having finished a lustful bout, they had relaxed into a quiet conversation in which Jessie had casually mentioned Stella Larson.

"She's Bart's housekeeper," Jessie clarified.

"Housekeeper, hell! Women like Stella don't clean

449

houses, they warm beds."

Jessie, knowing nothing of Stella's relationship with Harold, disagreed. "I think you're wrong. Bart isn't the type to have a mistress. Furthermore, I observed him and Stella while I was traveling with them. I think Bart is falling in love with her. Those two spent a lot of time together. He doted on Stella as well as her son."

A wicked smile crossed Harold's face. "I bet Stella didn't tell Bart that she's a whore."

Astounded, Jessie gasped, "A whore?"

"She worked at Belle's before she became my mistress."

"Your mistress?" she repeated, suddenly impaled with jealousy. She wondered desperately if Harold wanted Stella back. As anger rose inside her, she mumbled hatefully, "Why, that little slut! How dare she pretend she's a lady! She's quite an actress, I'll give her that much!"

"That's because she has a good teacher. I'm sure Selina Beaumont has taught her everything she needs to know to entrap Wilkerson."

"She won't have any problem getting him to the altar. He's obviously smitten with her."

Chamberlain chuckled spitefully. "He won't be so smitten when I tell him she's a whore and a thief. In the morning we'll ride to Bart's ranch. After all, it's about time I paid my respects."

Jessie rubbed her nude body seductively against his, and as her hand moved down to arouse his passion, she murmured anxiously, "Harold, you aren't wanting Stella for yourself, are you?"

"That depends."

450

"On what?"
"On how well you keep me satisfied."
She smiled confidently.

Thirty-four

Selina had her bag packed long before Layne was due to arrive. She was about to leave her room and go downstairs for breakfast when Stella rapped lightly on her door. "Selina, are you up?"

Admitting her friend, she said brightly, "I've been awake since dawn."

"Were you too nervous to sleep, or too excited?"

"Excited!" she exclaimed. "Oh Stella, I can hardly believe this is my wedding day!"

"I'm happy for you," Stella murmured, sounding quite the opposite. "I'm sorry. I don't mean to sound so depressed."

"Are you worried about Harold? Are you afraid he'll try to harm you or Paul?"

"No, not really. Layne doesn't think Chamberlain will hurt us — at least not physically."

Selina understood only too well. "Stella, you haven't told Bart about your past, have you?"

"No," she murmured. "But I intend to tell him this morning. After breakfast I'll ask if I can talk to him alone." She held back tears. "Oh Selina! I just know he'll think I'm trash!"

"I don't think he will. And, Stella, you aren't trash."

A self-condemning frown creased her brow. "No one made me become a prostitute. I took the job because it paid good. I knew it would keep a decent roof over Paul's head and food in the cupboard."

"Back then, you were an illiterate, backwoods country girl. You survived the best way you could. Bart will understand."

"I hope so," she moaned. "I never thought I could fall in love, but then, I didn't know a man like Bart would come into my life. Selina, I love him so much! If I lose him, I'll . . . I'll just die!"

Except for Stella, everyone ate a hearty breakfast. Bart was aware that she had merely picked at her food. He was worried about her and wished she trusted him enough to tell him what was bothering her. Although he was tempted to try and pressure her into a confession, he preferred that she come to him of her own accord.

Now, as the group sat about the table relaxing with second cups of coffee, Janet asked Selina, "When do you expect Layne?"

"Within the hour."

Janet pouted good-naturedly. "I wish I could be at your wedding. I don't see why you and Layne are so determined to elope."

Selina smiled, "We aren't exactly eloping. Besides, you and Doug are having a large wedding, and one elaborate wedding is enough."

Paul was in his highchair. It was placed between Bart and Stella. Tired of confinement, the boy began to fidget. Bart lifted him from the chair and onto his lap. Picking up a spoon, Paul began to happily bang it against the table.

At that moment Hattie, carrying a covered basket, emerged from the kitchen. "Miz Selina, honey, I packed a lunch for you and Mista Layne. It's a long ride to San Antonio, and even couples in love has gotta take time to eat."

"That was very thoughtful of you. Thank you."

As a loud, insistent knock sounded at the front door, Hattie gestured for Bart to remain seated, saying, "I'll get it Mista Bart." She turned a smiling face in Selina's direction. "It's probably Mista Layne. That knockin' sounds like a man impatient to get married."

She moved quickly to the door and opened it. As she stared wide-eyed into the visitor's face, fear shot through her and a cold shudder ran up her spine. "Masta Chamberlain!" she gasped.

Harold was poised on the other side of the threshold. Jessie was with him, and he had an arm wrapped about her waist. "Well, well," he drawled, grinning cruelly. "If it isn't Stella's black mammy."

Hattie, too numb to move, stood immobile as Chamberlain and Jessie barged inside.

"Hattie?" Selina called. "Is Layne here?"

Harold, following the sound of Selina's voice, entered the dining room with Jessie at his side.

The sight of Chamberlain sent Stella bounding to her feet. A wave of dizziness washed over her, causing her to sway unsteadily.

454

Bart stood up and handed Paul to Janet; then grasping Stella's arm, he asked anxiously, "Stella, what's wrong?"

She didn't answer; but her legs weakened, and she sunk back into her chair.

Meanwhile, Hattie had slipped quietly into the room and taken a stance in the corner.

"Bart, I hope you'll overlook this interruption," Harold said with a feigned note of apology. He then turned to Stella. "My dear, regardless of our past relationship, I can't stand idly by and let you manipulate a gentleman like Mr. Wilkerson."

"What the hell?" Bart demanded, "Stella, what . . ."

Harold quickly intruded. "I felt that it was my Christian duty to come here and let you know that Stella is not only a whore but also a thief. Also, in case you don't know it, her son is a bastard."

Silence ensued, and the strained quietness was so thick that it hung heavily in the air.

Finally, Stella rose to her feet. She looked at Bart and said with quiet dignity, "Mr. Chamberlain is right. I was a whore, a thief, and I've never been married. When I was sixteen, my father sold me to a slave trader. His name was Ben Chadwell, and he was Paul's father. He was killed by runaway slaves. Paul and I were left destitute. I found employment at Belle's. I'm sure you've heard of the establishment. It's the most infamous whorehouse in New Orleans. That's where Mr. Chamberlain found me. He threatened to kill Paul and me if I didn't become his mistress. Well, I stood his brutality for as long as I could. Then I stole a horse and carriage to run away to Texas." Her gaze not wavering from Bart's, she concluded, "You know the rest."

She waited with bated breath, hoping, praying, that he would understand.

Bart's rage was close to erupting. "You should've told me!"

"I was going to," she murmured.

"When? After we were married?" His accusation was raw and very angry.

She was about to defend herself, but he waved away her words. "No! Whatever you have to say, I don't want to hear it!"

Afraid he would completely lose his temper and say words that he might later regret, Bart moved stiffly across the room.

"Papa?" Janet called. "Where are you going?"

"I need to be alone," he grumbled. As he came up to Harold, he paused and glared into the man's cold eyes. "Chamberlain, you're a sadistic ass! I want you out of my home, and don't ever set foot on this ranch again!"

Bart left the house, slamming the door behind him. His horse was tied to the hitching rail, and swinging into the saddle, he turned the animal about and took off at a bolting speed.

Harold, unaffected by Bart's hostility, turned and looked closely at Selina. Her ravishing beauty overpowered him. Bitter disgruntlement washed over him as he again realized that he'd never savor her seductive charms. Losing Selina was a disappointment that he knew he'd never really get over.

Selina, wishing he would leave, got angrily to

her feet. "Harold, you heard what Bart said! He wants you off his property!" Gesturing at Jessie, she continued, "Take your little tramp and leave this ranch!"

"Tramp!" Jessie shouted. "How dare you!"

Harold chuckled and, taking Jessie's arm, led her from the dining room. "Don't get so upset, my dear. After all, you are a tramp."

As the two left the house, Stella, moving as though in a trance, stood up slowly. "Damn Chamberlain!" she raged quietly. "Damn him! Damn him!"

She had always despised Harold Chamberlain, and now, driven by hate, she moved through the dining room and outside.

"Miz Stella, come back!" Hattie called, hurrying after her.

Janet, still holding Paul, rushed outside with Selina. Pausing on the porch beside Hattie, they watched as Stella approached Harold.

He and Jessie were at their horses and about to mount when Stella said sharply, "Chamberlain!"

Her aggression took Harold by surprise. "You've acquired gumption, haven't you? Undoubtedly, Selina's rebellious nature has influenced you."

Stella held her head proudly. "I'm no longer the frightened, ignorant woman you used to abuse."

He chuckled humorlessly. "But you're still white trash, and you always will be." He suddenly appeared bored. "Now, why did you follow me outside? What do you want?"

"You never intended to kill me or Paul, did you? You held that threat over my head to keep me at your mercy."

"Of course I never intended to kill you or your bastard. Do you think I'd dirty my hands killing trash? My threat kept you submissive, though, didn't it? Not only submissive, but I had you literally crawling at my feet. You were a dirt farmer's ignorant daughter with pig shit for brains!" He laughed harshly. "Now, if you are quite through wasting my time, I shall leave."

"I'm not quite finished," she replied, her collected tone misleading.

He faced her. "Oh?"

Taking him completely unawares, she drew back her arm and slapped his cheek so soundly that his head snapped back.

"Now, I'm finished!" she remarked.

"You goddamned little bitch!" Harold raged, his eyes crazed with fury. He backhanded her across the face, the powerful blow knocking her to the ground. He moved to her quickly, jerked her back to her feet, and struck her again.

Paul screamed at the top of his lungs, and Janet covered his face to protect him from the violent scene. She looked about desperately, hoping to see at least one of her father's drovers. No one was about. Meanwhile, Hattie rushed into the house. She knew Bart's loaded shotgun was within easy reach.

"Stop it!" Selina yelled, running down the porch steps to Chamberlain. She grasped at his arm, but he shoved her aside so viciously that she lost her balance and fell. Springing back into action, she came at him again.

Releasing his hold on Stella, he grabbed Selina's wrist and twisted her arm behind her back. With a firm thrust he threw her to the ground, turned back to Stella, and was about to strike her with his fist when a thunderous blast sounded.

"Masta Chamberlain!" Hattie yelled. "This-here gun's got two barrels. I done fired one, but the other barrel's still loaded." She aimed the weapon directly at him. "You get away from them gals, get on your horse, and make tracks! You ain't never gonna hurt Miz Stella again, not as long as I's got breath in my body to stop ya!"

Harold's rage rose to a fever pitch. "You goddamn black-skinned wench! How dare you hold a gun on me!" That a Negro would defy him was beyond Chamberlain's comprehension. "Give me that gun, you stupid bitch!" He was too enraged by Hattie's insolence to be afraid, and driven by irrational anger, he moved toward her slowly but purposefully.

Jessie was standing beside Hattie, and she watched with growing apprehension. As Harold's steps brought him closer, dread mixed with fear whirled inside her. Without Harold her future was bleak, hopeless.

With each step, Chamberlain's jaw became firmer, his muscles grew more taut, and his rage climbed to a zenith.

"Don't come no closer," Hattie warned.

Jessie, afraid Harold would keep coming, made a wild lunge for the shotgun. She was trying desperately to take it from Hattie when it suddenly discharged. The gun's resounding boom exploded powerfully, then rumbled across the plains like distant thunder.

Harold was hit full force by the blast. Staggering, he clutched blindly at his bleeding chest, then he pitched forward and fell face down onto the ground.

Jessie threw back her head and let go a guttural, blood-curdling cry.

Bart hadn't ridden very far before coming across Layne and Doug. The three men had stopped and were talking when they heard the first shotgun blast. By the time the second blast sounded they were riding toward the ranch house at full speed.

When the men arrived, Selina and Jessie were kneeling beside Harold. Layne, dismounting swiftly, hurried over. Selina moved aside, giving him room. He quickly examined Chamberlain's ghastly wound. He knew the man was dying.

"What happened?" Layne asked.

Selina explained in as few words as possible.

"Smith," Chamberlain gasped, his voice terribly weak. "Get me to a doctor."

Layne knew he'd never live to reach a physician. "Chamberlain, did you kill my father?"

"Get . . . get me to a . . . a doctor," he groaned.

"Not until you tell me why you killed my father."

Jessie gaped at Layne as though he were a cold-hearted monster, but Selina knew otherwise. Harold's life was ebbing quickly, and nothing was going to save him.

"You . . . you bastard," Chamberlain choked out,

blood now trickling from his mouth.

"Tell me!" Layne insisted.

Harold groaned in pain. His whole body felt as though it were on fire, and a tortuous stinging burned in the pit of his stomach. He feared death and was so terrified that he would have sold his soul to the devil for a doctor's care. Desperate, he decided to tell Smith the truth. Later he could always claim he had made a false confession under duress.

"I killed him," Harold managed to moan. "He . . . he threatened to expose me to . . . to the authorities. I made it look like . . . suicide." A weak, rasping cough caught in his throat. He choked, spit up blood, then continued in an almost inaudible whisper, "Copying his handwriting wasn't difficult. Now, damn you, get me . . . get me to a doctor."

Layne intended to carry out his half of the bargain even though he didn't think Chamberlain would make it to the doctor. He looked over at Doug and was about to ask him to hitch up the buckboard, but before he could, a wheezing sound came from deep within Harold's throat.

It was Chamberlain's last sound, for his life was over.

Hattie paced the kitchen fretfully. She was alone, for the others were in the parlor talking to the sheriff. She had already been questioned by the law officer.

In an effort to calm herself, she poured a cup of

461

coffee, went to the table, and sat down. Her thoughts drifted back uneasily. Would she have willingly shot Chamberlain? If Miss Harte hadn't grabbed the gun, causing it to fire, would she have killed Chamberlain anyhow? She wasn't sure. He was a devil, and he deserved to die. Hattie felt no remorse over his death, if she felt anything at all, it was relief. Now he could never again hurt Stella or Paul. They were her family, and she loved them more than she loved herself.

Her hands were gripping the coffee cup, and she stared down at them, studying her black skin. Would the sheriff arrest her for murder? The shooting had been accidental, but she knew from experience that a Negro had no rights. She moved a hand to her throat, caressing it as though a noose was already fastened about it. Would she hang? Tears flooded her eyes, and her gentle face grew ravaged. She was almost certain she'd be executed.

The kitchen door suddenly opened. Stella and Janet hurried inside and sat down at the table.

Hattie, holding her breath, looked anxiously at their faces. When they responded with large smiles, her apprehensions faded away and joy filled her heart.

"Hattie," Janet began, "the sheriff has decided that the shooting was an accident. He also feels that you had a right to hold Harold at gunpoint. You were protecting Stella and Selina." Smiling warmly, she reached across the table, placed her hand on Hattie's, and patted it gently. "In this part of the country, the law doesn't look kindly on men

462

who beat up women."

"You mean I ain't gonna be arrested or nothin'?" she exclaimed.

The two women laughed gaily.

"Nothing's gonna happen to you," Stella assured her.

Getting to her feet, Hattie remarked cheerfully, "I's get you two some coffee. I also baked cookies this mornin'. I's get you some of them too."

Stella turned to Janet. "I want you to be completely honest with me. Now that you know about my past, are you still my friend?"

"Yes, I am," she answered truthfully. "There was a time not long ago when I wouldn't have been. But those days are gone. I'm a changed woman."

"You ain't really changed," Hattie intruded. "Miz Janet, you's always had goodness in you. It just took a man like Mista Doug to bring it out."

"Not only Doug," Janet replied. "But good friends. Like you two, Selina, and Layne."

Stella sighed depressingly.

"You're thinking about Papa, aren't you?" Janet asked.

"I've lost him," she murmured. "He'll never forgive me for not tellin' him the truth. Furthermore, he probably can't accept what I was. Your father's too much of a gentleman to marry a woman who was a prostitute and a mistress."

Selina suddenly entered the kitchen. "Janet, your father wants to see you in his study."

"Do you know why?"

"No. But Doug's with him, so it might have something to do with your wedding."

As Janet left the room, Selina moved over to Hattie and embraced her tightly. There was no need for words.

Thirty-five

Bart and Doug were talking when Janet entered the study. Her father was seated behind his desk, and Thompson was sitting across from him. At Janet's entrance, Doug stood and offered her his chair.

She preferred to stand, and slipping her hand into her fiancé's, she looked at Bart and asked, "Did the sheriff leave?"

"Yes, he left a few minutes ago. He took Chamberlain's body with him." Bart paused a moment before continuing, "There's something I want to tell you both." His gaze traveled over them warmly. "Janet, I had always hoped that you'd marry a Texan and decide to make your home here. Although I hoped it, I never thought it would really happen. But in case my hopes were fulfilled, years ago I bought up some excellent grazing land that I set aside to give you as a wedding gift." He looked at Doug. "I'm referring to my land on the north."

"That's good cattle land," Doug replied.

"It's now yours and Janet's." Worried that Thompson might balk, he went on quickly, "Now, Doug, I know you're very proud, but this land is rightfully Janet's. It's her inheritance. I want to sell you some cattle to get you started, and I'll also build you a house."

"Bart," Doug began, "I appreciate your generosity. The land is Janet's inheritance, and I have no intention of asking her to refuse it. I also accept your offer to sell us some cattle. But building our house is going too far. I'll build us a small cabin, and we'll live in it until I can afford something better."

Bart smiled agreeably. "You'll make a prosperous rancher, Doug. It won't be long before you can afford a good home." He turned to Janet. "How do you feel about living in a cabin?"

Her hand in Doug's tightened. "I don't care if I live in a cave, as long as Doug is living in it with me. Besides, if we work together for our future home, we'll appreciate it more."

Bart was proud of his daughter's maturity. "Then it's settled. I'll sign the land over to you and Doug." He stood up, reached across the desk, and offered Thompson his hand. "Well, it looks like we're going to be neighbors."

Doug's handshake was firm. "I can't think of anyone I'd rather have for a neighbor."

As Janet's thoughts went to Stella, she said somewhat hesitantly, "Papa, are you still angry at Stella?"

It was a moment before he answered. "No, I'm no longer angry. A little hurt, maybe."

"I'm sure Stella intended to tell you, but she was probably afraid you'd think badly of her."

"This morning when I stormed out of the house, I was too angry to think rationally. When I came across Doug and Layne, they talked to me about Stella. Layne told me that she had intended to tell me about herself, but was having a difficult time building up the courage."

"Do you still love her?" Janet asked.

"Why do you think I'm in love with her?"

Janet smiled brightly. "Papa, you wear your heart on your sleeve. This morning you blurted out your feelings when you asked Stella if she planned to tell you the truth after you were married. I didn't know, though, that you two had discussed marriage."

"We hadn't. But I guess we both knew our relationship was heading in that direction." He paused before asking, "How do you feel about a marriage between Stella and me? I mean, considering her past and our age difference."

"Her past is just that—the past. And I don't see why you're worried about your ages. Love is the only factor that matters."

"I agree totally," Bart replied. "Will you find Stella and tell her I'd like to see her?"

Janet said that she would, and she and Doug left the study.

Bart didn't have long to wait before Stella rapped lightly on his door and entered.

He met her halfway across the room. "Stella," he said, taking her hands into his. "I'm sorry. Please forgive me."

She hadn't been expecting an apology. "Forgive you?" she murmured.

He gazed into her large charcoal-gray eyes. He felt as though he were drowning in their deep depths. "I treated you abhorrently."

"I understand why you were so upset. But, Bart, I was going to tell you about my past! Please believe me!"

"I believe you," he replied softly, drawing her into his arms.

She went into his embrace happily. "Bart, about my past . . ."

"Shh . . ." he interrupted. "You owe me no explanations."

"But I want to tell you everything. Maybe then you'll understand."

"I already understand," he said, bringing her closer against him. Bending his head, he pressed his lips to hers, kissing her tenderly, endearingly. "My darling, we have plenty of time to get to know each other better."

Releasing her, he ran a hand through his hair in a detached motion, confessing quietly, "Stella, I'm scared of losing you. I was married twice. Janet's mother died when Janet was very young. I lost my second wife in childbirth. My son was stillborn. For years I avoided love and emotional involvements. Then you came unexpectedly into my life and touched a tender chord in my heart that I thought had died. You and Paul are now very precious to me." He took her back into his arms.

Sliding her hands about his neck and holding him tightly, she murmured intensely, "Bart, I'm scared too! Love's an emotion I've never felt before. I never dreamed I'd find a man I could love, a man who could awaken my passion. But, Bart, when you kiss me, my body, my very soul, cries out for you! I want you with all my heart!"

"Stella," he moaned huskily, "I want you too! Always!"

Moving her hand to the nape of his neck, she urged his mouth down to hers; love conquered their fears and uncertainties.

Selina, sitting on the porch steps, watched as Layne paced back and forth. She understood his restlessness. He was anxious to leave for San Antonio, for he wanted to get married as bad as she did. The shooting, the trip into town to fetch the sheriff, then the investigation had taken a long time. She sighed despondently. Now it was probably too late to leave. They would have to wait until tomorrow morning.

Layne suddenly stopped pacing. "Selina, I know it's kinda late, but, regardless, let's leave. We can camp out tonight, then ride into San Antonio in the morning."

A sparkle lit up her blue eyes. "Camping out sounds like a marvelous idea. Only I have a stipulation."

He quirked a brow.

"That we share the same bedroll."

"Miss Beaumont, you're a wanton little wench," he replied, sitting down on the step beside her.

"Yes, I know," she said, smiling. "Is it a deal? Do we sleep in the same bedroll?"

"You twisted my arm," he played along, kissing her softly. Then suddenly he exclaimed, "Damn! How could I have forgotten!"

"Forgotten what?"

Slipping a hand into his shirt pocket, he removed a telegram. "I received a wire from William Stratton. The sheriff brought it to me. It came in this morning. I've had so much on my mind that I forgot about it."

"William sent you a wire?" she questioned warily. A stab of fear shot through her. "Is it about my mother? Is she ill?"

"She's fine," he told her quickly. He gave her the wire. "Here, read it."

Unfolding the paper, she read aloud, "Elizabeth Beaumont and I plan to marry next year. Will give up my law practice and move to Cedar Hill. Elizabeth's health improves daily. Give Selina our best regards. Detailed letter will follow soon." She looked at Layne, her eyes filled with astonishment. "Mama and William?"

"You seem so surprised."

"Yes, I am." She was quiet for a moment, then as the shock began to wane, she continued, "I guess I shouldn't be so amazed. Mama and William have been friends for years. I can understand why their friendship has turned into love. They are both alone, and I'm sure they need each other. But my father hasn't been dead all that long. I guess that's why I'm so surprised."

"I'm sure that's their reason for waiting to get married. Your mother will honor tradition and your father's memory by remaining in mourning for a full year."

Selina handed back the wire. "William will take good care of Cedar Hill, and he'll treat its people fairly and compassionately. Now I don't have to

470

worry about them or the plantation." She felt as though a heavy burden had been lifted from her shoulders.

Layne took her hand and drew her to her feet. "Pack your bag, and let's leave."

She smiled pertly. "My bag has been packed since dawn."

At that moment Stella and Bart stepped out onto the porch, followed by Janet and Doug. Selina was pleased to note happiness shining in Stella's eyes. Evidently everything was fine between her and Bart.

"Although it's gettin' late," Layne told the group, "Selina and I have decided to leave for San Antonio."

"We figured you would," Doug answered, chuckling. "We just came out to watch you two ride off into the sunset."

Hattie came outside, toting Selina's carpetbag and a lunch basket. Handing them to Layne, she said heartily, "How come you two's wastin' time just a-standin' around? Don't you reckon you oughta get movin'?"

"We're on our way," Layne replied.

Riding up to Chamberlain's ranch house, Jessie dismounted swiftly and flung the reins over the hitching rail. She was no longer depressed over Chamberlain's death. Given a choice, she'd rather he was still alive, but nonetheless her spirits were high. She had remained at Bart's ranch until the sheriff was through questioning her, then during the long ride back to the Circle-C, she suddenly remembered that Harold had put his money belt in the safe located in the study. Her brother didn't know about the money, but even if he did, it would make no difference. She had decided to take the cash for herself, and no one was going to stop her. She wasn't sure of the amount, but she suspected it was in the thousands.

Jessie was so anxious to hurry into the study and count the money that she took no notice of the horse tied at the hitching rail, nor did she spot the stranger standing at the far end of the porch.

She was bounding up the steps when the man stepped forward, blocking her way.

Startled, she stopped abruptly. She stared at him with curious interest. He wasn't handsome, but there was an animal quality in his black-eyed gaze that appealed to her lewd nature. She sensed he'd be a demanding, untamed lover.

The stranger was finding her equally appetizing, and as his lustful gaze raked over her, he said, "I'm lookin' for Harold Chamberlain. He's expectin' me. My name's Jack. Are you Miss Harte?" Chamberlain had told him that the Hartes operated the Circle-C.

Jessie knew that Harold had been waiting for this man to join him. "Yes, I'm Miss Harte," she replied collectedly. "I'm sorry, but Mr. Chamberlain is dead. He was accidentally shot."

Jack wasn't grieved. "Well, I'll be damned." He shrugged indifferently. "In that case I guess I'll head back to New Orleans."

The man's plans fit perfectly with her own. "I'd like to hire you to take me with you. I want to go

472

to New Orleans, but I prefer not to travel alone."

"Whether or not I agree depends on how friendly you aim to be."

She spoke provocatively, "I'm sure we'll become intimate friends."

"Prove it," he replied, his tone daring.

Stepping up to him, she laced her arms about his neck, pressed her body against his hard frame, and kissed him aggressively.

Their tongues sought each other's out as Jack's hand went to her breasts, caressing them urgently. Her thighs rubbed against his stiff erection. It felt good, and she was eager to have him take her completely.

"When do you want to leave?" he asked hoarsely, letting her go with reluctance.

"Immediately." She knew her brother would soon be home. He always came in from the range an hour or so before sunset. She wanted to be gone before he arrived. She'd simply leave him a note. She felt no remorse over leaving him so brusquely. Jessie and her brother were opposites, and she had always considered him too honest and too straight-laced.

"Wait here," she said to Jack. "I'll pack a small bag. I can always have my clothes sent to me."

Darting into the house, she made a beeline for the study. Her plans for the future were running along well. New Orleans was full of rich bachelors, and she intended to snare one of them. Preferably an old one who would soon die and leave her his wealth. Chamberlain's money would give her the means to survive while she was searching for her future husband. A pleased smile crossed her lips. In the meantime, Jack's lustful temperament would undoubtedly make the trip to New Orleans an entertaining one.

She knelt in front of the small safe, unlocked it, and was taking out the money belt when she suddenly detected another's presence. Leaping to her feet, she whirled about.

Jack, standing close behind her, was grinning. "Hand me Chamberlain's money."

When she didn't obey, his hand shot out, snatching the belt out of her grasp.

"Give that back!" she demanded. "It isn't yours!"

"It is now," he replied. He took a step to leave but, changing his mind, turned and faced her. "You're welcome to come to New Orleans with me. We'll have a good time as long as the money lasts."

"Then what?" she questioned.

"Does it matter?" His eyes went over her voluptuous attributes. "Besides, a woman like you ain't got nothin' to worry about. You can always get a job as a whore. Belle would hire you on the spot."

"I wouldn't lower myself! I don't plan to become a prostitute! I intend to marry a rich man!"

"What's wrong with becomin' a prostitute? You're already a whore at heart." He was growing impatient. "Are you comin' with me or not?"

Jessie didn't have to think about it. She was too desperate to leave Texas. "Will you wait while I pack a bag?"

"Sure, just make it fast."

As she brushed past him, he said to her departing back, "I'd be willin' to bet my last dollar that you won't end up with a rich husband. You'll end up in a whorehouse workin' your tail off!"

His laughter followed her all the way to her bedroom. The stupid bitch! he thought gleefully. Did she really think he'd spend this money on her? He'd use her for his own pleasure, then when they reached New Orleans, he'd drop her. He'd do her a favor, though, and drop her in front of Belle's.

"Why does the sky seem more vast in Texas?" Selina asked. She was sharing Layne's bedroll and was gazing up at the dark heavens, sprinkled with twinkling stars.

"Haven't you heard?" Layne questioned teasingly. "Everything's bigger in Texas."

"Is that right?" she said saucily. They were nude beneath their blanket; and turning to him, she slipped a hand down to his maleness. "Everything is bigger in Texas? Is that what you said?"

"Yeah, and it's gettin' bigger," he replied laughingly.

As her hand continued its caress, his passion was quickly aroused. Clasping her to him, he kissed her fully, his questing tongue savoring the sweetness of her mouth. Without disrupting their kiss, he moved over her, fitting himself to her intimately.

As his hardness claimed her totally, Selina moaned with unrestrained desire. She clung to him tightly, her hips meeting his in love's erotic rhythm.

Engulfed in mindless rapture, they soared blissfully upward to passion's ultimate fulfillment. Surrendering to wonderous ecstasy, they soon crested love's glorious peak. With their hunger temporarily sated, they lay contentedly in each other's arms.

"Layne," Selina murmured, "I honestly believe I could make love to you for an eternity and still want more."

"The feeling is quite mutual." He drew her snug against him.

Selina placed her head on his shoulder, cuddling as close to him as possible. They were camped in an area surrounded on all sides by brush. The site was well secluded, but she felt doubly safe wrapped in Layne's protective arms.

"Why don't you get some sleep, sweetheart," he suggested. "Tomorrow's gonna be a busy day. You're safe, you know. My pistol's within easy reach."

"I'm not afraid," she replied. "Besides, my derringer is within my reach."

He chuckled heartily. "Are you still carryin' that toy with you?"

"I certainly am," she answered firmly.

"Selina Beaumont, you're quite a woman. No wonder I love you so much."

"In a few more hours I'll no longer be Selina Beaumont. I'll be Mrs. Layne Smith."

"That's right. This is your last night of freedom."

"Freedom?" she questioned archly, raising up and leaning over him. "Layne, I haven't been free since the day I met you. You captured my love from the first moment I looked into your eyes."

"I thought it was the other way around, that you had captured my love."

"Then I guess we captured each other," she murmured. "Now I'm your prisoner, and you're my prisoner forever."

"Forever," he agreed. Taking her into his arms, he pressed his lips to hers, sealing their commitment with a long, love-filled kiss.

THE BEST IN HISTORICAL ROMANCES

TIME-KEPT PROMISES   (2422, $3.95)
by Constance O'Day Flannery

Sean O'Mara froze when he saw his wife Christina standing before him. She had vanished and the news had been written about in all of the papers—he had even been charged with her murder! But now he had living proof of his innocence, and Sean was not about to let her get away. No matter that the woman was claiming to be someone named Kristine; she still caused his blood to boil.

PASSION'S PRISONER   (2573, $3.95)
by Casey Stewart

When Cassandra Lansing put on men's clothing and entered the Rawlings saloon she didn't expect to lose anything—in fact she was sure that she would win back her prized horse Rapscallion that her grandfather lost in a card game. She almost got a smug satisfaction at the thought of fooling the gamblers into believing that she was a man. But once she caught a glimpse of the virile Josh Rawlings, Cassandra wanted to be the woman in his embrace!

ANGEL HEART   (2426, $3.95)
by Victoria Thompson

Ever since Angelica's father died, Harlan Snyder had been angling to get his hands on her ranch, the Diamond R. And now, just when she had an important government contract to fulfill, she couldn't find a single cowhand to hire—all because of Snyder's threats. It was only a matter of time before the legendary gunfighter Kid Collins turned up on her doorstep, badly wounded. Angelica assessed his firmly muscled physique and stared into his startling blue eyes. Beneath all that blood and dirt he was the handsomest man she had ever seen, and the one person who could help beat Snyder at his own game.